THE HARRAD EXPERIMENT

A NOVEL BY
ROBERT H. RIMMER

BANTAM BOOKS
TORONTO · NEW YORK · LONDON

THE HARRAD EXPERIMENT

*A Bantam Book / published by arrangement with
Sherbourne Press, Inc.*

PRINTING HISTORY

*Sherbourne Press edition published May 1966
2nd printing . . . June 1966
Bantam edition published February 1967*

2nd printing

3rd printing

4th printing

5th printing

This book is dedicated to the men and women of the twenty-first century who may find it quaint but perhaps will consider it germinal.

ACKNOWLEDGMENTS

The author and publisher are grateful to the following institutions, publishers and individuals for permission to quote from the works described below. These works are copyrighted as indicated.

John W. Gardner and the Carnegie Corporation of New York for extracts from *Renewal in Societies and Men* by John W. Gardner, Copyright © 1962 by the Carnegie Corporation of New York.

Rudolph Von Urban, M.D. and Dial Press, Inc. for permission to quote from *Sex Perfection and Marital Happiness* by Rudolph Von Urban, M.D. Copyright © 1949 by Rudolph Von Urban, M.D.

Archibald MacLeish and Houghton Mifflin Co. for *The End of the World,* a poem by Archibald MacLeish, Copyright, © 1952 by Archibald MacLeish.

Pantheon Books and Alan Watts for *Nature, Man and Woman* by Alan Watts, Copyright © 1958 by Alan Watts.

INTRODUCTION

Six years ago, my wife Margaret and I wrote a paper for the *North American Journal of Sociology,* outlining a program designed to achieve sexual sanity. Essentially, our method consisted of teaching a new sexual ethic and moral code by conditioning and indoctrination throughout a four-year period to a select group of male and female college students of unusually sound character and high creative ability.

The paper was the result of ten years of work in family and marriage counseling and years spent studying the sexual habits and mores of man throughout recorded history.

My wife and I felt that, in order to survive, Western man must take the long step away from primitive emotions of hate and jealousy and learn the meaning of love and loving as a dynamic process. Such a program would counteract the decadence that is slowly infiltrating our society.

During their four years of college life, our students would live together, not only under the same roof, but (preselected on the basis of careful psychological tests) heterosexual couples would share the same quarters: a study room, a bathroom, and a bedroom with twin beds.

This unconventional living arrangement was the keystone of our proposal. The student body should be small, no more than 200 males and 200 females, and would be, in a sense, a pilot study. This study would provide the blueprint for a new sexually oriented aristocracy of individual men and women who were free of sexual inhibitions, repressions, and hate, and were thoroughly educated into the meaning and the art of love as distinguished from the purely sexual relationship.

This program is in sharp contrast to our present system of segregating boys and girls of seventeen or eighteen, when they are at the first peak of their emotional interest in each other, and forcing them into abnormal living patterns during their college life. Social pressure for prolonged continence often creates fear, anxiety, and actual repulsion between the sexes. The results: too early marriage ending in divorce, unwanted children born out of wedlock, sexual frustration before and continuing into marriage, and a sex-obsessed society with little or no knowledge of what dynamic love is. A society that deeply frustrates human interrelationships creates fear, hate, anxiety, and a feeling of loss of identity which are the keynotes of modern life.

Students living together under the proposed program would attend classes at established colleges or universities. Arrangements would be made for full accreditation. Functioning in this way, our student body would receive their educational requirements in an unusual social and intellectual environment.

One important feature of our proposal was a required four year seminar tentatively titled "Human Values." Every aspect of man's attempt to organize society religiously, sexually, economically, and politically would be examined. We felt our program would relate to the religious background of most of our students but that it would be wise to seek students who had a liberal religious background. We would be striving not to inculcate any predetermined values, religious or otherwise but rather hoped to open the door for each student to evolve his own philosophy and orientation of his own "self" to the world.

Since our program encouraged premarital relations among our student body, we would, very early in the course, make a complete study of contraception. Roommates might live together with or without sexual intercourse, and with the possibility, if desired, of having alternate roommates. Any marriage commitment during this period would be discouraged, but we assumed those students living together in this program would ultimately seek marriage with another student because they would have become so successfully conditioned by the program that they could not easily find an equally mature mate.

With a sincere belief that each individual should be made conscious of his responsibility to society and to any new life resulting from his mating, our proposal included the stipulation that couples who were responsible for the creation of new life would be dropped from the dormitory program and required to marry.

We expected that this program, if it continued in existence for any length of time, could lead to a healthy development in marital patterns for many of our graduates.

According to our predictions, a goodly percentage of our student body would ultimately become involved in monogamous marriage; we believed that there was the possibility that others would become involved in a close and lasting friendship with another couple of the same background. Because these two couples would have had their college and intellectual training in an atmosphere of controlled sexual freedom, they would be equipped to realize the many advantages of entering into any informal group marriage.

Without fear, jealousy, repression or inhibition they would recognize their need, not only for sexual varietism, but, even more important, the stimulus of living together would add depth, meaning, and breadth to the intellectual crosscurrents of life. Possibly, they would move into a common household and pool their financial as well as intellectual and emotional resources.

Keep well in mind that we are not recommending either this premarital program or this later possibility of group marriage for society in general. Obviously it would be too startling a change in sex and marriage behavior for the average person in our present culture. The point we made was that the time to begin is now. A start must be made somewhere. Too much is at stake to permit our basic social and family patterns to drift on the currents of haphazard marriage and distorted sex relations.

Our paper proposing a Premarital Living Program at the college level met with a great deal of unfavorable reaction. Margaret and I did not expect any definite action to result from our proposal, at least in our lifetime.

To our surprise, five years ago, and more than a year after the original article was published, John Carnsworth approached us with the offer to support such a program with an initial contribution from the Carnsworth Foundation of $10,000,000. In the past six years we have had the privilege of working closely with John Carnsworth. Without his guidance and perspicacity, undoubtedly Margaret and I would have made many unfortunate fumbles in creating Harrad

College on the grounds of the Carnsworth Estate in Cambridge, Massachusetts.

When Robert H. Rimmer, who has been closely associated with John Carnsworth, approached us with the suggestion of telling the story through the journals of actual students at Harrad, we gave a great deal of thought to the idea. The journals are kept by the students as a private record of their reactions and feelings to the Harrad Experiment. There were a great many advantages in permitting the outside public to see the Harrad program actually evolving in this way through the minds of the students. It became immediately apparent, however, that in making the selection from the wealth of material in these journals the students have freely turned over to us we could be accused of selectivity to prove our thesis. Rereading the journals that we have chosen from the various journals given to us by the first graduating class, I think we have avoided this pitfall. At times all Harrad students have had great doubts as to whether they were being educated in a sound environment. They too often wondered, especially in their freshman and sophomore years, whether the microcosmic society we have created at Harrad would be valid in the outside world. Occasionally, the program for individual students created its own insecure world, but largely the individual graduates of this first class discovered the roots of their insecurity and mastered them in a way that would be impossible in what we now label a normal premarital environment.

While the Harrad College Experiment will now for the first time be made public and subject to the winds of controversy, we are continuing our policy of not exposing our student body to the public eye. How students at Harrad are living their personal lives in this

new environment, who present Harrad students are
and where their homes are, and the kind of parents
that have permitted their children to attend Harrad
will continue to be closely guarded information. The
material from the journals of Harrad students which
comprise the body of this book has been carefully dis-
guised both as to the names of the students as well as
to any reference to local institutions or other points
that might make identity possible.

Harrad College is no more than what we accomplish
for the individual. In this book you have the rare
privilege of meeting exceptional individuals embarking
on a voyage into an unexplored land where the premise is that man is innately good and can lift himself by
his bootstraps into an infinitely better world. Margaret
and I hope a glimpse of this kind of world will enrich
your life; and, while you personally may have not been
educated in the manner of this Harrad Experiment,
you may give the option of leading a full premarital
life to your children.

PHILLIP TENHAUSEN
Harrad College
Cambridge, Massachusetts, 1966

EDITOR'S NOTE

The journals selected for presentation here are only four, culled from seventy-six possibilities. But since these four journals cover the activities of six individuals whose lives become irrevocably intimate and integrated, they are even more significantly indicative of the Harrad College Experiment.

No one journal is presented in its entirety. To do so would involve many volumes, since each student entering Harrad is asked to keep as detailed a record as possible.

As the reader will note, the journals are on an almost day-to-day level for the first year at Harrad. This frequently drops as we approach the third and final years, largely because the students have "adjusted" to the Harrad goals and are quite at ease in discussing ideas and reactions with one another, rather than setting them down on paper. Also, as the exchange of intimacy and ideas increases, the individual students tend to be less concerned about the privacy of their innermost feelings.

The only editing given the journals has been to remove complete days and months. But the continuity is accurate, and the journal entries presented here have not been altered in any other way.

THE HARRAD EXPERIMENT

FROM THE JOURNAL OF STANLEY COLE

September, the First Year

So this is Harrad College . . . ye Gods! How did I ever get myself in this place? My friends back in Public School 133 would call it mad. Strictly mad . . . or just plain kook.

Following instructions from the Tenhausens, all students at Harrad are expected to keep a journal . . . strictly private stuff of their reactions. Phil Tenhausen is a nice guy, a little owlish behind those glasses, and his wife Margaret . . . wow! Since when did Ph.D.'s come in such nice packages?

This morning we got the big indoctrination lecture in the Little Theatre, a new modernistic building located across the quadrangle from the Harrad dormitories.

"You are entering a new phase of your life, quite at variance, not only from your past emotional life, but from what present day society calls the norm," Phil Tenhausen told us. "After this meeting I'd like all of you to pick up spiral bound notebooks at the bookstore, and use these to keep a journal of the emotional and intellectual history of your days at Harrad. Write down who you are, your joys, your fears, your reactions to your roommate, your reactions to the Harrad Experiment. These journals do not have to be works of art. They are your private place to blow off steam. As time goes by we think they will be particularly helpful to you in assessing your growth, and the meanings and purposes of your life. While we don't make it compulsory, we do hope that someday before graduation, or after you graduate, you will turn your journals over to Harrad to be used, not only for improving our program, but also as guideposts as to what we have achieved or failed to achieve for you."

So, okay, Phil and Margaret, I am writing! Hunched over her desk is Sheila Grove, my roommate . . . a girl. A girl . . . with breasts, and a fanny, and a pussy, trapped with me! While I knew it was going to happen, I can't quite believe it. Some of the time Sheila is writing . . . when I look in her direction . . . but mostly she's staring out the window. The sun has almost disappeared, just a few rays catching at the upper branches of the elm trees that tower over all the grounds and seem to hide this building and the Carnsworth gardens. Maybe Sheila and I are lost in some magic forest, and outside the world has stopped.

Back to this morning. I might as well write down what Phil said. Who knows? Someday a thousand years from now if some one discovers this journal I may go down in history as the man who chronicled an upheaval in the male and female relationship. Phil's words!

Phil sat informally on the edge of the stage as he talked to us. "The purpose of this meeting is to get you into the Harrad groove. Many of you, in coming weeks, are going to wonder if the groove is a rut and if we actually know what we are doing, or if we have a definite program at all. Admittedly, some of our approaches in this first year are tenuous. You are in the enviable position of creating a new approach to life with us. If it doesn't work with this group, the project will probably be abandoned. Both as a group and as individuals you have the possibility of making our pipe dream come true or puncturing it rudely. After studying your scholastic aptitude scores and your various achievement tests, I can tell you that Margaret and I are more than a little frightened. I doubt if anywhere in the world there is an equivalent group of a hundred students who have a scholastic ability equal to this group. How this pairs with your emotional development remains to be seen.

"Tonight, without guidance and without preparation, you will begin to live in close proximity to a member of the opposite sex. At the beginning, you'll have to make your own adjustments to this situation. Next week our required course in 'Human Values' will meet daily five times a week, here in the Little Theatre, directly after dinner, from 7:00–8:00 P.M. We may later shift this to an afternoon schedule, depending on how your courses at the various colleges and universities in this area jibe with an afternoon time slot.

"Right after this meeting you will pick up your appointments, which have been arranged with the various colleges that you will attend. For the remainder of the week you are going to be busy with your prime responsibility of developing your own personal program of study. Practically all of you will be taking advanced placement courses, but in no case should you overextend yourself. The course in Human Values, which is the only required course at Harrad, is a stiff one. At the same time you will be expected to maintain in your other scholastic studies the same high standards that have permitted you to participate in this unique project. If any of you have the idea that your four years at Harrad will be an indolent sexual picnic, you had better resign now. The thought has actually occurred to us that you will be so busy we are not even sure you'll have time for sex."

Phil waited for the laughter to subside, and then continued. "Now, the problem of transportation. Realizing that we are a commuter based college, we have permitted all students who have automobiles to bring them to Harrad. We have forty-six cars available for one hundred students. Working cooperatively, we should be able to pool transportation and get everyone to classes on time. By Saturday we will announce car-pool arrangements.

"By this time you may have met your roommates. Margaret and I expect yowls of protest from some of you; first, because there have been no formal introductions. Keep in mind that if you were attending a regular college and living in a dormitory you would meet your roommate of the same sex without formality. We feel that this is the easiest way for rapid adjustment. Second, some of you may wonder how and on what basis you were selected for roommates. Let me tell you that Margaret and I, through our intense documentation on each of you, probably know more about you than you know about yourself. In a sense, at least temporarily, the faculty of Harrad is a composite parent choosing one possible mate for you, and doing this with more knowledge of you as a person than you yourself or your parents have. If you question our choice, we ask that you bear with it through the first semester. Many ideas you now have are going to change rapidly. However, we want you to know that there is no rigidity in any aspect of our program. It will be possible for students unable to make an adjustment to form their own splinter groups, and room alone, or if available, live with a member of their own sex. We are betting this won't happen, but we are not overlooking the possibility that it might.

"Because of your overall intellectual capacities, I assume you are all well aware of the hows and wherefores of human conception. But after this conference, you will all please pick up a copy of *The History of Contraception,* by Norman Himes, at the bookstore. This is a very detailed study from the earliest known history of man's attempts to prevent birth. While the book is about six hundred pages long, we expect you will read it within the next week and be ready to discuss it in our first conferences in Human Values.

"Ultimately, we expect you will have normal sexual relations with your roommate, therefore we want to reiterate a basic concept of Harrad. Heterosexual relations among strangers are very nonsatisfying relationships. Even though you may be living in close proximity, we actually assume that a love requirement (in a wider sense which will become clearer to you as the year progresses) will occur concomitantly or prior to any actual sexual relationship. Again, this is a personal matter and we simply want to make you aware of the pitfalls. With the present day knowledge of birth control methods available to you, and with the complete knowledge that we will give you of their use, there is no need for any of you to have fear of unwanted children.

"Moreover, we believe that until you finish Harrad College, you are all, without exception, too young to enter a monogamous family relationship. In a sense, you are the vanguard of future generations who, we believe because of the world population growth or explosion, as the press calls it, will be required by law to limit your progeny. The act of sexual intercourse will, if human beings are to survive, be an act largely of pleasure and emotional depth, and not one devoted to irresponsible procreation.

"We are fortunate in having attached to the staff of Harrad, Tom and Sandy Jelson, and Doctor Anson Fanner. Dr. Fanner does not live on the grounds of Harrad. He is an M.D. whose practice is in Cambridge. Dr. Fanner will discuss contraceptive techniques with you as a group and will be available for individual consultation with your roommate for specific methods to fit your own emotional needs and personalities.

"Tom and Sandy Jelson are a nationally famous husband and wife team who are in charge of our Physical Education program. They are also thoroughly familiar with contraceptive techniques.

"One of our responsibilities at Harrad is to maintain a sound mind in a sound body. Because we have accepted you in good health, we plan to keep you that way. One hour of Physical Education is compulsory daily. The hour you choose, or you and your roommate choose together, is up to you. In our long experience in dealing with high I.Q. students, we do not believe we can put Phys. Ed. on an honor system. We are fortunate in having on the Harrad grounds a fine gymnasium with a large indoor swimming pool. The pool and the gym will be open from 8 A.M. to 5 P.M. daily. Each student will have a time card assigned to him and must punch in and out daily. A minimum of one hour daily five days a week will be expected, and the only excuses will be on the basis of ill health or for female students during the time of their monthly period. Incidentally, Mrs. Jelson will maintain for each female student a complete record of their periods. This record will not only help students avoid obviously fertile periods in their sexual contacts, but will also quickly reveal any female who is overdue. Naturally, we hope this won't happen, but if it should, we have limited arrangements for married students. Of course, if all of you decide that you must immediately have children, then the Harrad Experiment will come to a rapid conclusion. The next four years of your life is not the time to have children. It is the time to prepare yourself for a responsible marriage.

"One other aspect of the Physical Education program will tie in with our seminar in Human Values. All sports, exercise, and swimming in the pool will be done in the nude."

Phil stopped talking, and grinned at the gasp of disapproval from the female students. "My lecture is over. For those who are shocked, I can only say that we are not nudists, *per se*. Nudism as a society or a way of life would be inconvenient. But we must face the fact that man took to clothing to keep warm and for personal adornment. You will find the gym well heated in the winter, and you'll be very comfortable without clothes. From a psychological aspect, we feel that it will prove extremely healthy for you to view each other calmly and objectively as naked human beings."

That was Phil's lecture. Actually there was a lot more, but if I keep going I'll fill this notebook in a couple of days.

I wonder what Sheila is thinking about? I'll bet she's scared to death. All the kids were raving and kidding at dinner, but Sheila didn't have much to say. We've been in the room for over an hour and she hasn't said two words. It's eight o'clock. Within a few hours one of us has got to make the move to go to bed. I'm not going first. I'm going to sweat her out. I'll bet a dollar no man . . . boy? . . . has ever seen Sheila in her birthday suit.

How did such a prim broad ever get herself into such a predicament? Maybe her mother thought this was the only way she'd ever get a man. Well, you're elected, Stanley Kolasukas. Yeah, elected; but you don't have to take office. Nothing in the Harrad rule book says you have to go to bed with your roommate. How the devil did they ever pick us for roommates, anyway? The only thing that I can figure that we have in common is that we are both the silent type.

Well, it's my luck. There's fifty other girls enrolled in this mad paradise. Some of them are really stacked, and I get Miss Prim-Dim for my one and only. Maybe she wouldn't be so bad if she wore a little lipstick. I wonder what's under that droopy sweater? It wouldn't fit tight on an elephant. She has a nice face, though . . . big sad brown eyes. Hell's bells, why get myself in a stew over a dame? I'm not really convinced, anyway, that this mad Utopian idea of living with a girl will ever work.

I was in love once, I guess, with Joan Austin. When we did it that night on the couch in her family's playroom it wasn't much fun. Joannie was scared to death. Hurry . . . hurry, she said, and she didn't want to look at me while I fiddled with that damned rubber. Well, I guess a man is no beauty . . . his prick red and kind of ugly looking . . . and then I was inside her, and I guess it hurt her. And then wham I came, and Joannie was crying, and I was telling her that I was sorry, and then we heard her father and mother drive into the garage, I was scrambling into my pants, and holding that sad little balloon filled with a teaspoon of what had been in me, and now was just as much trouble outside as inside, and I finally crumbled it in my handkerchief, and somehow there we were playing a phonograph record and saying hello to Mr. and Mrs. Austin, as if nothing had happened, and I was agreeing that it was late, and Joannie should be in bed. Then I was saying goodnight to Joannie and telling her that I was sorry, and she was saying that it was all right, but we would never do it again . . . would we? . . . until we were married? and I was wondering as I took the bus home, was that all there was to it? You got married just for that? I didn't feel any better . . . or any worse, than if I had jerked myself off. But the damnable thing was that the next day I didn't feel so depressed and was ready and eager to get Joannie's pants off again, if I could . . . which I never did. So what does it all add up to? How did a man get put together that he drives himself nuts to get his prick buried into a girl's snatch and when he succeeds neither of them . . . the man or the girl . . . think the result was worth the effort. I wonder what it is really all about?

Across the room Sheila is probably thinking the same kind of thoughts I am writing. I'll bet, if we could just talk about it and really say what we think and feel we could find the answers . . . or maybe understand. What the heck? In a couple of days classes will start. My schedule for honors work in History and Government is going to go a long way to keep my mind off sex and girls.

One thing I can say is: Phil Tenhausen has made it abundantly clear that he and Margaret will be willing to discuss any problems of sex and love but they are not going to be concerned with any student at Harrad who cannot maintain a top academic standing. Like one of the fellows said at dinner, "It's a conspiracy. Harrad hands you the lollipop on a stick, but if you start to lap it or enjoy it too much they'll snatch it right out of your hand."

I stopped writing last night at this point because right out of the clear blue sky Sheila started to talk. I guess that I might as well try to write down the conversation, because it was a lulu. I wonder if Sheila is doing the

same. Be fun someday to read what she is writing. Like
two authors given the same plot and out comes two
different stories.

"Do you think that I am kind of a drip?" Sheila
asked.

I guess I blushed. I'm wary of this kind of mind reading.

"How can I say? I only met you this morning," I
said. Might as well stall and see where this was going.
"You look just like any other girl . . . you know, girl as
distinguished from boy."

"That's just it." Sheila sighed. "Nothing special. Now,
you take you. You're the dreamboat type. You should
be groaning out gooey love songs to all the teen-agers.
You'd be a big hit."

"I don't sing . . . only croak," I said cheerfully.

"Well, if I had been doing the matching at Harrad,
I'd match up the beautiful and the homely separately
. . . seems more logical and less likely to cause problems. I'd have matched you with that blonde girl . . .
Beth Hillyer. She's really a knockout."

I really felt like agreeing with Sheila, not because I
think I'm any Hollywood type, but rooming with Beth
did seem to have its advantages. But being brought up
with four older sisters has taught me that you shouldn't
always agree with a woman on questions of this kind.

I said: "You look all right to me. You've got a pretty
face. Maybe because you wear your hair so tight it
makes your cheek bones stand out. Anyway, you know
what the song says: 'Always marry a woman uglier
than you!' "

I guess that wasn't very tactful, and it made Sheila
kind of mad, because she stopped talking for a while.
Finally, to break the silence which was getting a bit
thick, I said: "Look, this idea of having a girl for a

roommate is all right, I guess . . . and probably will be an interesting experience, but it isn't throwing me. I'm lucky to be here. My family are poor Polish people . . . couldn't afford to send me to a school for dog catchers. I just happened to win a Carnsworth scholarship . . . all expenses paid. The Tenhausens talked me into Harrad. I'm here to learn enough so that I don't have to go to work sticking nuts and bolts on automobiles like my father. If my old man knew what the set-up was at Harrad he'd probably say: 'Why in hell do you want to live with a woman at eighteen? Time enough to suffer when one hooks you and you get married.' "

Sheila smiled. "Maybe he's right. Maybe after four years of living with girls a man might decide it's better never to get married. I don't know how boys can stand girls, anyway. I don't like girls much. Most of the time I don't even like myself." Sheila paused. "What do you think of this journal idea anyway? Are you writing about me? Will you let me read what you have written someday?"

"Not on your life," I said grimly. "What's more, I think we'd better make some rules."

"Like what?"

"Anything in my desk is private. Anything in my dresser is private. Half of that bedroom closet belongs to me, and you keep your stuff in your half. My bed is the one next to the wall."

"Would you like to draw a chalk line across the room?" Sheila asked sweetly. "While you're at it, your rules for me apply to you in spades . . . plus, when I undress and get ready for bed, you stay out of the bedroom until I'm in bed. In the morning you can dress first . . . and I can assure you I won't look . . . and that bathroom is private. When I'm in it, you stay out. No visitors."

"Okay, settled," I said, "but what are you going to do about Physical Education. I won't *have* to peek then!"

"What do you mean?"

"What were you doing? Sleeping this morning? Didn't you hear Phil Tenhausen? He's read all the Utopias: Plato, More, Campanella. He's putting their ideas into practice at Harrad. One hour of Phys.-Ed. is compulsory at Harrad . . . Greek style . . . everybody bare ass."

"Oh yeah," Sheila said. "Not for this gal! I'm not stripping in front of a lot of men."

I shrugged. "Seems kind of unfair to you, though."

"What do you mean?"

"I'll see Beth Hillyer in her birthday suit."

"Oh . . ." Sheila said. She looked uncomfortable.

FROM THE JOURNAL OF SHEILA GROVE

September, the First Year

Sheila Anne Grove. That's me . . . born eighteen years ago on March 12th. Astrologically, I am a fish swimming upstream and downstream at the same time. In other words, I don't know whether I am coming or going. I guess that's a fair enough statement to sum me up for the first eighteen years.

I know a couple of things. I'm rich . . . well, not a millionairess, although I may well be if Daddy doesn't leave the rest of his loot to his second or third wife. Anyway, on my eighteenth birthday he put five hundred thousand dollars in my name. I guess Daddy figures by the time he dies he may have been through a few more wives, and this might have the effect of dividing up his wealth considerably. Since he earned all his money himself by founding the Grove Oil Corporation, what he does with his money is his business.

The second thing I know is that no one in this whole damned world loves me. According to some of the psychology books I've read, believing this entitles you to a front seat in the nut house. But not me. I don't care.

My life is pretty fouled up. Mother divorced Daddy when I was twelve. She couldn't stand two things about him, his desire to get rich no matter what . . . and the richer he got the more women he thought he could go to bed with. Daddy told Mother that it really was too bad she was divorcing him, because he loved her. But Mother's idea is that you can only love one person at a time. So, she married a nice homey man who takes her fishing in a rowboat and builds all kinds of jig-sawy things in his cellar workshop. Harold Tripp is his name, and he is an accountant of all things in the eastern division of the Grove Oil Corporation. As Mrs. Tripp, my mother has presented him with two boys and a girl in their six years of marriage. Either they like babies, or Harold has never heard of contraceptives. It is likely, however, that my Mother is responsible. She likes babies. She couldn't do much about it married to Daddy, who was too busy making money to want a family. My guess is, I was strictly an accident.

I have a room in the Tripps' home when and if I want to live there. But I feel like a fifth wheel, a living contradiction to the Edgar Guest poem framed in the front hall, which reads: "Let me live in a house by the side of the road, and be a friend to man." Such a poem would irk Daddy, who puts his trust in money.

To solve the problem of Sheila, I was sent to a very posh boarding school for a while, and then on to Brightwater Academy. For a couple of summers I tagged along to Europe with Daddy and the current Mrs. Grove. Somehow or other I must have got underfoot. The first thing I knew I was enrolled in a very proper school for French girls and spent my summer in middy blouses . . . very giggly, girlish, and far removed from male eyes.

This kind of life made me a book worm. Plunging into a book is for me the worst form of escapism. I guess I live in a kind of dream world. So what else?

Since I haven't had very much of what you might call an adjusted home life, I got the idea that if I read all of the Great Books, I might find why I had been born, anyway. Harold told me I needed God, and Daddy insists that God helps those who help themselves. I didn't like either of these ideas. I figured God needed me . . . but if He does, he hasn't given me any indication. All my reading accomplished several things. I have been at various times, in my mind, a Unitarian, a Jew, an existentialist, a communist, a brilliant teacher, a loving wife, a whore, a dictator, and a sad-apple, which I am at the moment. Sad-apple Sheila Grove, who graduated last June from Brightwater Academy with the highest marks in the history of the school. Summa Cum Laude . . . ugh! Three boys were Magna, and two girls and eight boys . . . Cum Laude. My boy friends, as you can see, were limited.

I guess I am a phenomenon . . . a spook of some kind. When Daddy informed me (by telephone) that I was half a millionaire, I told him that's nice. I'm half a virgin, too. That got him. Especially when I told him the unvirgin half was mental only, and how I was worried that even with a half million dollars I would probably end up a full time mental unvirgin.

I guess Daddy got the message because a few days later Margaret Tenhausen asked me to lunch. Daddy, who knows practically everybody with money, knows John Carnsworth, who was spending his life giving away to mad-cap projects all the millions *his* father and grandfather had begged, borrowed and cheated out of sober citizens for nearly a century.

Margaret is nice. I tried to tell her I'm rather shy and certainly introspective, and the idea of going to a college where I roomed with a boy was terrifying and scary. Margaret implied that I'd better get associated with other brainy types if I ever expected to lead a full life . . . that I would be an anathema to any solid, middle class citizen who wanted a fluffy, non-argumentative bed-mate. So I agreed and for two solid days I took every test the half-witted psychologists ever devised to find what makes another human being tick.

I must have met whatever standards Harrad is looking for, because here I am. Daddy knows. He laughed when he called me from Dallas.

"Relax and enjoy it, Sheila," he said. "I think the Tenhausens have a splendid idea. Maybe if I had got it as a balanced arrangement when I was a kid, I might have got it out of my system, and still be happily married to your Mother."

Knowing Daddy, I doubt it. He could never settle with one woman for life. Whatever kind of cake he is looking for, women are only the frosting on it, and he eats that first!

If Mommy knew, she'd die of shame. Those are her words. But all her life she has regularly died of shame, so I guess it isn't fatal. Mommy is happy to believe I am going to a nice college in Cambridge, Massachusetts. Mommy doesn't know too much about colleges . . . "Harrad College is a nice name, Sheila," she said. "It sounds better than those places called universities."

I drove up to Harrad yesterday from White Plains in my Buick convertible. I arrived in Cambridge about two-thirty. Using the mimeographed map the Tenhausens had sent to new students, I finally located the grounds. I would guess that few people in Cambridge know that Harrad College or even the old Carnsworth estate actually exists. The estate, which must be fifty acres over all, is completely surrounded by a stone wall about eight feet high. Set into the wall and rising another two feet above are sharp iron pickets. Ivy has obliterated most of the wall and conceals the pickets. Whoever built this wall was not interested in being stared at.

I finally located the entrance, a one lane tarvia road between two stone pillars that supported an iron picket gate. The gate was open. On one of the pillars a new brass plaque was engraved with one name: Harrad.

Feeling a little shaky, I drove slowly along a tree-lined drive. I had entered a nineteenth century world of ancient greenhouses, manicured gardens, tall trees, and carefully mowed lawns. Here and there a water sprinkler indicated that human beings did exist somewhere. About a quarter of a mile further in, I turned into a circular drive and stopped in front of a home that looked as if it might have been built by one of the nineteenth century robber barons. It was a huge imitation of an English hunting lodge. In sharp contrast at the rear of the lodge, was a modern three story stone and glass building about five hundred feet long. I saw some kids walking in front of it and a couple of girls sunning themselves in beach chairs. This was evidently Harrad.

Having got this far last night in my journal, I finally couldn't stand the silence on the other side of the room any longer. I don't really know how to write this . . . it is so crazy and impossible. Here am I, Sheila Anne Grove, sitting in a strange dormitory room with a boy I never saw until this morning. A boy whose name is Stanley Kolasukas . . . now Stanley Cole, because, as he told me, it was simple and he liked things simple.

Stanley and I ate dinner with a bunch of other kids in a very pleasant wood-paneled dining room with round tables big enough to seat eight people around them. We picked up our meal cafeteria style. All I remember (I was so jittery) was taking some roast beef and other stuff that was shoved on my tray. I guess I ate it, but I wasn't actually conscious of doing so. I wondered how I was ever going back to my (our) room with this smirking character Stanley Cole. He has wavy brown hair and his sideburns—at least an inch too long —are strictly Greenwich Village (my room-mate, God help me). I tried to keep abreast of a conversation with Harry Schacht and his roommate Beth Hillyer, who sat on one side of me. Across the table; Dorothy Stapleton and Valerie something-or-other belong (yucks, is that the right word?) to Herbert Snyder and Peter Longini. I felt like a blushing, tongue-tied simpleton. Especially so because Beth Hillyer is enough to scare any plain jane like me half to death. She has blonde hair, natural, blue eyes, a turned up nose, and everything else to go with it. I'll bet a dollar she would be asked to pose for one of those pull-out pages in *Playboy,* the kind where the girl, naked, is lying half on her hips so that in one glance you can see her breasts (big) and shapely behind, with a smile on her face that says to all boys with their tongue hanging out: "Wouldn't you like to cuddle me?" Beth has this and intelligence, too. During most of the dinner, she and Stanley carried on a long discussion about our foreign policy and the bad image the United States has created in African countries. Why the heck didn't the Tenhausens pick them for roommates?

Everybody was aware that I had a bad case of aphasia, and politely avoided directing any questions at me. Finally, we finished eating. Some of the kids went into a huge recreation room just off the dining room and played ping pong, others turned on a stereo phonograph and listened to Mozart, and still others went downstairs to a basement "nightclub" called the Cellar Club, where they danced to a juke box. I tried the Mozart group a while. Here, conversation was frowned upon. Stanley disappeared.

About an hour later Stanley walked in, said he had taken a walk. He then relapsed into silence, occasionally staring at me as if I were some kind of ogre. Finally, he decided to walk back to our room with me, where the silence continued until finally I couldn't stand it any longer. I asked him if he thought I was some kind of drip.

Stanley didn't agree or disagree. He tried to give me the impression that girls were girls and that I wasn't so bad. And then he, with his Rudolph Valentino haircut, tries to tell me that maybe my hair is too tight. Of course, all the time I know that he is thinking about Beth Hillyer. Then he pulls the old chestnut that handsome men should marry homely women. I felt like hurling this journal right at his smug face. So what if he looks like Hollywood's answer to a teen-ager's prayer?

I wonder what he is writing? I'd give ten dollars to read what he has to say about me. When I suggested the idea . . . real nicely . . . to him, what does he do but start a lot of guff about his privacy. He can have his nasty little privacy, but if I ever catch him leaving his journal around, all bets are off. Harold Tripp has some old World War II posters in his cellar with Hirohito on them looking very hideous, and underneath them in big red letters: KNOW YOUR ENEMY! Good tactics, I'd say.

Since we were making rules, I decided to get this going to bed bit straightened out. I had wanted to ask some of the other girls what they were going to do, but between the fact that I was too embarrassed to initiate the conversation with just any girl I didn't know, and the way the Tenhausens kept us hopping from one thing to another all day (I made appointments to talk with

the deans of "A" College, and "B" University),* I
never did solve the problem.

The funny thing is that by myself I'm not really mod-
est. I have often laid on my bed naked and read, or
looked at myself in a mirror. I have even touched myself once in a while and made believe that I was both
me and some nice boy who liked me, and once I must
have even masturbated. I guess I did, anyway, because
while it was happening it was just impossible to stop,
and then afterwards I felt awful. But no one has ever
seen me naked since I was old enough to wash myself,
and Stanley Dreamboat Cole isn't going to break that
record . . . at least, easily.

So, after we got these points settled, it was about
eleven-thirty. I told Stanley that I was going to bed. I
locked the bathroom door, did my business, brushed my
teeth, and scrambled into some new pajamas I had
bought. Then I turned out the bedroom lights and burrowed into my bed. I gave Stanley the all clear, but
remained very rigid. Let Mr. Cole try something and
he'd regret it, by gosh.

What did Stanley do? He sauntered into the bedroom, turned on his dresser lamp, looked at me with
my eyes squeezed tight, and then calmly undressed right
down to his bare skin. Okay, so I watched him through
my eyelashes. Didn't I say "Know your Enemy"? Besides, I had never seen a boy naked. Stanley looked
very nice. A little round-shouldered, a little hair on his
chest, a very small behind, and nestled in a soft growth
of hair, a fragile looking penis that wobbled when he

* All references to the actual names of colleges and universities in the New England area have been eliminated from these
journals. Students in these colleges who have become acquainted
with Harrad students assume that they are "day" students, or
"townies." This is in keeping with our purpose not to encourage
overt publicity.

walked to the bathroom. Somehow, he seemed much younger naked . . . as if he might be a scared little kid, too.

He finally got into his bed, still naked.

"Good-night, She," he said softly.

"Good-night," I whispered, and felt like crying. How did he know Mother and Daddy called me She . . . once, a long time ago when they lived together?

FROM THE JOURNAL OF BETH HILLYER

October, the First Year

Three weeks at Harrad and by this time I don't know whether I'm afoot or on horseback. Funny thing, it's not the environment of Harrad that's got me bugged. It's trying to find time to get all the work done.

Pops told me last summer, "Keep in mind, Beth, just because you come from a medical family you don't have to be an M.D. Your grandfather is still practicing. You've got one brother interning and one in Ohio determined to make a living as a General Practitioner . . . and there's me. Four Hillyers determined to help mankind is probably enough. Maybe a very pretty girl like you should take a nice easy college course at some girls' college, then get married and have children. After all, that's what your mother did."

Pops knows how to goad me. I love Mommy and all that, but I want to do more with my life than have babies. If you're a girl and you're pretty, everyone thinks you should be a dumb bunny who lives and breathes just because some man (your husband) lives and breathes. Reminds me of a story by Chekhov, *The Darling*. The poor girl in the story had no personality or individuality of her own. Just a big cipher. When her husband died she had to get another in a hurry . . . with each new husband she acquired a new identity.

"Listen, Pops," I told him. "It can be done. I love medicine. I've lived, breathed, and slept with Hippocrates since I was hatched. I'm going to do it. I'm going to be a doctor . . . I'm going to marry a doctor . . . I'm going to have babies . . . and my own husband will deliver me. And when your female patients see me hang my shingle out next door to yours . . . you're going to lose them all . . . especially the ones with big bellies, because I'll know more of what's happening in their head and in their womb than you and Gramp do if you live a million years."

So Pops, you can chuckle, but even this load of courses which includes: Advanced Chemistry, Sophomore Biology, German, English, and American History, not to mention the Tenhausens' course in Human Values, in which they assign books as if there is no tomorrow, doesn't frighten me. It's fun. Every day is new and exciting, with a million-billion things to learn.

What's more, I've got a roommate who is a brain . . . and he looks it, too! Harry Schacht. He wears big Hollywood-style tortoise shell glasses. Since he is nearly a six-foot string bean, the thing that impresses you most is that Harry looks like someone's day dream of a science-fiction superman. But Harry is only near-sighted. When it comes to fine print and reading just about everything that has been written, Harry terrifies me because he knows so much more than me. But there's compensations. In the ways of women, Harry is just a frightened boy.

Last night when I was undressing, Harry was lying on his bed, watching me.

"I can't get over it," he mused. "You're the most beautiful girl I've ever seen. The Tenhausens certainly wanted to keep the tea-kettle boiling. The only possible reason we could have been picked to room together is that we're both planning to go to medical school. You know what the kids have nicknamed us, don't you?"

Naked, I jumped on his bed and landed flat on him. He was wearing clothes, which I guess was lucky. "They call us Beauty and the Beast." I kissed him, a quick peck, and scrambled under the covers into my own bed.

"Don't you think that excites me?" Harry leaned on his elbow and looked at me.

"Sure, I guess so. Maybe I'd better not do it again. I just thought it would be nice to be friendly."

"Oh, gosh, don't stop being you. I look forward to it. I never dreamed I'd go to college and have a room-mate who kissed me good-night." Harry sighed and started to undress. "I really like you, Beth . . . you're so sunshiny, and I'm so gloomy." Still wearing his shorts, he turned down his bed.

"Why do you wear shorts to bed?" I asked.

"I don't know. I'm embarrassed to have you see me."

"I see you naked practically every damned day in the gym."

"That's different. There's a lot of other kids around." I laughed. "Your shorts don't conceal a thing. I can see your jamoke, and it's sticking in the air."

That made Harry laugh. He took his shorts off and stared at himself. Still laughing, he stared at it. "That's a pretty good name for it. How did you ever get the way you are, Beth?"

"What do you mean?"

"I don't know . . . so easy . . . so spontaneous . . . so unembarrassed."

"I guess it's being brought up in a family of doctors. In my family we call a spade a spade, and devil take the hindmost. Most doctors don't pussyfoot around about the facts and functions of life."

Harry got into his bed, turned out his bed light, and we talked about an exam that was coming up tomorrow in Chemistry. By the time we finished questioning each other for more than an hour, I knew we had it licked. I think we were practically ready to take mid-years instead of a lowly lab test. "Gosh," I said finally, "I've got to go to sleep. I'm not a night owl like you."

"Beth, can I ask you one thing?"

"Shoot."

"Do you think you and I will ever actually have intercourse?"

"I'm ready when you are," I said, grinning.

"You make it sound so casual."

"It isn't going to be casual with me. It's going to be nice and snuggly, and lots of fun."

"How can it be fun with a Beast?"

"Harry, you are not a beast. You're a nice warm skinny boy who is scared to death because he's living with a girl. Aren't you learning anything in the H.V. course? Love is in your head, and I am sure proud of what's in that head of yours."

"You mean you love me, Beth?"

"I like you a lot . . . that's a darned good beginning."

"Beth, have you ever made love with a boy?"

"Yes."

"Oh?"

"Harry, you sound gloomy again. I did twice. With a very nice boy. He was scared and I was scared. I was sixteen. He was nineteen. I kept wondering what if I had to marry him. He was very handsome. He sang all the popular songs, and knew the words by heart. In fact, the only words he knew to make love with, he parrotted right out of songs. Did you ever hear that song, 'Too Young' . . . he sang it all the time, and threatened to commit suicide if I didn't marry him."

"Did he commit suicide?" Harry asked hopefully.

"In a way. He got married last year. His wife is pregnant for the second time."

"You must have liked him. You kept track of him."

"Harry," I said, "go to sleep. He called me last summer, and wanted to have a date. He was bored with his wife, and told me we could make beautiful music together. I told him that I loved music but was only interested in music for unaccompanied violin. You didn't know that I can play a violin, did you, Harry?"

"I can play the piano," Harry chuckled. "We should try it sometime. They sound good together."

FROM THE JOURNAL OF HARRY SCHACHT

October, the First Year

I'm in love . . . not just with Beth Hillyer who is utterly, completely wonderfully feminine, but I'm in love with Sheila Grove and Dorothy Stapleton . . . in fact, I'm in love with fifty girls. "Bless them all, the long and the short and the tall. . . ." That's a World War II song my father used to sing . . . and there's another. "Thank Heaven for little girls." Only these aren't little girls . . . they are fully developed women with breasts and swaying behinds and soft round stomachs.

Every day when I go to Physical Education, there they are . . . girls . . . naked, swimming in the pool, playing volleyball, doing calisthenics . . . yelling, screaming, soprano-joyous. If I stand by the pool, one of them is likely to shove me in. When I come up spluttering in the middle of other girls, they splash me, or challenge me to a race, or toss a beach ball at me . . . and the hour goes by so fast that I can't really believe it is over . . . and then back to the room and I yell for Beth, only she hasn't come back from her classes . . . so I lie down on my bed and think awhile before dinner.

Mostly, I think I am a very lucky Beast. What good fortune saw to it that a homely guy like me should be

so lucky? Four weeks ago I had never been nearer to
a girl than ten feet. Even when that happened, I used
to get perspiry and so wound up inside that I couldn't
even talk to one if she ever happened to speak to me
. . . which was seldom. Now, it's easy to banter with
them or talk seriously, and they talk back to me . . .
easily . . . unashamed.

Like, yesterday . . . I was sitting at the edge of the
pool just watching about ten fellows and girls playing
water volleyball when Sheila Grove dropped out of the
game and scrambled up beside me. She was puffing from
the exertion. She pulled off her bathing cap, and with
her hands swished the droplets of water off her face and
breasts.

"Woof! I'm pooped." She grinned at me. "You know
just two weeks ago when I first came here and had to
walk out in front of everybody naked, I thought I'd die
of embarrassment. Now it seems the only way to be . . .
naked. Stanley isn't such a big shot, either. He told me
that he was really scared to death he'd have an erection
. . . right in front of everybody. He still gets a little
worried about it."

"It's mind over matter," I said, grinning at her. "Like
if I thought how nice it would be to kiss your breasts
. . . wingo, I'd be in trouble."

Sheila looked at me with a teasing expression in her
brown eyes. "Maybe I should keep you thinking about
it. Males are so funny," she chuckled. "Roger Wilnor
had it happen to him yesterday. Jane Atterman challenged him to a wrestling match. She said she could
wrestle better than any of the boys. I guess Roger was
thinking about something beside wrestling because suddenly he was really pointing in the air. Everyone who
saw him laughed and kidded him."

" 'You see why a boy can't wrestle with a girl,' Roger said, blushing.

" 'Don't you worry,' Jane told him laughing. 'Once I got you in a hammerlock, you'd forget all about that!' "

"He might relax and enjoy being suffocated," I suggested.

"Seriously, Harry," Sheila said, "what do you think of this whole idea of boys and girls living together this way? If what's happening at Harrad ever leaked out, an awful lot of people would be shocked. How do we know this kind of life won't make us all promiscuous? Maybe after males and females have been so casual with each other they never can really fall in love or will never want to settle into a monogamous marriage."

"I guess what the Tenhausens are trying to prove with us is that you can love," I said, "I mean, really love many people in your lifetime. How we will react when we get to the point of settling down with one person is a question that I'll bet even the Tenhausens don't know the answer to. We are sociological guinea pigs. Anyway, at the moment I'm quite happy."

"Have you gone to bed with Beth yet?" Sheila asked and then looked uncomfortable. "Maybe I shouldn't ask?"

"Why not? The answer is no. How about you and Stanley?"

"No . . . but it's bound to happen sooner or later."

"Would you go to bed with me?"

"You mean now . . . today?"

"I don't know really when. Sometime . . ."

"I don't really know, Harry. I think the Tenhausens expect it to happen."

"Did you ever stop to think that one bad little girl with nymphomania or something could wreck the place?"

Sheila smiled. "I doubt if that will happen. Remem-

ber, one of the cardinal rules is that a Harrad girl will
sleep only with one man between her monthly periods.
Any girl here will be pretty strict about that. After all,
if there is a slip-up, she'll want to know who the father
is. So, if some girl here develops nymphomania, she
isn't going to be able to play the field. At the rate of
one man a month, it would take her the whole four
years, including summer vacations, to accommodate all
the men in the freshman class. Anyway, Harry, most
girls aren't like that. The feminine psyche is pretty exclusive. I'll bet you that ninety-nine percent of the
girls here within four years will not have had sexual
experience with more than three men . . . four at the
most, and maybe lots of them with just one. Harrad
provides the female an exposure to many potential
husbands and gives her an opportunity to indulge her
natural sexual desire and curiosity without fear and
furtiveness."

"You sound like Margaret Tenhausen," I said. "But
what about jealousy? Supposing some month you decided to sleep with me. Suppose Stanley was in love
with you, but you weren't exactly in love with him."

"That could be messy," Sheila chuckled. "But you
overlook the way the Tenhausens are very carefully attempting to reorient our values. Every day we are being
shown, and I think convinced, that the individual human being is ultimately good. Jealousy is within our
own control. It's strictly a man-made emotion. Love
and sex are two different concepts, interrelated but impossible of satisfactory existence alone. You *can* love
man in general . . . but to really enjoy the peak experience of the contact of genital organs with one specific
person, you must know that individual deeply . . . emotionally, in . . . a thorough empathetic contact based
on a desire to rationally understand the other person

and care for him. The mucous will flow in my vagina and your penis will become erect without this understanding, but the result is simple rutting. Animals do that. Man persists in saying that beneath the cultural veneer he remains an animal . . . but it simply doesn't have to be true any longer. If individual men can be taught to make the effort, they can learn to love other human beings in a brand new way that gives the male and female security and value in each other's eyes . . ."

"You mean," I said, "if I were in love with you and valued you, that you wouldn't be jealous of some other person I might think I was in love with?"

"Harry, I don't know." She playfully flipped water on my penis with her toe. "I'm Sheila, spouting Tenhausen gospel. I'm not Beth. If you slept with Beth, I don't think I could ever understand why you'd want to sleep with me. Would it be because you wanted variety? And if you wanted variety wouldn't you devalue me, and yourself?"

I laughed. "It's fun to try and find the answers. I think my own answer would be that I am studying to be a doctor because I find human beings endlessly fascinating. The awe-inspiring mystery of what makes you Sheila, and not Beth, could still make sexual intercourse with either one of you . . . without devaluing either of you . . . a wonderful exploration. Come on, I'll race you to the shower, and I'll scrub your back because it's Sheila's back and very nice and fragile and freckly . . . and I'm glad you exist in my world."

FROM THE JOURNAL OF STANLEY COLE

November, the First Year

Last Saturday I went to "E" College for a football week-
end. Sheila arranged it. Tom Brierly, a fellow she met
in her Pre-Elizabethan drama course at "R" College, has
a brother at "E" who is a sophomore. Sheila was Tom's
date and I had Tom's sister, Ruth, for a date. Sound
screwy? Well . . . more to come. I went along as Sheila's
brother . . . Stanley Grove!

Of course, one thing we have all been cautioned
about from the very beginning is that Harrad College
doesn't exist. If students at other colleges ask us where
we live, we pretend we live somewhere in the Greater
Boston area and commute to classes. This is probably
good sense. If the outside world were aware of Phil
Tenhausen and the Mad Hatter world he has created,
we would be all living in a fishbowl with a million sober
citizens up in arms screaming that the Tenhausens were
destroying the morals of the country . . . those are
Phil's words and we all agree that he could double them
in brass.

While this secrecy has its complications, it gives Harrad a sense of unity, and most Harrad students seem to

think it's a ball to be the "villains" in the drama. Sheila is no exception.

"I think we should see how the other half lives," she said. "Please . . . please it will be fun to pretend you're my brother."

"Other than picking up your bra and panties, and trying to find my way into the bathroom through a forest of nylons, I might just as well be your brother," I said, teasing her.

"At least, you've seen me in my birthday suit," Sheila grinned. "I can assure you Tom Brierly isn't going to have that privilege."

"Big deal . . . I've seen the entire freshman class of females at Harrad in their birthday suits at one time or another."

"Has it given you a let down?" Sheila asked. "No more feminine mystery . . . just girls, big, skinny, plump. Do they drive you crazy? . . . Do you think about sex all the time? I think you should let me read that monstrous journal of yours so I would know better what you are thinking."

"Stay out of my journal," I warned her. "And don't get yourself in a tizzy. I've been studying so hard these past three weeks that I scarcely know you exist."

"Then why do you watch me when I dress and undress?"

"To tell you the truth, I can't believe that you'd ever get so relaxed."

"Neither did I," Sheila said, grinning. "For ten days I self-analyzed myself and wrote at least thirty pages in my journal . . . all of which sounds silly. Now I take it for granted. You're just like some girl I could be living with."

"That statement, my full-breasted friend, is, to use the current vernacular, the living end!"

"Well, I admit I like your anatomy better than a female roommate's. It's more interesting, and there's no competition . . . please, Stanley . . . will you go as my brother?"

So we went, and I guess it was a good idea, because it gave Sheila and me some sharp contrasts between life at Harrad and life at a small New England all male college.

Contrast #1: SEX. Sex is number one topic of discussion both at Harrad and at "E" College. But the difference in approach is night and day. At Harrad if you get into a male discussion of sex . . . the question is when . . . not IF. I know, for example, that I will eventually make love to Sheila. We talk about it often, and have long discussions about man and woman. But we aren't really intense about it. I think we'll know almost simultaneously when we want to make love. Things are considerably different at "E" College.

We left Boston about nine-thirty and arrived at "E" about noon. When we finally located Bill Brierly's fraternity, we found it jammed from attic to basement with fellows and girls. The men were drinking beer and the girls had weak Tom Collinses.

Bill Brierly, full of at least two quarts of beer, grabbed Susan like a starving man. "Gotta hug my bug," he said, enthusiastically kissing her. "Don't worry if we get separated," he told his brother. "We'll be around."

I could see where this was going to become complicated. Sheila had one Tom Collins. Dubiously, she watched Tom attacking bourbon with beer chasers. I kept Tom company in his drinking, and we reached a happy state of euphoria.

Bill introduced us to a mountain of nondescript *hors d'oeuvres,* telling us how he and his fraternity brothers had worked on them until midnight. We ate politely, showed more enthusiasm at some boiled hotdogs, then began the trek across campus to the stadium.

Walking through the pine woods toward the football game, Bill joyously began feeling Susan's behind. Tom walked closely with Sheila, talking to her intimately. I was polite and circumspect with Ruth, who seemed none too pleased with me.

I was obviously not behaving according to "E" College patterns, since I had made no offensive based on the simple fact that Ruth was a girl and I was a boy. Ruth is pretty enough. She is a freshman at "L" College just outside of Boston. As she made quite clear on the ride up to "E" she isn't going to college to learn anything in particular. She had just read Betty Friedan's *Feminine Mystique,* and in Ruth's opinion the author was plainly a kook.

"Sure," she said, "there are girls at 'L' who are planning to be scientists or what not . . . but they're creeps. I feel sorry for them. They have no choice. If a girl has anything at all, she'd darned soon rather get married and live in suburbia. The hell with how dull it was. Anyway, darned few men want to marry a brainy woman. They want somebody to tell them they are wonderful, and be ready to cuddle with them or baby them."

"Maybe a girl can be intelligent and cuddly, too," I suggested.

"Sure, intelligent," she replied. "She can read the best sellers and take on little civic problems in her women's club . . . but let her really get her own interests . . . let her not be completely children and house oriented . . . then watch out, she's in for trouble. Take you, Stan. You're going to major in History and Government. I don't really give a damn about history or who runs what. Now, just supposing that I married you and I was a career woman, a doctor, or make it simpler, a dress designer, or worse, for the hell of it, a lawyer. Do you think we'd stay married long? Heck no! Most men want three things out of a woman . . . a nice social hostess for their friends, a good mother to their kids . . . and a sex pot in bed."

"Supposing we were married, and you *were* like that?" I could see Sheila, sitting in the front seat of the car, straining to hear our conversation. "What would we talk about?"

"Gossip, kids, sickness . . . your job . . . what's in *Time Magazine* . . . what's the sexiest best seller, who some movie star is shacking up with . . . what some neighbor is doing to some other neighbor's wife . . . and television when we ran out of higher thoughts." She looked at me archly. "That's what my father and mother say and do. What do you want in a wife . . . in a marriage anyway?"

Since I wasn't so sure I knew, I dropped the subject. I also had the feeling that if I weren't careful, Sheila wouldn't be able to stand eavesdropping any longer, and both Sheila and I would end up expounding marriage à la Tenhausen to her.

By the time we stumbled over more sober spectators and finally located our seats, the first quarter of the game was nearly over. This was the football game of the year pitting "E" College against their arch enemy "G" College. In sixty years, according to the program, "E" was only one game up on "G." I sat with Sheila on one side of me and Ruth on the other. Tom had a flask of straight bourbon which he passed around. "E" College was aggressively murdering "G" College. By the half the score was 21 to 0, and three men had been carried out of the game on stretchers while the cheerleaders paid special tribute to them with frenzied cheering. Everytime "E" College made a small yardage gain, or it looked as if "G" College might recover the initiative, Tom, Bill, Susan, and Ruth would jump up and scream wildly and cheer in voices cracked and shrill from previous cheerings.

It was nothing new. I had done it myself at football games. The last year at high school, when I was captain of the football team, three colleges had offered me football scholarships . . . but I had suddenly got fed up with it. Get yourself murdered . . . for what? A lot of screaming maniacs . . . a crowd that is only interested in you for the moment. Only two guys came to see me in the hospital after that last game I played. So I was a limping hero for a couple of weeks. Big deal.

From the quick glance Sheila tossed in my direction, I could tell she was reacting to this spectacle of mayhem much the same way I was. In the second half, "G" College, evidently goosed to activity by the coach and old-grads, came to life. After wreaking their share of vengeance on "E" College, they were only a field goal behind.

I guessed that Sheila and I both felt like anthropologists studying the tribal rites of some vanished, primitive civilization. After two months of exposure to the Tenhausens' Human Values course, I was beginning to sense the eventuality of all of us at Harrad, for good or bad, evolving into a new form of man and woman. Not that I was disgusted at the game or even aloof. It was interesting enough. But I knew I was observing and not reacting like a typical college student. It was an odd experience.

This, then, is CONTRAST # 2. Group spectator sports seem atavistic to Harrad students. If they arrived at Harrad with this as a feeling, Harrad will eventually make it articulate. Not that Harrad students aren't aggressive. I think they are considerably more aggressive than most students, but they are not competing against each other. They are unified against a common enemy . . . man's own lack of knowledge, and the immensity of things there are to know in the world.

This leads to CONTRAST #3 which is a by-product. The entire Harrad environment has been created for and revolves around individual competition. It isn't a competition of man against man, rather it is man, like the Greek heroes, against Nature (meaning all that man doesn't know). Result: Harrad students don't rebel against studying. A good example is the course in Human Values. Sometimes, I think the Tenhausens feel we shouldn't sleep. In addition to the six courses I'm carrying (all practically at the sophomore college level) we are required to read an average of a book and a half a week in the Human Values course. In eight weeks we have read *The History of Contraceptives,* by Norman Himes, *The Meaning of Love,* by Ashley Montagu, *Motivation and Personality* and *The Psychology of Being* by Abraham Maslow, *Becoming* by Gordon Allport, the *Art of Loving,* by Erich Fromm, and three books on how-to-do-it sex, by R. Street, Van de Velde, and Albert Ellis.

This reading course and the level of discussion in the daily group meeting produces a rapid and fundamental change in everyone at Harrad. Thus, the story of what happened at "E" College as recorded by me, Stanley Cole, self-appointed Harrad historian and observer, seems to reveal to me that the Tenhausens are obviously succeeding in reconditioning most of the Harrad students. Anyway, one advantage of being a *human* guinea pig is you can always ask the question, Even if they succeed . . . then what? Harrad students may end up wiser, and, superior citizens, but they will be the smallest minority in the world, and democracy somehow or other has a neat way of trampling over minorities who deviate.

After the football game, which "E" finally won, 27 to 21, we brought the girls back to the Weatherly Inn, about a half mile from the campus, where Bill Brierly had rented a room for Sheila, Ruth, and Susan. We left them for two hours to get cleaned up for dinner at the frat house.

Back in the frat house, Bill and Tom and a dozen other brothers swarmed into Bill's room. Stripped to shorts and T shirts because the weather was god-awful hot for a November twelfth week-end, we drank endless cans of beer and discussed the game and women and sex.

I learned that Bill had met Susan last summer. Susan had just finished her freshman year at "L" College. They had pursued their summer love at beaches, on her father's Chris Craft, and in drive-in movies.

"She's as sexy as the devil, but she doesn't put out," Bill said morosely. "Some nights I could get her bra off . . . some nights her panties. Never both at once. One night I said, 'Listen, Sue, we've been French kissing, hugging, and touching for two hours. You're whimpering and I'm bursting. How about doing it the way men and women are supposed to do it . . . just for a change.' She says, 'Oh, Bill! I want to . . . I want to! . . . but, I can't . . . I can't.' "

"Why not?" one of the brothers asked.

"She can't until she's engaged," Bill said, laughing.

"That's the big hint, brother," Tom said. "Why didn't you pin her and get it over with?"

"Hell, it wouldn't be honest. A lot of guys in this house do that, but not me. I've got principles. I'm not using my pin to seduce virgins. If I ever got that hard up, I'd just go downtown. There's plenty of girls working at the mill who'd just as soon screw as piss."

"All the college broads are the same," one of the brothers said, philosophically sucking on his pipe. "They'll neck like hell with you, let you play with their boobs. After you get to know them awhile they'll even relieve you of your misery . . . by hand, and they'll let you return the favor . . . but they are scared to death to go all the way . . . and, brother, if they do . . . kiss yourself good-bye . . . you're hooked! Remember Joe Tingsley. The poor slob is a runner down in Wall Street. He couldn't finish his junior year. He knocked up that little doll he had up to house parties. Her old man got him a job as prat boy in his brokerage firm to help support his darling daughter. So that's the sum total of it. If they let you go all the way, it's like playing Russian Roulette. Not for me, buster. I'm playing it cool . . . play it their way. Let them play with your pokey . . . but be darn careful where they put it!"

"You fellows don't know what love is," one of the older brothers, evidently a senior, said. "When you meet the right girl . . . you'll forget all about your little animal self. You'll go around starry-eyed, and virginal!"

"Sure, and when you meet this one and only, and you're up here in the woods at this male monastery, writing her bloopy, soulful letters, the chances are that she'll be out necking her ass off with some other guy."

"The gals have to get experience," Bill Brierly said. "The more they know, the better they are. Speaking of experience, what's the strategy for tonight? I got the key to Sam Tobey's shack. It's a hunting lodge, Stan," he explained for my benefit. "There's a couple of sacks and a fireplace with a bear-rug. We'll toss for who gets the bearskin . . . very conducive to romance. One thing is for damned sure, I don't want to hang around here and spend the night arguing with Susan, and trying to persuade her that every other creep in this house without a date isn't watching us . . . which they will be. The Fertility Room, that's the cellar, Stan . . . will be jam packed. Down there you could be kissing your best girl while your dearest brother, who wasn't making out, was feeling her rear end."

Tom shook his head. "I don't know, Bill. Tobey's place is going to be kind of awkward and confusing. Remember . . . you got relatives mixed up in this. Ruth is our sister . . . and Stan is Sheila's brother. Are you going to throw our sister to a wolf like Stan?"

"Are you a wolf, Stan?" Bill asked, grinning at me. "No . . . you look more like a dirty dog."

"I don't mind some hugging," I said. "But if you are really protecting your sister's virtue, I'll be careful."

"Don't worry about Ruth . . . she knows the score. If your old man has got any dough and/or your prospects look good, she'll add you to her waiting list, and tease you just enough to keep you dangling and sighing for her. Ruth is using her four years at college to line up a sufficient selection of males so that the day after graduation she can get married in the chapel . . . and, if possible, arrive in her marriage bed *virgo intacta*."

"What about Sheila?" Tom asked me.

Poor Sheila, I thought. You asked for this. "To tell you the truth, Sheila is really my stepsister. I haven't seen too much of her in the past year. She's been traveling in Europe with her father."

Tom brightened. "Everything being equal, I think perhaps we should run out to Sam Tobey's shack after all. Maybe we can stay for breakfast."

At dinner, when I alerted Sheila to our new relationship she looked at me angrily. "You think that you're a wise guy, don't you," she hissed. "You'll be sorry . . . tossing your roommate to the wolves. From now on when you feel like discussing Mediaeval History with me, I'll refuse to listen."

"Okay," I told her, "Beth Hillyer has a sympathetic ear."

"You dog," Sheila scowled at me. "I hope you fall madly in love with Ruth Brierly and live with her in suburbia with ten pimply children while your matronly wife reads all the best sellers and eats chocolates until she weighs two hundred pounds, at which point she will finally achieve her life long ambition and be elected President of the Women's Clubs of America, and drag you around with her to meet all of her chubby friends."

. . . I stopped writing at this point, yesterday, because Sheila finally persuaded me to let her read my journal. She decided it would be more interesting if, in the future, we used our journals as a place to write back and forth to each other. This way we could say things to one another we might not actually want to discuss aloud. She got so enthusiastic about the idea that she wanted to suggest it to the Tenhausens. While I agreed, as a temporary idea, I think some problems may arise.

"Even in a marriage," I told her, "a person has to maintain some private area of his own. Once I know and you know that we are reading each other's journal, neither of us will really say what we think. We will write what we think the other person wants to hear."

"I don't agree," Sheila said. "The most important thing in a marriage is that two people be very close . . . so close that their intimate thoughts are revealed to each other."

Since you are now reading this, Sheila . . . I say to you as your roommate, as your lover . . . as your husband (if that should happen) I'm not too sure you'd like my most intimate thoughts if I revealed them to you. I'll give you an example. In addition to thinking of going to bed with you, I also think of making love to Beth Hillyer. How do you like that? Bet you a dollar that thought makes you see red!

FROM THE JOURNAL OF SHEILA GROVE

November, the First Year

I'm floating on a soft dreamy cloud, Stanley. I love you.
I love you. Yesterday, you let me read all the wonderful, crazy things you've written in your journal, and I
let you read mine. When you got to the point where I
hoped you would have a long, dull placid life with Ruth
Brierly, you stopped writing about our week-end at "E"
College.

"Stanley," I protested. "You haven't finished it! Just
when it was going to get interesting."

We were lying in your bed. Outside, the temperature
had dropped more than forty degrees, and even Indian
summer had given up the ghost. A slushy New England
rain was splashing against our window.

You kissed me and said, "I've got to get back to the
cruel world, and study. I've got an exam in European
Government tomorrow. Anyhow, since you have convinced me that we should in the future read each other's
journals . . . there's no sense in duplicating. You haven't
written a thing about yesterday. All you have done most
of the day is sleep with an angelic smile on your face.
When are you going to study?"

"For your information," I said, "when I knew that
we were going to 'E' College, I did all my work in ad-

vance. I'm really covered through Tuesday except for Vatsayana's *Kama Sutra,* which we are supposed to have finished by Tuesday for Human Values. I'm in good shape."

"You can say that again," you said dreamily. You snuggled against my breasts, sucking first one nipple then the other. I could see you were ready to start all over again, and I wasn't going to need much encouraging.

"Not now," I said practically. "You might wear it out . . . and I wouldn't want that to happen. What bothers me, if I finish the story in my journal it won't be the same . . . your reactions would be different from mine."

"See, I told you," you said. "Like all females, you want your cake and eat it, too. Anyway, in the infamous history of our week-end at 'E' College, I don't think our reactions would be too dissimilar."

"You may be right," I said. "I'd rather be me in bed with you than be Ruth or Susan . . . but I can't believe the boys in the fraternity are so bad. They are just frustrated and confused."

"I didn't say they were so bad," you said. "I just feel sorry for them. They're not only frustrated now, they *will* be for years. Anyway, remember what I said. From now on, since you are determined that we read what each other writes, even if I disagree with you, I'll write it down."

"You already have," I said. "And it nearly made me choke! But now . . . after this wonderful morning and afternoon . . . do you feel the same? . . . or are you more selective?"

So okay . . . Stanley Cole . . . don't answer . . . but what could you do with Beth Hillyer that we haven't done in the past six hours . . . that's what I'd like to know, by golly! Anyhow, here's the rest of the story of "E" College seen through the eyes of the late, *but not mourned,* virgin . . . Sheila Grove.

As you know, after dinner at the frat house, we all went downstairs to the Fertility Room. I finally got you alone at the bar for a few minutes.

"Don't be a complete rat," I begged you. "I've figured out Tom Brierly's tactics. He's trying to get me loaded . . . and when I'm good and tipsy he thinks I'll relax and enjoy 'it.'

" 'It' . . . is . . . according to the best tradition in dating circles . . . Four Finger Feelies. With his right hand and arm Tom keeps me in a suffering position. FFF logically proceeds to simultaneous P.O."

"What the heck is P.O.?" you asked.

"I can see that you are not well acquainted with defensive action that is the female stock in trade. P.O. is Peripatetic Osculation usually attempted from head to toes."

"Not a bad idea," you said.

"Maybe . . . but for me . . . not with just anybody."

"Okay, where do I come in?" you asked.

"Well," I said, "I understand we're going to some place called Tobey's. It sounds to me like a S.D. . . . Seduction Den. My gosh, Stanley, you are nineteenth century. Anyway, I figured the only way to get out of a really serious clinch with Tom Brierly and do it gracefully is to pretend that he has succeeded beyond his wildest expectations."

"I don't follow your torturous thinking," you said hurriedly. "But you better get it off your chest fast, because Tom is arriving with a Mephistophelean smile on his manly face."

"Listen," I told you hastily, "If I pretend I'm really whooshed . . . believe me, I'll only be pretending. I'll just be hoping that the 'E' College ethics dominates Tom's morals, and he wouldn't be interested in making love to an inebriated girl. If I guess wrong, then I'm counting on you to save me."

I know this plan seemed cock-eyed to you but I think you'll agree that it should have made for harmonious relations and a more pleasant evening than if I pursued the untouchable virgin formula. By this time, I was back in Tom's clutches, so I couldn't discuss it further with you. Tom told me that Bill, Susan and Ruth were all raring to go to Tobey's. Bill had run downtown for food to make breakfast, and in no time at all the car was loaded with liquor and we were on our way.

You can say that a more logical approach to the evening was to freeze Tom in his tracks every time he made a pass at me . . . or make it abundantly clear to him that I was a nice girl; but you must remember that most of my (adult?) life has been *sans* boys, and I was quite curious to see in practice what I had only heard second-hand. I honestly agree with you that Harrad is changing our lives, but at the moment even you are not entirely sure where all of us are going . . . and whether the results will be better than the tried and true way of female defensive countering male offensive until they end up in marriage and live unhappily ever after.

So, if I acted like a prude, I was obviously going to put a damper on the whole evening so . . . well, darn you anyway . . . why explain my motives until you explain your bombshell day-dream of enjoying Beth as well as me?

We drove to Tobey's, and I admit that even with you sitting in the front seat beside me while Tom drove, that maybe, after all, I was really playing with fire. Because while I was only playing a game, maybe you were playing for real.

Oh, Stanley . . . this morning and afternoon have been so nice. I never guessed that having you touch me and being so big inside me could be so warm . . . hungry . . . gentle . . . tender. Are there any words in the world to describe how I feel?

"I love you," you said, and you told me you weren't really interested in Ruth. But before I "passed out," I did see you entwined with her on the bear-skin rug in front of Tobey's fireplace. Well, I'm not jealous. After all, we don't own each other, do we? Would you want to own me? I kind of agree with the Tenhausens that if our love survives Harrad and continues throughout our life, it will be because we have inextricably interwoven the threads of what really is the real you and me. Here and there, threads might unravel, or we might drop a stitch and have to go back and unravel it, but the total pattern would be constantly emerging and assuming a "Gestalt" that was the unity of us. Ye gods . . . I'm becoming a philosopher. But any other way would be dull, stagnant, and boring. Wouldn't it?

Enough of Sheila pontificating.

After driving through miles of woods and dirt roads full of pot holes that jounced you and Ruth even closer together, we arrived at Tobey's, which turned out to be a log cabin on the edge of a moonlighted lake that extended black and silver-rippled into the night. I was correct. This was a place where a maiden screaming for help would only get her own echo for reply. Inside were knotty pine walls, open ceilings, two bedrooms to the right and left of a huge fieldstone fireplace, and outside plumbing. Tobey is a former Chi Psi, or Deke, or something, who used the place in the summer for fishing (Ho! Ho!). He'd loaned the key to some brother or other from whom Bill had conveniently borrowed it. Bill and Tom had obviously been there before. (With whom?)

Big dark mystery, but obviously dames . . . chicks . . . broads—such interesting names men have for us!

We danced. That is *you* danced with Ruth to a hi-fi phonograph. Almost immediately Bill and Susan disappeared into one of the bedrooms. Slowly, inexorably, Tom Brierly plied your heroine with Tom Collinses first and martinis next (faster?). He didn't grab or try to touch; just talked in soft endearing whispers until I began to wonder if I would "pass-out" in reality and not have to pretend at all. Such a conversation. Here's a small extract:

"You are really quite a fascinating girl, Sheila."

"Really quite ordinary," I said.

"No . . . you have a unique charm. A *savoir-faire* aloofness that is captivating."

"Oh?"

"I find myself vibrating to you. Even your hands-off manner is a kind of invitation."

"Invitation to what?"

"Call it reciprocal response. Beneath your cool exterior lies a full grown, fiery woman. Do you ever let your hair down?"

"You mean literally?"

Tom grinned, and before I could stop him he had unpinned my up-do and my hair was on my shoulders.

"You're quite experienced in handling women's hair," I said.

"Sheila, with your hair down you're breath-taking! May I kiss you?"

"I'm afraid to get too close," I said. "I'm a little dizzy. I'm afraid I'd see you double." There was some truth in this.

"You don't have to look," Tom said agreeably. "You're supposed to close your eyes."

"And sigh passionately?"

"Sheila, I'm a little crocked, too. It's warm enough. What do you say for a little swim in the lake?"

"It would be too cold for me. Besides, I have no bathing suit."

"It's amazingly warm for this time of year. Come on. We can skinny dip."

"No thanks."

"Take off your shoes and stockings. We can walk in the water along the edge."

"No thanks."

"Sheila," Tom said, passing his hand over his face. "I'm really crocked. Would you mind if I lay down in the bedroom for awhile?"

"Of course not. Go ahead!"

"Well, you can't hang around out here watching Stanley and Ruth. Will you come and sit beside me?"

You can see, Stanley, that I was finally trapped. I followed Tom cautiously into the bedroom, and he actually did lie down. He looked as if he were not long for this world. I went out in the kitchen, and pumped some water, and put a damp rag on his head. Then when I was being a really good and tender nurse . . . he grabbed me. "Oh, Sheila," he moaned, imprisoning me in his arms and kissing me enthusiastically. "Forgive me. You're so lovely, I can't help myself!" With a swift movement he unzipped the back of my dress and released the snaps on my bra. I fought him desperately while he held me in a bear-hug, whispering. "Sheila, Sheila . . . I won't hurt you . . . just relax. You knew when you came in here what the score was. Bill and Susan are in the sack right now. You don't hear her struggling. You can't go back in the living room. Stanley and Ruth are bound to be in a clinch. Honestly, I promise. I won't try anything funny."

"What you are doing right now is funny enough!" I

hissed at him, trying to first unclasp his hand from my breast, and when I succeeded, I discovered that his other hand was prying at my middle. "Take your hand away this instant!"

"All right," he said, "But let me take your bra off."

At first I refused, and there we lay. Me silently wriggling and trying to escape, and Tom inching his fingers inside my panties. It was time for the *coup d'etat . . .* MINE . . . not his!

"Tom," I said, "I'm awfully dizzy. I think I'm going to be sick . . . or just pass out." So saying . . . I "passed out" and lay absolutely limp across the bed. I crossed my fingers. Would he be a gentleman? Tom let go of me, jumped out of bed and lighted a lamp. I made believe trying to rise, but instead slipped gracefully to the floor in a heap, breathing as if I were about to toss my cookies. Obviously aghast, Tom lifted me off the floor and dumped me back on the bed.

"Oh, I'm so dizzy!" I moaned.

He took the damp cloth I had gotten for him and put it on my face, telling me that I'd be all right. And then what does he do but proceed to *thoroughly undress* me, telling me all the time that I'll be just fine . . . that I need to unloosen my clothes, and there's really no need to get my dress wrinkled. In two seconds I was lying like a naked corpse on the bed, not knowing what to do. If I jumped up and revealed I was really quite sober, it would go over like a lead balloon. If I yelled for you to save me, things would be even worse. While I was trying to find a course of action, Tom stripped and jumped in bed beside me whispering that his lovely Sheila would be fine . . . just fine. He took my limp hand and folded it around his penis. I was shocked. You can laugh . . . Stanley . . . but never in my life had I ever touched a man . . . not even you, until this morning. After two months at Harrad, a certain naïveté in my previous character has vanished. Even so, I never imagined what size a man can grow to, and I never really believed that this long heavy apparatus would fit comfortably inside a woman. I snatched my hand away. Murmuring passionately at me, Tom placed my hand back on his weapon. We went through this routine at least five times. All the time Tom moaned lugubriously, telling me to just move it for him.

Suddenly . . . I don't know why . . . I felt very sorry for him. He was obviously quite distraught with emotion. So I held him hard and felt him move against my fingers. After ten seconds and a groan of sheer desperation, it was over.

I pretended not to know what had happened, I lay there with my eyes closed while he wiped my hand and himself. And then, I got a terrible emotional let-down and started to cry . . . sobbing hysterically. I knew I was a little drunk, and I know you were shocked then when you burst into the room and found me lying there naked, and Tom struggling into his pants, in dismay, at the havoc he had created. But what you didn't know was that I was crying my heart out for the world, and the way it was and the sheer, animal drive that made Tom seek something he so desperately needed . . . love . . . affection, only to end up with such a hollow triumph. And I wondered if this was what the Tenhausens were trying to achieve at Harrad; a world where men and women can and must relate their sexual drives and needs for one another into a unified whole so that the act of sex is a perfectly wonderful consummation of a much larger ecstasy and pride and joy and respect for the amazing fact that each of us, man and woman, are human beings, and we loved because we liked each other. Overflowingly liked each other as human beings.

Didn't Phil say one day that each individual should live as if he personally were the God who created other individuals? From such a perspective a man or woman could not judge; they could only love. For each person in the world would be each other's own creation, and be the best creation that he, acting as God, could accomplish at the moment. Maybe if there is a God, he has created men imperfect to give them this potential . . . and as they realize it they become God themselves.

But, of course, Tom standing there . . . disgusted at me . . . at himself . . . didn't know what I was thinking. To him Sheila was a mechanical hand that had done what he had been compelled to do by drives momentarily beyond his control.

So . . . we didn't breakfast at Tobey's. There was no way back. The whole thing had taken on a nasty aura. Ruth, Susan, Bill thought I was a typical virgin bitch, and you, as my brother, volunteered to take me back to Boston by bus. Bill drove us glumly to the bus station. I had ruined their week-end.

But somehow, on that lonely two A.M. bus ride home, walking the empty streets of Cambridge back to our room at Harrad, and the long wonderful night that we held each other, naked in your bed . . . not making love, but just feeling the warmth of each other . . . without words, somehow we had swept away the gap that exists between people. Ten weeks ago we were strangers, Stanley. I'm glad that the Tenhausens found us for each other. Can I say I love you? I don't like to use the word lightly . . . it's beyond love. I just *like* you immensely. I even like your sideburns, and I'm sorry I teased you so much that you shaved them higher. Only . . . only, you really wouldn't want to sleep with Beth? Could you . . . after today?

FROM THE JOURNAL OF HARRY SCHACHT

November, the First Year

A long week-end that went by too fast. Tomorrow, classes. But my mind is not on Chemistry or Physics to-night. I have an uneasy mixed-up feeling I can't quite pin down.

For more than an hour, pretending that I have been writing in this journal, I have been watching Beth study-ing. Her hair is twisted with curlers. "So that you can see how disillusioning living with a girl can be," she told me grinning. She is wearing a white terry-cloth bathrobe with nothing under it. I can't help thinking how her body looks. Seeing right through the bathrobe . . . see-ing her spine, curved as she hunches over her desk . . . seeing her full breasts, one unconcernedly crushed against the edge of the desk as she leans her head on her elbow and ponders the book she is studying . . . seeing the curve of her belly which is so flat when she stands up and now must be a warm ripple of flesh merging into curly pubic hairs . . . seeing her calves, soft, the muscles relaxed into two graceful mounds firm on her chair and ending in her bare knees, fixed as she im-patiently jiggles her legs and digs her toes into the rug in the pursuit of answers to the problem she is working on.

In a little while she will ask me to talk with her about Chemistry or Biology, and her eyes will flash with pleasure if she has arrived at equivalent solutions, or if she hasn't we may end up in a long discussion, and I will be listening and carrying on with perfectly sensible answers with one facet of my mind, and at the same time I'll be thinking . . . Beth, Beth, I love you . . . the way you are . . . your flashing enthusiasm, your breathless intensity, the warm flesh of you . . . and I am more than a little frightened that a homely, ordinary man like me has permitted himself such delight . . . such an overwhelming feeling of tenderness toward another person. I am very vulnerable, and that vulnerability is predisposed toward . . . toward what?

Stanley and Sheila with Peter Longini and Valerie Latrobe were here a little while ago, and we talked about the English Literature course we're all taking.

Something has happened this weekend. I could sense it with them, and earlier at dinner. Not just because it finally happened to me, but something intangible almost . . . a deeper sense of affection. Stanley and Sheila seemed wrapped in a little cloud, and they seemed unable to stop a sort of hand touching game between them. While we all talked generally I got the feeling we were all wondering on a subliminal level if we shared this wonderful sense of involvement with each other. How hard it is for people to communicate the feelings that make them what they are. This has been a mating weekend. If Phil and Margaret took a survey tomorrow, and everybody was truthful, I would bet that there are few virgins left at Harrad.

Not that anyone said anything openly. Love is a private experience . . . incommunicable despite the desire

. . . often the need to communicate it. But you could sense it in the various roommates' reaction to each other. Most of the sexual flippancy and embarrassment of the past weeks was gone . . . the bantering . . . the teasing, suddenly seemed superfluous. They have had coitus. They know they will again. No girl or boy (man or woman) at Harrad can ever respond to one another quite so independently again. As if we all had been a brand new litter of kittens, fumbling around for weeks with our eyes closed, we suddenly now see each really for the first time, and for some of us, at least, the other person seems to be wearing a unique halo.

At dinner those at our table got into a discussion of premarital petting. Some sexologists in the books the Tenhausens have assigned us to read, evidently feel that the gradual, fumbling approaches a boy makes toward a girl, and vice versa . . . weeks . . . months . . . years of sexual touching . . . withdrawal . . . exploration . . . even finally mutual masturbation when a relationship has proceeded to this point, is a very necessary and important prelude to marriage and that without it the male, in particular, might never achieve the necessary practice to create a responsive and happy wife.

"Maybe," Dorothy Stapleton said, "but the environment of doing it . . . in a car . . . on a living room couch . . . in a motel . . . catch as catch can probably makes the average boy and girl feel guilty. Guilt, because what they are doing is against all religious codes; guilt, because society in general says one should wait . . . and mostly fear, because, no matter what the sex books say, it isn't healthy for a boy and girl to fumble at each other for years and build up repressions against doing what is natural."

"Yes, but take our situation at Harrad," Valerie

Latrobe said. "Does the very nature of this environment automatically exclude romance?"

Everyone at the table smiled in gentle disagreement.

"Okay, laugh," Valerie said. "Right at this moment I get the impression that a lot of us are floating in a wonderful multi-colored bubble. But how do we know that ultimately, before we are finished with Harrad, that a male and female won't just jump into bed . . . no preliminaries . . . no petting, what an ugly word! . . . and then just wham bang, with the boy maybe polite enough to wait for the girl; but that's about all. What I mean to say is: won't making sex so easy finally devalue the whole experience? Everything you read about marriage indicates that finally in the average marriage sex gets boring . . . a sort of 'oh, hell I've done this so many times attitude,' that the whole business no longer has any meaning."

"Do you feel that way now, Val?" Peter asked.

"No," Valerie murmured, and I was surprised to see her, so usually composed, blush a little.

"There is one considerable difference at Harrad," Beth said laughing. "Namely . . . we aren't married! Hence the area of possessiveness that engulfs and swamps a lot of marriages doesn't exist here. In a marriage, somebody *owns* somebody because the magic, legal, and sacred words have been said. Here, unmarried, with no claims except a genuine liking for each other, we must automatically work at retaining that *like* or love. Mostly, married people don't bother. The woman says: 'I've got a wedding ring.' The man says: 'Without me, you'd starve . . . and anyway, who'd want our kids except me?' They call marriage a tender trap; more likely it's a barbed-wire, booby trapped, No Man's Land."

"You overlook one thing, Beth," I said. "The roommate system right here is a trap. How do you get out of it? It is completely unlikely that any given set of roommates are going to arrive mutually and instantaneously at an agreement that they are unhappy or not fully adjusted to each other."

"You may be right," Beth said seriously. "The Tenhausens may ultimately find themselves acting as divorce lawyers for the student body."

I suppose it is silly, but the way Beth responded sounded like a complete refutation of the complete amazing surrender of ourselves yesterday.

"Oh, Beth . . . I am really writing this to you. So far I haven't been a very faithful 'journal keeper' . . . but what happened I must write down as best I can. You may never read it. Or maybe someday years and years from now I would read it to you somewhere in another world and you would remember and smile happily as we recalled our wonderful craziness. Do you feel the same way as I do? I keep looking at you, and I want to say, 'I wasn't dreaming . . . was I, Beth. Yesterday actually did happen, didn't it?' "

They call a day like yesterday Indian Summer. A blue-sky placid day, soft and balmy, with the temperature climbing almost to eighty degrees. Harrad was deserted. Most of the kids had gone to football games. A gang of them were going over to "A" College stadium. They had invited Beth and me to go along. When I asked Beth why she hadn't gone with them, she said: "You didn't invite me. I didn't want to go alone."

"I'm sorry," I said. "See, I told you that I was an odd-ball. I guess I don't really like football. But I would have gone if you wanted to."

"Harry," Beth said, "I'm the cheerleader type . . . didn't you know? Rah . . . rah . . . har . . . rah . . . Harrad! Go, Team! Go! Dopey, if I had wanted to see a football game, I would have twisted you around my little finger. But don't think I haven't got ulterior motives. You and I, Harry, are going exploring!" Beth's smile was mischievous, a blonde pixie. "See this box. In it are two ham and cheese sandwiches . . . by tomorrow you may be dead mixing *milchik* and *fleischik*. In this thermos bottle is some dago red wine that cost me one dollar. See, I have all the ingredients and I'm proposing: 'A loaf of bread, a jug of wine' " . . .

"I'm thou," I said fervently.

"No, I am Thou," Beth said. "You're Omar, the Tentmaker."

So we went exploring. Beth held my hand, and I carried the sandwiches and the wine. She brought a book of Dylan Thomas' poems which she promised to read to me with my head in her lap.

"That's the way it's done in all the romantic movies," she said, smiling happily. "I'll bet you don't know it, but I found a book about the first John Carnsworth. It tells of the days he lived here in Cambridge. Somewhere in the middle of these grounds, running right through them, is a brook. Years ago they had a fish hatchery, Carnsworth kept it stocked for his millionaire friends. The Tenhausens have been so busy teaching us about love and life, they've overlooked the pastoral things."

Beth, dressed in a green skirt and white V-necked blouse, skipped along like a six-year old, her blonde hair flying, her face flushed with excitement. She, hastening me along a wooded path, was a reincarnation of Rima, transplanted from a South American jungle . . . but now quite real and tangible. I measured my ordinary pedestrian steps to her rhythm and soon I, too, was buoyant as the leaves floating unhurriedly as they glided down from the nearly naked maples and elms.

"Isn't this our day, Harry?" she asked me. "For a moment we are the only two humans in the world."

And it was our day. It held us in its sunny hands and filled our nostrils with the dry musty odor of millions of leaves, earthy and crumbling beneath our feet. And then we found the brook, about twenty feet across, studded with alluvial rocks and running rapidly with clear bubbly water flowing over a mulch of soft black muck and slippery leaves.

Near the brook on a dirt road two gardeners who took care of the Harrad grounds were unloading a Ford pick-up truck piled high with leaves. They waved at us good-naturedly.

"We've found other humans," I suggested to Beth.

"Not really humans." Beth took off her shoes and paddled in the water. "Just a picturesque back-drop to the stage we are acting on."

We sat on a rock near the edge of the brook and dangled our feet in the water. The gardeners drove away in their truck and then came back with more leaves. We watched them while we ate our sandwiches and took swigs of wine from the thermos bottle.

"They must be collecting leaves from all over the grounds," I said. "Should we go somewhere else? . . . Rude practicality has invaded our dream world."

Beth shook her head. "It's Saturday afternoon. They won't work much longer." We watched several of the piles grow to more than ten feet high. "What are you going to do with them?" Beth asked one of the gardeners.

"Too dry to burn them . . . We'll compost them next week," one of them replied, wiping his brow and looking longingly at the water. "Cripes, if I were a kid I'd strip bollicky and go swimming in this little puddle."

He scooped up some water and splashed it across his face.

"Come on," the other gardener said. "It's twelve-thirty. We're knocking off. You kids go to Harrad?"

We nodded.

"What kind of monkeyshines are goin' on there? I heard a rumor you kids sleep together. Is that true?" he demanded.

"Does it sound likely?" Beth asked, her eyebrows raised.

"Hell's bells, with the younger generation anything is likely. I tell my son, I know you won't be good . . . but for godsake be careful."

They drove away chuckling, leaving us with the blippety sound of the water and the skeletons of the trees. I stretched out on the ground beside Beth and I looked up at the few remaining leaves wispy and brown against the clear blue sky. Beth read, in a deep throaty imitation of a Welsh voice, Thomas' *Fern Hill, Do not go gentle into that Good Night, Poem in October* and *In my Craft or Sullen Art* while I listened dreamily, charmed as much by her seriousness as the words of the poems.

We finished the wine, and for a long time, her back against a tree, her eyes closed, Beth said nothing. Then softly:

"Harry, I think sometimes I am a very erotic person."

"Why?" I asked.

"I get very sensuous ideas. Once in the middle of winter, I took off all my clothes and ran out in our back yard. It was snowing and blustery. Drifts four and five feet high swirled into small knife-edge mountains. The snow was soft and powdery. For a moment, though I knew I was half frozen, I felt that I wasn't me. I was snow itself, and I was whirling in a mad snow dance.

Then you know what I did? I jumped and rolled in the biggest drift and rubbed the snow all over me."

"Did you catch cold?"

"My, you are practical, aren't you, Harry?"

"I would have liked to have been there," I said.

"Would you have jumped in the snow with me . . . or would you have watched?"

"I guess I am practical."

"Well, jiminy I could have used you, anyway . . . to snuggle against. Afterwards, I got into bed and shivered all night? Why did I do that, Harry?"

"I don't know. Maybe you were all tense, and it relaxed you. You seem to have a wonderful ability to just let go. Everybody has to find some form of release."

"No, I don't think so, Harry. I think it was a throwback."

"Throwback?"

"Did you ever see a dog or cat roll on the ground . . . right in the dirt?

"Or a pig or rhinoceros in the zoo just wallow in the mud?"

"Sure. My guess is that it is a sexual response of some kind."

"Maybe masochistic?"

"Ugh . . . no! Just plain sensual. After all, man is linked to the earth. One's body crying for the earth from which it came, and an ecstasy at being re-united."

"If you'd like to roll in the mud," I said laughing, "go ahead. I'll roll with you."

"Let's play in the leaves instead. Did you ever play in the leaves when you were a kid, Harry?"

"Sure. We had leaf houses and burrowed in them, and had leaf fights and itched for days afterwards. But they weren't our leaves. They belonged to the city. Maybe that's why I never got the urge to roll in the snow. We have no back yard, and when it snows the city cleans it off the streets within a day."

"Come on, Harry," Beth said. "Stop mourning your youth. Take off your clothes and follow me!" In seconds she stripped off her blouse, skirt, bra, and panties. Yelling with sheer joy, she plunged naked into huge piles of leaves. Tossing them about her in mad abandon, she sank deep into them and disappeared from view.

Naked myself, I followed, burrowed in after her, and grabbed her. Laughing hilariously, we tumbled and leaped and jumped, and worked our way deep into the pile, tossing leaves at each other, and in the air . . . and then we rolled together and Beth hugged me as we sank deep into the crackly pyramid. Sunlight filtered down through the leaves covering us. Beth kissed me fiercely.

"What is love?" she whispered.

"A girl, a boy, their hearts beating . . . happy with simple things like leaves and each other," I said.

"You look like Pan . . . or maybe like Bacchus. At least you're full of wine," she said. "Harry, you said a boy and girl. Not a man and woman? Love is youth? When you are fifty, and a staid old Doctor, you wouldn't roll in the leaves naked, would you? I guess not. Daddy and Mommy wouldn't . . . but I will, Harry, because I believe love is laughter, too."

I couldn't answer her. I could only see her through a film of tears that came in my eyes. Oh, Beth . . .

"Rub the leaves on my body, Harry," she sighed.

And she lay there, luxuriating, sensuous, while the leaves crumbled in my hands and turned her white breasts and shoulders and stomach dusty brown.

"We're going to need a bath," she chuckled, rubbing leaves over me until I was as dusty as she.

"Harry," she whispered, lying back in the leaves, her legs wide apart. "I am a very devious person. I prac-

ticed with that diaphragm this morning. It's kind of
god-awful . . . but . . ."

"But what?"

"I left it in."

"I never did it before, Beth," I said.

"According to everything I have read in the books,
you are ready enough." She grinned at me and carefully
picked the leaves off my penis. "Please, Harry. We've
waited long enough."

She shuddered and raked my back with her finger-
nails. "Harry . . . Harry . . . hold me . . . I'm afraid
. . . I'm afraid . . ." she whimpered, and then with a
banshee wail she clasped her legs around me, rocked me
fiercely, kissing me and sobbing while I kissed her dusty
face and breasts and held her so hard that her poor
body must ache even now. We lay together for a long
time in our leafy womb, and I could feel the soft undulating movement of her vagina keeping me happily
within her.

"Was that love, Harry?" she asked.

"Yes . . . and this whole day, and yesterday and tomorrow is love, too."

She gave me one million two hundred and thirty-nine
thousand little kisses, and then, laughing and screaming
at the cold chill of the brook water, we washed the dirt
and powdered leaves off each other, and dried ourselves
as best we could with my shorts and her panties.

And then last night she slept in her own bed; and today she has been very serious and subdued. When I
said: "I love you, Beth," she smiled affectionately, but
she didn't say: "I love you, too, Harry."

Oh, Beth . . . why am I afraid to just ask you what
you are thinking?

FROM THE JOURNAL OF BETH HILLYER

November and December, the First Year

Suddenly it's no longer simple. Because I had intercourse with Harry, am I supposed to love him? I like him, in fact I like him very much, but I don't have an overwhelming feeling of love.

Making love in that mountain of leaves was more than just playful fun. I think I almost lost consciousness. I was no longer me. My brain lost control and I surged . . . profoundly . . . ecstatically . . . much like surf gathering on an ocean shelf, cresting unbelievably high, and then pounding helplessly on the shore, cresting again and again as if the mass of water rising toward the sky would never tumble back to earth . . . and when it finally did I was swirling in a vortex, and a flood of tears unaccountably poured from my eyes. Nice. Not one orgasm, but a recurring of orgasms . . . for a moment, two Beths . . . one helpless, a creature of emotions . . . and the other a dimly perceiving and appreciating brain.

But. Must there always be a but? I couldn't relate it to Harry. He was the instrument . . . the leaves . . . the musky day . . . the sunlight, were the exotic setting, but all the time I was really only interested in me, Beth

Hillyer, whoever she is. Not once during that wild culmination did I care about Harry or what was happening
to him. I was completely centered in my own emotions.
It frightens me. Given the moment, the setting, the
mood couldn't any man have produced the same response? I am afraid that may be true.

With Harry it was different. His awareness, even during his violent ejaculation, was mostly for me. He was
afraid he might be hurting me. He was almost nauseat-
ing in his tenderness toward me, worried about the
scratches the dried leaves were making on my body,
later over-solicitous as he tenderly dabbed away the dirt
and mud. How could I respond to tenderness when I
would have welcomed a fury of passion equal to my
own?

And, now, in the last few days Harry has assumed a
terribly proprietary manner toward me, not in a masterful way but anxiously, worriedly. I know he expects we
should sleep together practically every night.

"I love you, Beth," he said last night. He got into bed
beside me. I lay on my back, and he snuggled against
my breast like a child, kissing it and sucking it. When I
didn't respond he was unhappy. "What's the matter?"
he asked, still kissing. "Are you sorry it happened?"

"No, I'm not sorry," I said. "We'll probably do it
again."

"It was three days ago, Beth. I could make love to
you every day."

"We aren't married," I told him. "If we do it every
day it would probably get boring."

"I guess I don't understand you," Harry sighed.

"There's nothing to understand." But there was, and
I knew what it was. Harry as a friend, as a roommate, was fun . . . someone to kid with. Harry as a
lover, demanding, fawning on me, expecting me to hold

his head against my breast and be a baby sucking a teat again, just didn't inspire me to return his emotion. Oh, damn! I'm too confused to keep writing. What is the matter with me, anyway?

I haven't written in this journal for four weeks. The study pace at Harrad is so fast and so demanding that while we all live in a presumably titillating environment, most of us forget the sexual aspects much of the time. Harry finally stoped trying to probe into what was the matter with me. Do I know myself? We resumed our earlier friendly, bantering relationship. I like studying in our room at night with him. Harry has a wonderfully keen mind. We act as a catalyst on each other. I know that we will both finish the term with straight A's. The kids in our chemistry course have labelled us Monsieur and Madame Curie. Several students at the university have tried to date me, and look at me incredulously when I tell them I am going steady with Harry. Wouldn't they be surprised (shocked?) if they really knew!

"You mean that you are going to marry him someday?" Jon Wainstrom, who sits beside me in Honors English, asked. "Good God, your children will be swinging from trees!"

I got kind of angry at him. "Harry is just as nice looking as you, and what's more, he doesn't have a face full of pimples."

Jon chuckled good-naturedly. "But Harry will always have an eagle's proboscis."

Another boy in Chemistry laboratory, when I refused to go out with him, said. "But Harry's a Jew. You won't marry him. Jews only marry Jews."

I wonder if that's true. Of course, I *know* it isn't true. Anyway, I don't plan to marry Harry. Why is it that every time I start to write in this damned journal I get all tangled up with my emotional reactions to

Harry? I guess it is because I know that I am going to have to make a decision. Most of the roommates, so far as I can determine, are enjoying sex with each other on a more or less regular basis. I have avoided Harry ever since that day in the leaves. What should I do? What can I do?

Oh, dear . . . oh, dear God! I guess I feel more like crying than writing. I couldn't get it off my mind. After the Human Values course today I decided to talk with Margaret Tenhausen. I tried to tell her how I was reacting to Harry.

"The truth is that I don't really love him," I said. "I don't know why. I just don't."

Margaret sat behind her desk and listened while I told her about this morning.

"I was awake before Harry! I was half dozing, looking over at him in his bed and watching him sleep. Suddenly, I noticed his eyes were squeezed together tighter. His body had stiffened beneath the blankets. He jerked spasmodically, and then in a few seconds he opened his eyes and looked at me . . . unseeing at first, and then bewildered. He blushed, 'You know, I guess I've been thinking about you too much!' he said. 'I just dreamed I was making love to you, and it happened.' He got out of bed and looked at himself ruefully. His stomach and his hand were wet.

" 'Oh Harry, I'm so sorry!' I couldn't hold back the tears in my eyes.

" 'No need to be sorry, Beth. It happens in the best of families. Besides, it was a nice dream.' He took a shower, and at breakfast I asked him why it happened.

" 'I don't know,' he shrugged. 'Man knows very little of the whys and wherefores of the human body. Maybe if we ever become doctors, the interaction of the brain on the body would be worth studying.' "

Margaret made no comment on my tearful recital. "Do you think maybe Harrad is a bad idea, Margaret? A boy and a girl living so close together and not doing anything?"

She smiled. "Harry would have seminal emissions whether you were rooming with him or not, Beth. It is a natural bodily adjustment for the male. Nature protests, perhaps, but provides the solution."

"I guess I should sleep with Harry whether I love him or not?"

"What is love, Beth?" Margaret asked. "From what you have told me and the way you have reacted I think in many ways you actually do love Harry."

"I like him," I corrected her. "Love is something else."

"What else?"

"I don't know. Something more dynamic, all-consuming. Something that makes you want to kneel down before somebody, humble yourself to him. Give yourself irrevocably."

"In other words, the way Harry feels about you?"

I looked at her, puzzled. "Yes . . . but woman to man . . . not man to woman."

"I hope this happens to you, Beth," Margaret said. "I think you may react differently if you ever experience this overpowering loss of identity to another person. If it happens to you at Harrad, I hope you will tell me your feeling then."

During the two weeks before Christmas vacations, I slept with Harry five different nights. Harry was delighted. Wonderfully gentle, deeply possessive, hungrily oral as he fell asleep on my breast. And all I learned is that I am a terribly passionate woman. I scare myself. Each night was a repetition of the fury of our introduction in our mountain of leaves. But while I was an explosive, sexually wracked body enjoying the demon Beth's violent coupling, a part of my brain stood aside and watched. I was, unhappily, not in love. My God . . . what is love?

Sometimes I wonder whether I am fully responsible for what happened or whether Sheila Grove was purposely testing Stanley. A week before Christmas vacation she offered Stanley her Buick for the Holidays. He could drive it to his home in Detroit if he wished. Sheila wasn't going to use the car since her father had invited her to fly down to Palm Beach for Christmas and New Year's. To Stanley, who comes from a poor family, this was a king sized gift. He immediately planned a junket which included driving me to Columbus, and then proceeding on to Detroit.

As Stanley's plan grew in magnitude it finally embraced an idea contributed by Jack Dawes, who lives across the river in New Jersey, that as many as possible of us meet in New York City for a New Year's Eve blast. Harry was enthusiastic, and soon Jack had organized twenty of us with a contribution of fifteen dollars apiece to hire a hotel suite and provide food, liquor, and entertainment.

We were all due back at Harrad January 5th. As many as wished could squeeze into Sheila's car for the return trip. Those left over could fly or take a bus. Jack made reservations at the Hotel Astor because of its proximity to Times Square.

By this time I think Sheila was sorry that she was involved with her father. While she couldn't promise she was determined to try and fly back from Florida and spend New Year's Eve with all of us. Some details of this junket would have to be glossed over with my family, who would much prefer that Beth spend a less merry time in Columbus, but I figured I could convince Pops.

On a freezing cold afternoon of December 20th, after our final classes, Stanley and I, alone, in Sheila's car, drove to the Mass. Turnpike. We were on our way to Columbus. Neither of us had mentioned the obvious. Columbus was more than seven hundred miles away. We were either going to drive all night or stay overnight in a motel somewhere enroute. Stanley was singing as he drove and seemed unusually happy and gay.

"Do you think Sheila approves of this?" I asked, snuggling into a corner of the seat near the window.

"Why not?" Stanley asked. "She wanted me to use her car."

"But she didn't expect that you were going to drive me home, and then pick me up a few days after Christmas and drive back to New York City."

"You aren't saying what you really mean," Stanley grinned.

"Oh, you think not?"

"I know not. You really mean: will Sheila approve of us sleeping together?"

"What makes you think that we are going to sleep together?"

"Beth, don't be devious. You could have taken a train or flown home in half the time. Why were you so eager to drive with me?"

I was silent. It is disconcerting to have the truth served up ungarnished.

"Besides," Stanley continued, "even if we don't sleep together in the same bed, we will sleep together under the same roof, because we aren't going to drive all night. And, furthermore, to the contrary, not withstanding, and all that gleek . . . no matter what, the die is cast. Sheila will believe we slept together."

"Stanley, do you love Sheila?" I asked.

"Yes, I do." Stanley smiled at my reflection in the car mirror. "The Tenhausen theories have captured me. I love you, too, Beth. I loved you from the first night we got into that argument about American foreign policy. I thought what a wonderful thing it is that Beth is a girl . . . that her eyes flash, and for this moment we are two interacting, thinking human beings."

"You mean you like me . . . not love me."

"I love you. I couldn't love you if I didn't like you."

"You can't love two women."

"I think you can love every woman . . . every man, if you really try. I honestly believe that the Tenhausens are right. Both you and Sheila evoke a responsive chord in me. As females you make me feel male . . . protective."

"Ha . . . you have vanquished your own argument!"

"How?"

"You couldn't love a girl like Valerie Latrobe, who is quite blustery and dominant."

"I do love her." Stanley chuckled. "Aren't you confusing love with going to bed with someone?"

"I don't think you can love everybody, even the way you term it, whatever that may be. It sounds kind of ucky to me. Like the Salvation Army or Candide. Anyway, so far as going to bed goes, I don't really enjoy going to bed with Harry. I like him . . . but I don't love him. He doesn't make me feel feminine . . . only motherly. The sad fact is, I have no mother instincts. At the moment, anyway."

"Have you told Harry how you feel?"

"No. Harry and I can talk endlessly about our studies . . . but when it comes to our intimate feelings, we can't seem to communicate."

"God," Stanley sighed. "The Tenhausens are right.

Man is at a low level in the art of expressing himself."

"How is it that we talk together so easily? I don't really know you the way I do Harry."

"Because I love you as a person. I'm not afraid of you so I can accept you as Beth for whatever you are or may be. Such an attitude creates a magnetic field of compulsive attraction." Stanley smiled at my look of disbelief.

"Stanley . . . you're not for real," I said. "You're too good to be true."

We arrived at Niagara Falls at eight o'clock. It was Stanley's idea of an appropriate place to spend the night together. At a Holiday Inn Stanley registered us as Mr. and Mrs. Cole, and with great enthusiasm insisted on carrying me across the threshold of our room.

"This is nutty," I giggled as he tumbled me on one of the beds. "We're not married."

"We might be," he grinned, and tossed a pillow at me.

I flung it back, and for ten minutes we engaged in a free-for-all pillow fight which left the room in shambles and me stretched out on the bed, weak with laughter and lack of breath.

"Come on," Stanley said, puffing while he undressed. "We'll take a shower together and then eat. I saw a candle-lighted dining room as we drove in."

In the bathroom he horsed around in the shower. Dripping wet, we covered each other with soap from head to foot, then walked around the room admiring ourselves in the mirrors. Stanley took great delight in soaping my breasts and pubic hairs and behind. I responded by thoroughly soaping his penis until he pleaded "uncle." Then we let the needle spray shower restore our equilibrium.

Rubbing my back with a towel, Stanley kissed me

between the shoulders and whispered, "You are very beautiful, Beth . . . and fun."

At dinner, while slowly drinking a bottle of red wine we ate veal parmesan. I asked Stanley how he resisted making love to me before we ate. "I was ready," I said softly. "So were you."

"I'm making love to you now," Stanley said happily. "Just talking with you, feeling that glow that emanates from you is an exhilarating experience."

"It is for me, too," I said. "I know what you're trying to say. How can we sustain this moment? If we lose it, how can we make it come again?"

"Did you read Maslow's book, *Motivation and Personality?* Remember when he talks about *peak experiences*. The last hour with you, Beth, has been like that . . . an experience of sheer wonder at the loveliness of you as Beth a physical person, and you as an ineffable mystery . . . a mystery that even now makes your eyes glow and trembles on your lips. I think I could recapture this feeling with you thousands of times . . . even though I knew you a lifetime."

"Have you had the same feeling with Sheila?"

"Yes." Stanley noticed that I seemed more subdued. "Beth, it doesn't lessen the moment with you, it heightens it. I'm becoming gradually aware that such a feeling as Maslow describes is not wholly mystical. I think it can be recaptured at will. It means simply developing a willingness to respond to all the infinite mystery of life and do it from a perspective of joyous humility at just being alive and able to participate."

"To see the world in a grain of sand, and heaven in a wild flower," I said, grinning. "William Blake said it . . . the Tenhausens are saying it. Will the world itself ever listen?"

"Are you?"

"Yes, I think so, Stanley. Anyway, right or wrong, it is a positive philosophy. It is better than the apathy that seems to have most of our generation in its grip. I read an article yesterday that said dissent has largely vanished from America . . . that the average American is in an emotional vacuum with an overwhelming feeling of uselessness engulfing everybody. Everyone is demanding something worthwhile from the world and can't seem to discover it. Maybe Harrad College will succeed in ushering in the Age of Positive Dissent."

"It's dissent, all right," Stanley said, "but it is going to take some awfully good minds to encompass it . . . believe in it . . . and make it work in a general way. For example, would you be able to explain Harrad up until now . . . or tonight, to your father and mother?"

"No. Would you?"

"Absolutely not!"

Back in the room as I was undressing, I told Stanley I was expecting my period. "I've got twinges already . . . so I may be an uncomfortable mess by tomorrow."

"Should we make love?"

"It's not that," I said. "You know the Harrad rule . . . no more than one boy a month. I've been with Harry this month."

Stanley smiled. "I guess Phil overlooked the fact that proper timing would make it possible for a girl to negotiate two men in a month without risk of pregnancy."

"I doubt that most of the girls would be interested. Anyway, in most cases events wouldn't coincide to make it possible."

We lay on the bed, naked, and watched television for awhile. I held Stanley's hand and nibbled his fingertips; and then we didn't hear the television, though it continued to play; and the light it made danced on the ceiling, and when our ecstasy was over Stanley lay himself half across me, his face against my breast. I suddenly felt very tender toward him, and caressed his back softly while he dozed. For awhile I wasn't sure whether I held Stanley or Harry. Did it really matter? I guess that somehow or other I loved them both . . . and I . . . me . . . whoever Beth was, was destined to be the archetypal mother to her men.

FROM THE JOURNAL OF STANLEY COLE

January, the First Year

Recapitulation is in order. I haven't written in this journal for more than a month . . . and small wonder. Events have moved faster than Stanley Cole, the historian, could record them. Historian. That's me, all right. Historian of my own demise . . . the man who wrote his own obituary.

At the moment, according to Phil, I simply lack perspective. Someday, through the soft mists of time, I will be able to look back and laugh at Stanley Cole's miseries. Maybe. But I doubt it.

I'm writing this as though I am bursting with laughter . . . the truth is that I am punctured, deflated, with the last hiss of despair emerging from the balloon that was Stanley Cole. In the chessboard that is Harrad I have been put in check not by one queen but by two. Check and mate! All my queens have vanished. I have a new roommate . . . Harry Schacht! Some difference! Beth has moved in with Jack Dawes, and Sheila is living alone. In fact, right after the Holidays I would guess that about twenty-five percent of the Tenhausens' house of cards went through an internal reshuffle. This probably taxed the Tenhausens' patience to the breaking point, and must have made them think the whole structure was in danger of collapse.

How did it all happen? I'm not sure I know, myself. I suppose it stems back to me, blithely accepting Sheila's car for the Holidays. But that's only the surface factor. Eventually I would have slept with Beth, somehow. Anyway, I am firmly of the opinion that Sheila was guilty of testing me. Did she really expect me to act like some kind of mediaeval hero and sleep beside Beth encased in steel armor? The simple truth of the matter is that Sheila is jealous. Unnecessarily, of course.

"Not particularly of you," she told me very coolly. "I just can't adjust to the idea of sharing *any* man I might love with another woman. I might have loved you very much, Stanley . . . but my love is possessive. I discussed it with Margaret and Phil, and they finally suggested that I live alone, for awhile, at least."

"Why don't you let Harry Schacht move in here?" I suggested. "He needs solace from his wounds."

"I'm not going to make a career of mending hearts that Beth Hillyer has broken," Sheila said stiffly. "Thank you just the same."

"My heart is not broken," I grinned at her. "I love you, too, Sheila."

"Ugh!" she said.

So . . . I'm not sorry. I slept with Beth twice. Once in Niagara Falls, my own very good idea (and of course Beth *had* to tell Sheila), and once in New York City, in the Astor Hotel, which was undeniable, anyway, because Sheila found us in bed together.

Just in case I ever become your roommate again, Sheila Grove, and you get the idea that you should read my journal, I'll tell you right here and now that I am not mad at Beth, and I love her. Beth is confused. She is determined to find the ideal man, and then, very practically when that has been "taken care of," get on with equally valuable parts of her life . . . such as being a doctor. Beth is very practical . . . except in bed, and there her body takes over and Beth is a feverish, passionate woman; and not all subdued like you, Sheila. Where you surrender, Beth wants to be conquered. My own male reaction is that you both need a little of each other. But why am I bothering to write you words you will probably never read? If you do, they'll no doubt make you even more angry. But I would do it all over again. Even if it were a foregone conclusion that I would end up living with Harry Schacht!

Christmas was sticky. Arriving home with Sheila's car convinced Ma that I wasn't really going to college in Cambridge, that I must have fallen in with cheap gangsters. When she occasionally dropped the subject, it gave my old man (who has a vague idea of what is going on at Harrad) an opportunity to try to discover if I really had a female roommate and if I had slept with her. I told him the whole business was strictly chaperoned and I really wasn't nearer to going to bed with a girl than I had been with Joan Austin.

This pleased him. He admitted that a young man couldn't avoid chasing "skirts." God made him that way, and all that, but that I should keep in mind that the chase was more fun than the capture.

My sisters invited me to a Polish Christmas dance with their husbands, and I spent one god-awful night dancing polkas with a big-breasted, high school senior who was overly impressed at dancing with a boy who went to college. Breathlessly, she introduced me to her father and mother, and I could see a picture of me marching down the aisle in all their eyes.

On December 29th I drove back to Columbus and stayed overnight at Beth's house. Beth's family is very nice, but her mother and father are in complete disagreement over Harrad. I was subjected to a third degree and was glad that I wasn't Beth's roommate. I think I would have been embarrassed to discuss the fact that I was sleeping with their daughter, which from their standpoint I wasn't, but, of course, I actually had and was planning to do again.

Beth's mother believes the entire Harrad program is quite impossible . . . that her daughter is certain to regret it . . . that they have a family understanding that no one in Columbus nor anyone outside the family will ever know about it . . . that Beth is a headstrong girl, too much indoctrinated with modern ideas of feminine achievement . . . that Beth's father is much too easy with her . . . that all modern parents are letting their children dominate the family, which is decidedly wrong, etc., etc., and what did I think about it? Beth's father listened quietly to all the discussion, a little smile on his face. I have the feeling that he really isn't so much dominated by Beth, but he has a great deal of confidence in her. Anyway a lot of things were left unmentioned in detail such as the fact that Beth's roommate is Jewish. To them, insulated Mid-Westerners that they are, this was somewhat surprising. Oh well, they would be even more surprised if they read the details that follow.

After much hugging, and various admonitions and restatements of the fact that they loved her very much, and to please be careful driving, Beth and I finally left Columbus about three o'clock in the afternoon on December 30th. I suggested to Beth that we could stay overnight again in Niagara Falls and get to New York by noon on the 31st.

"Never go back to a place where you had fun," she advised. "You can't recapture it. Let's drive straight through to New York City and sleep in the suite at the Astor. We should be able to get there by nine or ten o'clock tomorrow, and sleep until three or four. We'll have it all to ourselves. None of the Harrad kids will show up until seven-thirty or so at night. Jack Dawes said the Astor was right in the middle of Times Square."

It seemed like a logical idea. We split the assignment and drove right through the night and finally arrived in New York City, got the car parked, and were in the Astor, looking red-eyed and somewhat beat, by ten-thirty in the morning. A bellboy brought us to the suite and started opening connecting doors. Jack had reserved two connecting suites. Despite the fact that there were three bedrooms, two baths, and two living rooms, it was going to be a good question where ten couples were going to sleep. Beth's reaction was, "Who wants to sleep on New Year's?"

"You must be expecting a gang," the bellboy commented.

I nodded, feeling somewhat glum. I pictured a noisy all night blast . . . a lot of drinking, and tons of drunken conversation. At the moment at least, a big feather-bed with Beth, snowed in somewhere in the North Woods for several days, seemed a lot more interesting.

By the time I tipped the bellboy, I had to search through the bedrooms to relocate Beth. She had pulled down the shades and was undressing.

"I'm too pooped even to shower," she sighed. "All I can see before my eyes is miles of super highway . . . like a bad dream of hell where you might enter a purgatory condemned to drive an automobile forever and ever." She plopped into bed naked. I joined her.

"I can't keep my eyes open," she said, "and I'm probably somewhat smelly."

"But you wouldn't mind being kissed," I said, kissing her belly and then her breasts. "It's been torture sitting beside you for twelve hours and not being able to touch you for fear we'd both end up highway statistics." I slowly sniffed her from head to toe. "You smell surprisingly nice to me."

"On second thought," she said sighing happily, "if we didn't waste too much time, it might calm our nerves." She rolled on top of me. "Let me be the man."

"I thought you were exhausted?"

"Don't worry, Stanley," she whispered, kissing me enthusiastically. "It will only take a minute."

Well, maybe it took three. Joyously satiated, she collapsed on top of me, pretending to snore; and then she really was asleep.

I awoke slowly . . . certain that I was dreaming. Suspended over our heads was a giant balloon. I stared at it through slit-open eyes, trying to make up my mind what strange dream I was immersed in. Beth was sprawled on her stomach, one arm across my chest. Her face was half turned on the pillow. She was softly breathing in my ear. I closed my eyes tight, convinced it was a dream, and then the balloon broke. Several tons of water cascaded down on our heads. Sputtering and yelling angrily I knew it was no dream. Almost simultaneously the room was filled with an explosion of laughter, and Beth and I, dripping wet, were surrounded by Jack Dawes, Peter Longini, Herb Snyder, Valerie Latrobe, Dottie Stapleton, Jane Atterman, Roger Wilnor, and at least a dozen others, all screaming and choking with laughter. As I wiped the water that was dripping from my hair into my eyes, I recognized Harry Schacht and Sheila Grove in the background. Valerie was doubled over with laughter.

"Look at them! They look like two half-drowned cats."

"We thought that damned condom would never break," Peter Longini said, gasping with delight. "We've been tip-toeing around this room for more than twenty minutes filling it, trying to find a good way to hang that safe full of water over your heads. If you two hadn't been sleeping under it like there's no tomorrow, you would have heard us."

"Of all the god-damned fool kid tricks," Beth yelled at him. She sat up on the bed, clutching the soaking wet blanket around her. Her wet hair was plastered against her head. Her blue eyes were wide with murderous rage. "What crazy, bastardly son-of-a-bitch thought this one up?"

"Me," Jack Dawes said, smirking. "I just wanted to prove a properly made contraceptive could hold the semen of a Gargantua. Not to change the subject, Beth, but you look as if you've been had by Stanley-the-Giant-Killer. How long have you kids been at it . . . since Christmas?"

"Five days in bed!" Roger Wilnor groaned. "Obviously a world's record. Stan . . . what will your roommate think?"

I didn't have to answer . . . Sheila standing at the foot of the bed . . . speechless. The tears in her eyes, living testimony to what Sheila thought. I saw Harry Schacht standing near the door. His face quivered a little. Then he walked out of the room. Sheila followed him.

Jack, obviously feeling the effects of several drinks, tried to yank the blanket off the bed. Beth struggled to hold it, and then gave up. We were both sitting in bed naked.

Beth jumped out of bed. "Now that you've had your nasty little fun," she snarled, "please have the decency to get the hell out of here while Stanley and I take a shower and get dressed."

Beth had more aplomb than I. Still sitting on the bed I watched all of them leave, listening to their giggling and crazy laughter. Slightly stunned, I tried to figure out what to say to Sheila . . . or Harry. We had been caught . . . how do they say it in law courts? . . . "in flagrante delicto."

Leaning dejectedly against the washstand in the bathroom, I watched Beth calmly take a shower.

"What is the matter, Stanley? Are you sorry for your sins?"

"No, I'm only sorry that Sheila thinks they are sins . . . and so, obviously, does Harry."

"I know," she said. "Three months at Harrad hasn't reversed tried and true morality . . . for them, at least."

"Has it for you?"

"Heavens, Stanley," Beth said, stepping out of the tub. "Dry my back and stop being mournful. It's New Year's Eve. We are the cynosure of Harrad's eyes. Everybody in the other room is probably clucking about it . . . We are the first promiscuous ones."

"I can still see the expression on Sheila's and Harry's face. They were shocked."

"I know," Beth said, and shrugged. "But I'm simply not worried about it. We made love. We like each other . . . quite a lot, I think. Isn't that what the Tenhausens expected would happen?"

"Will you room with Harry again?"

"No," Beth said, fastening her bra. "He wouldn't be happy with me."

"Would you room with me?"

"No, because I'm only partially amoral. You said you love Sheila. Sheila would have to love me . . ."

"It's too complicated," I said . . .

"Too impractical, you mean," she said and slapped me on the behind. "Come on, Stanley-the-Giant-Killer . . . get ready. A New Year is coming up!"

FROM THE JOURNAL OF SHEILA GROVE

December, January, February and March, the First Year

Well, I did it! I made it possible for Stanley and Beth to be together. If you love a man, do you consciously test his love? Could I love Stanley so much that I wouldn't be jealous of him if he went to bed with Beth? Could he love me and even consider such a thing? Could I love Stanley and permit myself to have intercourse with Harry? No! . . . No! . . . No! . . . unless I loved Harry. Could I love both Stanley and Harry? According to the Tenhausens this is possible. But loving and having sex with two men . . . that's decidedly different. I couldn't do it . . . I don't think. Anyway, that's not really the point of my problem. It just comes down to this . . . I do love Stanley. In a hundred ways we think and feel alike about so many things. Stanley is gentle, affectionate, and a wonderfully passionate lover. I would marry him. What is love? What is marriage? A person with whom to share your loneliness? Isn't this what every human being must have . . . someone who lets the little tiny thing that is really and truly "you" out of the shadowy hiding place in your brain, and accepts this strange "you" and loves whatever this something is that makes you what you are . . . loves the mercurial "you" that maybe even sometimes you don't understand yourself? And you love him in return in the same way, though there are no words for it and it "passes understanding." Is that kind of love possible except between one man and one woman? And if you could love two men, wouldn't something be subtracted out of each relationship?

God, it's confusing. Tonight, while I was eating at the most exclusive country club in Palm Beach, dressed in a three hundred dollar evening gown, trying to smile at Gregory Caldwell, and respond to him, Beejee Grove, my third mother, by adoption (insisting in a whiskey tenor that Gregory was a good catch and his family owned just piles of Humble Oil Stock), . . . tonight, while I drank two martinis, four glasses of champagne, refused oysters and wasted a huge lobster . . . . the leftovers from all our meals would have fed a family of four (and who was really happy?) . . . tonight, Stanley Kolasukas (whose family probably couldn't even afford a Christmas turkey) and Beth Hillyer are somewhere between Boston, Massachusetts and Columbus, Ohio, in my car. I wonder what they ate for dinner. I wonder what they . . . No, damn it, Sheila, stop it . . . stop it!

Why did I come to Palm Beach, anyway? I had two choices. Mother's house, with a Christmas tree and all the kids, and Sheila feeling like a maiden aunt while she helped her step-brothers and step-sisters play with their dolls and games. Or Daddy's current winter-time house, where my newest mother, Beejee, is entertaining an endless procession of sleek friends; confiding in any male who cared to listen that sex with Daddy was hellza-poppin, and who said a man of fifty wasn't any good? Where Sam Grove got the energy she would never know . . . saying all this with a piercing look, hoping (I bet) that the listener might challenge her husband's bed prowess. During the holidays I noticed several men who seemed eager to enter this kind of Olympics, and perhaps did. Beejee is a remarkably good-looking woman, and being only thirty-seven probably has a stamina for combat that would surprise Daddy, if he knew.

"You know, Sheila," Beejee told me, "your father is a very energetic man. Unfortunately, sex for him is only a necessary incident to sandwich in between other occupations. See what I mean." She waved at Daddy, who was in the library making a long-distance phone call. "You know what he is doing? He is calling Iran. He wants to check the political situation and see whether the student uprising will spread to the Grove Oil properties. You know what he was doing twenty minutes ago? He was in bed with me. Ten minutes before that he was on the telephone to San Jose. Some fun!"

So, Beejee plays the field. And during the incessant round of parties and continual drinking, I began to wonder if any sane person would be really shocked by Harrad College. A good portion of the (adult?) world was obviously on a sexual merry-go-round, with everyone who was married trying to catch a new brass ring as it whirled by. But the laughter and high spirits seemed to have a hollow sound. It reminded me of Archibald MacLeish's poem "Sonnet to the End of the World." I learned it by heart at Brightwater.

"Quite unexpectedly as Vasserot
The armless ambidextrian was lighting
A match between his great and second toe
And Ralph, the lion, was engaged in biting
The neck of Madame Sossman, while the drum

Pointed; and Teeny was about to cough
In, waltz-time, swinging Jocko by the thumb
Quite unexpectedly the top blew off.
And there, there overhead, there, there hung over
Those thousands of white faces, those dazed faces
There in the starless dark, the poise, the hover
There with vast wings across the cancelled skies
There in the sudden blackness, the black pall
Of nothing, nothing, nothing—nothing at all!

Oh damn, damn to hell with such morbid stuff. I know
. . . I really know the answer. It was all so clean and
good . . . those weeks in November with Stanley. For
him, too, I'm sure. Can we recapture it? Can I recapture it . . . or will I build a cross out of Beth and nail
Stanley to it?

The day after Christmas I couldn't stand it any more.
I begged off a very special party aboard the Caldwells'
fifty-foot Chris Craft. I was sure Greg would find me a
"good miss," anyway. I mooned around the swimming
pool, thinking it would be fun to have it all to ourselves
and swim naked in it with Stanley, and then make love
lying on that rough Florida grass, and watch the stars
and the black sky through the palm fronds. Finally I
decided that wishing wasn't going to make it so, and
I went to bed in the big guest room that Beejee had
given me for the holidays.

To keep my mind off Stanley and Beth and sex
and God knows what wormy thoughts were slithering
through my brains, I turned on the late show on television. Propped up in bed I watched an old movie
called *Wings of the Eagle*. Now this *was* a mistake!
Here's John Wayne, portraying a man who actually
lived, Frank "Spig" some-thing-or-other, who was a
naval hero. John is married to a very nice woman,

played by Maureen O'Hara, and they have a baby boy. Are they happy? Well, John is. He spends his time crashing up airplanes (for fun), or establishing new flying records, or mostly brawling around with the "boys." He hasn't much time for Maureen or any sissy-like stuff that a man and woman might do together. Then their baby dies. Does John put his arm around Maureen and want to be close together in their tragedy? Hell, no! He sits in the living room; holds his head in his hands and smokes a pack of cigarettes. Big strong men don't cry . . . see? Anyway John doesn't get drunk. He just tries to get cancer in one night. Next scene. Why worry? There's more babies where that one came from. Here come John and Maureen, *each* pushing a baby carriage. Each with a daughter. Obviously a few years have snuck away. But John is still itchy . . . not for Maureen. Hell, no . . . for the Navy! He is now flying around the world and hasn't been home for years. Maureen has to take her daughters to the neighborhood movie theater to see their Daddy in the newsreels. Mummy, is that man with the goggles really my Daddy? (No . . . no . . . that not my Daddy. My daddy not ugly so!) Then lo and behold! Daddy John comes home. The children don't recognize him, but Mommy does! She's sex-starved, I bet you. After years and years they finally go to bed in *twin* beds. Daddy John wakes up in the night (his first night home), Maureen is snoring in the other sack. Does he hear his darling children crying in the night? He does. Rushing out of the bedroom (the jerk has been away so long he's forgotten he's sleeping on the second floor), he tumbles down two flights of stairs and breaks his neck. Literally, no kidding!

Does this make him a better man? Do Maureen and John come closer together? No, sir! John knows he's been a bastard. So now he'll be the big strong hero and not tie Maureen down to a poor crumb who has to stay on his stomach for ever and ever. How does he evacuate, I begin to wonder . . . stretched out like that? This bothered me so much that I lost the thread of the plot for awhile. Anyway, Maureen loves John, broken neck or broken thing-a-ma-jig. But John is adamant. She must get out of his life! She should have skipped out singing! Not Maureen. She slinks bravely down the hospital corridor, struggling to contain her tears.

After months and months on his stomach (unable to evacuate, I guess, and hence pretty constipated) John, with the help of a Navy buddy who loves him, manages to wiggle his big toe, proving that whatever brain he had was finally equal to this effort, anyway. After this singular accomplishment, John becomes a famous writer (I was getting pretty sorry I had turned on the knob that started this whole mess). John makes a fortune writing stories, movies and plays about the wonderful boys in the Navy. Does he miss Maureen, who lives alone in another city? Misty eyed and slightly bald, he occasionally looks at photographs she has sent him of herself with her daughters. Time has passed—the kids are wearing baccalaureate hats. Finally, the guy who has taught him to wiggle his big toe convinces him that he might need a wife to take care of him in his old age.

Unannounced, after what must be ten years or more, Big Daddy John calls on Maureen, his hat in his hand, a bumbling, sheepish boy. He finally persuades her that "home is the sailor" or some such gush, and she, figuring perhaps that since the old boy is on crutches, maybe he will stay put while she fetches his pipe and slippers. They turn on the radio. Wham! It's December 7th, 1941 . . . Pearl Harbor. Goodbye, Maureen . . . my country needs me! Our hero hobbles to Washington, offers his services, invents an ingenious plan to beat the Japs, wangles his way onto an aircraft carrier, practically wins the Pacific War and then has a heart attack. Is he dead? Sweat through the deodorant and cigarette commercial. Nope . . . Big John has three months, six months to live, who can tell? Get out your handkerchiefs, wipe your sniffly nose. Here comes John hobbling across the aircraft carrier while all the men stand at attention and the bugles play. With tears in his eyes, he salutes his "boys" and he is escalated off the carrier to a waiting destroyer . . . homeward bound. While it isn't shown in the picture, you know that Maureen will get the pleasure of burying him.

By the time this movie was over I was really depressed. Was this supposed to be the story of a good man? Obviously. The big wonderful lovable brute could destroy the lives of his wife and daughters, but he was really and truly a man . . . a hero, and isn't love a secondary pursuit, after all?

I sometimes wonder if the Tenhausens seriously believe what they are doing. Man, so amazingly ingenious at mastering his environment, creating such incredible things as automobiles, airplanes, television, computers, controlling life and even death; man, dreaming of the stars and the universe, has so little interest or feeling or desire to really know and love another person. All you have to do is read the morning newspaper to know that it must be easier to invent a hydrogen bomb than to put your hand out to someone and say, "I understand . . . I sympathize . . . I love you because I am you."

My life so far has been a tryst with loneliness, an overwhelming longing to find someone to run to, to hold myself against, to find someone in the world I could surrender to, to blend myself with; not essentially in a physical sense, but in a mutual involvement that was so strong that we would come to each other willingly as naked, defenseless human beings.

Does man ever achieve this with man, or are we all so fearful with one another that even after years of living together most men and women are afraid to surrender to each other completely? I guess surrender of one's self is against all concepts of the Western World which demand self-mastery; virility beyond any man or woman's real capacity for virility. I would think people in love, in marriage, could do this with one another and yet for the most part I guess they can't. We are all little, fearing souls . . . afraid . . . afraid of what? . . . Of being scorned . . . of being laughed at. This must be the reason that there are priests, psychiatrists, and social workers in the world. Someone a person can go to and attempt to be what he really is. But for me neither the priest nor psychiatrist nor social worker would be able to release the springs of my being. They would be unable to be involved with me, try as they might. Unless they, too, lived and responded to me in a defenseless way, I would know they were not really participating but inevitably would be judges. So most people never really have anywhere to turn.

Today and yesterday, alone here at Harrad, I have been reading *Toward a Psychology of Being*. Maslow sums it up: "Expressing one's nature . . . refers to effortless spontaneity which permits the deepest, innermost nature to be seen in behavior. Since spontaneity is difficult, most people can be called 'human impersonators,' i.e., they are trying to be what they think is human, rather than just being what they are."

What I'm really trying to ask is why couldn't I have *really been Sheila* New Year's Eve? I arrived in at La Guardia Airport buoyant, happy. I was going to see Stanley again. I would be with all the kids at Harrad, and the uneasiness of my Palm Beach "vacation" would dissipate.

About four-thirty, I walked into the Harrad Suite. A bunch of the kids were sitting in the living room. Bottles were stacked on the coffee tables. Although everyone was drinking, they were talking in whispers and their eyes were bright with excitement. They hushed my noisy greeting. Jack Dawes, followed by Peter Longini, Roger Wilnor, and Harry Schacht emerged from one of the other rooms. I thought Harry had a strange, flushed expression on his face. Jack Dawes broke the embarrassed silence.

"Sheila," he whispered, "I hope you are in a good mood and still have a sense of humor." I took off my coat and looked at him, puzzled. "What the heck is going on . . . it looks like a meeting of the Communist International."

"Beth and Stanley are in one of the bedrooms . . . sound asleep. We've rigged up a surprise for them." Peter chuckled.

"It's awful," Dorothy Stapleton said, but she obviously didn't think so. "We all got here an hour ago, and Jack discovered them. They haven't even heard us. Jack and the boys filled a 'safe' with water and hung it over their heads. It's hanging there like a huge bloop ready to burst any minute. It must have a gallon of water in it."

"You mean they slept through all of this," I asked, feeling as if the pit of my stomach had sunk through the floor to the lobby.

I followed them through the connecting suite and into the bedroom. It is a wonder that I didn't burst into tears. Beth was sleeping with her arm across Stanley's chest. Stanley looked as peacefully happy as a male angel.

I didn't have time to even gasp in disgust (was it

disgust? or hate? or more a feeling of terrible submission before the lash of a whip?), because the safe collapsed, and deluged the sleeping cherubs. Jack yanked the blanket off the bed, and Stanley and Beth, naked and dripping wet, awoke from their sweet dreams to a world of yelling and screaming maniacs.

I ran out of the room, followed by Harry Schacht, and finally the rest of the kids. Was that a mistake? Maybe. Harry and I could have stayed in the bedroom with Beth and Stanley. For the rest, it was none of their business. Maybe somehow I could have spoken the rush of emotions I really felt. Stanley, I love you, I'm not really shocked. Only a little frightened to know that I have shared you . . . that maybe while you were making love with Beth you were laughing at me.

Later, back in the living room, with Harry silently drinking and Beth much too convivial with the rest of the Harrad kids, Stanley said to me: "I'm sorry if I hurt you, She."

"Why don't you just sock me in the jaw?" I asked sarcastically. "You might just as well finish the job."

Stanley looked at me sadly. "Loving isn't a game of subtraction. I love you no less."

"It isn't a game of multiplication, either. Let's not talk about it."

And we didn't . . . nor could I, no matter how much I wanted to, talk with Stanley the rest of the evening. Like Faust I let my soul go to the Devil (not for knowledge) but for pride. All I really had to do was try to talk with Stanley . . . or listen. I could tell by the expression on his face that if we were alone for a minute he would have kissed me or touched my hand and maybe somehow have made me believe that what had physically taken place between him and Beth did not automatically undermine the joy we had and still might have with each other. Although I dimly perceived that in some utopian world it might be possible for several men and women to interweave their lives so their sexual acts with several mates not only did not diminish them individually, or for each other, but actually might become a cornerstone on which an even greater arch of love and life might be erected, it was only a dim perception. So I grabbed Mephistopheles' skirt and plunged into New Year's Eve. Or was it really a Walpurgis Night that began with a condom swaying from the ceiling over two lovers and ended on Hartz Mountain with Sheila nearly raped by horrible demons?

The second meeting with the Witches began when Valerie Latrobe, instead of letting the whole episode sink into oblivion, insisted (in the true Harrad tradition) on cleansing the wound in public.

Harry Schacht tried to shut her up, but her persistent probing and laughing re-hash of what had happened in the bedroom finally commanded the attention of the entire group.

"I really don't see why you are so darned shocked, Harry," she said imperturbably. "So . . . if Stanley and Beth slept together? Isn't that what you expected would happen at Harrad?"

Harry shrugged. "Drop it, Val. I don't feel like discussing it."

"It's better to discuss it than drink yourself to death. Do you think that's sensible? We are supposed to be a superior group. You are acting like television's idea of a spurned lover."

"What am I supposed to do? Jump for joy?"

"No . . . if Beth likes Stanley, find some other girl. There's Sheila. Why don't you two switch roommates?"

"Valerie," I said, "you better get off the subject. I

like Harry, but I'm not providing a haven for Beth Hillyer's wounded lovers."

"What's so wrong with loving Harry and providing a haven just because he is Harry, and he's wounded?"

"You cuddle him on your breasts and pat his head," I said nastily. "If you're so concerned, why don't you invite him to room with you and Peter? You can love them both. You're big enough."

Valerie just laughed. "Boy, that's a grouping the Tenhausens haven't considered. Maybe we should try it, Peter? Would you be agreeable?"

Peter looked at her sourly. "Val, you've had too much to drink."

"Damn it, Peter, I asked you a question. I am not drunk. I would never drink to excess. I like to have a clear mind. Now, I can see clearly that we don't really have a fluid situation at Harrad at all. We are stuck just as firmly as if we were going steady at some regular co-ed college. Maybe worse. We have an irrevocable commitment to the roommate we started with."

"That's the truth," Jack Dawes said enthusiastically, "I agree with you, Val. Only you are really missing the point. The Tenhausens are pussyfooting around. I think we should get this sex business right down to essentials. All this romantic stuff is just a cover-up. I don't know how the girls feel, but I'll bet there isn't a boy here wouldn't like to swive . . ." Jack paused, chuckling. "Hey, that's a good word . . . Swive every girl in this room."

"Jack, you are crude," Roger Wilnor said.

"So, I didn't say fuck! Anyway, euphemisms aside, I'll bet, despite the fact that the Tenhausens picked you as a soul-mate for Jane Atterman, that if Beth Hillyer took off her clothes and shook herself at you, you'd point right in the air and be ready to take her on."

"Would you, Roger?" Jane asked. I could see Beth grinning. Roger was out on a limb.

"I've seen Beth naked a hundred times in the Harrad gym," Roger said weakly.

"Sure, in the Harrad gym. But here in New York with a drink in your hand the moral climate is different. Frankly, the way I feel about it, there is only one solution, males being what they are, and maybe females for all I know, we should all just communally fornicate whenever we feel like it. If we did that Harrad would make sense. We would get rid of sin and itchiness and be able to concentrate on learning as much as we can to survive in this unpleasant world."

"Wham! Bang! Thank you, ma'am!" Beth Hillyer laughed. "I don't think Jack really believes it. He's just bitter. In case you don't know, Eleanor Rupp quit Harrad. Jack is our first 'bachelor.' "

"There you are, Sheila," Valerie said triumphantly. "You don't have to room with either Stanley or Harry. You can move in with Jack."

"You're a nice kid," Jack put his arm around me. "But, I'm not your type, Sheila. A few minutes ago I asked Beth if she would room with me. She's thinking it over. Who wants to punch me in the nose first? You, Harry? Or, you, Stanley?"

I looked at Stanley. He shook his head with a weak grin, but he was obviously shocked. Harry, propped against a chair, stared at the ceiling. "Beats jumping in the snow or rolling in the mud," he said.

Beth looked at him queerly. She poured herself a drink from one of the bottles of Scotch perched in the middle of the floor along with an ice bucket and a wastebasket filled with ice and cans of beer. "I'm sorry, Harry. I partially agree with Jack. We've got four years at Harrad. Maybe we are taking it too seriously. I know it sounds really crazy, but I love you all. It just makes me feel warm and good that we are all here . . . talking, thinking; discussing things most people are afraid to discuss. I can't help it if I don't feel possessive . . . and yet I do. As long as I live, I hope I feel this way . . . just as if I could run around this room and kiss you all, or if my arms were big enough, give you all a big hug, I'm glad you're alive in my world." Beth looked at me, "You don't feel that way, do you, Sheila?"

I wonder what would have happened if I'd said I did . . . or that I was so confused that I didn't know how I really felt. Would I have saved myself a Faustian trip through New York? Instead of trying to put my muddle of thoughts into words, I said, "No, I don't feel that way. Some things in this world are between two people . . . and two people only."

"You sound like Eleanor Rupp." Jack Dawes fished a letter from his pocket. "Here's some extracts from what she wrote me: 'I was brought up differently from you and the others at Harrad. My mother and father have always let me do what I wanted to do, but even when they agreed to let me go to Harrad they didn't like the idea. Now I know that they were right. I guess I never believed that a boy and girl who weren't married would actually sleep together. I know that you wanted to sleep with me, Jack. You kept telling me how all of your friends had slept with their roommates. I guess I am a puritan, but I think it is terrible. It may be all right for a girl to room with a boy and get to know him as a friend, but just to hop into bed and casually do 'it.' That's bad. If the Tenhausens believe, as they say, that marriage can come later they are wrong. What's going to happen to a Harrad girl who sleeps with her roommate or several different roommates, but who never marries any of them? What happens when she goes back home and tries to find a husband? Supposing a man who never went to Harrad finds out about her? She'd be no better than a whore in his eyes!' "

Jack crumbled the letter. "Ellie is a good kid. But the way I feel about it the Tenhausens are overdoing the love aspects, even more than Ellie. Sure, a guy wants a woman . . . but Christ almighty, he can't make a woman and all her petty little daisy plucking his whole life. Sure, a man and woman have to get married eventually. She thinks they vibrate together, maybe he does, too. Maybe, they want to have kids . . . ego glorification or something, but the girl is always pulling the petal that says 'he loves me not' . . . and the guy isn't giving it a thought one way or the other because he knows that it isn't really basic. Somehow, he's got to keep them and their brood from starving. Finally, what really is the biggest force in his life is not the woman and not his children but his own big desire to be somebody . . . to succeed in the world. The Tenhausens are overlooking that we are all cogs in an economic machine, and we either find the place we mesh with the other cogs or we will strip the gears of the whole cotton picking mess and grind ourselves to pieces."

"You mean you never made love to Ellie?" Herb Snyder asked.

"Hell, no!" Jack said. "The only time I ever saw her naked was in the gym. Isn't that a laugh? I knew a dozen girls in New York who would hump just for the exercise . . . so I spend four months at Harrad, the sex college, living like a male monk."

"What's all this conversation adding up to?" Stanley asked. "So far as I can see, Harry, you and I are going to move in together and commiserate with each other. Unless some guy has quit Harrad, or unless some nice girl will welcome us for roommates, you and I are going to live a celibate existence."

"There's only one solution," Jack said. "Once a week we should all have an orgy. Come on, girls, what do you say? When we arrive back here tonight we all will take off our clothes and have a New Year's Saturnalia. After a night of good clean fun, all these little worries about sex and who sleeps with whom will assume their normal perspective."

Jack kept returning to his idea of a rip-roaring orgy. He pictured all nineteen of us naked, running from room to room, playing swapsies all night long until we collapsed from exhaustion.

"I think you're ugly and repulsive, Jack," Dorothy shuddered. "Is that all men think of . . . just sex, and nothing else?"

"Jack is obviously suffering from frustration," Herb said. "His rutting instincts are dominating his otherwise clear mind."

"You're right," Jack said, laughing. "Seeing all the Harrad girls naked for four months, walking around with a perpetual erection, has driven me off my rocker. Won't some girl here please take pity on me?"

"Why don't you do a hundred push-ups and sublimate yourself," Beth suggested. "Then maybe we can go out. It's New Year's Eve. What are we going to do?"

Jack flopped on his belly, pushing himself rigidly up and down, while he explained to us, puffing, that we were all invited to a private party at a night club in Greenwich Village called The Last Gurgle.

"A friend of mine, Bad Max, owns it," he gasped. "It's a tourist trap. Bad Max wears an uncombed beard, uncombed hair, and tight dungarees. Admission is ordinarily three dollars and fifty cents a head. For this you get folk singing, beat poetry, from-hunger ballets that Bad Max conceives on Sundays and Mondays when The Gurgle is closed. Ordinarily he uses his time more profitably investing his ill-gotten wealth in the stock market. Weekdays, Bad Max sneers at the tourists and tells them they are dirty capitalists."

Jack collapsed on the floor, perspiring. "You're right, Beth. I've purged my sinful self. To hell with women." Standing up, Jack undressed down to his skin, calmly flinging his clothes around the room. "After a hot and cold shower I'll never think of pussy again!"

All nineteen of us, yelling and offering inane advice, crowded into the bathroom and watched him take a shower. To get rid of us, he turned the place into a steaming inferno. After we got him dressed, all of us noisily invaded the lobby of the hotel, until finally the manager and several bellboys escorted us into Times Square. Not knowing what to do, or how to adjust to the fact that Beth had calmly shucked off both Stanley and Harry, and with an it-serves-you-right feeling toward Stanley, I ignored his protestations and bundled into a taxi with Harry, Roger and Jane. Harry sat in the front seat, uncommunicative, while I, in back (a fifth wheel), watched Roger and Jane snuggling together, holding hands, and ignoring me.

In the small lobby of what had been a former off-Broadway playhouse, Bad Max greeted us and explained that tonight The Last Gurgle was closed to the public. Instead of muddy coffee, he was serving Gurgle punch made from one hundred-and-ninety proof alcohol. All of his Village friends had been invited. Entertainment was to be spontaneous, self inspired, and anyone who wanted the stage could have it.

Proudly, Bad Max showed us the club trademark: A bathtub drain with the final water in the tub disappearing into the sewerage with an unrestrained bloop of despair. "I'm having it revised," he said, "so that a hairy hand emerging out of the drain is clasping a naked ankle about to drag the body down, too. It's symbolic of the state of the world."

Seeing me standing alone and obviously unescorted (I had repulsed Stanley so thoroughly that he made no further overtures), Bad Max took me by the arm and forced me to reveal that I was Sheila Grove.

"You can be my girl tonight," Bad Max said, leering at me. "I'm at least twice your age, so you are safe with me. My own true love, Frankie, a very unpleasant trollop, caught me making love to Captain Bligh . . . or was it Nellie? . . . She has temporarily deserted me. Truthfully, last night she got so steamed up at me that I took a pitcher of water off the table, and to the delight of the tourists, heaved it at her. Several ice cubes struck her in the face, and she entertained, unrehearsed, for ten minutes with the most fascinating and far-out cussing I've heard since I was Captain of a four-master rounding the Cape of Good Hope. That was in my youth, of course. Tonight, Frankie is in bed with pneumonia, a black eye, and pre-menstrual tension. As her husband wearily takes her temperature she is no doubt telling him in a wheezy voice (I'm psychic, by the way) that it all happened when she fell down skating at Rockefeller Center with two girl friends."

By this time we were inside the club. While he talked Bad Max had managed to feel my behind, approved the fact that I wasn't wearing a girdle, and suggested that if I felt like doing a strip act that he had invented a new one. "You just come on . . . see, in a special gold evening gown. You walk upstage, light a cigarette, and then very coolly walk back and forth smoking it. As you walk, the music is growling. The audience is licking its lips. You stare at the audience. Then you crush the cigarette out. Blackout. Get it?" he asked, patting my rump. I shook my head. He sighed. "Hell, it's symbolic. The audience stripped you while you smoked. The dream beats the reality."

As we worked our way past the tables, greeting friends of Max, I discovered that fresh air had disappeared forever. The Club was lighted mostly by candles dripping into wax-covered bottles. The cigarette smoke was thick and the whole place seemed to be in motion, with silhouetted people weaving between the tables or rubbing against each other on a tiny dance floor.

We finally located several empty tables in a far corner. Bad Max led us to a huge iron-strapped barrel and invited us to join the crowd around the spigot. He filled a coffee mug for me. It tasted like plain grapefruit juice, but I was soon aware that it could make me seriously dizzy in a very few minutes. In the dim light I had lost track of most of the Harrad kids, but noted that Beth and Jack, chaperoned by Stanley and Harry (who looked somewhat glum), were at a table next to us.

Bad Max, proprietarily taking over, encouraged me to have another Gurgle. Waggling his beard in my face, he demanded to know if I believed his story of Frankie. "Of course, it isn't true," he explained. "I'm really ambisexual, delighting in sexual congress with both men and women. My wife, an elderly lady of sixty-four, supports me and puts up with my heinous behavior so long as I service her regularly on Tuesday and Thursday mornings at half-past ten. Don't laugh," he said. "This schedule leaves me in shape for my own preference in belly bumping on Fridays and Saturdays."

"I'm not laughing; I'm crying," I said.

"We are all crying," murmured a hollow voice from the opposite side of the table.

In the flickering candlelight I discovered that our

table companion was a sunken-eyed skeleton. A curved emaciated nose protruded over the skeleton's neatly trimmed black beard. The skeleton's face, staring at me mournfully, sucked a cigarette which grew out of the corner of its mouth. Occasionally the skeleton emitted a stream of smoke from its nostrils.

"Meet Warner Bondieu," Bad Max said. "We call him Good God for short. Good God, this is Sheila Grove."

"Grove? Grove?" Good God asked. "An interesting name. Used in the Authorized Version of the Bible as a camouflage."

"Good God is a poet," Bad Max explained. "He wears a tomb of useless knowledge between his ears."

"Max is correct," Good God said, grinning. "Let me demonstrate. Grove is the translation that was given to the Hebrew word *Asherah,* which actually means *yoni* or the female sex organ, viz: *First Kings, Chapter Fourteen, Verse Twenty Three.* I quote: 'For they also built them high places and images, and groves, on every hill and under every green tree.' It seems that our early forbears were happy worshippers of the sex organs. As time went by this was not considered a very elevating idea, so the translators of the Bible substituted grove for *yoni.* As you can see, re-writing history was discovered long before the Communists."

"Very enlightening," Bad Max said morosely. Cautiously, he sipped some of his own punch. "The way I feel about it, we should reinstitute this useful custom. If Miss Grove has no objection, we will begin by worshipping her pussy. Salaam!"

"In that event," Good God chuckled, "we should go the entire way. Let me turn your companion into a sex symbol. Take *Sheilah* . . . a name of Irish origin . . . related no doubt to the *Shelah-na-gig:* a curious carving of a female exposing her genitals, found in the keystone arch of ancient Irish places of worship. An emasculating snatch obviously put there to scare the crap out of the devil."

"My middle name is Anne," I said, fascinated in spite of myself.

"From the Hebrew, *Hannah,* meaning Grace. A nice contradiction which, of course, is typical of life. Max, my brain is stimulated. I will now offer this curious assemblage of the thinking rabble a personal reading of my latest poetry."

Bad Max stood up and yelled to someone in the balcony. "Turn the green spot on the stage. We are about to be blessed by a rendition from Good God."

I can't hope to write down Good God's poem, or remember half of what it was about. It lasted at least a half hour and seemed to be a wordy diatribe against poets, artists, businessmen, politicians, sex, marriage, children and the world in general. During the last fifteen minutes, as Good God recited, a girl with long black hair hanging down below her behind, sat on the edge of the stage and emphasized his snarling words with dissonant chords struck on her guitar. Toward the end of the poem, Good God took off his shoes, then his stockings, then his T-shirt, and finally, in a gesture of despair, unbuttoned his dungarees, and continued to recite as they slipped around his ankles, leaving him a naked, swaying, green skeleton, bowing happily to the cheering spectators.

Still naked, carrying his clothes, he and his guitar-playing companion rejoined us at the table. She was introduced as Petey Love.

"Another symbolic name," Bad Max said. "She adores diminutive peters. Put your pants on, Good God, before she demonstrates."

Struggling into his tight dungarees, Good God demanded to know if anyone had written down his poem. "It's lost forever," he said, brushing the tears out of his eyes. "All my greatest work is extemporaneous. I shall never achieve such heights again!"

"It was derivative," Petey said. "You have been influenced by Allen Ginsberg's *Howl*. But never mind. You took off your clothes with more *éclat* than Allen ever did."

"Thank you, thank you, for that accolade," Good God sighed happily.

I excused myself to find the ladies room, and was followed by Petey. The only vacant stall had no doors, and worse had one of those damned female stand-up toilets. Petey watched me hoist my skirt and fumble with my panties, while I silently cursed the man who thought a woman could urinate standing better than sitting. To make matters worse, Petey watched the whole procedure with interest.

"You'll burst your bladder holding that long," she remarked.

I tried to ignore her invasion of my privacy.

"Women make the best lovers, don't you think so?" she asked.

"For men?"

"No, silly . . . for women."

I didn't wait to watch Petey. I scrambled back to the table wondering if she meant it, and feeling slightly sick. Some of the Harrad kids waved at me. Stanley and Harry had disappeared. I noticed that Beth and Jack were talking intimately. A new "act" had started on the stage. I told Bad Max I was leaving.

"Leaving? Where to? It will be midnight in two hours. Then the place will really start jumping. Besides, you don't want to leave The Last Gurgle without seeing

Bad Max's bedroom. I'm going to show it to you personally at midnight." He pushed me back into my chair and pointed at the stage. "Just watch this. This is the sexiest strip act ever put on in New York City."

Reluctantly, I watched the stage while Bad Max gave me a play by play description.

"This is a modern interpretation of the story of Prometheus. I whipped it together one weekend. Tonight you'll see the uncut version. On weekdays, for the tourists, we clean it up."

Accompanied by the high squeal of a cornet and thundering bongos, two male dancers leaped into the center of the stage and were followed by lightning flashes of purple and yellow spot lights. One dancer tugged against chains that looped his body, the other, brandishing a dagger, forced him to the rear of the stage. While the bongos beat furiously, the dancer with the dagger fastened the other dancer to a red brick wall, where he weaved and struggled hopelessly against his chains.

"The one with the dagger is Hephaestus," Bad Max explained. "He is sad at being forced by Zeus to bind Prometheus to the Rock. But Zeus is adamant. Watch."

His face distorted with despair, his hands aloft, Hephaestus offered his dagger to Zeus. Evidently refused, he turned suddenly in a grand *jeté,* landing in front of Prometheus and slashing his clothes, until the writhing and twisting Prometheus was naked against the wall.

"How was that?" Bad Max breathed in my ears. "It took some doing to devise Prometheus' robes so that Hephaestus could slash them off without cutting him to pieces. The first performance, Prometheus was wiggling so damned much that Hephaestus nearly de-balled him."

In spite of myself I couldn't help staring at Prometheus. His tall, naked, muscular body, hairless except for the pubic area, fought against its chains in an agonized movement that was obviously meant to portray frustrated sexuality.

"He's a handsome brute," Bad Max sighed. "All the women want to take him to bed. But he's a man's man . . . as was Prometheus. Does the idea shock you?"

I shook my head. I wasn't shocked. I just wanted to cry.

Five girls, naked except for diaphanous skirts wound lightly around their hips and unshaved pubes, appeared *sur les pointes,* and danced mincingly around Prometheus.

"They are the daughters of Oceanus," Bad Max explained. "They are angry with Zeus, and in despair because they know that Prometheus will never be forgiven."

As they danced by him, the daughters of Oceanus lightly caressed Prometheus, who arched his pelvis in suitable reaction to their touch.

"Good thing he prefers men." Bad Max grinned at me. "How do you like the way I've sexed up Aeschylus?"

Another naked girl, wearing horns on her head and a tail suspended from behind, danced onto the stage and did a *pas de poisson* into the arms of Hephaestus. She was pursued by another male dancer, who snapped a whip at her.

"That girl is a damned good dancer," Bad Max said, clapping. "She is Io who was turned into a heifer by Hera. Hermes is pursuing her. Do you know the story?"

I nodded. "Io was loved by Zeus. Hera punished Zeus by turning Io into a heifer and forcing her to wander the world endlessly."

Hermes was now dancing menacingly around Prometheus.

"I am the originator of the nude ballet." Bad Max grinned at me. "You can readily see that the movements of the body are expressed in the entrechats, the lifts, the *pas de bourree,* are much more entrancing when seen naked—a beautiful flow of controlled flesh in motion. Now, watch! Prometheus has refused to tell Hermes the name of the person who will eventually usurp Zeus' power. Hermes indicates that for his defiance of Zeus, Prometheus must suffer interminably. Here is the *tour de force.* I have made the eagle, who will gnaw endlessly on Prometheus' liver, a woman!"

For a second all the stage lights went out. While a cornet snarled and the bongos thumped in an increasing intensity, the floodlights slowly turned the stage a misty green. A woman, naked except for black wings strapped to her arms, literally flew on stage. Floating down from above and inside the curtain, she glided toward Prometheus, her face made up like a vulture, her body held incredibly straight and rigid with only her arms moving slowly up and down. It was impossible to see how she was suspended. When she alighted on the stage, she hurled herself, naked, against the naked Prometheus. The stage slowly darkened, the bongos thundered, and the cornet wailed until the sound became supersonic.

Good God broke the trance. "You should have made the eagle a man. The end would be more Grecian and not nearly so nasty."

"Why didn't you make them both women?" Petey asked.

"Christ Almighty," Bad Max exploded. "How do you please everybody?"

I finally escaped Bad Max by telling him I wanted to talk with some of my friends. Locating my leopard coat under a heap of fur coats in the unmonitored cloak room, and without daring to look behind me, I dashed to the street and freedom.

Signalling wildly at taxis that ignored me, I discovered Harry Schacht, quite drunk, leaning against a street light on the corner of MacDougal Street.

"Hi," he said, peering at me without recognition.

"I'm Sheila," I said. "Come on, we are going back to the Astor."

"I'm sick," Harry said. "Don't feel good."

"Well . . . not good."

"Well . . . Well . . . Down in the Well," he sang as I moved him into a taxi that finally heeded my frantic signalling.

Inside he collapsed against me, murmuring: "Beth . . . Beth. . . . I spun the *dreidl* and lost . . . lost all my candy down the well."

"Your boy friend?" the taxi driver asked.

Harry slumped against me. I took off his glasses and put my arm around him. By the time we got back to the hotel he was snoring. Somehow, I piloted him through the lobby and up the elevator to our rooms. Harry ran for the bathroom, and I could hear him vomiting. I held his head over the toilet fearful that his wracking spasms would shake his frail body apart.

"Oh, Sheila . . . I'm very sorry," he moaned. "I never really drank anything in my life before except beer."

"Why did you drink tonight?"

"Because I lost the only girl in the world that was ever nice to me."

"I'm being nice to you."

"But you don't care about me."

I kissed the back of his head. "I care for you, Harry. Come on, I'll help you get into bed."

He sat on the toilet, and I washed his face and un-

buttoned his shirt. Guiding him into one of the bedrooms, I pushed him into a twin bed, took off his trousers, shorts, and shoes, and after a great deal of tugging,
finally got him under the covers. Then I couldn't help it.
I sat beside him on the bed and sobbed.

"You crying, too?" Harry opened his eyes and stared
at me.

"No. Go to sleep."

I knew I couldn't stay in the hotel and wait for the
Harrad kids to come back. I couldn't face Stanley or
Beth or any of their New Year's gaiety. I had to go. Go
where? Anywhere. I wrote a note on the hotel stationery. "Stanley, I've gone to LaGuardia to take a plane
back to Harrad. You can drive my car back. Take care
of Harry. You owe it to him." I pinned the note to
Harry's trousers, grabbed my suitcase, and ran for the
hotel lobby.

It's March. It's snowing. Harry just went back to his
room. "Aren't you lonesome?" he asked just before he
left.

"Yes," I said. "But I'm not ready for a roommate."

I haven't been able to write in this journal since the
week after New Year's. Harry is the only one who
knows the frightening conclusion to my New Year's
Eve. Even now when I remember how terrified I was
. . . so sickeningly afraid that I actually wet my pants
. . . I don't like to think about it. But I know I have to
write it down. If only to try and stop it from endlessly
unreeling in my brain like a slow motion horror movie
. . . if only to ask as I have a thousand times since; why?
why? God . . . why does love escape us?

When I dashed out of the Astor, I was ruthlessly
sucked into a maelstrom of screaming, yelling, laughing,
cursing, drunken, whirling, twisting, world-gone-mad
people, all hovering on the brink of midnight. Thou-

sands and thousands of them, drinking from bottles, throwing streamers and confetti, cracking noisemakers, hugging, grabbing, goosing, kissing, slobbering against me as I tried to find my way to 42nd Street, and a possible taxi. It was hopeless. I was shoved deeper and deeper into the crowd in the opposite direction.

"In five minutes it will be New Year's Eve," someone screamed in my ear. A man swung me around and kissed me with wet slippery lips. Trying desperately to hold my suitcase, I couldn't fend him off. He kept kissing me, his breath heavy with whiskey and cigar smoke. I screamed, and he was dragged away with the crowd.

"Dearie, it's awful," a woman muttered. "A lot of people are going to get trampled to death before this is over."

Someone whirled me around and blew a noisemaker in my face. I stumbled back . . . was pushed forward . . . and then I tripped and fell to my knees. I could feel my nylons split under the sharp impact. Someone grabbed my suitcase. A hand clutched my armpit. Strong fingers bit through my fur coat and jerked me to my feet. Numbly, my knees aching and bleeding, I stared into the faces of three boys who had formed a wedge against the crowd.

"Hey, we found ourselves a doll," one of them yelled.

Another, brandishing a fifth of whiskey, shoved it in my face.

"You're slopping it all over her, man," the one holding my arm said. I could smell the cheap liquor on his breath. "Where's your boyfriend?"

"Would you help me get a taxi?" I begged him. His hand was still a vise on my arm. Hundreds of faces, laughing, angry, contorted, flowed by us like water pouring over a dam, never ceasing, an endless stream of grinning eyes, and mouths shouting Happy New Year.

The boys stood their ground, viciously punching at anyone who tried to push them into the swirling, undulating mass.

"I dub thee Sir Galahad." The boy holding the whiskey sprinkled some on the one who held me. "I dub thee Sir Launcelot." He splashed some on the other boy, who angrily jabbed him in the ribs.

"Cut the crap and stop wasting that stuff."

"Don't talk to me like that. I'm King Arthur. Get on your god-damned white horses. Break a path through this stinking pile of humanity. We will rescue Lady Tit-Quim from the mad dragon-bagons."

King Arthur, who had long black sideburns, pulled me away from Sir Galahad and shoved him and Sir Launcelot into the crowd. I noticed that the back of their jackets were lettered with the word "Chasers."

"We're tit-and-pussy chasers," King Arthur said, laughing raucously as he propelled me forward.

Pushing, shoving, flaying their arms, Sir Galahad and Sir Launcelot flung themselves against the tide of people who were moving in the opposite direction. They stamped on feet, straight-armed, jammed people in the middle, and cursed them. When one man angrily refused to give ground, they lifted him by the armpits and tossed him bodily into the crowd. Ignoring the cries of hoodlums and punks that were screamed at them they finally reached the corner of 47th Street. At last we were free of the helpless revellers. I tried to thank them and asked for my suitcase.

"You won't get a cab here until the crowds thin out," King Arthur said. "We'll walk you through to 9th Avenue."

I tried to assure them that I was all right.

"We haven't finished saving you, Lady Tit-Quim," Sir Galahad said.

"Have a drink and calm down," Sir Launcelot said. "We are jolly knights of the round table." He grabbed my other arm. With Sir Galahad leading, they pushed me along 47th Street.

"Please, please! Let me go!" I screamed.

"She's looking for a place to have a leak," Sir Launcelot explained to the curious passersby.

King Arthur held me menacingly. While Sir Launcelot and Sir Galahad stood in front of us, preventing anyone from seeing what was happening, King Arthur snapped open a long switch knife and pushed it deep into my fur coat. "If you yell like that again, I'll slit you in two from your skinny neck right down to your hairy crotch. Get the message?"

We were now quite a distance from Times Square. The few people hurrying by ignored us completely. The noise and bright lights had disappeared. Our footsteps echoed on the empty street.

"Please," I begged, paralyzed with fear as they forced me to walk faster and faster. "If you want money, take my pocket book."

"What are we going to do with her?" Sir Galahad asked.

"This looks like a rich quiff," King Arthur said. "I think we'll look into her suitcase."

"There's nothing in it, please, please . . ." I said, unable to hold back my tears. "Let me go!"

"Take her damned pocket book," Sir Launcelot said. "Let's get the hell out of here. I don't want to get tangled with the fuzz."

"There's an open-air garage across the street; we can take her there. Check it out, Chaser."

Sir Galahad ran across the street and disappeared. We waited on the corner. Helplessly I watched the automobiles speeding by us, praying they might see the terror on my face. A taxi slowed down, but Sir Launcelot waved the driver on.

In a few minutes Sir Galahad returned, puffing. "There's a stairway to the roof floor. Nobody up there. A couple of trucks is all."

When we reached the garage, Sir Galahad yanked open a metal door leading upstairs. I screamed. King Arthur shoved me inside and slapped me twice across the face. "Try that again, sister, and you've had it."

They dragged me up the stairs to the roof. I was sobbing hysterically, only dimly aware that it was freezing cold. In the background the tall buildings of Manhattan and the shimmering lights looked frigidly down on us . . . disinterested stone and glass.

Sir Galahad jumped up on the tailgate of one of the trucks. "This crate is empty. Toss her up here. Let's get out of the wind before we freeze to death."

They pushed me into the truck. Sir Galahad explored my face with a pocket flashlight. "Stop blubbering. We aren't going to kill you."

King Arthur pushed me to the back of the truck and forced me to sit on the metal floor. Slumping down beside me, he took a swallow of whiskey from the bottle Sir Launcelot handed him, and then grabbed me by the back of the neck. "Open your mouth," he hissed. Digging his fingers into my neck he pulled my head back. I finally opened my mouth. He poured the whiskey slopping it in my face, forcing me to swallow, I finally gagged.

"For Christ sake, leave her alone," Sir Launcelot said. "Let's grab her dough and get the hell out of here before we all freeze to death."

"I thought we were going to shag her," Sir Galahad said. "This looks like good stuff."

"Shut up, you fag," Sir Launcelot opened my suitcase

and dumped it on the floor of the truck. Using pocket flashlights they pawed through the mess. King Arthur held up my brassieres and panties and sniffed at them. "There's nothing in the suitcase. Dump out her pocketbook."

Whistling with amazement, they counted the money. "Two hundred and thirty-two smackers. We've hit it rich."

"What kind of coat is this?" King Arthur demanded, rubbing the fur.

"It's leopard. Please, for God's sake, let me go."

He grabbed me by the arm. "How much is it worth?"

"Fifteen hundred dollars."

King Arthur started to pull my coat off.

"Let her go. We're not snatching her coat." Sir Launcelot said, pulling him away from me.

"This is a rich bitch," King Arthur snarled. "Listen, you crumb, when did you ever get so near a babe who wore a thousand buck coat?"

"Her snatch must be made of gold. I want to stick my shaft in her little gold mine," Sir Galahad pinned my arms with one hand and tore open the top of my dress with the other. "You first, King Arthur. I'll hold her."

I kicked my legs wildly but King Arthur managed to push my dress up. He ripped at my panties. "Jesus, she's pissing herself," he said, drawing his hand away. And I was. So terrified that I no longer had control. I locked my legs together, but it was hopeless. King Arthur stuck the point of his knife against my navel. "Open your legs up wide, sister, or I'll stick you." He drew the knife across my belly, increasing the pressure until I was certain that I was bleeding. Moaning, trying to writhe away from Sir Galahad who held my breast I finally

opened my legs. King Arthur examined me with a flash
light.

"Looks like any other tail . . . only damper," he said.
"Maybe it feels different." He unzipped his pants.

"Okay," Sir Launcelot snarled. "You've had your
fun. Let the kid go!" I heard the snap of a switch knife.

"You're off your rocker," King Arthur said, ignoring
him. "Take a drink and watch a man knock off a piece."
His penis in his hand he started to lower himself on me.

Sir Launcelot shoved him with his foot. King Arthur
fell forward on me yelling angrily. He jumped up. I
heard a knife swish through the air. Sir Galahad let go
of me and tried to stand between them.

"Cut it out, you two! What the hell are you fighting
about?"

"I told him to leave her alone," Sir Launcelot said.
"Get the hell out of my way."

"You crazy bastard, I'll kill you," King Arthur
snarled. He pushed Sir Galahad away and lunged at Sir
Launcelot. Then he fell back, screaming in agony,
clutching himself.

"You slashed me," King Arthur sobbed. "Jesus, I'm
bleeding. I'm going to bleed to death."

"Why in hell did you do that?" Sir Galahad demanded. He examined King Arthur with a flashlight.
"He's bleeding like a pig."

"He's a pig, all right." Sir Launcelot said grimly.
"It's only a slit on his belly. He's lucky I didn't slice his
prick off." Sir Launcelot grabbed me by the arm and
pushed me out of the truck. "Come on, get the hell out
of here before things get rough." He rushed me down
the garage stairs. At the bottom of the stairwell he
pushed me against the wall. I was shivering so hard
that I could scarcely stand.

"Are you going to run to the cops?" he demanded.

"No! No!" I shuddered. "Just let me go. Please!"

He still held the open knife in his hand. "Aren't you going to thank me for saving you?"

I really looked at him for the first time. He had a sunken, pock-marked face. Except for his eyes, which seemed sad, he was frighteningly ugly. He couldn't have been more than nineteen. Trying to stop sobbing, I shrank against the wall. An open light bulb glowed dully on the staircase landing. Frantic with fear, I was certain I was going to faint.

"Maybe you didn't care. Maybe you wanted him to do it."

"Please. I thank you. Please. Let me go."

"Are you afraid of me?"

I nodded dumbly.

"Don't you want to know why I saved you?"

To rape me yourself, I thought, but said nothing.

"I would have liked to screw you," he said. "I never had a girl. Girls wouldn't have anything to do with me. I can't help my face. But I wouldn't ever want a girl that didn't want me. Do you think a girl like you would ever make love with me?"

"Yes," I said, and my teeth were chattering. "If you were nice to her, and protected her, a girl would want to make love with you."

He stared at me for a minute, trying to determine if I meant it. "Okay, you can go. I'm sorry about your money and your clothes."

I'll never know why, but I kissed him.

"Thank you, thank you," I said, and I ran. Afraid that he might be following me, I looked back. He was just standing there. Sir Launcelot.

Somehow, I got through the lobby of the Astor without attracting attention. I looked at the clock unbelievingly. It was only twelve-thirty. Less than forty-five minutes ago I was holding Harry's head while he spewed out his stomach in the toilet. None of the Harrad kids had returned from The Last Gurgle. Harry was sleeping where I had left him.

I stared at myself in the full length door mirror. Tears were pouring down the face of the girl who looked back at me. Her hair was disheveled, her lipstick smeared, the top of her dress was ripped open, and her stockings were ravelling around her ankles. As I looked at the stranger in the mirror, the full horror and shock of what had happened struck me. I ran into the bathroom and threw up.

As I leaned over the sink, I felt a hand on my back. I screamed, and then recognized Harry's face in the mirror. He was naked . . . skinny; looking at me worriedly. I rushed into his arms and he held me while I sobbed uncontrollably.

"I'm so lost, Harry . . . so very lost. I just can't face anyone else tonight."

"We'll lock ourselves in the bedroom," Harry said softly. And we did. Harry washed my face and helped me take my dress off. Tenderly, he washed the caked blood from the scratches King Arthur's knife had left on my stomach. Shivering in his arms, crying my heart out, I told him what had happened.

"I just can't believe it, Harry. Those boys must feel some love toward *some* girl. Maybe they've even held a girl close to them, protecting her, soothing her fears, caring for her. If they've loved someone in their lives, cared for someone once, how could they deliberately hurt a stranger?"

"You haven't been reading your history lately," Harry said. "Has man made any progress in the last twenty years? Really? The Nazi and Commissar mentality is still rampant. Man's an emotional infant. When it comes to love, we are all strangers."

"I don't feel strange lying here naked with you."

Harry held me close to him. We didn't talk. Though his penis felt big against my belly, he didn't try to make love. I wondered if we would be lovers one day, and I was glad we could be quiet with each other and still be happy and secure. When the rest of the Harrad kids came back to the room and banged on the door, Harry refused to open it. "Go away," he yelled, "I feel antisocial. There's plenty of room to sleep on the floor."

No one asked where Sheila was. Perhaps no one cared.

FROM THE JOURNAL OF HARRY SCHACHT

February, March, the First Year

Four weeks ago I was determined to quit Harrad. I told Phil Tenhausen it was the only sane thing to do. I would take a room in Cambridge or Boston, finish out the year, and then in the fall transfer to a regular college . . . preferably male.

"You are giving up at your first crisis," Phil said. "Somehow, it doesn't sound like you, Harry. I thought you were a pretty clear thinking young man."

"Not when it comes to love, Phil," I told him. "I've thought a lot about it. I have two counts against me. I'm homely . . . maybe ugly, and I'm Jewish. That not being sufficient, I lowered my guard, and let myself fall in love with a WASP (White-Anglo-Saxon-Protestant). It's not your fault there are no Jewish girls at Harrad. I'd bet there will never be any . . . nor any Catholic girls. The whole idea is too much in conflict with traditional beliefs and theology. Really, in a way, it's a good thing for me that Beth didn't play me along. When I went home for vacation I suddenly saw my family through Beth's eyes. My mother and father are not really orthodox, but they respect our customs. I could imagine Beth's home with a Christmas tree, holly, a big turkey dinner, Christmas carolling . . . all the excitement that goes with Christmas, and I contrasted it with Chanukah, and my mother lighting the candles in the menorah for eight nights, our token gifts, and our endless procession of relatives joining us for *latkes*. As I listened to all the excited conversation, interspersed with Yiddish slang, and Yiddish jokes I knew that if Beth had been there she would have felt foreign . . . a *shicksa,* and while my mother and father would have tried to make her welcome, Beth would never feel a part of this life . . . anymore than I could ever be honest with myself singing *Hark the Herald Angels Sing* . . . or what have you? What I would like to know, Phil, is why? Why did you ever put Beth and I together as roommates?"

Phil smiled. "We chose you as two potentially intelligent people who have a great deal to offer each other. We expected and hoped a switching of roommates would occur. In all probability, even the current shifts will not be final. All Harrad students are in a unique position. They have the opportunity to know and understand more than one person of the opposite sex intimately and develop emotional relationships with them that are far more mature than any similar relationships occurring in what we term a normal premarital environment. While we have suggested that the best approach to each other would be for roommates not to particularize their love; we guessed that inevitably, having been raised in a culture which believes that love between male and female must be specific excluding all others, that many of you would repeat the same role at Harrad; demanding exclusive love in return for exclusive love."

"I was never demanding of Beth," I said, angrily.

Phil chuckled. "You expected because you loved her

. . . that she would love you in an identical way, didn't you? That's an extremely demanding idea. It can lead to the following conclusions. You either blame yourself, telling yourself that Beth didn't love you because you are ugly or you are Jewish or any of a host of masochistic ideas that you may dream up to whip yourself with; or you take a more positive approach and tell yourself that Beth is really not a good person because she didn't respond to your good love. The first approach will destroy your identity and probably lead to insanity, the second approach which is more typical, will ultimately bring you to the following: 'I really dislike Beth. She is promiscuous and will never love any one except herself.'

"Depending on how strongly you react, it is a simple step to move from her apparent rejection of you to your rejection of her. This makes life simple. You reduce your problems to black and white. In this case: 'I hate Beth.' All of this is extremely unrealistic thinking. You are planning to be a doctor, aren't you, Harry? In our opinion many of the illnesses that you will encounter will have been triggered by this type of thinking. Hating is a self-indulgence that eventually leads to self-destruction. Where are you at the moment, Harry?"

"I guess I've already arrived at the second phase. Yesterday, Beth had the cool nerve to ask me if we could study some Chemistry problems together. Jack is planning to major in economics and he is only taking a bare minimum in sciences. So you need me after all, I thought. I may not be a smooth operator like Jack Dawes, but you are glad to pick my brains. I almost told her no; then, I agreed. We studied in her room. Jack had gone to an evening lecture at 'D' University. After dinner, when I went to their room, Beth greeted me dressed in her terry cloth bathrobe. She knew that I knew she never wore anything under it.

"She was shy and formal. 'I appreciate your coming, Harry. I'm glad you aren't angry with me.'

"I tried not to look directly at her. We reviewed several chapters and solved two of the problems that were bothering her. I started to leave.

" 'Can't we just talk, Harry?' she asked.

" 'You must be crazy,' I said angrily. 'What do you think I am? Nothing but a Great Stone Face? In a few hours Jack will be here, and you'll take that damned bathrobe off. I'll be back with Stanley, imagining you making passionate love with Jack. What are you trying to do . . . drive me insane?'

"Then do you know what she did? She took off the bathrobe and sat in my lap, naked, and kissed me. 'I like you, Harry,' she said, 'I always will. Take me in the bedroom and make love with me.'

" 'Why don't you screw a red light over your door and go into business?' I asked. 'How many men do you want, anyway?'

"Beth stood up and put her bathrobe back on. 'I finished my period yesterday. If I had made love with you tonight, I would have told Jack,' she grinned at me. 'See, I'm a good Harrad girl. If you should get me pregnant, I wouldn't want Jack to think he was the father. Honestly, Harry. You have no sense of humor. Look at how grim you are. You think I'm promiscuous. I have had sexual intercourse with three men at Harrad, and you are one of them. From each person I've made love with, I learned something . . . mostly that the act of sexual congress is simply not so damned death-defying, all encompassing serious. It is not the alpha and omega of love or marriage. It's fun. The really wonderful thing about it is, if you come to the act of love defenseless, willing to give yourself to another person, and the other person shares this feeling, then for a few moments in your life it's possible to be wholly and completely the real you. If two people make love this way, and stop playing roles with each other, and can enjoy and accept each other for the frightened little people they really are . . . then sexual intercourse becomes a way of saying "I am for a moment no longer me, I am you!" ' "

"I like that," Phil said thoughtfully. "What did you say?"

"Nothing. I went back to my room. Truthfully, for the moment I hated Beth. If I had made love with her it wouldn't have been nice, I just wanted to conquer her. I wanted her to admit that she was wrong . . . that she couldn't love me and Jack and Stanley. Why did I ever fall in love with her, Phil?"

"Supposing you could have perfection?" Phil asked. "Supposing Beth reacted just exactly as you wished."

"I would love her forever."

"Wouldn't you really be loving your own reflection. Narcissus gazing in the pool, enamored with himself. You are too smart for that, Harry. You would get bored. I'm sure that if you stay at Harrad you will find another girl. When you do . . . love her for her uniqueness as an individual. Love her as a particular female with all the wonderful attributes and mystery of the generalized female and human being. Stop worrying about whether she loves you. One thing is fundamental; if you give love instead of asking for it, if you love openly, defenselessly discarding forever the proposition, 'I'll love you if you'll love me,' which most people live by, then you will discover a wonderful serenity in your life. Give love, tenderness, affection, warmth, interest, be unafraid to share your fears and worries, show people that you need them, too, and you will have love in abundance."

"Sounds Christian to me," I said. "Turn the other cheek."

"It was a Jew who said it."

When I told Stanley, he said: "Harry, I think Beth has you bugged. Why didn't you make love with her? I would have. You enjoy your suffering. You're so convinced you've failed with a woman that the failure is more real to you than Beth. Yet it hasn't thrown you entirely. I've watched you studying. If Beth is affecting you so much, how can you concentrate and prepare your courses so thoroughly? Not to mention the fact that every night you go across the hall and visit with Sheila for at least an hour. On the other hand, take the sad case of Stanley Cole. Sheila doesn't find me an exciting conversationalist the way she used to. Beth will argue with me on any subject *at dinner*. Yesterday, I went skating with her. She gave me a great hug when I laced up her skates, but she didn't invite me to study with her."

"Maybe it's deprivation," I said. "If we were going to a regular college we probably would never have made out on a regular basis with any girl. But here at Harrad we have both experienced the delights of the bed. After a wonderful idyll, it's hard to go back to reality."

"What is reality?" Stanley asked. "If someone from some other college or university around here had been listening at the keyhole to our discussion, I wager he wouldn't consider it reality. It would sound like a pipe dream. Anyway, since both Beth and Sheila seem to have lost interest in Stanley Cole, Valerie Latrobe has decided that she might like to room with me for a month or two. Next week Peter Longini is going to move in with you."

I looked at him, astonished. "This sounds like a kid game of musical chairs. You mean to say that Peter isn't angry?"

"He suggested it. He wants to see what will happen

when an irresistible force meets an immovable object. Meaning that Valerie needs a mental spanking, and I've been elected to give it to her."

"This place is getting pretty damned casual about the whole business," I said. "I wonder where it's all going to end up. It looks to me as if we are building our future on sand. After four years at Harrad no one will really love anyone very much, and none of us will have a secure love relationship."

"I think you're wrong, Harry. I agree with the Tenhausens that a rapid shifting of sexual partners in the outside world would certainly devalue the sexual and interpersonal relationships, but here at Harrad we are very much a contained community. All of us are developing on a high intellectual plane and simultaneously being indoctrinated into a much saner view of the male and female relationship. I am much more than the Stanley Cole who arrived at Harrad seven months ago. I am me plus Beth and plus Sheila and plus all the other influences that I have absorbed as well as the courses I am studying. Not one minute that I have spent with Beth or Sheila has been casual. When we made love it was not sex for the sake of sex. It was because we liked each other and wanted to share the depth of that liking in a natural release of our affections. The real joy in the act of love is when the normal human defenses are down, when role playing and posturing are gone. This is the key to everything I've learned at Harrad. Most people go through their whole lives and never learn that in the act of love the great catharsis is not the orgasm. That's too short-lived. It's the simple, blinding revelation that you and this female you care for are both small fumbling creatures needing to be loved. The world, man in aggregate and the blind forces of nature which man will never understand, are not hostile; they're rather disinterested. So the only peaceful harbor is the warm, bubbling laughter of individual man's love for each other and for his wonderful, ridiculous humanity."

"Everybody at Harrad spouts the Tenhausen gospel," I said. "I'm still provincial. How could you make love to Beth now . . . knowing she made love with me as well as Jack Dawes? That's all I would think about."

"Why not? Is she less a person? If she still retains the delight of love and doesn't become bored and casual, which she won't if she has any real intelligence, then she may actually have become more rather than less. You know, Harry, there's one amazingly beautiful thing about the act of love freely given between a man and woman who trust each other. If they understand what is happening, they're no longer just existing; each one is becoming. You are *you,* extended in the delight and confidence of the other person. It would be a wonderful world if what the male and female could learn in this interaction could be extended to embrace every human interrelationship. As Phil Tenhausen says, 'We are living in a world that sneers at idealism, or sentimentalizes it. The mission of Harrad is to make all of us practical idealists!' "

As I try to write down this conversation between me and Stanley, I suddenly realize that many of the words I put into the mouth of Stanley are really my own words, but if I read them back to Stanley, he'd accept them as his. It's interesting and somewhat frightening. Since most of us come to Harrad without any real philosophy of life, after four years most of us probably will have absorbed the Harrad philosophy. God help us if the Tenhausens are wrong and the tried (and true?) ways of society are right.

Last night after supper I walked with Sheila to her room. She seemed unusually quiet, remote and withdrawn into her own world. I noticed she'd brought a painter's easel. On it stood a strange painting of shadowy, blue-black houses with window shades drawn nearly to the bottom, revealing pale yellow lights behind them, and in the sky a moon, mostly obscured by black-edged clouds.

"I didn't know that you were an artist."

"I'm not," Sheila said. "I've been taking a course in art. We learn to appreciate by attempting to paint. It's far more enlightening than just looking at a picture. You learn how difficult it is to handle oils, or water colors, and express yourself at the same rate."

"This looks pretty good to me."

"It's neither good nor pretty. It's symbolic."

"Symbolic of what?"

"I don't know . . . loneliness."

"Well, symbolic things irk me! Why does everything in art have to be symbolic, or have hidden meanings, or be written on two planes? Why does man want to be so damned subtle and put a shroud around the world? Life itself has so much mystery that man should spend his life trying to uncover it rather than muddying it up with symbols. Why don't you and I say what we think with each other?"

Sheila smiled. "All right. Here's what I've really been thinking in the past few minutes. I have cramps. I got my period this morning. Why do I flow so much? Will Harry leave soon . . . or will I tell him I have a headache? I really have to go to the bathroom. I'm sure that the tampon isn't working. I think I better use sanitary pads for the first two days. Do I have an odor? I know I do. I really have a headache. I think I'll lie down. I feel like crying. I think I'll put a heating pad on my belly. I'd like to snuggle against Harry. Maybe his hand would feel good on my stomach."

"Hey," I said, delighted. "That's much more fun. Now that I really know what you are thinking, the way you've been acting makes more sense."

Sheila shrugged. "What I told you is only a part of what I've been thinking. No human being dares lay himself completely open to another person. You'd better go, Harry, I really feel quite messy and unconversational tonight."

"What about wanting me to snuggle against you? I'd be happy to warm your stomach."

Sheila looked at me with tears in her eyes. "When I told you that I was thinking, Harry . . . I was really thinking Stanley."

"Oh," I mumbled. "Well, I'll see you tomorrow."

A few hours later I told Stanley what Sheila said. "She's miserable. Why don't you go see her? She really wants you."

Stanley shook his head. "Harry, you have absolutely no confidence. You should have put your arm around her instead of bumbling off like a ninny."

"Oh, for God's sake, Stan. Why should I comfort her when she is thinking about you?"

Stanley laughed. "You know what would happen if I went to her? She wouldn't be happy at all. She'd start a long discussion on how I would rather be with Beth than with her. In ten minutes she'd make herself more miserable than she is."

"Brother," I said. "I just decided to hell with women. They're too complicated for me."

"What Sheila and you both need is some laughter." Stanley looked at his watch. "It's twelve-fifteen. Sheila has gone to bed. She never stays up beyond eleven-thirty. Come on. We'll both jump in bed with her stark naked. We'll tell her we've come to warm her belly. It's high time Sheila stopped being so damned exclusive."

Sheila's door was locked, but Stanley was not to be deterred from his idea. We ploughed through the snow to the maintenance shop, got a ladder, and propped it against Sheila's study window. Stanley went up first. Shushing and shirring each other, we finally eased the window open and squeezed through, into the study. Hastily undressing, we tried to orient ourselves without turning on the light. I tiptoed silently behind Stanley toward the bedroom door, and then he bumped into the easel, tripped and fell against it with an ear-shattering crash.

Sheila, in a shorty night-gown, opened the door, snapped on the lights, and stared at us unbelievingly.

"Oh, my good lord," she gasped, unable to stop laughing. "Look at the two of you! Naked as jaybirds."

"We came to warm your belly." Stanley said, trying to look dignified as he ruefully rubbed his knee.

"See," I said. "No subtlety. No symbols. No secrets."

Stanley grabbed her and pushed her into the bedroom. "Since you really can't make up your mind, get in bed. We're both going to sleep with you."

And we did! Wedged between us, Sheila finally stopped laughing and solemnly kissed us each goodnight.

"Thank you, Harry. Thank you, Stanley," she said.

"For what?"

"For caring."

FROM THE JOURNAL OF BETH HILLYER

April, May and June, the First Year

Last night when Jack came back from the lecture at "D" University, I told him I had made love with Harry Schacht.

"That's nice," was all he said. "I hope Harry is smiling again for a change."

"Aren't you jealous?" I demanded.

"Nope," Jack said. "I know you like Harry."

"It means I can't make love with you for a month."

"That's nonsense," Jack kissed my ear and then took a little bite on my neck. "You've been taking those pills religiously. How could you get pregnant? Anyway, you know the only reason that the Tenhausens set that once a month rule with one boy was really just to slow everyone down a little until they could brainwash us."

"Supposing somehow I did get pregnant?"

"I'd marry you. What else? You'd be a doctor and I'd be an economist and we'd live happily ever after."

"Supposing it were Harry's baby?"

"If you buy a cat or a dog, is it your cat or dog?"

"Sure, I guess so."

"Why?"

"Because you love it and feed it and take care of it and it loves you back."

"Quod erat demonstrum," Jack laughed. "It's a wise father that knoweth his own child, anyway. Harry and I both have brown eyes, and brown eyes are dominant."

"Do you really believe all this Tenhausen stuff?" I asked him. "Everyone here spouts it, but when the chips are down, then what? Don't you really think I'm immoral? In less than a year, I've made love with three different Harrad boys. You've only made love with me."

"I'm happy. Besides, we've got three years to go."

"Would you want to marry me even if you didn't have to?"

"Do I have to?"

"No! Damn you!"

While this conversation was going on, Jack undressed. I followed him into the bedroom and watched him get into bed. "Open the window, like a good kid," he sighed, and closed his eyes.

"I'm not a good kid," I said. "I really *didn't* make love with Harry Schacht."

Jack looked at me, amused. "I could have guessed that. If you had, you wouldn't be so discursive. Really, Beth, your basic nature is that of a big, hungry, affectionate mother. You want all your boys to love you. Harry, Stanley, Jack. You want to hold us fiercely against those lovely tits of yours, pat us on the po-pos, pin on our mittens, and send us to school with tears of sheer joy in your eyes. You go around with the notion that you want a man to dominate you. You think you could be a slave to some willful man, but the few times I have tried the masterful approach on you, you act as if I'm some kind of nut. The plain and simple truth is that you need at least three men and a dozen children to absorb your overflowing affectionate nature."

I snuggled beside him in bed. "I'm really bad, aren't I?"

"No," he said, burying his face in my breasts, "I find you comforting."

The nice thing about Jack is that he doesn't take me seriously. I told him I would only be serious about studying. I was going to medical school come hell or high water, just to prove to Pops that I could do it. But I wasn't going to take anything else seriously. If I live to seventy, I have fifty years to be serious, so I'm not starting until I get at least half way.

Jack pointed out that I was serious about love. I admit it. I'm in love with Jack, Harry, and Stanley, and that's nothing to laugh about. Still, it makes me bubble with laughter. Lately, I've been falling in love with Sheila, too.

Somehow, since early in March, we all seem to have crossed the troubled waters and landed on a quiet island. It started when Harry and Sheila decided to room together. Then Valerie moved in with Stanley. That lasted four weeks. The other night at dinner Stanley told all of us at our table that he and Valerie had decided to give up the Experiment.

"We like each other better," Valerie said, grinning at him. "But we have both discovered that not everybody can room together, even if they get along in bed."

She wouldn't tell us any more, but that night Sheila, Harry, and Stanley visited with Jack and me, and we gradually pumped the story out of Stanley.

Jack and I bought a hot plate, and though it is against dormitory rules, he was making coffee, and warming up some pizzas Sheila brought from her refrigerator. Because all of our rooms are at the end of the corridor, and because we'd become more sexually involved with each other than with the rest of the Harrad kids, the six of us had got into the habit of meeting around ten o'clock to discuss the world in general and us in particular. For the past four weeks Valerie had arrived with Stanley and joined in the discussion. Now, since Valerie had decided to room with Peter again, Stanley was alone. Dressed in a sweat suit he'd used for cross country running, and ignoring my comments that he definitely had a gymnasium odor, Stanley sprawled on the floor doing a bicycle exercise with his feet.

"My last night with this group," he said puffing.

"Just because Valerie has left you?" Jack asked.

"Sure . . . no room for a Onesie among you Twosies."

"That's silly," Sheila said. "After all, we do know each other quite well."

"Yeah," Stanley grunted as Jack handed him a wedge of pizza. "The last time I slept with you, Harry was on your other side, staring at me all night. Not conducive to romance in my book."

"What are we going to do about you?" I asked Stanley. "Obviously, the Tenhausens overlooked this in their calculations . . . one person of the opposite sex too many."

"They can even it out with the freshman class in the fall," Stanley chuckled. "I'm patient."

Jack suggested that Sheila and I share the problem of Stanley. He proposed Sheila and I work our way around a circle, week by week, composed of the three of them.

"That would give Sheila the dubious pleasure of sleeping with me every third week," Jack said, grinning at Sheila, who looked quite shocked. "Well, you did say a minute ago that we were all well acquainted, Sheila. I seem to be the only male who hasn't experienced nuptial delights with all the females present."

"Why do men think that every female is different in bed?" Sheila demanded.

"I pass," Jack said. "I am a Harrad neophyte. Ask Stanley or Harry."

"Don't answer," Harry laughed. "Next thing, she'll want to know qualitative differences."

Stanley chewed a second piece of pizza philosophically. "My own opinion is that the variation in experience in bed is only limited by the number of women in the world and the male's willingness to appreciate the infinite and subtle differences which are not truly sexual but mental . . . hence while the physical characteristics and the physical movements may be similar, like the notes in a scale, you can compose anything from concertos and symphonies to low down Basin Street . . . but usually not with the same woman."

I shrugged. "Most women seek security in love. How did the world ever get created so that women are perfectly content all their lives with one good man, while most men would crawl in the sack with as many different women as possible? The best solution is for Sheila and I to room together. Then these three males will all be equally deprived."

Though I was jesting, Sheila immediately agreed with me. "I think that's a very good idea. Sometimes, this whole business gets me worried. When I stop to think what I have done and what is going on here, I can't believe it. I never thought I'd actually make love with two boys and not be married to either of them. The idea of rotating among three men isn't nice at all. It would make me feel cheap . . . like a sexual object rather than a person."

I wondered if Sheila was right. Here were two girls and three boys, all unmarried, sitting around a room in their night clothes, drinking coffee and eating pizza.

Sheila's breasts were clearly visible through her night-gown. My legs and the lord knows what else were ex-posed under my bathrobe. Jack was in jockey shorts. Harry wore pants but no shirt. And Stanley had calmly decided his exercise had made him so warm that he had removed the bottom of his sweat suit. Any stranger to Harrad seeing us would condemn our semi-nudity as extremely immoral. But is it immoral? After eight months of seeing boys and girls naked in the gym and in the communal showers of the dormitory, I not only don't usually give it a second thought, I simply can't conceive being naked as anything but an interesting fact of life.

Are there really any absolute standards of morality? Maybe there is one. Sheila skirted the fringe of it when she said she didn't want to be a sexual object. Once any of us in this room ceased to care deeply for each other, we would move into the category of object, not person. The moment that occurred, we would be be-having immorally. I tried to evoke this idea.

Harry agreed. "But none of us knows whether a human being is capable of maintaining a sexual rela-tionship with several persons without having the whole business become casual and devalued."

Jack flopped on the floor beside Stanley. "Most of the early writers on love, from Ovid to Balzac to Sten-dhal, feel that all human love proceeds inevitably to the phase of boredom and casualness, and that even great lovers like Romeo and Juliet, or Paul and Virginia, or Heloise and Abelard, if they had entered into any long relationship, or, God forbid, marriage, the charm they would have had for each other would soon have van-ished." He shook Stanley who was, lying on his back, staring at the ceiling. "Now here we have an authority who can throw some light on the subject. How come you and Valerie petered out so fast?"

"You know," Stanley said, "it's amazing. Even the students at Harrad get the surface idea that everyone here is doing nothing but climbing in the sack night and day. Yet, I'll wager that the actual amount of sexual intercourse to a climax is relatively small. Before I answer your question, Jack, tell me how many times you have had intercourse with Beth in the last two weeks?"

Jack grinned at me. I blushed. Conversations at Harrad between males and females and even nonroommates have become very matter-of-fact and blunt. But I'm still devious enough to think everybody shouldn't know everything.

"All right," I said finally. "Twice."

"How many nights did you sleep with each other?"

"Six or seven."

"There you are." Stanley said triumphantly. "In case you don't know it, here in a free sexual environment we are all functioning on a much lower quantitative sexual level than the Kinsey statistics for newly-weds." He looked at Sheila. "What about you?"

"Once," she said shyly.

"Now how in hell do you figure it?" Stanley demanded. "I roomed with Valerie two weeks and we had intercourse twice. If any of us had functioned as normal married men, we would have considered it our moral duty to 'knock it off' every other night, at the very least. Why is Harrad different?"

"We aren't married!" Sheila and I chorused.

"It's not only that," I continued. "Without realizing it most of the girls want to be very sure of love, and the security I mentioned, before they are psychologically able to surrender themselves. I think the continual hammering by the Tenhausens that our love motivations evolve on a rational basis . . . that I love Jack because he has a pimple on his behind and I know it hurts him, or that I love Stanley because he, or his gym suit, or both, need to take a shower, that I love Sheila because she is timid, that I love Harry because he looks so absent-minded and can't find his money to pay a restaurant check . . . all these new evaluations we are learning about ourselves in relation to people make everything about the sexual relationship to Harrad more mature. We are learning, early in life, to evoke what people long married may know but can't even put into words."

"It's the difference between the thrill of a roller coaster ride," Sheila said, "and the pure joy that exists between two people when they are simultaneously reacting to experiences outside themselves in an identical way. Not that I don't enjoy the roller coaster ride, too." Sheila laughed.

"The reason that Valerie and I decided not to room together," Stanley said, "was because there never was any capitulation. Basically Valerie believes in complete equality between a man and a woman, I don't. I need a woman to protect. Valerie is completely self-sufficient. Peter is able to coexist with her. I desire interpenetration of my personality with a woman. Anyway, while we decided we could love each other as surface friends, we knew we could never work out our lives together."

"Have you found any girl who meets your qualifications?" Sheila asked.

"Yes . . . you and Beth."

"Good God," I said, "where does that leave us?"

We couldn't arrive at any solution either for Stanley or for our composite futures, but I think there is one thing we could all agree on: The five of us were developing an inter-dependency and need for each other. I have noticed many similar groupings of friends have occurred at Harrad. We've discovered that the room-mate system is greatly enhanced by multiplying our relationships on a discussion level. In this way, we share the thinking of several minds. In the process of pooling our reactions to the world, to our experiences, to our fears and hopes, we expand the horizon of our own life on a level not usually achieved by ordinary friendships.

I wonder where this is all leading us. After four years at Harrad, will the five of us, or six of us (we've obviously got to find another girl) . . . or any Harrad student who has shared this communal approach to life for four of their most formative years . . . (communal love, ugh . . . somehow I hate that expression. It's inadequate somehow) . . . will any of us be able to settle down into a strictly monogamous relationship? Could I, right now, marry Jack, move into suburbia, have children and exist as a housewife? If I finally manage to get through medical school . . . then what? Could I live life where I practiced medicine and live like Pops in a world of doctors who know little else but their specialties and the patients they practiced them on? No. I'd want somebody around me like Sheila or Stanley, who'd enrich my world with their very different worlds. If I married Jack, I'm not sure I wouldn't want to go to bed with Stanley or Harry. Where does *that* leave us, Phillip Tenhausen?

I haven't really led a sane life since I moved in with Jack Dawes. He plays the guitar and sings his Economics homework in crazy rhyming songs I listen to in spite of myself. Jack believes he has been endlessly reincarnated and occasionally slips into complete historical and cultural dissertations on the world circa 500 B.C., or during the Middle Ages, when he claims he was reborn again, as well the specific year, 1778, when he claims that he was eighteen years old and a soldier in the Revolutionary War. He dates his next rebirth sometime in the twenty-fourth century; and if I'm around, he promises to say hello to me. He is a faddist, plunging into the study of things, like Astronomy, Religion, Witchcraft and ·Alchemy, and then after littering the room with books and talking incessantly on the ideas these pursuits have generated, he drops the whole subject and moves on to something else.

One thing about Jack: he is never dull. The moments when I'm not trying to reform him and make him come down to earth, I suddenly realize he is making me wonder who I am. Which of the Beths I show the world is the real Beth? Is it possible for anyone to be completely whole and honest with any one single person in the world?

I, Beth, certainly am not really me so far as my mother and father are concerned. I am their daughter. I look like a composite them. In many ways I can share my overt thoughts with them. I want to be a doctor. So when I talk about medicine I can talk with Pops. I suppose that I will be a wife and mother one day. So I can talk homemaking, children, and cooking with Mother. I can also talk about music with Mother because she is responsible for my taking violin lessons. Mother plays the viola well and belongs to a group that meet once a month and play chamber music all night. Pops not only finds chamber music exceedingly boring, he refuses to make any attempt to understand it. Any discussion of his musical deficiencies ends up with him proudly explaining that he has a "tin ear."

To Pops, I am Beth who loves medicine. To Mother I am Beth who loves music. To neither of them am I Beth who likes to go to bed with a boy. Beth who likes to have a man's hands and lips touch and kiss her breasts and her genitals.

One night a few weeks ago when Jack was gently kissing me between my legs and I was kissing his penis, I started to laugh and couldn't stop until I almost had hiccoughs. When I asked Jack what his mother would think that after twenty years he had his head between another woman's legs he began to laugh, too. We nearly forgot to make love.

So, to neither Mother or Pops is Beth a sexy woman. Nor can she ever tell them she is. From Pop's standpoint, if Beth ever has a child, I am sure, despite all his familiarity with the necessary methods of impregnation, Pops will consider one more immaculate conception has occurred.

Will Harry Schacht ever know the complete Beth? Yes, on the score of interest in medicine and music. Never, of course, the multiple Beth that could make love with him as well as Stanley Cole and Jack Dawes. Each man I have known releases a different Beth. I have never really been able to be my giddy, zany self with Harry. I just couldn't be silly or pout or tease him, because Harry would be bewildered. If we were in the act of intercourse and he was having a wonderful metaphysical rapport with me, and I, too, should have been having other-worldly thoughts, and then if he would ask me what I was thinking, instead of replying some heavenly nonsense such as: "I am ecstatically floating on a cloud of love" . . . if I dared reply: "I was wondering if I should put my hair in curlers," or, "I really love you, Harry . . . but right now you are crushing my left breast beyond recognition" . . . Would Harry have laughed, or thought it kind of funny? No. Harry has a very tender ego. It can't stand laughter. When it is laughed at, it runs away and weeks are needed to coax it out of hiding.

What about Stanley? Stanley would soon know Beth, the sex-pot, inside out. In fact Stanley, as a lover, would leave no nook or cranny of Beth unexplored. Stanley's ego is tougher than Harry's, so he can laugh at himself a little, too. Not so much as Jack Dawes, because Stanley is essentially the poor boy who has licked his environment but always feels the danger of the past reaching out and clutching him back. He is a man who, even if he becomes wealthy, will always live his life as if one foot is caught in the quicksand of poverty. Would Stanley ever know the Beth who loves medicine? Would either of us ever thoroughly understand the other's drives? We might live together fifty years, make love regularly, have children, and still neither of us be able to reveal fully the deep-down inside person of ourselves that makes us really tick. So while Stanley would know the Beth who was a hungry sexual animal, he would never know many aspects of the Beth that could really unite us; two separate people.

What about Jack? Jack is a year older than me, but that doesn't give him any right to treat me like a wayward child. Yet, I always have the feeling with Jack that I am a little girl. Sometimes I am a bad little girl and I yell and scream at him, but he doesn't yell back. Jack works on the principle that you simply can't get mad at bad little girls. You just scoop them up in your arms, open their bathrobes, or pull up their dresses, and kiss them very thoroughly from head to foot. If they beat you with their hands and legs, and nearly scratch you to bits while this is going on, well, this is just one of the hazards of dealing with naughty little girls; you just chuckle or sing little songs, such as "Sing hallelujah, hallelujah, put a nickel in the pail, get another piece of tail," or "Ball of yarn, ball of yarn, it was then I spun her little ball of yarn," or "ay, ay, yi ay, in China they do it for Chili" . . . and pretty soon the bad little girl is a laughing, co-operating little girl.

Does it all mean everyone in life is doomed to be one-dimensional to everybody else? Margaret Tenhausen told me this wasn't really the problem. The important goal and what most people failed to achieve is understanding *ourselves* in three-dimensions.

I asked her what she meant.

She said: "When the spiritual, mental, and physical Beth is unified and you are cognitively aware of your real self, all the many Beths you now perceive will vanish, and you won't be one-dimensional, to yourself at least."

Since April, Harry, Sheila, Stanley, Jack, and I have spent Saturday nights together. We usually go to Boston and eat in Chinatown, or poke around Hanover Street and eat in some Italian restaurant. Last Saturday we had tickets for *Who's Afraid of Virginia Woolf?* which was being rerun at the Charles Playhouse. We ate in Omonoia, a small Greek restaurant, which Jack had discovered in a very dreary part of Boston. Upstairs we were in another world, enjoying the resin-flavored Greek wine, shish kebab, bakalava, and Greek coffee, all served to a background accompaniment of Greek folk music. We drank two bottles of Pendelli, and to me everybody seemed bathed in a soft halo. I was in my usual I-love-everybody mood when Stanley spoiled it by announcing he wasn't going to sweat through Albee's play. He'd read it and listened to it on the original cast recording. To him it was sickening.

"It presents a very good case for never getting married," he said. "Two very stupid couples who are presumably representative of the typical college faculty, and by definition middle class America, hate each other out loud for about two and a half hours, and then have a drunken catharsis as a result of shock because they nearly slept with each other's spouses." Stanley grinned. "Phil Tenhausen should use it as a good example of the moral bankruptcy of Western society. A sick country that exalts a sick playwright. Anyhow, tonight I feel like going exploring."

"Exploring?" Jack asked. "Where . . . for what?"

"For a woman," Stanley said coolly. "What else? I've been celibate for nearly eight weeks. Do you think I'm made of stone?"

"You mean you'd just go to bed with anyone?" Sheila asked.

This started a discussion in which Stanley demanded to know why should he be so angelic and other worldly as to not want sexual relations. He asked Sheila if she would sleep with him, and when she didn't answer, he asked Harry if he would loan Sheila to him.

"I don't think you are very nice," Sheila said stiffly.

Stanley just shrugged. "There's any number of people who wouldn't think you or anybody at Harrad was very nice but wouldn't give a second thought about a college boy on a fling about town. What I propose to do is the accepted morality. What you and everybody at Harrad is doing is downright illegal and immoral."

We knew Stanley was trying to aggravate us, and since we couldn't dissuade him, we finally persuaded him to meet us in the lobby of the Hotel Bradford around eleven-thirty, after the play.

I like the Charles Playhouse and its three-quarter stage. Jack bought another bottle of Greek wine, which we drank between the acts in paper cups. Maybe it was because I was in a pleasant state of alcoholic euphoria, but I enjoyed the play. If you don't take Albee literally, but simply respond to the laughter of an unhappy man and woman excoriating each other, and then watch the surface hatred get out of control and move toward tragedy, it is an interesting experience. Judged from the Harrad viewpoint the whole play is unnecessary. But one thing even the Tenhausens fail to emphasize enough is: Harrad isn't the world . . . yet. We must live our lives with one foot in Utopia and one foot in reality.

We waited in the Bradford until a quarter of twelve, me defending Albee against Jack, Sheila, and Harry, while we waited for Stanley. We were about to give up. Jack had us convinced that Stanley was probably in bed with some whore, when Stanley walked in looking slightly wan and uncommunicative.

Jack grinned at him. "As my old man used to say, did you get your ashes hauled?"

"Let's not be crude," Stanley said. He refused to discuss what had happened to him. "I drank five bourbon and sodas and I'm as drunk as a Kentucky Colonel."

Back at Harrad, I asked Jack if he'd mind if I went to Stanley's room and talked with him.

"Mother Beth is worried about her little boy," he said, smiling at me.

"Stanley was kind of moody on the way home," I said as I undressed and put on my bathrobe. "I think he needs a good listener, someone to talk with."

"You mean to sleep with, don't you?"

"Are you jealous?"

"No. I don't own you."

"Do you want to own me?"

"In a sense, I believe I do own you, Beth. I'm beginning to believe the die is cast, and somehow, you, Stanley, Sheila, Harry and I will always be involved with each other. In that sense, I think we have made a commitment deeper than ownership."

"You *are* serious tonight, aren't you?"

He kissed my cheek. "Go see what's eating Stanley. If you don't come back tonight, I won't be angry."

I found Stanley sitting at his desk, naked, writing in his journal.

"Maybe I should have locked my door," he said disagreeably. "Good God, nobody has any privacy here. Suppose you walked in without knocking and found me masturbating . . . or something?"

"Are you trying to shock me?"

"Sure . . . why not? I have masturbated on occasion."

"If I had found you so occupied, I would have helped you."

"Happy days! You can start now!"

"Not until I find out what happened to you."

Stanley closed his journal. "I was going to write it down, but knowing you I might as well give up and tell you. Only there's a catch. If you want to find out what happened, you'll have to sleep with me." He stood up and grinned at me.

"My . . . you are quite excited for a man who only an hour ago . . . what did Jack say . . . 'had his ashes hauled.' "

"Would you make love with me anyway?" Stanley asked.

"Not until you had scalded your jamoke. Do you think I want to get diseased?"

"Let's stop kidding," Stanley said. "After a year at Harrad I have discovered that I make love with my brain, not my penis. I spent an impotent evening. The title of the play I saw was: *Who's Afraid of Vapid Vulvas?* . . . and the answer is me: Stanley Cole."

"All right," I said, taking off my bathrobe. "Let's get into your bed while we talk."

I waited while he kissed my eyes, and lips, and nose, and breasts. I kissed him back gently.

Finally, he said, "You know, Beth, it's a God-awful sad and futile world. I found this joint I had heard about. It was filled with men lined up against a long bar, or sitting at tables around it. Behind the bar a continuous procession of girls were going through the motions of stripping . . . ending up with their breasts in nets and their mounds covered with triangles of rhinestones. They shook and gyrated dispassionately for a while, and eventually were followed by another girl who went through the same routine. Those poor sad men, drinking and staring, have no other way of seeing a girl naked. They probably have to make love to their wives in the dark. If they are married, their wives are the only women, from their wedding day on, they are supposed to get close to, or touch. Each one of these strip 'acts' had three phases of teasing, and lasted at least a half hour before this boring denouement was achieved. During the acts and between them, the girls, fully dressed, sold cigarettes and propositioned the men. The price: twenty-dollars for one hour.

"Finally, after four bourbons, I decided that I, Stanley Cole the sociologist, would invest twenty dollars to discover the whys, whats, and wherefores. I picked a pretty brown-eyed woman about thirty years old. She had just finished her act. She was quite well-shaped."

"You were thinking a lot more than the whys and wherefores, Stanley Cole," I said, interrupting him. "You mean you would have actually resisted a pretty woman who offered herself to you? I don't believe it."

Stanley shook his head. "No girl offers herself without conditions to a stranger, so the question answers itself. The conditions make it possible to resist. Anyway, I followed her around the back of the bar into a kitchen of the joint, and then down a flight of stairs and through a passageway that led into the next building. In the basement, next to the garbage and trash cans, was a service elevator that she explained would take us to her room in the hotel which was next door to the barroom. We got off at the eighth floor. I followed her down a hall that smelled of centuries of sweat and dirty underwear to a room which she unlocked and carefully relocked when we were inside.

" 'Okay,' she said. 'Twenty-dollars . . . in advance.'

"I paid her and sat on the edge of the bed, which had been stripped to a mattress and a sheet. In about two movements she was stripped naked and tried to shove her bush in my face.

" 'No tit squeezing or sucking,' she said, making the rules. 'I don't trust you college kids. You think they're made of rubber. Here's a safe. Put it on.' She lay on the bed with her legs open.

" 'I want to talk awhile,' I said.

" 'Oh, Jesus,' she said disgustedly. 'Not that routine. Come on, get it over with, then you won't feel so conversational.'

" 'Why do you do this?' I asked her. 'You are pretty enough to have a husband who would support you.'

" 'Kid,' she sighed, 'I am married. My husband makes a hundred bucks a week. Some weeks I make six hundred. We have a Cadillac and spend the winter in Miami. Why don't you can the Freud approach and do what you paid for?' She started to rub my pants."

Stanley chuckled. "I could see I was playing out of my league. I told her I wasn't really interested in sex. Quick as a wink she got dressed.

" 'Okay, let's go,' she said.

"'I paid for an hour,' I told her. 'I've got forty minutes coming.'

"'I could have you tossed out of here on your ass,' she said nastily.

"'Go ahead.'

"She sat on the bed and stared at me despondently.

"'There's no love in the world,' she said. 'Woman is to man a good fuck or a bad fuck. My old man worked in a foundry. He seared his eyeballs. When he was fifty he started to go blind. Every fuck my mother ever had was one more kid until she was finally bedridden. She had fifteen fucks in her life, three of which ended in miscarriages. All I ever wanted for the first fifteen years in my life was something to eat besides potatoes. I found a way. This is a good living while it lasts. If I manage to save up a million dollars from fucking and moved to Newton or Wellesley, society would accept me with open arms. How could anyone complain even if they knew how I earned it? Most of the rich people in the world, or at least their grandparents, fucked somebody one way or the other to get their money.'"

Stanley sighed. "I certainly had gotten in deeper than I had anticipated. You know what she did then? She cried. For the next half hour she sobbed. I stroked her face and tried to soothe her.

"'Thanks, kid,' she said finally. She wiped her eyes and stared sadly at me.

"'I'm sorry,' I told her.

"'Forget it.' She took me out of the hotel through the lobby, and I found her a taxi. As she was getting in the cab she gave me a kiss on my cheek. 'You know something,' she said. 'I'm not married, and I was never poor. I read all that crap I told you in some damned book written by an ex-prostitute. I tell it to all the college kids. It will make good reading in your term paper.'

" 'Why did you cry?' I asked her.

" 'For you and me and the god-damned world,' she said."

Stanley shook his head. "Thus ends the saga of Stanley Cole." He kissed me. "What's life all about, Beth? Where are we all going?"

I couldn't answer. I kept thinking about that girl. Stanley held me close . . . as if I might somehow vanish. We made love with a deep need for each other. Finally, I said, "I think she was really looking for something besides potatoes. She needs someone, somewhere, in her life who needs her."

"I guess that's what life is really about," Stanley said.

FROM THE JOURNAL OF STANLEY COLE

September, the Second Year

People who faithfully keep a journal or a diary, like Samuel Pepys or James Boswell or Arnold Bennett, do so out of a need to communicate as well as evaluate what is happening to them on a daily basis. Casanova, on the other hand, wrote his Memoirs in his lonely old age largely as an escape from the bitter present and as an attempt to relive his youth spent joyously jumping in and out of the beds of lovely ladies.

Phil Tenhausen assigned all six volumes of the Memoirs as summer reading in Human Values. The other day Sheila informed us in the seminar that she had counted the women Casanova had made love with. She arrived at the total of one hundred and twenty-two. But I am wandering. The real point is I have had no need to keep a journal either out of loneliness or the need to communicate. Harrad and the way we live here almost eliminates these feelings . . . at least as problems. For me the value of this journal is for recapitulation. Since June, events happened to me so fast that for the most part my reactions have been objective and not subjective.

Not without cause, either, because this past summer

has been "My Sam Grove Summer." Since June fifteenth until I landed back in Boston on the twenty-fifth
of August, I was dominated by Sam Grove, and Sam
Grove qualifies in my book for the most objective and
completely self-oriented man I have ever met.

Sam met me in June at the airport in Houston. "I
don't usually go to such trouble for a young squirt,"
he said. "But since you are a potential son-in-law, you
merit special attention."

"You may have a doctor for a son-in-law," I told
him as we drove to the headquarters of the Grove Oil
Corporation. "Sheila and Harry Schacht have moved
into an apartment on Beacon Hill for the summer.
Sheila is studying piano at the Conservatory of Music
and Harry has attached himself to the Mass. General
Hospital as a bed-pan orderly."

Sam stared at me. "So, my virgin daughter has at last
become a woman. Did you sleep with her?"

I told Sam I had. "I like Sheila. Not because she
conned you into giving me a summer job, and not because she is rich. I like her because I never believed a
girl with so much money could be so honestly straight-
forward and undevious. Money means nothing to her."

"Despite what you might have heard to the contrary, money is not the motivating factor in my life,"
Sam grinned. "Sheila intimated to me that you screwed
around with some other broad . . . but I gather she still
likes you. I don't give a damn who Sheila marries, just
so long as she is happy. Beejee, Sheila's stepmother, is
always trying to arrange a merger with some other oil
money, but Sheila ignores her. She is a lonesome kid
. . . had a fouled up life, largely because of me, I suppose. That's the way the ball bounces. Some men can
sacrifice themselves to the ideals and goals of a particular woman. I couldn't.

"Sheila's mother is a happy peasant. The salt of the earth type but really dull, boring, and fixated on her little problems of survival. In love with everything that is certain and stable and routine. It is a characteristic of modern man, though most of them will deny it vehemently. Each generation must produce a few Sam Groves or the world would sink into the mud of contented lethargy. If I had been born in another generation, I would have been with Alexander or Caesar, trying to unify the world, or with Ericson or Columbus or Magellan, trying to find a new world. I only click with people trying to achieve the unattainable. Grove Oil has millions of dollars sunk into space research. My only regret in this life is that I may not personally get to the planets. I have an intense curiosity about everything. I violently disagree with Phillip Tenhausen. He is most certainly cracked, but I find him challenging. He appeals to me because he is flinging himself against the impossible. Human nature will always remain the way it is, and whatever is good in it will easily be swayed and dominated by the crass, the vulgar, the ordinary." Sam chuckled. "I look at the newspapers every morning, expecting to find the biggest scandal since the Boston Tea Party . . . the story of Harrad College."

Sam was still talking when we arrived at his Penthouse on the thirtieth floor of the Grove Building. He took off his shoes, stockings, and shirt, and strode around his office, a barrel-chested, slim-hipped man, stripped to the waist. "The rest of this building is air-conditioned," he said. "Nobody tough left in the world. All most people want is their little creature comforts. Give them that, and they'll trade you their souls. The trouble with people today, they're all scared to death of a little sweat. I get in bed with Beejee, and she smells as if she had been sleeping with some Paris couturier. I tell her I like the smell of her skin, to wash off that crap. She tells me I stink. What kind of man are you, Kolasukas? You changed your name. What's the matter? Are you afraid of your origins? That's one count against you. You couldn't hold my daughter because you screwed another woman. That's two counts against you."

By this time I was getting pretty fed up with Sheila's egotistic father. "You haven't managed to hold your women, either," I said angrily. "Sheila says you've been married three times. I'm not asking any big favors from you. Just give me a job in one of your oil fields. I'm not afraid of sweating, and I'll earn my keep."

Sam chuckled. "I can hold my women, son. The only reason I have been married three times is that I get bored with the scenery . . . not the physical scenery of pussy, tits, hips, ass and legs, but the mental scenery that puts the physical scenery in motion. Women, by and large, are mentally dull. Most of them never find one damn thing to occupy their minds creatively. Rich females subsist on the lastest fashions, doing what is socially 'in,' seeking admiration from men for their sexual appurtenances, and daydreaming of ideal love. Middle class females imitate the rich ones. The poor female simply propagates endlessly because that is her duty to her husband, who arrives with a stiff cock in his hand, ready to discharge like a helpless salmon swimming upstream against the current, because his seminal vessels tell him he must spawn before he dies."

"What are you doing for the world?" I asked him. "What makes you so much more valuable?"

Sam looked at me thoughtfully.

"I created a business that employs some twenty-three thousand people . . . most of whom are intent on overpopulating the world and making their grandchildren's existence here considerably less tenable than their own. I don't believe in philosophizing. I am forty-eight years old. I can live twenty more years or drop dead tomorrow. . . . My major problem at the moment is that my only heirs are a daughter, two ex-wives, and one current one. My personal estate is in excess of thirty-six million dollars, and this does not include my holdings in the Grove Oil which will be transferred to the Grove Foundation when I die. I'd like to transfer control of this product of my imagination into the hands of my non-existent grandsons."

"Are you afraid of dying?" I asked.

"Hell, no! What's that got to do with it?"

"Then why do you care what happens to Grove Oil? What's really bothering you is that you're not immortal. In lieu of that, at the very least, you'd like to look down from heaven at this tower and your oil producing properties, rub your hands together, and say to God, 'Look what I did . . . and there's my grandson, Samuel Grove III still running it.' Why don't you impregnate your current wife? That's the only way you're going to get a male Grove in the picture." I had taken off my shoes and stockings and propped my feet on Sam's magnificent blond mahogany desk. "If I married Sheila and she inherited this empire, her first official act would be to elect me President, after which I would immediately change the name to the Kolasukas Oil Corporation."

Sam looked at me gloomily. I later learned he'd had an operation on his seminal tubes and couldn't have children. "Stanley, you are a nervy bastard," he said. "Don't they teach you to mince words at Harrad? All I have to do is push a button and have you chucked out of here. You are still wet behind the ears. No one in the Grove Oil Corporation dares to talk back to me.

Get the hell out of here. Tomorrow report to the per-
sonnel department on the eighth floor. I'll find something unpleasant for you to do this summer."

Sam was good as his word. Three days later I was
on a jet plane to Iran. At the Abadan airport I was
picked up by a grinning Iranian who was driving a
Grove Oil jeep. He drove me to Agha Jari where the
Grove Oil operates producing wells under licenses from
the National Iranian Oil Company. Grove is a member
of the Consortium that plans Iranian Oil production.
A new well had just come in. Molloy, a taciturn Irish-
man in charge, explained that this baby would produce
25,000 barrels a day. He told me to report to Gach
Saran, where a gravity pipeline was being built to
Khark, a small island in the Persian Gulf about a hundred miles south.

All summer I sweated continuously, ate sand and
slop from a field kitchen, slept in the open, inhaled the
odor of camel dung and urine until I was certain it
was my own odor. With a team of Iranians, we inched
our way across grubby country, working from sun up
to sun down, and laying a quarter of mile of pipe a day;
welding it, wrapping it, and burying it, until one day it
would become a continuous tube of slow moving oil,
flowing to storage tanks on the island of Khark. With
the *Memoirs of Casanova* to read (the only books I
could carry on the plane and stay within the weight
limit), and for companionship Neville and Sincher
(Britishers, in charge of the construction, whose idea
of recreation was endless games of pinochle accompanied by oceans of gin and orange squash), by August I had convinced myself that Sam Grove's plan was
to turn me into a screaming idiot. I was ten pounds
lighter and deeply tanned, but I had received no pay.
When I questioned Neville on the subject, his opinion

was that I must be on the headquarters payroll, since no provision had been made for me on the field payroll. Since there was no place to spend money, anyway, Neville's feeling was "why worry about it . . . think of the experience you are having."

On the second Saturday in August, two official Grove cars from Abadan led by Sam Grove in a jeep, which he was driving himself, screeched into our current location and stopped in a cloud of dust.

"I see you survived," Sam said, grinning at me. "Get your stuff together; you're coming back with me."

An hour later, hanging onto the edge of the seat for fear I would be catapulted out of the jeep, Sam drove us at top speed over dirt roads toward Khark.

"Sheila is mad as hell at me." Sam clutched the steering wheel with both hands to steel himself against the bumps and road shocks. "She got your postcard in June from Abadan, and hasn't heard from you since. I told her I'd come out here and either escort you home or give you a military funeral."

"You can pay me, too," I said. "I've worked for Grove Oil for ten weeks. I figure that you owe me at least six hundred bucks, tax free, as depletion allowance on human flesh."

Sam handed me his billfold. "Take ten one hundreds. I wouldn't want to underpay a possible future son-in-law."

His bulging billfold must have had at least one hundred hundred dollar bills in it. "It's only money, son," he said, noticing me staring at it. "I always carry five to ten thousand. Never know what might turn up where you can use a fast buck."

I took the thousand and asked him how Sheila was. He told me she was living alone in Boston. Harry Schacht had gone out to Columbus to visit with Beth

Hillyer until school opened. Some interesting wheels had been turning, but Sheila hadn't given Sam any detailed information on Harrad developments.

In his hotel room in Abadan, as we drank gimlets together, Sam became expansive. "I operated out of a suitcase for years," he told me. "I was worth five million dollars and I didn't even have a desk. It's easy to make money, son. Just think of it as a commodity. Borrow it as cheaply as you can and make it work for you. I made my money using other people's money. If I needed a hundred million tomorrow, I could raise it in twenty-four hours. Do you want to be rich, Stan?"

I grinned. "Anyone who is poor wants to be rich. But I don't want to be so rich that I don't have love."

"That's Hollywood and television crap, son. I can have any kind of love you can think of. Love . . . screwing . . . that's not a man's whole life. A man lives for what he can personally create in this world. Not children. Children are simply one product of his creative energy . . . but the recreation of this world, his environment; a man's ability to design the tallest building and then have it constructed, dig the longest canal, conquer the ice and snow of Antarctica, literally project himself into the stars . . . that's man's purpose, and if there is a God, that is why he created man . . . to emulate Himself. Man is closest to God when he is determined to achieve the impossible, seek the unattainable."

The next morning on a jet plane to Calcutta, where Sam had a conference with the officials of an Indian refinery controlled by Grove Oil, we continued the discussion.

"The Hindu is closest to God," I told him, "and achieves the Brahmin state when he no longer seeks the material wealth, possessions, and attainments of this world. He achieves the Unattainable with a direct merger of his own being. All else is *maya* or illusion. When he has pierced through the veil of materialism he returns to Nirvana and reunites himself with the unending consciousness of the Universe."

Sam laughed. "All the mystics and the logicians in the world ever offer man are rationalizations for poverty. Jesus Christ preached to forsake all others and follow him. If the Christians had taken him seriously, the way the Hindus and Chinese have taken Ramakrishna and Buddha, the Western World would be wallowing in dung. If all men lived their lives for the next world, man would never have invented the flush toilet. He'd be up to his ass in his own shit. Wait until you have seen the dregs of Calcutta, son. You'll see what living for the next world can do to man in this one."

At dinner in the Great Eastern Hotel in Calcutta, we were still at it.

"From what you told me about Harrad and the Tenhausens," Sam said, "I'm convinced the whole idea is unrealistic. Their theories of educating a man in such a close contact with women will ultimately feminize the male. The average male today has already gone too far. He seeks the female ultimate . . . security."

"If virility is hydrogen bombs," I grinned, "it may not be such a bad idea."

"Do you expect you and Sheila will achieve this perfect love and maintain it for a lifetime? It sounds a little sloppy to me."

"I don't know, Sam. I do know that if Sheila and I, or some other woman, develop and grow together, it won't end up in the vast wasteland of modern suburban marriage. The marriages the Tenhausens envision would have constantly evolving strength and drives, not for money or power but to project for all men a higher image of themselves. The idea behind Harrad is infinitely larger than pre-marital sexual adjustment. Ultimately it is a belief that man can take one more step up the evolutionary ladder . . . lift himself by his own bootstraps, and develop a society and culture that is emotionally and mentally in control of itself. What we would be seeking may be just as unattainable as the goals you set for yourself. The difference is that the values that drive us are not so ego centered as yours."

The next day Sam took me on a tour of Calcutta. "I want you to see a small portion of this best of all possible worlds, Kandy Kolasukas." He was delighted with his own joke. "Get it, son? Candide? . . . Kandy? Okay, Kandy Kid, look around you."

Adamantly, Sam expounded his philosophy of hopelessness. In a taxi driven by a Sikh we drove through miles of poverty-stricken shambles overflowing with Indians living little more than an animal existence. We pushed our way through markets crawling with flies, plunged into alleys reeking with slop and sewage, forced our way into mud and bamboo houses that gave shelter to families of ten or more plus chickens and cows all living in one or two rooms that completely eliminated privacy. In the sweltering heat, on the edge of a muddy tributary of the Hoogly River, we watched men and women bathe, washing themselves while they still wore their shabby saris and dhotis, in water thick with silt.

For a few rupees Sam convinced one Indian family to share their meal of grimy rice and fish, and grimly insisted that we both eat the tasteless concoction, while they watched us with grinning approval. We finished the day at the burning ghats, a funeral practice of which Sam heartily approved. "Millions of them die before their time. Very sensibly, they realize that any man's life on this earth is not much more than a few puffs of smoke."

The next night Sam had to go to a formal dinner at a British Polo Club, but he continued his campaign to unnerve me, hoping, evidently, that I would renounce my "pollyanna" philosophy. He had reserved separate rooms for us. In case, as he put it, something turned up. I think he was disappointed when I told him that I was going to bed early.

Around nine o'clock, just as I had flopped on the bed with a sigh of relief, I heard a knock on my door. I scrambled into my shorts, opened the door an inch, and was staring into the saucer brown eyes of a very pretty Indian girl. She was wearing a red sari, a simple necklace, a tinkling profusion of bangles on her arms, and tiny bells on her ankles. She smiled timidly at me, revealing very white teeth that contrasted with her mocha skin. She handed me a piece of paper. It was a note from Sam: "Less than an hour ago this girl was given a thorough medical inspection. She's clean, healthy. No V.D. She knows at least ninety positions and will demonstrate them with no thought of love on her mind. She isn't even a good business woman. She's yours for the night. Fifteen rupees. Pay her when you finish. Compliments of Sam Grove. She didn't ask to be born a whore. It just happened that way in this best of all possible worlds."

"I'm sorry," I said to the girl. "I wouldn't enjoy it."

She just stared at me, refusing to understand. If possible, her eyes grew even larger as they overflowed with tears.

"Do you understand English?" I asked her.

"Please, sahib," she whispered. "I have no one. I need money."

"Didn't Sam Grove give you any money? Where did he get you, anyway?"

She looked at me, puzzled. "The other American. They call Sam. He not want me tonight. Not give rupees. Too many of us. Say all his money not give every Indian even one rupee. So why start?" She grinned at me as if this made good sense. Sam was handing me the world's problems in a microcosm. Still, it was difficult to restrain my anger. If most men were as thick-skinned as Sam, the world probably was hopeless.

I invited the girl in the room, wondering what I was going to do with her. She sat dumbly on the edge of the bed, waiting for me. I touched her breast through her sari. She suffered my explorations in silence. I suddenly realized my penis was erect. My body and some uncontrolled part of my mind was telling me to have dispassionate intercourse with this girl, pay for the (pleasure?) and send her on her way. Sam was betting that after ten weeks in the Iranian desert that my sexual desires would overwhelm the Harrad philosophy I had been spouting. I told the girl to take off her sari, and when she did, and stood naked in front of me, not more than five feet three inches tall but beautifully formed, I felt a terrible sadness. She was a fragile, defenseless child, offering the only thing she had of value in the world.

"What's your name?"

"Asoka Devi," she said eagerly. "I part Indian. My father American soldier."

"Does he know about you?"

"Long time ago. He not know. Not care. My mother very sick. She die. Small village in Assam. No one want me. I go to government school."

"How old are you?"

"Fifteen, I think. Maybe fourteen."

"Will you marry?"

Asoka shrugged. "Indian man marry Indian girl. Not me. No dowry. Very bad."

"How many men have you been with?"

She didn't understand me. I don't know why I pursued it. I felt as if someone had punched me in the stomach. Finally, she said, "First man . . . twelve. Hurt bad." She smiled. "Many men."

"You have baby some day?" I found that I was matching my English to hers. It made conversation easier.

She shrugged. "I not want."

When I tried to discover what she was doing to make sure that fate didn't have other plans, she didn't understand me. "Indian women have many babies," she said.

I pushed her down on the bed. She lay there passively, staring at me, wondering, probably, why I didn't climb on her and get it over with. I turned up the air-conditioner, turned off the lights, got in bed beside Asoka, pulled a sheet over us, took her in my arms, kissed her cheek, and told her to go to sleep. When she finally realized I wasn't going to make love to her she sighed, curled up against me, and snuggled her face against my chest. In the morning I awoke first and found her curled in a little ball, sleeping like a child in the womb, two fingers in her mouth.

It was eight-thirty. I telephoned Sam's room and could tell from the sound of his voice that I had awakened him. "Your Indian girl friend is here in my bed," I said.

"For God's sake get rid of her," Sam chuckled. "We're leaving for Bangkok on a six o'clock plane. Tonight you can try some Thai shmooie. Quite a different flavor than the Indian stuff. I hope you have some strength left."

"Do you know this girl is only fifteen years old?"

Sam laughed. "They start young in the Orient. I hope you aren't getting sentimental, Kandy."

"What if she were your daughter?"

"She isn't. You can't cry for the world, Stanley. Forget it. See you at breakfast in a half hour."

I tried to convince Sam that since Asoka was half-American he could adopt her, or endow her, or do something for her. "What would it mean to you, Sam?"

"Oh, for Christ's sake, grow up!" Sam hung up the phone.

I called him back. "Sam, if you don't do something for her, I'll tell Sheila." I slammed the phone down before he could hang up again.

I found Asoka squatting on the toilet. I waited until she finished, and then ignoring her protests pulled her into the shower with me and soaped her from head to foot. A vague thought was slowly blossoming in my mind. I made her unknot her hair which was tied in a bun. While she gasped in indignation, I washed her hair clean of the rancid-smelling oil. When I finished, it was obvious that, among other things Asoka would need a haircut.

I finally got her to breakfast in the hotel dining room, where we were greeted with some shock and surprise by the Indian maître d' and the Indian bearers who waited on us with great distaste.

Not knowing what mad thing I'd do next, Asoka scarcely touched the food. "Not good," she said. "Not belong here."

Sam finally joined us in the dining room. "All right," he said. "I decided to humor you. I telephoned a friend and got her a job as a maid with a British family. They are sending their driver for her." He stared at Asoka, noticing her hair hanging down her neck. "A good looking doll. I see you couldn't stand the smell of chicken fat in her hair."

"I'd like to put some money in the bank for her."

"You must be kidding."

"No, I'm not. What's more, I want to meet the British family where she will live."

Sam stared at me, dismayed. "You don't trust me."

"No."

"Okay. There's no British family. The driver will bring her back to Dum Dum where she lives. It's about twenty miles from here. Now, let's get to reality. Life isn't moral or immoral. It just is, and you can't change it." He handed Asoka twenty rupees. "There you are. My treat. You can tell Sheila anything you want. I couldn't care less. She knows by now that her father is no paragon of virtue."

I decided the only way to deal with Sam was by not letting him know the low bastard I was convinced that he was. I told him that since Asoka was paid up I might as well enjoy the rest of the day with her. I would meet him at the airport in time for the flight. After Sam had thoroughly applauded my conversion to reality, I took Asoka back to the room. It took me nearly an hour to convince her Sam really loved her and wanted her to come to the United States. By ten-thirty I located a department store, commandeered a British manager, and explained that I wanted to buy Asoka a complete Western style wardrobe. Leaving Asoka in his charge, I asked for the loan of a typewriter, and using some Grove Oil stationery I had borrowed from Sam on the plane, I wrote a to-whom-it-may-concern letter explaining that Asoka Devi was an employee of the Grove Oil Corporation and was being transferred to the United States for one year to work at the Company headquarters at Houston, Texas.

By noontime Asoka, wobbling a little on her high heels, ecstatic over her new clothes, and still dubious over her amazing good fortune, greeted me with tears in her eyes. There was still something missing. She needed a fast haircut. I found a hairdresser, pawed through a book of hair styles, and watched while Asoka was being shorn, and transformed into a sexy looking waif with an elfin style, windblown Italian hair-do. When they finished I had no doubt she would pass for eighteen or nineteen years old. With her large brown eyes and coffee cream complexion she was strikingly beautiful.

By two o'clock I had her in the American Embassy and within an hour convinced an undersecretary to arrange a passport. While Asoka watched, I filled out the forms. No one questioned why Grove Oil was hiring an Indian employee who couldn't write English. By three-thirty Asoka had been photographed and was holding her passport and airline tickets on a flight to Houston. I arranged with the airline officials to take care of her on any stop-overs or transfers. As the coup d'etat, I put in an overseas phone call to Beejee Grove. It took until four-thirty to connect. By this time I was really sweating. I had no doubt that Sam would leave without me if I failed to show up at the airport. The telephone connection was erratic, but Beejee finally grasped who I was. I told her Sam had asked me to call her. I told her she was to meet Asoka at the Houston airport in approximately two days; to take care of Asoka until Sam arrived; that Sam would explain it all to her when we got back.

After paying for Asoka's clothes and the airline fare, I had seventy-five dollars left, which I put in Asoka's pocketbook. I hugged her and told her that she was going to have a wonderful new life. Two days from now she would be in Houston, Texas. The airline hostesses would take care of her all the way.

"I not know your name," she whispered in my ear.

"Mud." I grinned at her. "My name is mud from now on."

When our plane took off for Bangkok, I asked Sam when he planned to be back in Houston. "No hurry," he said, "I need a little vacation. Tonight we shall *both* enjoy the ultimate pleasures of sex with some lovely Thai girls. I promise you an experience without which you have not lived. Then when we get bored, we will take off to Los Angeles. Maybe we will run down to Tijuana. A few days in that quaint little town will give you a new perspective on Harrad College. Sex is simply a commodity on the periphery of life. Now that you have learned this in Calcutta you have taken the first step. The Tenhausens are attempting to give sex a sacredness that neither the act nor the aftermath is equal to."

I was beginning to wonder if I was going to have the courage to tell Sam about Asoka Devi. "Sam," I said, "I think you are wrong. The Tenhausens are not only trying to teach that there is no ultimate pleasure in the orgasm unless a particular man and woman are deeply involved with each other as individuals. They go further and envision a society where all men and women care so much for each other that the basic dishonesty or inability to communicate in most human relationships is completely eliminated. Imagine a world where I could say: 'Sam, that Anglo-Indian girl is a human being whose heart beats, who can eat food, digest it, and defecate, who has a vagina and a womb to bear children and breasts to feed them, and above all, a brain that remembers and correlates her memories. She is a blinding miracle. How could I treat her simply as a warm sheath

into which I ejaculated?' Imagine a world instead where
every human being was trained from birth that every
other human being was the most amazing, wondrous,
beautiful fact of existence."

Sam stared at me. "Jesus Christ," he muttered.

"No," I grinned. "Even Jesus failed to understand.
He insisted on something beyond to explain the miracle,
and then the theologians gave man something to lean
on. A God who exacted retribution, or answered pray-
ers. If there is a God, why should He expect more from
man than to appreciate the miracle of his own existence?"

"You don't believe it," Sam said. "You are spouting
words. Man is not good. He has the capacity for evil.
He is selfish, hedonistic. In business for himself. Your
ideas won't work in this world. Kandy Kolasukas.
You'll grow up one of these days and discover it for
yourself."

I looked at my watch. It was seven-thirty. We would
be landing in Bangkok soon. By now Asoka was on a
jet to Honolulu. I decided now was the time to tell
Sam. He listened to me in complete disbelief. He told
me I was trying to get his ass. He told me I could never
have accomplished it in eight hours. It was impossible to
convince the officials and get a passport so quickly. All
the time he talked, he was both cursing me and trying
to laugh me into a confession that it was all a hoax.

"Sam," I said chuckling, "I thought I'd better tell
you now. Just in case, tonight, I got feeling the same
way about some Thai girl. I haven't any more money,
but the first thing you know I'd be asking you for a
loan, and you would end up with a harem in Houston."

"I suppose you told Beejee this girl was a whore I
had slept with," he said sourly.

"No. I simply told her Asoka was fifteen, an orphan, and you had decided to take care of her education."

"If it's true," Sam said, grimly fastening his seat belt, "I'll put your ass in a sling. No one ever pulls a fast one on me and gets away with it." He grinned at me nastily. "Keep in mind, Kandy, I haven't had your Harrad education. I don't believe in this namby-pamby crap. For Christ sake, there's four hundred million Indians and just as many Chinese. What would it prove if I saved one miserable human being?"

"You aren't going to save her, Sam. You are going to save yourself. There's a lot more important things in this world than discovering oil or flying to the moon."

Sam's only response was "Bullshit!"

When we landed in Bangkok and were in our room at the Ratanakosin Hotel, he put in a long distance phone call to Beejee. "Don't get in an uproar," he said when he finally was connected. "I was just confirming Stanley's call. I know it sounds a little unusual, Beejee. Just meet the kid at the airport. I'll explain it to you later." He hung up and stared at me. "You miserable son of a bitch," was all he said, but I detected a note of admiration in his voice.

We didn't go in search of Siamese whores, nor did Sam show any further interest in Tijuana. By the time we landed in Houston, three days later, conversation between us had deteriorated to such a point that I was able to finish volume Four and Five of Casanova's Memoirs. Beejee met us with Asoka, who had arrived the day before.

"Sam," she cried, bussing him enthusiastically, "she's a darling child. Are we going to adopt her?"

"She's no child," Sam said angrily. "She's a whore."

"Sam, don't tell me you slept with her?"

"No, damn it! I didn't sleep with her," Sam exploded. He looked at me warningly.

"Where did you get her?"

"Never mind. It's all a joke. We're sending her back."

"There's no back," I explained to Beejee. "Asoka has no father or mother." I told Beejee Asoka was the daughter of an unknown American G.I., that neither Sam nor I had slept with her, and that Sam was really only perturbed because I was so tender-hearted, that Sam really wanted to give the kid a chance in life but felt that she, Beejee, would think he had gone soft.

"Oh, Sam," Beejee said, crying and hugging him to his great embarrassment, right in the middle of the crowds in the airline terminal. "It's the nicest thing you have ever done." Tears were running down Beejee's cheeks. "I never would have believed it. We ought to adopt hundreds of kids and help them. It would make our lives worthwhile, somehow."

The next morning Sam took me back to the airport to catch a plane for Boston. He handed me a thousand dollars. "Are you going to tell Sheila the truth?" he demanded.

"There's worse things than caring for the woman you slept with," I said, grinning at him. "If you adopted them all, you'd have quite a harem. I'm sure Sheila would be proud of you."

Sam chuckled. "If you want a job next summer, Kandy, please apply to Saint Peter. Grove Oil can't afford you."

When I arrived back in Boston at Logan Airport, I took a taxi to a little street on the north side of Beacon Hill. Trudging up five flights of stairs in an old brick apartment house that had probably been built before the Civil War, I arrived at the top, puffing. I heard someone playing a piano. I knocked, but there was no answer. Finally, I opened the door, and there was Sheila, her back to me, engrossed in Bach's Goldberg Variations. I tip-toed behind her, grabbed her and she fell screaming into my arms.

"Oh my God, Stanley," she sobbed happily. "It's you. I've been so darned lonesome." She kissed my lips, my eyes, my cheeks, enthusiastically. "I was about to kill Daddy when I heard what he did to you. Oh, Stanley. I've missed you . . . missed you."

"What became of Harry?"

"He and Beth corresponded. Then she telephoned and insisted he spend a few weeks in Columbus before school opened. Harry tried to tell her that it wasn't a good idea. He was afraid of her father and mother's reaction. Oh, Stanley, Harry really is so very gentle and such a good person. We've had a lot of fun this summer."

"But you finally decided that you loved me most," I said, messing up her hair and kissing her quite thoroughly.

"How did you know?"

By this time I had unbuttoned the boy's shirt she was wearing and unzippered her plaid skirt. "Sheila," I groaned as I pulled her slip over her head, and discovered a bra, panties, garter belt and stockings. "I'll never get through all the layers and find you."

"It's only three in the afternoon," she sighed lying in my arms. "This is a crazy time to make love. How many girls have you slept with this summer?"

"A couple of dozen."

"I don't believe it," she chuckled, "You act starved."

"Are you going to room with me this year at Harrad?"

"I'm going to marry you, Stanley, and have babies

with you! But I may still want to be with Harry or Jack once in a while. Will you be jealous?"

"Ho . . . a new Sheila speaks!"

"Yes," she said. "And here's some news for you. Peter Longini decided to quit Harrad. His father has been transferred to Switzerland and he's going to the University of Zurich. Jack is going to room with Valerie Latrobe. Beth and I decided we might just as well simplify things and all of us live more or less communally for the next two years."

"That's simple?" I asked, nibbling her ear.

"Well, it's simpler than being jealous."

"You said two years. What about our senior year?"

Sheila snuggled hard against me. "About November of our last year I'm going to get pregnant by you, and Beth is going to get pregnant by Harry."

"Ye gods . . . what about Jack and Valerie?"

"Silly . . . we don't know about them yet. Maybe they won't want to get married and have children."

"But you and Beth do?"

"Yes!"

"And who supports all this brood?"

"Well," Sheila said seriously, "Beth and I figured it this way. She and Harry are planning to go to medical school. If you and I apply to do graduate work in the same university, we all ought to be able to get scholarships. Next summer and the following summer we will have a fund of nearly five thousand dollars. Then, when we graduate from Harrad we can take an apartment together or rent a house, and all of us can move in with the children. We can hire a woman to take care of the children when we aren't there. But, anyway our classes will probably work out so that one of the four of us will be there most of the time."

"Sheila," I chuckled and pulled her behind against

me so that I was deep inside her. "Do you mind if I change your name?"

"To what?" she asked.

"To Kandy . . . Kandy Grove. And when you write your father be sure and tell him!"

FROM THE JOURNAL OF SHEILA GROVE

November, December, January,
the Second Year

All of the second year class at Harrad are experimenting with a method of sexual intercourse which Margaret and Phil call sexual communion. I can see now that Phil has been preparing us for it gradually. Since September in the Human Values seminar, he has assigned John Woodroffe's *S'akti and S'akta,* John Noyes' *Male Continence, Diana,* by Henry Parkhurst, *Karezza* by Alice Stockham, *Art of Love,* by W. F. Robie, *Sex Perfection* by Rudoph von Urban, finishing with *Nature, Man and Woman* by Alan Watts.

This is by no means all the books we have had scheduled. Phil feels the only sound basis of education is exposure to thousands of ideas. By forcing us into continuous evaluation, he expects our own frames of reference will be eventually enlarged into a workable philosophy of life.

When we groaned that we didn't need to read any more books on how-to-do-it sex, Phil asked us to be patient. "I would never assign these books to the freshman class. As freshmen you weren't mature enough. Even now with most of you in your twentieth year it may be questionable whether you can fully grasp these concepts. In the next few weeks we are going to explore the psychological, the metaphysical, and the religious quality of sexual intercourse. Whether you profit by it now, or in later life, the door has been opened. I predict that eventually you will embody these ideas in your love experiences. To our knowledge, outside occasional references to these ideas in various sex manuals, the books we have assigned are the only writings available on the subject. Yet we will be dealing with a very ancient idea. In practical married life, perhaps many people have learned these ideas by trial and error without ever becoming aware of their tremendous potential in developing communication in its deepest sense between the male and female.

"The original concept stems from the Hindu Tantric literature and is based on the worship of Sakti, or the all pervading life principle in the Universe. As John Woodroffe points out: 'the whole of life, without any single exception, may be an act of worship if man makes it so.' Thus, the Hindu Pancattattva offer five ways for man to unite himself with the fountainhead of the universe. One of these ways 'Maithuna' is sexual intercourse of a very special kind. The Tantric philosophy conceives the physical union of man and woman as part of the Divine Nature in action. Thus the body is Sakti. Pursued to its ultimate, man himself is God. When the Divine Mother is seen in all things, man achieves true liberation. In seeking these truths, many means are available. Sexual intercourse, properly understood, is one of the important ways for man and woman to eliminate the polarization of their bodies. In the act of coitus, a man and woman can unite their consciousness into a single pole with the unceasing Consciousness of the Universe. In the sexual act, bodies are left behind and the minds of the participants can merge into a state called by the Hindu Samadhi."

"You can see," Phil said later, during one of his lectures to us in Harrad Little Theatre, "that sexual intercourse taking place in this mental environment is actually an act of worship. By definition it becomes elevated, pure without lust. We are not suggesting that the act of coitus need always be endowed with such high spirituality, but we do have in this yoga discipline a definite and obvious requirement that the male participant be able to delay his ejaculation not for a typical half-hour, but perhaps for a whole evening."

There was a lot of laughter, groans, and comments that it might be possible if the girl would cooperate and not move a muscle. But what fun would that be, anyway?

Phil chuckled. "We are neither prescribers, or enforcers . . . just exploring with you an idea which we believe can enhance and enlarge your own values. So far as we can determine, the Tantric idea which is extremely repugnant to orthodox Christianity and Judaism because it idealizes sex, and uses sex as a form of worship, has lain dormant in the West for centuries. Whatever knowledge of the basic concepts that have filtered through to the West are ultimately identified with a sexual orgiastic behavior, and little has been written about them.

"The possibility of delaying the male ejaculation was rediscovered in 1846 by John Humphrey Noyes who described it in a book called *Male Continence*. Noyes' discovery came about through his great love for his wife who had suffered through five pregnancies, with all but one child prematurely born. Noyes persuaded his wife to experiment with prolonged intercourse without ejaculation or orgasm. Keep in mind this was little more than a hundred years ago. Contraceptive techniques were largely unknown. In Noyes' words: 'But what if a man knowing his own power and limits should not even approach the crisis, and yet be able to enjoy motion *ad libitum*. If you say that is impossible, I answer that I know it is possible . . . nay it is easy.'"

"He's crazy," Harry Schacht said when a group of us continued the discussion with Phil after his lecture. "First, a man who had intercourse without ever ejaculating would have aching testicles, and second, I doubt its efficacy as a method of birth control. Some semen would escape into the vagina whether there was ejaculation or not."

Dr. Anson Fanner, who had been attending this series of lectures, shook his head. "I won't agree that male continence is a healthy approach to sex, but it is a method that probably would be effective for birth control. Basically in prolonged intercourse some semen is released into the urethra. This slight release probably saves the male from what you refer to as aching testicles. Since there are no violent muscular contractions in the man who accomplishes this feat, the pressure of the vagina on the penis may tend to crowd any liquid from escaping from the seminal ducts into the urethra back toward the bladder, rather than forward to the meatus."

"You mean a man doesn't have to wear anything until he ejaculates?" Valerie demanded.

Dr. Fanner smiled. "If you are depending on sheaths for birth control, you can probably blame the failure of the sheath at the point of ejaculation rather than the simple insertion of a penis into your vagina for an hour or two. Since you have birth control pills available to you, the problem is academic."

"We want you to realize," Phil Tenhausen told us a few days later, "that we are simply tracing an idea.

Noyes' theory of male continence was adopted for a time by the Oneida Community who, at the time, depended upon it as a means of birth control. This community shared wives communally. Male continence probably permitted them to determine with some accuracy a particular father, as well as limit the combined progeny of the group. The real value of the theory is the awareness that the male can control his ejaculation and develop such a yoga like control that it is possible for the female to have several orgasms over a period of several hours without the male losing control."

"This may be well and good in theory," Jack Dawes protested, "but I fail to see the advantage of such lengthy intercourse."

"Only personal experimentation can prove the value of this approach to sex," Phil said, "In the various books we've read, a common body of unique experience indicates that individuals attempting prolonged intercourse may make some interesting discoveries. We, of course, believe that ultimate orgasm for both participants is desirable. As you read these various books, I suggest you collect a series of impressions from them that may point up for you the psychological and mystic experiences that others have obtained from sexual communion."

Stanley hasn't been keeping a journal for the past few months. "I'm too happy to write in a journal," he grinned at me. "I have no problems. *You* underline all the ideas that impress you. When you're finished, we'll give sexual communion a real whirl. We'll climb in the sack and you can read them to me while I'm inside you. Be sure you have enough material to last all night, because I am really a strong yoga."

I challenged Stanley there and then, and he had to eat his words. But Saturday night he demanded a return match, "to prove the power of mind over matter." By nine o'clock I was in bed with Robie's book, *The Art of Loving,* von Urban's *Sex Perfection,* Alan Watts' *Nature, Man and Woman,* and *Summerhill* by A. S. Neill. I told Stanley I was ready.

"What has *Summerhill* got to do with this?" Stanley demanded, trying to ignore naked me, and looking over the books I'd piled on the night stand near the bed.

"Just in case we ran out of material," I grinned. "In point of fact, you don't look as if you'd last ten minutes, let alone several hours."

Stanley snuggled against my breasts for a moment, kissing them softly. "It's probably going to be quite a project," he whispered. "I'm losing confidence already."

"Come inside me," I said. "Then we'll turn on our sides, and we'll lie very quietly while I read to you."

For a minute or two Stanley seemed to have other ideas. He found his way into me with great conviction. Feeling him moving slowly inside me, I was quite certain we weren't going to prove anything. "All right," he said giving me a final kiss and rolling me on my side, "I can see that it's up to me to restrain you . . . you demon! Go ahead and read to me."

"This really is a nice way to read," I murmured into his ear. I was reluctant to open the book, enjoying the pressure of his hand on my behind as he held me close to him.

"You'd better start reading," Stanley chuckled. "I don't dare breathe. I need to think of something beyond how enjoyable this is."

I perched Dr. Robie's book on the pillow just over his head. "This is fun," I said feeling quite bubbly. "Seriously, Stan, I think one of the most interesting things about this book is that it was written more than forty years ago. Dr. Robie was away ahead of his time

in understanding sex and love. Here's some of the things
I've underlined: 'Men now find that it is a delight to
prolong the love union, and soon discover that mutual
— delight is given and received under complete control . . .
During a lengthy period of lengthy control the whole
being of each is submerged in the other, and exquisite
exaltation is experienced . . . Perfect control comes by
patience and determination and the reward is happy,
— united lives and each attain to their higher selves . . .
To be able to continue the reciprocal movements of
communion for an indefinite time without arriving at
the orgasm is a matter of education, and will only come
after continued endeavor.' "

"He can say that again," Stanley said tasting my nipples. "When I kiss you like that, I feel your vagina
contract on me."

"It will do more than contract, if you don't stop.
Cooperate and listen," I said, continuing to read. " 'I
seem to sublimate my partner into a paradise of tender
peace and romantic reverie and thrill her to a sort of
soul intoxication of magnetic bliss. The orgasm would
seem quite the antipodes of this and a crude shock by
contrast . . . All my aim is to establish this wonderful
magnetic rapport and this romantic, Poetic ecstacy . . .
Words fail . . . We are literally angels in heaven in our
innocence and conscious purity an untellable mutual
love. Who would care for an orgasm in such an emotional state of divine realization. It would bring all to
an abrupt end. Do not even think of it or mention it.'

"Stanley," I shivered, "stop running your fingers
over my belly before I explode. Listen to this. A female
doctor wrote this to Dr. Robie more than forty years
ago: 'You ask how long the desire for emission should
be inhibited . . . You seem to consider reservatus (extended sexual intercourse) as *re*pression while I think

of it as *ex*pression of the highest order. As all progress in civilization has been by means of the volitional part of the brain gradually taking over more and more of the processes that were formerly reflexive or instinctive, so the sexual nature is the last to be taken over. Evolution demands that this be done. Fame waits at the door of him to whom is given the task of so educating humanity that it may come to see sexual intercourse in this light.'

"Are you going to last, Stanley?" I asked.

"No trouble at all," he grinned. "You look so sweetly serious while you are reading, your breasts feel so nice and warm, and your heart is beating so quietly that I really am magically floating on your words."

"Let me finish Robie . . . then you can read from von Urban. Here, this is interesting! It's from the *Handbook of the Oneida Community,* written nearly a hundred years ago: 'Oneida Communists have a special theory in regard to the act of sexual intercourse . . . two distinctive kinds of sexual intercourse ought to be recognized; one simply social, the other propagative, and that the propagative should only be exercised when impregnation is intended and mutually agreed upon. Sexual intercourse *without the propagative act* (except when propagation is intended) is all that we tolerate in Free Love; . . . So far as this matter is concerned, Free Love, in the Oneida sense of the term, is much less free in the gross, sensual way than marriage . . . We have left the simple form of marriage and advanced to the complex stage of it. We have no quarrel with those who believe in exclusive dual marriage and faithfully observe it, but, for us, we have concluded there is a better way. The honor and faithfulness that constitute an ideal marriage may exist between two hundred as well as two; while the guarantees for women and children are much greater in the Community than they can be in any private family. The results of the complex system we may sum up by saying, that men are rendered more courteous, women more winning, children are better born, and both sexes are personally free.' "

"I wonder why other groups haven't tried to form communities like Oneida?" I asked.

Stanley smiled. "There's a lot more than sex in the Oneida concepts. They pooled the results of all their labor. The very thought is abhorrent to the average American. We are too individualistic. There were a dozen or more of those communistic societies in the United States in the 1800's. Most of them were based on very stern religious codes, and dominated by one or two leaders." Stanley wiggled away from me and took von Urban's book.

"Hurry back," I sighed. "I feel better when you are inside me."

Joined again, Stanley turned the pages to my underlinings. "This is from a letter to Dr. von Urban: 'Dr. A. B., a former patient of my sanitarium, told the following story: (A week ago I married a beautiful young Arabian girl. We were both very much in love. The strange happenings between us were so remarkable and exciting, that I felt impelled to tell them to an expert. My wife and I lay for an hour, naked on a couch in close bodily contact, caressing each other, but without sex union. The room was in total darkness, entirely blacked out. You could not distinguish anything. Then we separated from each other and stood up; thereupon my wife became visible. She was outlined with a nimbus of greenish-blue mystic light which radiated from her. It was like a halo, except for the fact, that it encircled not only her head but her whole body, showing its configuration in a hazy way. As she stood there, I moved my hand slowly toward her. When my palm came within an inch of her breast an electric spark sprang from her to me, visible, audible, and painful. We both shrank back) . . . Experience has convinced the author that there is a difference in the bio-electrical potential in the bodies of male and female which can be exchanged in proper intercourse, leaving both partners relaxed, happy and satisfied . . . During the following weeks this young couple made further experiments on my behalf . . . During the course of these experiments it was ascertained that if the couple did not lie naked for a half hour or longer, in close physical contact, kissing and caressing, but instead started intercourse immediately, the strange radiation did not emanate from the body of the girl, nor did the sparks fly between the two lovers when they stood near each other afterwards, even though the sex union lasted less than twenty-seven minutes. Further the lovers found that every intercourse lasting less than twenty-seven minutes induced an urgent desire, in both, for a repetition of the sex act. But, if this desire was fulfilled by another too brief act, both became nervous and irritated, and sometimes they suffered physical ailments afterwards (headache, heart-palpitation, asthma, etc.). This seemed to show that the tension in the sex organs was reduced, but not the tension of the entire body . . . Intercourse for less than twenty-seven minutes increased the distance at which the sparks would jump to more than one inch, indicating that the tension in their bodies became stronger with each intercourse of brief duration . . . On the other hand intercourse lasting half an hour or more was followed by entire relaxation from nervous tension.' "

"My God . . . what does that prove?" I asked pressing myself even closer against Stanley.

"It's simple. If people like you and me rush into

intercourse, and whack it off, the coroner may find only the charred remains. We would have electrocuted each other!"

Stanley stopped for a minute to kiss away my laughter and then he read: " 'The natives of the Trobriand Islands, in British New Guinea, ridicule the sex life of civilized people, caricaturing before mixed audiences, the sketchy, limp and clumsy technique of Western lovers. The audience is amused by this burlesque of a lower state of erotic culture; but they believe that they exaggerate because, in their experience, no people could enjoy a sex act so lacking in preparation, and so hurried in consummation. The explanation they offer is this: "After one hour the souls of the ancestors awaken and bless our union." For these Island Lovers, the long duration of the sex act is obligatory, a duty to their ancestors. Too brief a sex union would torture them with feelings of guilt and remorse . . . The man does not lie over his mate; to do so would imprison her . . . During a long sex act this would become unbearable . . . Sometimes they lie together with their heads at opposite ends of the sleeping mat, the two open pair of legs fitted together like two pincers in such a way that the sex organs come into the closest possible contact without penetration of the vagina. In this position they sleep together at times when no sex intercourse is intended.' "

"I think we ought to try that for a minute," Stanley said grinning. And we did! . . . But pretty soon Stanley had edged his way back from my toes and was kissing me between the legs. "This is better, and more interesting," he said. "You taste quite nice."

"I can't get over the feeling that it's not a nice thing to do," I said.

"You don't like it?"

"I didn't say that. But the books give it such horrible Latin names."

"All the books say it's quite normal marital behavior. Hey! You bit me!"

"Only nibbled," I chuckled. "But what I want to know is why? Why do you have the compulsion to kiss me that way? Nothing I've ever read explains why."

"You don't feel the compulsion?"

"A little," I admitted. "But not so much as you."

"But you do like it when I kiss you?"

"Stanley," I shivered. "You don't need an answer to that . . . and if you don't stop, this experiment is going to have a rapid conclusion. You still haven't answered why."

"Aren't most animals attracted into propagation by the male and female odor?"

"Stanley . . . please, stop. I'm afraid I may have an odor."

"You do. You smell like warm hay drying in a barn. Very aphrodisiacal!"

"Okay . . . that does it! I'm going to read to you from Watts' book."

Once again joined, I started to read but Stanley interrupted me. "The last chapter called *Consummation* is the best thing I have ever read on the male-female relationship."

"I agree," I said fervently. "Listen to some of the things I have underlined: 'This makes it the more strange that conventional spirituality rejects the bodily union of man and woman as the most fleshy animal and degrading phase of human activity—a rejection showing the extent of its faulty perception and its misinterpretation of the natural world. It rejects the most concrete and creative form of man's relationship to the world outside his organism, because it is through the love of a woman that he can say not only of her but what is other, "This is my body." . . . All this is peculiarly true of love and sexual communion between man and woman. This is why it has such a strong spiritual and mystical character when spontaneous and why it is so degrading and frustrating when forced . . . Sex is therefore the virtual religion of very many people, the end to which they accord more devotion than any other. To the conventionally religious minded this worship of sex is a dangerous and positively sinful substitute for the worship of God. But this is because sex, or any pleasure, as ordinarily pursued is never a true fulfillment. For this very reason it is *not* God, but not at all because it is "merely physical" . . . Sexuality is not a separate compartment of human life; it is a radiance pervading every human relationship . . . A relationship of this kind cannot adequately be discussed in manuals of sexual hygiene . . . Their use is consequence rather than the cause of a certain inner attitude, since they suggest themselves almost naturally to partners who take their love as it comes, contemplatively, and are in no hurry to grasp anything from it . . . and to see that pleasure grasped is no pleasure . . . According to Tantric symbolism, the energy of the *Kundalini* is aroused but simply dissipated in ordinary sexual activity. It can, however, be transmuted in a prolonged embrace in which the male orgasm is reserved and the sexual energy diverted into contemplation of the divine as incarnate in the woman . . . Long before the male orgasm begins, the sexual impulse manifests itself as what can only be described, psychologically, as a melting warmth between the partners so that they seem veritably to flow into each other. To put it in another way, "physical lust" transforms itself into the most considerate and tender form of love imaginable . . . Sexual love in the contemplative spirit simply provides the conditions in which we can be aware of our mutual interdependence and "oneness" . . .'

"Stanley . . ." I stopped reading and kissed him. "I think this man, Alan Watts, has given, in this book, the most important insights on sex and love I've ever read. It gives me goose-pimples to read it . . . a sense of identity with another person who thinks and feels the way I feel."

"There's only one trouble," Stanley said. "To achieve the heights that Watts says are possible requires a tremendous ability to surrender yourself to another individual. The key then is a high degree of education not only in sex as practiced this way, but also along the lines of philosophy, psychology, in fact every aspect of education. What I mean is that two neurotic people could not make love this way. They simply wouldn't know how to escape from themselves . . . into the other person."

"Let me read a little more," I said trying to ignore his happy kisses on my breast. "Listen: 'One finds out what it means to simply look at the other person, to touch hands or listen to the voice. If these contacts are not regarded as leading to something else, but rather allowed to become one's consciousness, as if the source of activity lay in them and not the will, they become sensations of immense subtlety and richness . . . The point is to discover the wonder of simple contacts . . . The psychic counterpart of this bodily and sensuous intimacy is a similar openness of attention to each other's thoughts—a form of communion which can be as sexually 'charged' as physical contact. This is the feeling that one can express one's thoughts to the other just as they are since there is not the slightest compulsion to assume a pretended character. This is perhaps

the rarest and most difficult aspect of any human relationship, since in ordinary social converse the spontaneous arising of thought is more carefully hidden than
anything else. Between unconscious and humorless people who do not know and accept their own limitations
it is almost impossible . . . To unveil the flow of thought
can therefore be an even greater sexual intimacy than
physical nakedness . . . If no attempt is made to induce
the orgasm by bodily motion, the interpenetration of
the sexual centers becomes a channel of the most vivid
psychic interchange . . . The marvellously overwhelming urge to turn themselves inside out for each other
. . . Rare as gaiety may be in cultures where there is
a tie between sex and guilt, the release from self brings
laughter in love-making . . . The height of sexual love,
coming upon us of itself, is one of the most total experiences of relationship to the other of which we are
capable . . . For what lovers feel for each other in this
moment is no other than adoration in the full religious
sense, and its climax is almost literally the pouring of
their lives into each other. Such adoration which is due
God, would indeed be idolatrous were it not that, in
that moment, love takes away the illusion and shows
the beloved for what he or she in truth is . . . not the
socially pretended person but the naturally divine.'

"Stanley . . . Stanley . . ." I whispered undulating in
response to him. "We've done remarkably well for our
first attempt. Don't you agree?"

Watts' book thudded on the floor beside the bed.

"Unquestionably, Sheila." Stanley grinned at me.

"Do you want to fall asleep this way?"

"I'm afraid I've passed the point of no return."

I kissed him wildly. "Oh, God! Darling . . . darling
. . . so have I. So have I!"

FROM THE JOURNAL OF HARRY SCHACHT

August, after the Second Year

So I am writing this in jail. A few miles west of Provincetown. In this first half day of incarceration the philosopher, latent in me, bubbles through to the surface. I can now prove something or other. Possibly, that males and females even after some years of familiarity with the pros and cons of each other need not necessarily lead dull and unimaginative lives. Or perhaps, like some other famous personages in history, Thoreau and Gandhi for example, I have discovered that the confines of a narrow cell are conducive to reflection.

The truth is that in the past year the Tenhausens' journal keeping project simply hadn't dovetailed into the pace of the fast life I have been leading. Admittedly, calm appraisal in the jug and via the pen is somewhat difficult. I have two argumentative cellmates, Jack and Stanley, who feel that I should participate in their heated discussion about the vagaries of destiny and fate, versus the general perversity of the human animal. Forsaking me, a scribbling idiot, they are now carrying on a long-distance discussion with Beth, Sheila and Valerie. Yes, our female compatriots are likewise imprisoned in this red jail house. They are out of sight, for propriety's sake, in another row of cells at the rear of the building. But definitely, shrilly . . . they are not out of hearing.

The six of us, quietly baking, as a hot August Saturday afternoon sun beats on the flat roof of this dreary penitentiary, seem to be the only occupants of this steaming Cape Cod oven. Stanley, Jack and I have stripped to our shorts. In what state of undress our female mentors are is impossible to determine since we can't see them.

Tearful, rescue-us telegrams have been dispatched to my father and Phillip Tenhausen . . . but as the sun sinks slowly in the west it seems quite obvious that no one is going to arrive to bail out the impenitent six before Monday. Beth, Valerie and Sheila have either been excoriating the plumbing or giggling and laughing hysterically as they recall the events that led up to our capture by the town constable, Ebeneezer Schnook. It really should be his last name! Now the girls are harmonizing . . . "Write me a letter. Send it by Smokey . . . care of this little ol' Cape Cod pokey."

All of which brings me back to the facts of life. If my father arrives before Phillip Tenhausen, I am obviously going to listen to the longest lecture in the history of long lectures on the subject of Harrad College. The rest of my cellmates are indeed fortunate. Their parents live a considerable distance from this stronghold of Puritanism. I can only pray that Rachel and Jake are in the Catskills on vacation. If they receive their telegram before Phil Tenhausen, and after a mad dash to the Cape, they discover their only son's peccadillo first hand; well, they may be able to laugh at the subject of *yentizing* around when a Jewish comedian on the borscht circuit makes a "funny" but as a practical family matter it quite obviously won't be admitted as a fit subject for laughter.

So please, Phil . . . discover us before Jake (my father's name is actually Saul but he tolerates Jake) arrives with his moustache bristling, and behind him my mother wailing; "Es passt nit! I told you, Saul, Harry's not too old for a *potch* before he becomes a *paskudnick*."

Before InSix (as we are now known) started out on this mad junket, I had worked the summer at Mass. General Hospital and then spent a week at home. Jake was pleased, and Mother with tears of joy displayed her future doctor to all the ladies of Hadassah. She was careful to mention only Cambridge, Massachusetts as the locale of my endeavors, hoping, obviously, that by association her friends would assume her son's pedagogical training was being acquired at a more venerable institution in the same area.

Several times Jake corralled me for a man-to-man discussion. "Harry," he said, "I'm worried about you. Why don't you quit this Harrad College monkey shines and switch over to a regular college?"

"Why?" I demanded. "Phil Tenhausen tells me that reports he has on me from 'A' University are absolutely tops. All I have to do is keep in the same groove and I can walk into any medical school in the country."

"Oy, such a groove," Jake sighed. "How can you keep it up, Harry? My God, a little piece of. . . ." Jake smiled apologetically. "Well, sex is all right. A growing boy has to learn . . . but everyday you are living with that little blonde *meidele*. Day in, day out. You'll wear yourself out!"

"Jake," I grinned. "It's like any muscle. It grows stronger with exercise!"

"Ha . . . you make jokes. But I still say it isn't

healthy. I was reading yesterday about morals on the campus. All this sex so young. You'll grow bored. I was never with a woman until I was twenty-two. Now ... everywhere you read, boys and girls in college going to bed in their college rooms, yet. And brassy enough to insist this is their right without having even earned it. *Mach a leben* and *then* you have the right. The world has gone to hell. Now a man can only 'get himself security,' I read it! . . . In bed with a girl. Some security."

I knew it was hopeless but once again I tried to explain Harrad to Jake. "You are wrong about the boredom and security bit," I told him. "You see, the stuff you have been reading is not Harrad.

"It's the way most colleges and universities are right now. Harrad accepts the male-female relationship as completely normal for men and women in their late teens and accepts sexual relations without the requirement of marriage. Harrad has simply leapt forward fifty or one hundred years. The colleges you are reading about and their sex problems are simply not equivalent to Harrad. At the typical college today, the kids are fighting for sexual freedom without social meaning. Sure they will become bored. By the time they are juniors in college many of them have settled into a kind of early monogamy without marriage. They seek love in a moral climate that says if pre-marital sex must exist, then it must ape monogamous marriage; that way it is still guilt ridden but it is permissible. I feel sorry for them. In this environment these students are in effect pretending marriage; playing at being husband and wife. They are discovering that neither the boy nor the girl can give the security or identity that they are demanding from each other. A broken engagement becomes a divorce.

"Harrad students don't do that. One of the common denominators the Tenhausens use in accepting students at Harrad is based on an early analysis made by Abraham Maslow; what Maslow labeled 'a dominance feeling syndrome.' People of this type are 'self confident, socially poised, relaxed, extroverted, have high self-esteem, are self assured, have a feeling of general capability, are unconventional, have less respect for rules, have a tendency to "use" people, have freer personality expression, are somewhat more secure, have an autonomous code of ethics, are more independent, less religious, more masculine, less polite, and have a love of adventure, novelty and new experience.' "

I grinned at Jake who was listening to me in a state of semi-shock. "Not all the Harrad kids have these attributes, but they have some. After a year or two, they acquire more. As a result they don't seek 'security' from each other. In fact they don't expect or demand anything from one another but a willingness to accept the other person as an amazing human being. It is an interesting side-light on Maslow's study that people of this type, when they are married, do not as a rule end up in divorce courts. They make the most successful marriages particularly when they mate with a person with similar attributes. Now place this Harrad student in an environment where sex is accepted as a quite normal enjoyment, and love is based on admiration and deep liking for another person as a person, you have something entirely different from the Western concepts of romantic love and passion. Because I love Beth and she loves me doesn't exclude Sheila or Stanley, and other kids that may come within our orbit of interests. United, we stand to have more interesting and vital lives than we would performing independent love duets. With only two of us seeing our own reflections in each other's eyes for a lifetime, a certain glazing would set in caused simply by overexposure . . . not lack of love."

"Oh, my God," Jake exploded. "All you college kids do is spout words. Do you honestly know what the hell you are talking about?"

"Sure," I said, "but I can see that you don't."

"Look, son . . . it's an insane idea . . . and now if I understand you, you are trying to tell me that every one in your school is going to bed with everyone else."

"The males with the females, not the males with the males, or the females with the females," I chuckled.

"I should hope not," Jake said sourly. "But you can't do that all your life."

"Why not? A great many married people in this country are doing just that right now . . . and it all ends up in divorce courts, or gets pretty messy."

"You are going to be a doctor. Who could trust a doctor who lived like you do at Harrad? You'd have no patients."

"You trust Doctor Neisner. I heard Mother telling a friend of hers that Doctor Neisner has a girl friend. His wife knows it and couldn't care less. Old Jewish custom, really. Have you read the Old Testament lately?"

Jake scowled at me and changed the subject. "So someday you are going to marry this blonde girl."

"Her name is Beth."

"Will she change her religion?"

"Who cares?"

"I do. Your mother does. You will. If your wife does not change for you, you can never become a member of the congregation. A good Jew's wife is an extension of himself."

"Not Beth. She will be herself."

"What kind of Jew will you be?"

"A happy man first, and a Jew second."

"You would give up your faith?"

"No. I have endless faith . . . in man."

Jake looked at me, puzzled. "So this is the kind of education I am paying for?"

I hugged him. "This is what happens when you love . . . as any good Jew knows."

If Jake was bewildered then, he's going to be more bewildered when he finds his son arrested for indecent exposure, and on a morals charge involving orgiastic sex behavior. Ebeneezer Schnook just returned with our supper. Baked beans, of course, donated by the Women's Auxiliary who are having their Saturday night supper and bingo game in the cellar of the church across the street. With Ebeneezer were two reporters from the local newspaper.

"This will make the wire services, Eb," one of them said, gleefully. "You'll be famous. You can run for selectman this fall."

The other character tried to persuade us to grasp the bars of our cell and shout angrily while he aimed his Graflex at us. Failing to get our cooperation he edged his way to the cell, in the rear, where Beth, Sheila and Valerie were imprisoned. He was back in a second blushing. "Jumping Jesus," he yelled. "Those dames are standing there stark naked! Is that the way you found them, Eb?"

Ebeneezer, snorting, ran to see. "Put on your clothes," we heard him shout angrily.

"You didn't give us time to bring our nightgowns," Valerie answered indignantly. Beth and Sheila were choking with laughter. "It's your fault, you dirty old man. Do you expect us to sleep in our clothes? The least thing you could do is turn on the air conditioning."

On reflection, the reporter with the Graflex stared

back to the girls' cell, but Eb held him back. "Who are they, Eb? Where did you arrest them? Let me snap a couple of pictures."

"Nope. No dirty pictures in my jail! I don't know who they are. Can't get a damned thing out of them. A bunch of wild college kids is my guess. They moved into Bill Sykes's place up at Nob Point. Been up there nearly a week . . . running all over the place bare-ass . . . taking movies of each other, singing, dancing and drinking all night long. Don't know what in hell this generation is coming to. Couple of them live in New York, I think. Probably beatniks or bums from Greenwich Village. A damned shame. Stuff like this gives the Cape a bad name."

"If it's bad for business," Stanley asked, "why do you want to put it in the newspapers, Eb old boy? I'd hush the whole matter up if I were you."

"Keep your fresh mouth shut!" Ebeneezer snarled.

"Where do you kids go to school?" the reporter asked.

"On a little known planet in outer space," Jack said, a very serious tone in his voice. "We are emissaries from the planet Sub Rosa. We arrived two days ago in our space ship which is carefully concealed in one of the lonely sand dunes nearby. These are not our normal bodies. In actual fact on Sub Rosa we had no bodies but are simply emanations of spirit. To bring our message to your leaders we have temporarily assumed the terrestrial bodies of six nice earth children."

"See what television has done." Eb looked at us sadly.

"It's true," Jack said solemnly. "Within the next few hours you will discover that certain earthlings have disappeared. Contact the parents . . . send them to view us. They will recognize the bodies of their loved ones

. . . but will tremble at the dark spirits inhabiting them."

I suppose from the viewpoint of more practical and moral earth creatures our Cape vacation and final incarceration does have an other-worldly quality about it. It really all started last March. InSix wasn't planned. It just grew spontaneously as a result of our nightly get-to-gethers at Harrad. Looking back, I would guess that Jack Dawes was really the germinating factor. The night that he accompanied himself on his guitar and sang us a screwball, satirical rhyming version of the news of the day, we kept testing him to see if he could do it extemporaneously. Jack, never at a loss for words, was able to sing off-the-cuff, jazzed-up calypso interpretations that had us all gasping with laughter. A few nights later, Valerie, who can mimic almost any gesture or voice, joined Jack with a skit satirizing the first flight of a man with a woman (she had a slight case of nymphomania) as they orbited out of earth into space together. For the fun of it we worked out several other skits. Sheila, who had mastered the accordion, joined with Jack on the guitar. Stanley provided a beat by banging on any available pan or bottle. He finally got so enthusiastic, he bought a set of bongo drums. Jack taught Beth how to play chords on the guitar, and before long I had mastered it well enough to plunk along with them.

By April we had a repertoire of eight musical sketches. Sheila refused to do any acting. She couldn't let herself go like Beth and Valerie. Somehow, Beth always seemed to get cast as the dumb blonde sex-pot, and Valerie as the sophisticated hep-cat. Stanley's enthusiasm held us together with his pipe dream that we were good enough to "go professional." The money we could make would help put us through graduate school.

None of us took Stanley seriously until the night he and Jack told us we were "booked" the following Saturday at Joe Gonzi's coffee house in Cambridge. Even then we didn't believe him.

"We're not that good," Sheila objected. "It would take too much rehearsing."

"I'd be scared silly with an audience," Beth said.

"It's only the 'Grinning Eye,' " Jack said. "Gonzi isn't going to pay us. It's just for experience."

Three weeks later Gonzi offered us one hundred fifty dollars a week for our Friday and Saturday night appearances. Our skits on the parietal rules at "B" College, with Beth and Val paralyzing the audience as the virgin co-ed on their visit to a senior's room, and Jack and Stanley playing the roles of the Mephisophelean seducers of young womanhood; our outer space skit, and a skit with Beth as the naive blonde who comes to college to be a drum majorette and is either constantly dropping her baton or is nearly exposing her breasts as she whirls it in the air, created standing room only at the Grinning Eye. Gonzi upped his admission price. A local recording company told us that if we could "clean up" all eight skits, they would make a long playing record of us.

Still none of us took it very seriously. "It's a lark," Beth said when we all got back to Harrad after one Saturday show, "but it could take too much time. I think we should play it for what it's worth within limits. None of this business of racing around the country or signing a contract the way that agent wants; we are a local fad. We're 'in' for the moment. I wouldn't want to live my life in a sweat of wondering how to stay 'in.' The whole racket is too fickle."

All of us agreed. But Beth had named us. We were temporarily, at least, InSix. Jack and Stanley decided we should be incorporated with the purpose of our corporation to put all the stockholders through graduate school. We finally made the recording and exhausted our repertoire. Much to the relief of Margaret and Phil Tenhausen, by June we had forgotten the whole business.

But unwanted success is sometimes hard to dispose of. We had a money bull by the horns. As President of InSix, Inc. Jack kept in touch with us through the summer. Our lack of desire for publicity created interest, mystery and intrigue. Our record began selling beyond all expectation. The recording company wanted to make another one. By mail and telephone, Jack badgered us until we finally all agreed to spend the week before Labor Day on the Cape. Object, to write and rehearse a half dozen more skits.

Sheila and Stanley agreed to meet us in Boston with Sheila's new station wagon, purchased so that InSix could travel together. To our amazement, Jack and Valerie arrived at the South Station followed by porters carrying enough movie equipment to fill a small truck without any passengers. After much hugging and bussing one another (while the local citizenry watched us with their mouths open) Jack finally explained. "I borrowed the stuff from Bad Max. All summer he has been making experimental movies. Ten or fifteen minute jobs that are supposed to give the cinema a new artistic depth and meaning. One of Bad Max's friends won a twenty thousand dollar award from the Ford Foundation. Seems the foundation is encouraging new types of cinematic expression. The joke is that some of the awards were given for 'pornies.' "

"What the devil are pornies?" Beth demanded.

Jack grinned. "Flickers a little on the pornographic side. The public loves them. Makes them feel they can be esthetically interested and still not bored to death. Kook stuff. Nudes with skulls where their breasts should be; a girl sitting like Whistler's mother but dressed only in her garter belt; a girl carrying her tits on a tray; naked witches riding broomsticks, etc., all mixed up with political crap and God knows what, supposedly created by artists and poets who have some mystical message to convey. I decided InSix can do better!"

We finally wrestled all the movie stuff, together with Jack and Valerie's trunks and bags, into Sheila's station wagon. With the six of us squeezed between tripods, floodlights, guitars, accordions and what not, there was scarcely room to turn and look at each other. Stanley edged the car slowly through the Boston traffic.

"Get us to the Cape before the transmission is scraping on the highway," I groaned.

On the expressway, Sheila managed to pry a few more details out of Jack and Valerie. "Aren't we going to work on a new record?" she demanded. "Where is making screwball movies going to get us? Where the heck are we going to stay on the Cape with all this junk?"

"Typical female," Jack said hugging her. "Three questions at once. You bet we are going to make another record. InSix is famous. If we want to go on a national television hook-up it's all arranged."

"Nothing doing," Beth said. "I promised Mother and Pops and Margaret and Phil that we wouldn't go any further from Harrad than the Grinning Eye. The last straw would be their nubile daughter barnstorming around the country . . . and believe me Harrad College is next to the last straw, as far as they are concerned."

"I agree," Valerie said. "Let the world come to us."

"The world won't have to come to us," Jack chuckled. "We are going to the world with a movie.

When it is finished it will be the rage of the Village. Bad Max promises to run it twice a week at the Last Gurgle. Behold, you knaves! Sitting next to you is Jack Dawes, producer and director of the new epic, a twenty minute satire on the women's fashion industry. InSix is going to change women's fashions and clothing styles singlehanded. We'll be famous and infamous. Tell 'em, Val."

Val groaned. "Jack has lost his marbles. I refuse to comment. Whatever mad project he has afoot we are going to come to grips with it at Nob Point. Bill Sykes, a kind of uncle-ish friend of my father (unbeknown to that good man) loaned me the key to his cottage, a slight token of his affection and appreciation of behind patting privileges I have rendered him since I was a little tot. It's a nice lonely spot on a sand dune overlooking the Atlantic, conducive to lovemaking and reverie."

A few miles from Eastham we turned off the highway; bumping and careening along a lonely dirt road that led to the ocean, we finally located the Sykes cottage. It seemed isolated enough. The Atlantic a hundred feet below us was a red glaze in the afternoon sun. A few other cottages were nestled in dunes at a respectable distance. After we had lugged all the stuff inside and surveyed the living room, single bedroom and kitchen, it became apparent that we were going to have to rearrange the sleeping facilities. Hilariously we tossed the mattresses from the two single beds on the floor. Sideways with our feet hanging over the edge all six of us lay down. We were as neatly packed as sardines.

"Those with sex on their minds will have to find a lonely sand dune," Beth yelled from the bottom of the pig pile we all made on top of her.

"Who wants sex and with whom?" Val said hugging Stanley.

We all looked at each other, embarrassed for a moment. Beth broke the tension. "Remember me? I love you all!"

"So do we," Sheila and Val chorused. The girls merrily proceeded to kiss Stanley, Jack and me.

Deciding that food was more important than kissing and hugging, at least for the moment, we drove back to the highway, found a supermarket, and bought enough groceries for a week, and Jack bought two cases of aged-in-the-bottle champagne, telling us we earned it for devotion to InSix, besides we had to celebrate our re-union.

An hour later, wearing sweat-shirts that the girls had embroidered with the word InSix lettered inside a heart, and shorts and panties, we slid down the sand cliff in front of the cottage to the beach below. Stanley slid a case of champagne down the cliff and popped the corks at us showering us with geysers of foaming wine. We cooked hot dogs over an open fire. Wrapped in blankets as protection against the cold night air (somehow or other I found Valerie, a sinuous caterpillar, curled up beside me) we chattered incessantly about the world, life and us.

"I guess you've got me for the night," Valerie wiggled closer. "Are you sorry?"

The conversation had become sporadic. I pulled the army blankets partially over our heads and Val and I burrowed into our shelter. The fire of drift wood had turned into a red glow. The sand beneath us was still warm from the sun. Not far away, Beth and Stanley, Sheila and Jack were huddled mounds on the beach. I watched the shadows the firelight made on the planes of

Val's face. I held her hand. Silently, we watched the stars in the evening sky.

"Are we bad . . . all of us?" Val asked softly.

"What is bad? That I care for you? That we are just human beings alone . . . and yet somehow wonderfully knit together?"

"Doesn't it frighten you?"

"This moment isn't meaningless. It's wondrous. You know, my guess is that Stanley and Beth and Sheila and Jack are asking each other the same questions. I like the way the six of us surrender ourselves to each other. We have eliminated dishonesty . . . shame . . . pretense."

Val sighed. "I don't know why any of you, Jack, Stanley or you would want me. I'm too tall . . . too awkward. An ugly duckling compared to Beth and Sheila."

I leaned on my elbow and looked into her face. "Val, you have a lovely face; strong, clean cut, big saucer eyes that glisten, a nice body. If you are looking for the ugly duckling in the crowd, you are lying beside him."

"Men shouldn't be pretty. You have character. You look like a genius. But me . . . in high heels I'm at least two inches taller than any of you."

"I haven't heard Jack complaining."

"Do you think we should be mixed up like this? Won't someone get hurt? You probably wish you were with Beth."

I grinned at her. "I'm not giving it a thought. I think we have all discovered that any two of us could get married and live together so, in effect, we are all married to each other. What's more I think that the 'Idea' of us will last. I used to think we might fight and get jealous of each other. In the first year at Harrad most of us did. And then we simply eliminated jealousy by discovering that it was a very boring and selfish pre-occupation. In its place we have developed a strong sense of unity and a fast instant communication."

Val kissed me. "Pull up your sweatshirt, Harry. I want to feel your flesh against me." Later she wiggled out of her panties, and we fell asleep enmeshed.

I awoke with the sun a red crescent on the horizon. Night was reluctantly leaving the sky. Val was holding my penis lightly, half asleep herself. Our climax was sleepy-sweet and hungrily joyful. I was asleep again in her arms when Stanley yelled, "Come on, all you young lovers. Last one in the ocean is custard the dragon."

A yelling screaming churning mass of gasping naked flesh, we all plunged into the icy morning water. Shivering and half frozen we scrambled out within minutes. Our courtly naked ladies, their nipples erect, hooted and howled at our shrunken, wizened penises and our dismay at discovering they had practically disappeared in pure shock at such an outrage.

After breakfast, Jack and Valerie opened their Pandora trunk. Jack proudly held up what looked like a roll of cloth, about five yards long. While it looked like ordinary cloth held on the vertical axis it was transparent as clear vinyl plastic.

"This," he said mysteriously, "is something new in the world. It is actually plastic but it is perforated with millions of microscopic holes. In the vernacular of Madison Avenue, it breathes, and behaves like any ordinary cloth. It is not on the market yet, and probably won't be for a few years until the manufacturing costs are reduced. A friend of mine pilfered it from the research laboratory of one of the large chemical companies."

"What will anyone use it for?" Beth demanded.

"Beth!" Jack chided her. "You obviously didn't get enough sleep last night. Your clear mind isn't functioning. It will be used for clothes! What else? Show them your handiwork, Val."

"This wasn't my idea," Val grinned as she fished in the trunk. "If I hadn't been working for a very good-natured dress designer this summer, Jack would never have got them made. A fortune of labor went into them." Val handed Beth a dress which looked quite normal to me until Beth held it up to examine it.

"Jack Dawes, you are mad!" Beth yelled. "Completely off your rocker! Look, everybody . . . the damned thing has a transparent behind!"

Sure enough, carefully merged into the seat of the dress in the shape of a perfect heart was a piece of Jack's plastic cloth.

Val produced a similar dress for Sheila. Altogether Val had three street dresses and three evening gowns. The evening gowns had the additional feature of transparent breast cups as well as transparent behinds.

While the girls were excitedly putting them on, their behinds undulating and clearly visible as they walked, Stanley and I tried to stop laughing long enough to listen to Jack.

"How do you like them?" he demanded. "Most entrancing style ever developed for females. Something absolutely unique in female fashions. Original creations by Jacque. That's me! When Val first modeled them for me I nearly gave up my dream of being a movie mogul and departed for Paris to set up a fashion house. But that will have to wait. First InSix is going to make a movie. It will be a satire on the fashion industry. Since I will, of necessity, have to be cameraman and director,

I think that Harry and Stanley should take the parts of famous French fashion designers. Get the picture? As the movie opens the entire fashion industry is clamoring for the first view of the fall fashions."

Jack delved into his trunk, and chucked two rubber apemasks at Harry and Stanley. He then produced two full dress morning suits with striped pants. "I bought you costumes for two dollars each from the Morgan Memorial," he chuckled. "Probably taken off rich corpses before they interred them," Jack grinned at Stanley and me who were suspiciously sniffing the shabby moth-ball impregnated clothing. "Now my idea is that our famous designers should appear in full dress, wearing ape masks. This will permit Harry and Stanley to take other parts as the movie develops. So, I give you the idea. Take it from there! The basic point is that women will wear anything if the Paris or Italian designers make it sufficiently *outré*. All we have to do now is to put together a zippy script."

"Don't kid yourself," Sheila said. "No woman would ever bare her fanny to the public."

"These styles are kind of intriguing," Stanley mused. "Imagine walking along Fifth Avenue judging and comparing women's behinds."

"The wheels of industry would stop turning," I chuckled. "All traffic would stop, the male population would develop permanent priapism, the girdle and brassiere industry would languish. . . . Maybe we should call the movie, *The Day the World Ended*." I waited for applause but no one got the pun.

"I've got a better title," Beth chuckled, flipping her behind. "Since the style would only appeal to men, it is obvious that drama should climax with the women castrating the designers. Why not call it *The Short Saga of the Fat Asses?"* Beth bent over to see what else was in Jack's trunk.

"My God, Beth," Val warned her. "In that dress you should stoop, *not bend!* We just saw your tonsils!"

"I think the style will catch on," I laughed. "It reveals entirely new areas of the female anatomy."

"How about *Cheeks of Delight* for a title?" Val asked. She was immediately bombarded with pillows.

For two days we swam, sang, wrote a script for the movie and as the mood seized us, hysterically rehearsed our parts. Stanley and I were given the name Apeneé Brothers. I suggested the addition of meshugana. We finally agreed that the title "Meshugana Frères Apeneé" had a nice esthetic sound that should entrance the critics. By the fourth day, Stanley and I, nearly asphyxiated by the odor of naphthalene, had abandoned the size 40 striped pants. Dressed in tailcoats, ape masks and nothing else, we horsed through the mysterious motions of designing women's clothes.

Exasperated, Jack insisted that our costumes were too pornographic. The production came to a halt until Sheila and Beth got the idea of designing cod-pieces for us with grinning faces stitched onto them. Their masterpieces were a concoction of brassiere cups, padded, embroidered and sewn onto our jockey shorts. They insisted on sewing on the cups while we were still in our shorts and poked their needles at us with scary abandon!

"A much more intriguing style," Val insisted, "than bare female buttocks."

Since this was to be a silent film with eventual appropriate sound track furnished by InSix, we had to act our parts with broad hammy facial expressions. We finally concluded that Les Frères Apeneé shouldn't wear the ape masks until the last scene! The masks would be the faces the public naturally expected on the first fateful showing of the new fashions.

Jack, amazingly serious, in his role of director kept shooting miles of film, and even filmed all our insane rehearsals. "This movie will finally be the product of my expert editing and cutting," he said pompously. "I visualize it opening with a whirling montage of breasts, behinds, legs and unshaved deltas. These will gradually dissolve into the interior of the famous Apeneé House of Fashion. It will end with Les Frères Apeneé being pursued right out of their salon into the street by slobbering, hysterical, adoring women. To escape the howling mob Les Frères will discover a convenient ladder and climb to the roof of the establishment. Below the women, ecstatic, happily swooning are ready to literally eat their heroes."

Jack spent considerable effort and ingenuity to transform Sykes' cottage into a passable version of a French fashion salon. Though we were dubious as to the effect, he was undaunted, insisting that the comic elements would sustain the somewhat garbled backgrounds.

Sheila, Val, and Beth played the parts of fashion models wearing wigs that Jack had brought. They swayed their hips and behinds modishly as they modeled the gowns. Wearing rhinestone sun glasses, no wigs, but with suitable admiring and haughty expressions they also played the parts of the female audience.

Although Jack kept insisting that somehow he would end up with a serious experimental movie, and he spent half his time either lying on the floor shooting scenes or hanging from the rafters of the cottage to get interesting camera angles, each rehearsal for a particular scene became more horsed up and insane than the previous one. Most of the time we were helpless with laughter at our own antics. Jack's pained expression of frustration reduced Sheila and Beth to hysterical laughter and finally they got hiccoughs from drinking too much champagne. This morning the whole meshugana project finally came to an abrupt end. Jack set his tripod up outside the cottage. Stanley and I (wearing the ape masks, Henri and Cecil Apeneé) were to run past his camera pursued by Val, Sheila and Beth. Our coat tails flying, wearing our jockey shorts with the grinning cod-pieces, we scrambled up the ladder to the roof. Below us the girls were begging us to come down. They adored our Fanny and Titty Fashions. In a happy inspiration the girls took off their dresses and tossed them up at us. We responded by tossing our jockey shorts back at them. And that's the way our world ended. Not with a whimper but with a literal bang!

Ebeneezer Schnook emerged from the bushes, actually shooting a revolver over our heads. He was followed by his deputy, both screaming hoarsely. We were a disgrace to the human race. Like Doukhiboors, naked but unbowed, Sheila, Val and Beth stared at them contemptuously angry at their invasion of privacy. Stanley and I tried unsuccessfully to make our exit over the opposite side of the roof. Jack, a model of propriety, in his bathing trunks excoriated Ebeneezer and his deputy, who paid no attention to him. Triumphantly they corralled Stanley and me, their guns levelled at us in a very determined, no nonsense manner.

With horror and pure shock on their faces at their discovery of us, our heroes herded us into the cottage, searched the place for loot, impounded all of Jack's exposed film, denounced our lack of morals, and then with their siren blasting drove us hell bent to the pokey.

Sunday, Phil and Margaret rescued us. They arrived with a lawyer who knew somebody who knew Schnook.

Mr. Big (whoever he was), the lawyer's friend, never put in an appearance. Ebeneezer finally tossed in the towel and accepted the one-upmanship with grim reluctance. He even returned the movie equipment and all the exposed film to Jack.

"Just like a gangster movie on television," Beth said admiringly to Phil. "Even the fuzz don't fool around when the Big Man speaks. Sometimes, Phil, it is obviously true that power speaks louder than love in this best of all possible worlds."

But Phil didn't feel philosophical. "Damn it," he exploded when we were out of Ebeneezer's hearing. "I expect more maturity from Harrad students. You've been acting just like typical college brats. An escapade like this could land Harrad and all of us in the newspapers."

I defended us. "There is considerable difference, Phil. Who were we harming? Were we destroying property or making a general nuisance of ourselves? On the contrary, Schnook invaded *our* privacy. On the opposite side of the fence, my father, for example, feels that all of us at Harrad are going to end up a grim, humorless lot, exposed to sex too early, tied down to marriage, and generally sour from having assumed too much responsibility at an immature age. We disagree. We, In-Six, are all in love. We have discovered the fun and laughter and sheer joy of each other as mortal, sexual human beings. We all have Phi Beta Kappa level marks and we're far from being dull. You have no right to be angry with us. If you are angry, *you* have lost the key to Harrad."

"What's the key to Harrad?" Phil demanded, interested in spite of himself.

"The ability to slide out of your skin, be your own *'Doppelgänger.'* At a moment's notice to be able to step aside and laugh happily at your own serious, concerned, frustrated, conforming other-self."

Phil sighed. "Okay, I asked for it. All of you pack up your junk. Any further movie making will be done in the confines of Harrad. It's obvious that the world and Old Cape Cod aren't quite ready for you!"

FROM THE JOURNAL OF BETH HILLYER

March, the Third Year

Because Mom and Pops decided they had earned a Caribbean vacation, I am spending Spring vacation in New York with Jake and Rachel. Actually, this took some doing. Rather than have their daughter exposed to Passover, they would have gladly planned their Easter vacation to coincide with my Spring vacation. I received several letters from them extolling the merits of Jamaica, and the value of exposure to other influences than Harrad and Harry Schacht. I owed it to myself to compare and examine all the pebbles on the beach. It is patently impossible to explain to them that having already experienced the delights of the bed with three boys, and being able to continue this joy with great regularity, I scarcely need to extend myself by lying down with other pebbles. They finally grew impatient at my malingering and departed for Jamaica without their ungrateful daughter.

I love New York, and I love Harry's big house filled with uncles and aunts and kids and a grandmother all living under one roof. I really believe they're no longer afraid of me. Still, Rachel worries about her boy.

"Saul and I wanted a big family," she told me yesterday when I was helping her make supper. "I had four brothers and three sisters. Saul had two sisters and a brother. Then after Harry was born I had female troubles, and finally, after an operation, there was to be no more children. So maybe we worry too much about Harry. Being an only child is not good."

"You've done very well with Harry," I smiled at her. "I love him, too."

"Are you going to get married soon?" Rachel asked. She looked hopefully at me.

"Next year. Harry and I think that is soon enough. Are you afraid of having a Gentile daughter-in-law?"

Rachel sighed and hugged me. I like her quick affectionate nature. "Saul and I are confused. Our friends, the rabbi . . . our religion, you see, Beth, we love you, but I guess we wonder why you love Harry. You are so very pretty . . . and so Goyish. Your father and mother . . . they've met Harry. They can't possibly approve. And then there's Harrad. Oi-vey, I'm afraid this can only end in great unhappiness."

I kissed her cheek. "Rachel, I love Harry. When I first knew him I was afraid, too. He was Jewish, the way he thought, the expressions he used, they all seemed foreign and insular to me. When we first made love, I didn't think I liked his deep concern for me. I thought somehow it wasn't virile . . . that a man should dominate a woman. And then suddenly I saw Harry for the person he really is, dynamic, kind, gentle, affectionate . . . I visualized him as the doctor he will be and I knew that somehow he was my real ideal of a man. I actually feel like socking people who say to me; 'but Beth you are so pretty,' meaning that Harry is homely. Harry will be lean, craggy and quite impressive when all the pretty boys have gone to seed, and have developed potbellies. After three years, Harry and I have learned we're opposite sides of the same coin. Separated we don't function. Together we are a perfectly adjusted, reasoning, emoting whole person. We deeply understand each other's foibles, and love each other for them."

Rachel listened to me while she rolled out and thinned her blintz dough. "These are very nice things you say about my son, Beth. I am glad. But I will feel better when you are married. When you come to our house you both sleep alone in a separate room. I hope you understand. I know you room together . . . go to bed together at *that* college . . . but here in my home, unmarried . . . well, somehow it doesn't seem right."

I wanted to hug Rachel. She looked so concerned and worried. "Really," I laughed, "it's not so much different. If Harry and I were going to a regular college, we'd probably be sleeping together in motels, or what have you. But I do understand. When I come to visit in your house both Harry and I respect your feelings." I didn't tell her about late last night, Harry sneaked up to the third floor where the guest room is and we snuggled together until dawn.

Of course, I realize that Rachel's worries have some basis in reality. Altogether over the past two years, Harry has spent a month with my family in Columbus. Mother and Pops have been cordial with him but it still is a distant cordiality. Harry may be the finest boy in the world but, inescapably, to them, he is Jewish first and a man second. There is no overt anti-semitism in anything my family have said to me. It is indirect. They point out that the Jewish doctors stick together. The Jewish families maintain their own solidarity. They have their own functions, their own groups, their own organizations. It is useless to point out to them that the gentiles have similar walls to hide behind.

Mother and Pops belong to a country club that seeks new memberships very carefully. Thus they avoid a "Jewish takeover." "You can't fight it," Pops told me. "It's the basis of their religion. They don't want us either. From early history the Jew has insisted on his uniqueness in relation to God and non-Jews." When I countered that this was the only basis of Jewish survival in a hostile world, Pops insisted that was beside the point. The past couldn't be changed. Now it was too late. The Jews did not want to be assimilated by any nation; not even Israel if it came to that. Their religious indoctrination, in a larger sense, simply placed them in their own minds above the mainstream of any particular culture. "And, you Beth, you will be neither flesh nor fowl." Pops sighed. "The Jews will never fully accept you, and you will be shut off from your own kind."

It is a sad commentary on the world, but Jake and Rachel could agree with Mother and Pops on one thing, if nothing else. Harry and I shouldn't marry. It bewilders me. If you accept their philosophy to its ultimate, the world would be a collection of inbred cultural islands. Possibly there would be an exchange of goods and some superficial contact between the tribes, but deep interchange of cultural values and of course intermarriage would be avoided. Years ago I discovered a book in Pops' library by a man named Wendell Willkie. He ran for President. Several wars ago, Willkie was campaigning for *One World*. Do we make progress ten steps backward to one forward? Poor Mr. Willkie. There are now twice as many nations in this one world and all of them grind their axes in New York. They must have named it with grim humor . . . United Nations.

Last night, with Harry deep inside me, my face snuggled against his neck and shoulder, I was in a blissful, talkative mood. "It is incredible to me, that I lived twenty years and never tasted Jewish food until I knew you. Life would be very dull without potato latkes, bagels, lox, sweet and sour meat balls, stuffed cabbage, kishke, knishes, kreplach, chopped liver, gefilte fish, all the wonderfully crazy pareve food, all the enchanting desserts without leavening that have been invented for Passover . . . even borscht . . . which took some doing."

Harry interrupted my breathless recital by kissing my breasts and gently probing them with his tongue. "I like the taste of your breasts better than any food. What's more, this diet is not fattening!" Harry stopped kissing for a minute. "You know what Jake says, Beth? 'Good food killed more Jews than Hitler.' When we are married I'm going to watch your diet. You may have a tendency to get too plump. I like skinny women."

"Skinny women with big tits," I said offering him one.

"And firm behinds."

"And a warm vagina," I said oscillating slightly.

"Amen," he affirmed rather loudly.

"Talk softly," I whispered. "If your father walked in here right now he would go into a state of shock. Anyway, you interrupted me. Jewish food is only one of the things I have discovered. I have inherited a whole new group of holidays. Rosh Hashonoh, Hanukkah, Passover to mention a few, and with them a whole new understanding of the origins of Christianity. And, I'm learning a whole new Yiddish vocabulary. Hundreds and hundreds of useful onomatopoeic words, *Schlecht, pisk, metziah, plotz, schlemiel, fresser, shicker, shmendrick, bobbe, kvetch . . .*"

"Hocken a cheinik," Harry interrupted me.

I bit him. "I am not banging on a tea kettle, or however you translate it. In fact, I'm so entranced and there are such useful words for cursing, too, that I am compiling a dictionary of them. Your father is helping me. And words are not all I've learned, Harry. I've discovered a new Jewish way of looking at life. A new way to worry humorously. Jews have a way of laughing at themselves that is particularly appealing and psychologically healthy. And I like the intensity of Jews, and their keen desire to learn and study. It strikes a keynote in my own philosophy of living." I kissed Harry. "There's a hundred other things. I'm so happy. Thank you for loving me, too."

Harry hugged me. I kissed the tears in his eyes. "Did you ever stop to think, Beth, that the basic idea of Harrad is ultimately against a world within a world like the Jews have made. These are the cultural differences from one religion, or one race, or one nation that set us all apart. All the things you admire about the Jewish culture would have disappeared long ago if the world had been able to assimilate the Jews. If you want to consider it from the standpoint of national or racial differences the same thing applies to the Italians, Greeks, Scandinavians, Germans, Japanese, Chinese, or any nation or culture you can name. In a few centuries these ethnic differences will have mostly vanished. Maybe it is necessary for peace in the world that the foreign aspects of humanity are eliminated, but when you look at Japan, for example, as a product of American influence, it is a little terrifying. In a few centuries the Japanese will be as minus a cultural heritage . . . and hence a sense of past and identity in the world . . . as are the Americans."

"I don't believe that the Harrad idea is to obliterate cultural differences," I said. "It seems to me we're being taught to be citizens of the world. We're building our own bridges between cultures. That's the whole

educative process, if you really analyze it. Everything
that makes a particular culture unique should be pre-
served. But anything in the folklore of a culture or
group that denigrates man or destroys the love of man
for all men should disappear from the world. In my
world I don't need your Scroll of Laws. I don't need
your Moses or the prophets who proclaim Jews are the
favored children of God. I don't need Christ on the
Cross, or the Virgin Mary, but I *do* need the idea of
Christmas and Hanukkah. Just as in the larger sense of
love and awakening of the world to Spring, and rebirth,
I need Easter and Passover." I kissed Harry and he responded eagerly. "You've come out of me," I said, a little disappointed. I helped him find his way back.

"I got so interested in listening I forgot about sex,"
Harry grinned at me. "A man's mind won't always let
him do two things at once."

"Are we talking too much?" I whispered.

"No," Harry said. "In our lifetime, let's have billions
of words probing our world and our lives. I believe it is
the cornerstone of love."

I kissed him in fervent agreement. "One thing I
didn't mention: I enjoy the strong sense of family unity
you, and many Jewish families, seem to have. You have
grown up in a family where aunts, uncles, cousins, sisters, brothers, grandmothers and grandfathers are genu-
inely concerned and involved in each other's lives. Even
disparity in age and income doesn't separate you. Your
holidays cement what personal disruptions and conflicts
the days in between may have wrought. And if Jewish
families are small, they identify quickly and deeply with
other Jews. Maybe it's self-protection, or a feeling of
being a minority. You are all . . . what does your father
say? . . . *Landsmen.* Nevertheless, I think even Jewish
families are having a hard time holding out against a

philosophy of marriage that believes each generation should live their own lives."

Since I was so talkative, Harry decided to listen to me as he kissed my belly. I let my fingers trickle over his penis and kissed it lightly. "I'm glad that you let me rant and rave, Harry. I love you."

"I'm enjoying it. Your fingers feel like feathers tickling me. Very exotic!" Harry grinned. "I know what you are driving at, Beth. It's a part of our mass culture. The economic wheels turn better when the younger generation creates their own little two-by-four nests. This way twice as many automobiles, television sets, refrigerators or what have you, can be sold. One night, a few months ago, I walked through a middle class suburbia, a few miles from Harrad. The houses are not like this old firetrap with fifteen rooms plus a huge basement and overflowing attic. These new suburban houses are all built to the pattern of families with two or three children. Possibly they have a bedroom for each child, and generally a family room where most of the leisure time of the wife and husband is spent viewing television with their children, when they are not all engaged in dreary little 'do-it-yourself' projects. In the summer the man and wife manicure their little five thousand square feet of crab grass using all the latest mechanical gadgets from Sears Roebuck so that the job can be done in a half hour or less thus freeing them at last to join all the bored people travelling the highways with their broods where they finally purchase a Dairy Freeze or a Howard Johnson ice cream cone. A modern family's Sunday adventure in togetherness. I don't think I could live like that. On the other hand, I suppose there aren't many families left who live like we do. My father and his brother Milt started in business together during the depression. The only way they could afford

to get married was to move their wives in with their
father and mother. My grandfather built this house
with three floors and fifteen rooms because he liked a lot
of people around him. Originally, my *bobbe* and *zaide*
had so much room they took in boarders. As children
were born and they needed the space, the boarders were
pre-empted.

"Finally the wheel came full turn. Two of their children moved back with them and filled the house with
their own families. At times with Jake, Rachel, his
brother Milt, his wife Annie, their three children, me,
Grandma, Gramp and a great aunt who has since died,
there have been eleven or twelve people living here at
one time. Yet there has been surprisingly little conflict.
Everyone managed to develop their own inviolate re-
treat within the house. A place to escape the general
confusion whenever they desired. We have no grass,
but Grandma has a garden in the back of the house, a
space about twelve by fourteen that isn't occupied by
clotheslines and ash barrels. In the summer Grandma
has something growing in every inch of it as well as
growing up the walls surrounding it. On warm nights we
sit on the back porch, and the neighbors next door sit
on theirs. We watch Grandma who continues gardening
with an extension light. All of us put in our two cents
worth of advice on gardening, or we talk and discuss
and argue late into the evening. Finally, we can't even
see each other's faces. We are simply disembodied
voices, and the words we are saying are like friends
holding hands on a summer night."

"Your kind of world, and this house is dying," I said.
"Man in the mass will have to find a new way to live.
What will happen in the next fifty years when men will
inevitably be forced by law to limit their offspring?
We'll all have to discover new ways to live closer to-

gether and search for values as groups, not individuals. The human animal needs the constant stimulation of the never quite attainable, and I don't mean things or possessions, I mean the never-ending lure of knowledge and understanding."

While I was talking, Harry had rejoined himself with me. "I think the Tenhausens are pointing the way to the future," he said. "With InSix, for example, you and I, Jack and Val, Sheila and Stanley; we've replaced the vanishing family. We can give it an even larger existence and strength. Our personal commitment to keep learning in the fields of our general interests, effectively breaks down specialization and hence lack of communication, and our love for each other both idealistic, sexual and practical creates a constant renewal of wonder and delight in our humanness and our place in the larger world."

I hugged Harry hard against me. "You know, making love this way, extending the delight, heightening our closeness to each other reminds me of when I was a little girl. I loved ice cream cones. I would eat one ever so slowly, making it last and last. I feel the same way now, blissfully ecstatic. Your lips and mouth taste better than any ice cream cone," I grinned at him. "You won't melt will you?"

Harry laughed. "Not so fast as an ice cream cone, anyway."

Last night at supper I thought Jake was rather preoccupied. He kept looking across the table at me with a strange expression on his face. He answered Rachel's and Annie's conversation in a monotone, and he didn't probe Alan and Sammy (Annie's and Milt's kids) about their school work or parry business conversation with his brother Milt concerning their day at their dress factory.

"So quiet you are, Saul. Is the business failing again?" Grandma demanded sarcastically.

"In the dress business always we are failing," Jake said morosely. "Styles . . . women . . . phooey. Better women should go naked." He looked at me speculatively.

"Sometimes going naked is nice," I said wondering what I had done that was obviously bugging him. "You don't have to worry though. There will always be a women's clothing business. Women know they are sexier with clothes than without them. How else would women lure men and impress other women?"

"Not naked!" Rachel snorted. "That's for certain sure."

When we finished eating, Jake made a point of inviting me and Harry into his "hideaway," a little room on the third floor that he maintained sacrosanct to escape the family and mess around with his fishing gear and a stamp collection. We sat on a studio couch facing his desk. From under a pile of albums he unearthed a copy of *Cool Boy Magazine*. As he silently flipped the pages to the center gate-fold, I suddenly knew what the trouble was.

"Oh my God, Harry," I yipped. "They must have finally published that picture of me."

Jake grimly held it up as silent testimony. A full length, full color, naked me stared at us with a decided come hither look on her face.

Harry examined it excitedly. "You are the sexiest looking Cool Girl they ever published. I never thought with all the commotion and argument they would ever get one that good."

"They should have, they took enough poses."

Jake listened to our conversation with an incredulous expression on his face. "Harry, you knew about this?

The girl you are going to marry . . . naked for every-body to see. Beth, tell me it's not you! When I opened this magazine suddenly my hands were burning. What if Rachel, or Annie, or Grandma saw it? What would your father and mother think, Beth? Their daughter a sex-object!"

I held up my crossed fingers and grinned at Jake. "Let's pray none of them ever see it."

"You don't have to worry about Grandma or Rachel," Harry chuckled, "I can't imagine they would ever spend a dollar to look at naked women. What puzzles me, Jake, is you. I'd never have imagined you spending good money for such a magazine."

Jake looked embarrassed. "I don't buy it," he mumbled. "I look at it down at the drugstore. Since when should a father have to explain to a son? I look to see what a mess the younger generation is in. Maybe I like to look at pretty girls too. But not my future daughter-in-law! Beth, why would you ever do such a thing?"

I hugged Jake. "For a thousand dollars," I said laughing. "And you don't have to worry about my morals. I was well chaperoned. Harry was there, as well as Stanley Cole, Jack Dawes, Sheila Grove and Valerie Latrobe."

"A thousand dollars!" Jake repeated, somewhat mol-lified. "You mean they paid you a thousand dollars. My God! Any girl in my factory would take her clothes off for fifty dollars."

"Most of them have eaten too many latkes," Harry said. "Even for fifty dollars they would get no takers. Beth looks like every man's idea of the woman he should have married."

"Oh shut up, Harry," I said. "Honestly, Jake, I think the whole thing is as silly as you do. The only reason that they sell that foolish magazine is that men don't have the opportunity to see women naked, naturally, in their everyday living. If boys and girls grew up swimming together at public beaches, naked, took gym together naked, walked around their houses naked in warm weather, and simply wore clothes to keep warm, then all this voyeur, frustrated desire to see the naked human body of other human beings would vanish in smoke, and *Cool Boy* would go out of business."

While Jake listened, obviously wondering whether to continue to play the role of the horrified parent, we gave him a partially expurgated account of how I consented to pose for Cool Girl of the month.

The whole business was crazy to say the least, but of course the thousand dollars gave it an air of practicality. One Friday, last fall when InSix had finished their act at the Grinning Eye, a hefty character, smoking a cigar, invited us to his table and introduced himself as Otto Ogleby, publisher of *Cool Boy*. "We are scouting Boston for a prospective Cool Girl," he told us looking at me with X-ray eyes. "Miss Hillyer has the face for it, and may be the type. Would you be interested?"

"Not much," I said staring back at him. "I wouldn't feel comfortable hanging on college and barrack walls while sad little boys played with themselves and pretended that I was their girl friend."

"My God!" Otto marvelled. "That's a whole new reaction. Most girls can't wait to jump out of their clothes for the opportunity."

"How much would Beth get paid?" Stanley demanded, being eminently practical.

When Otto mentioned the fee, and added that it would give InSix records a real publicity push since the average subscriber to *Cool Boy* was a heavy buyer of way-out records like ours, I knew from the expressions on all the faces that I was sunk. Immediately, Val,

Sheila, Jack, Stanley and even Harry began to think the idea was worth considering.

"These are my managers," I said grinning at Otto. "If they vote in favor you've got yourself a new Cool Girl."

"Take it easy," Otto said when Jack and Stanley started to ply him for further details. "We have to see the merchandise before we buy."

"You mean that you want to see me naked?"

"Naturally. You have a lovely face, Miss Hillyer, and you seem to stock up very well in clothes, but you may be wearing falsies, have a wooden leg, appendicitis scars, or other ailments the flesh is heir to. These would naturally eliminate you as a Cool Girl," Otto guffawed. "Of course, in other respects you may be quite cool. Incidentally, I assume you are of age and free to dispose of your person in ways the law sees fit to allow."

"I'm of age," I said. "Where is the auction block that the merchandise is displayed? And what happens if there is no bid?"

"Nothing," Otto grinned. "We give you back to your owners, shake hands and say goodbye. When you get old and droopy you can tell your friends and children, who won't believe it anyway, that you were once almost chosen for a Cool Girl."

Otto handed me his business card. "There's an address written on the back. It's an apartment overlooking the Charles that belongs to an improper Bostonian. Ideal for display and photography. If you want to have us take a look and give you our decision, be there tomorrow morning at ten o'clock. If the decision is favorable you can sign the contract and we'll shoot the pix right away."

"Who's us?" I demanded.

"Me and Hy and Sy Fleshman, our *Cool Boy* photographic team." Otto leered at me. "They guide my thinking and save me from making erratic choices dictated by reasons other than photogenic. By the way, I hope you are not having your period. We've got to get back to Los Angeles on the Monday plane."

"What did he mean by that?" I asked the kids. I was still somewhat in a fog, as Otto departed.

Sheila giggled. "He's afraid you'll arrive wearing a sanitary belt and sanitary pad. Hardly a sex symbol, old girl, by *Cool Boy* standards. The very thought of such things freezes Cool Boys in their tracks."

We argued about Otto's proposition all the way home to Harrad and into the small hours of the morning. "It's great for all of you to be so damned agreeable," I argued. "You are offering your best friend, like a fatted calf, to the wolves. None of you have to bare your blushing body to a lot of panting strangers." Little did I know that in addition I was going to be poked and pushed and bent and curled into extraordinary positions, (to best reveal the exotic me) as well as stared at from every conceivable angle from floor to the ceiling.

"You are going to do it for InSix," Jack grinned. "I can't wait to see professional photographers at work. Just think, Beth, you will be able to contribute a thousand dollars to our education fund. I don't see why you're so scary about showing yourself naked. You're bare-bottom every day in the gym, and right now all you are wearing is Harry's shirt. So what's different?"

I found out the next morning. At the apartment overlooking the Charles, Otto greeted us at the door with a look of dismay. "We only want you, Kid," he said, putting his arm around me.

"These are my chaperones," I said demurely. "They automatically save your reputation in case anything leaks out."

Paying no attention to Otto, Stanley, Sheila, Jack, Val and Harry invaded the apartment, admired the phallic drawings on the walls, tried the low-to-the-floor sofas, gasped over the view of the Charles from the picture window, and finally captured the stools in front of a long well-stocked bar. "Cheer up Otto, old boy," Jack said from behind the bar. "We have brought you the Cool Girl to end Cool Girls."

"My enthusiasm is ended," Otto said, somewhat disgruntled by this takeover. "Meet Sy and Hy Fleshman." He pointed to two men who were watching us swarm over the place. "This is our pigeon. She brought all her little friends."

Sy smacked his lips. "Let's see if the second and third acts are as good as the first."

"There's a sense of drama in the disrobing," Hy explained unnecessarily.

"Let's play it cool," I said. "There are some ground rules. Harry, tell him."

"It's like this," Harry said. "We've been looking over some previous pictures and stories on Cool Girls. In the case of Beth, beyond the fact that she goes to college in the Boston area and is a part of the InSix singing act, nothing must appear in *Cool Boy* concerning her personal life. You'll have to make that a part of the contract."

"We couldn't care less about Miss Hillyer's brains," Otto grinned. "One of our staff writers will explain that our Cool Girl isn't married, that she likes Beethoven and Mozart quartets, revels in modern jazz, reads Immanuel Kant with her breakfast coffee, cooks a mean cheese fondue in the wee hours of the morning for tall dark men who drive X-KE Jaguars, but sleeps alone and without night clothes. This will be cleared with Miss

Hillyer before publication. For the fee, we reserve full rights in perpetuity for all the pictures we take of her."

They showed me the bedroom which obviously belonged to a bachelor. If he were married why would he need such a gargantuan bed? I poked around and discovered an extensive wardrobe of men's clothing. The headboard of the bed, however, was the cynosure of the room. It contained bookcases, a radio, a drawer with contraceptives, and numerous illustrated books of erotica, a small refrigerator, television controls to the picture tube which was embedded on the ceiling amidst mirrors. Evidently in case you got bored watching NBC, you could turn it off and watch yourself and companion cavorting; the idea had a certain charm. Since I now had my clothes off I lay on the bed and stared at myself, and forgetting the business I had come for I nearly yelled for Harry to join me. My reverie was interrupted by Otto pounding on the door.

Coolly, the Cool-Girl, I walked into the living room, naked. Sy and Hy croaked their approval. Otto nodded his head savagely. The kids all banged on their champagne glasses. And me! Darned if I didn't blush. I could feel the pink heat spread right from my toes. I clutched myself like September Morn and was about to run. I suddenly realized it's one thing to be naked with other naked people, but it was something else again to be naked with six men and two women all staring at you. I felt like a cow hung on a meat hook while the butchers were deciding which slice would make the tastiest steak.

"Perfect," Sy said. "Otto, you've done it again!"

Hy nodded agreement. "A perfect blending of face, breasts, legs and buttocks. She'll have to shave her bush!"

Everyone laughed while it slowly dawned on me

what Hy meant. "You're crazy," I snorted forgetting that I was pretending to be a Greek statue, arms shielding her femininity. "This kid only shaves her legs and under her arms."

Otto examined all that I would let him see. "You should thin it once in a while, Miss Hillyer. There's a few blonde strands encroaching on your belly button."

"To hell with that. Do you want me to look like a ten year old? Shaved, I'd feel like an unframed picture."

"Look, sister," Sy said trying the sincere arm-around-you approach, which I fluttered away from, "we don't care what you look like in your private life! Only in nudist magazines do they have a beaver. Did you ever look at a nudist magazine? My God, really naked women aren't sexy! When we pose you, two million Cool Boys are going to stare with their tongues hanging out. We'll show everything the law allows, right down to the edge of your cleft, which from all appearances is considerably beyond that blonde nest. But hairs! No! Only on your head."

"It's deeper than that," Hy said. "Nobody airbrushes a Fleshman photograph. We don't permit it. So if a few hairs get in the way we lose our best shots. The law says it and we agree; pubic hair isn't artistic."

"You got to see the whole picture," Otto said realizing that I was still adamant. "Cool girls aren't really females in the ordinary sense; they're just wet dreams."

"I haven't got a razor," I said lamely.

"There's one in the bathroom and plenty of shaving cream," Otto said.

"I wouldn't know how to shave myself down there."

"I'll help you," Harry said smiling broadly. Sheila, Val, Stanley and Jack collapsed with laughter.

I glared at Helpful Harry, but, aided by Frozen Daiquiris, he was already too far in the spirit of things.

"Let's sign the contract first," Stanley said, practicality suddenly constraining his hysteria.

"I have a better idea," I said grimly. "I'll sign the contract, I'll let Harry desecrate my femininity . . . but first every damn one of you can take off your clothes. I'm not standing around here being stared at like a freak. It makes me feel inferior, as if all of you were born fully dressed and I'm the only one that has skin and sexual organs."

Otto with his paunchy belly, and Sy and Hy, skinny wrecks with too long hair and sideburns, all looked at me in dismay. They shook their heads in vigorous protest. Sheila, Val, Jack and Stanley voted their immediate approval and started to doff their clothes. At least InSix sticks together.

"Suffering Jesus!" Otto moaned. "I've been had by six nuts. I tell you the younger generation is going to hell, you offer them a sweetheart deal and right off they start to make conditions."

"I won't do it," Hy said emphatically. "How can I concentrate on taking pictures of a naked dame when I'm naked myself?"

Four drinks later, after Otto, Hy and Sy had tried every gambit from being too fat or too skinny, and even genuine tears that they would be too embarrassed to be flopping around without clothes, we finally convinced Otto, who by now was a little bleary, to undress. Propped in a sling chair, a scotch and ice resting on his white hairy belly, Otto was blubbering that he felt like an ass. Sy and Hy, hairy white skeletons with dangling penises, cursed Otto as they set up their lights and cameras and complained that there must be a better way to make a living.

But Harry, as I sprawled on the bathroom floor, and screamed at the indignity of being plastered with shaving cream in such a vulnerable area, scraped my lovely hairs away, and told me he was going to apply for a job as Cool Girl Scalper, First Class.

Jake listened to our slightly revised version of the story and shook his head. "It's too much for me, Harry. My lips are sealed. *Abi gezunt,* pray your mother and *bobbe* never hear about it."

The day before we went back to Harrad, Grandma took me to the attic. "I have something to show you," she said mysteriously. "Promise you will never tell Harry's father." From an old trunk she exhumed a yellowed book and opened it to pictures of a young naked woman entitled "Woman, walking and turning while pouring water from a watering can." "That is Saul's grandmother," she said smiling at me craftily. "A man named Muybridge took them. My mother was a pretty woman in her day."

I nodded, pretty sure of what was coming next.

"Uncle Levi, the junk man, found a copy of that magazine in an ash barrel. He showed it to me. Burn it, burn it, you old meshuganah, I told him." Grandma sighed. "Men are all the same. He hung it in his junk shop. Seventy-two and he still has ideas. You are a pretty girl, Beth. Pray that Harry's mother never hears about it."

"Does she know about Saul's grandmother?" I grinned.

Grandma winked. "She should worry! A picture! The body is dust."

I looked at Harry's great grandmother pouring water from her watering can. "I'll be darned . . . they didn't make her shave." When I told grandma what I meant she thought it was a great joke. "I'm glad we have a secret, grandma," I told her, and kissed her withered face.

FROM THE JOURNAL OF SHEILA GROVE

October and November, the Fourth Year

Even when I'm the happiest, most joyful and life is bouncing along in C Major . . . simple, uncomplicated, I always seem to have a minor key melody playing softly and unobtrusively in the back of my brain. Sometimes I can't hear this sad requiem playing in my conscious mind, it is still there ready to be triggered alive often by unrelated incidents.

Mostly a lilting song floats on the surface of my mind. It bubbles and effervesces and makes the entire one hundred and four pounds of me a misty gift of love. Tomorrow evening in the Little Theatre, Stanley and I will be married. Now, I truly know that tomorrow night, when I snuggle in Stanley's arms, there can't possibly be a deeper emotional and intellectual involvement than we already have, yet there is something in the commitment that will legalize our relationship and will validate the children we will have that is essential to the human psyche. At Harrad we have learned that society cannot legislate love, but we also know that the very existence of society, and hence man, depends on regulating and defining the boundaries of sexual behavior.

Last night about eleven o'clock, when Stanley and I

were finished studying, he tiptoed behind my desk, picked me up and carried me into the bedroom. From the look in his eyes I knew words were unnecessary. I kissed his face and cheeks and head while he took off my blouse and brassiere. When my skirt and panties had dropped to the floor and I stood before him naked, I felt suddenly shy.

"Why do you look at me like that?" I asked him, seeing the tenderness in his expression and tears in his eyes. "I'm not very beautiful. My breasts are too small. I'm too skinny." I sat on the edge of the bed. Stanley didn't answer. For a moment he knelt before me and kissed my knees, my belly, my breasts. I hugged his face fiercely against me.

"Sheila," he whispered. "Every time I'm with you like this I'm awestruck, amazed at the sheer wonder of you. As you sit there now, fragile, feminine, your heart beating, your eyes liquid and half open, as you hugged me against you I know that every time I make love to you is the first time, and though I have actually had intercourse with you a hundred times, and will make love to you in our lives thousands of times, the physical joining with you is only a small fraction of my need."

"I know," I said smiling. "Your penis in my vagina is only a small attempt. Maybe you feel the way I do. You want to be simultaneously you and me. I want to vanish inside you and look at the world through your eyes."

Joined, we lay silent for a long time. I was happy in a pensive kind of way. I knew that deep in my subconscious I was contrasting our marriage tomorrow, a beginning, and the strange death of my father in September. A grim finality.

In the telepathic accord we have, Stanley's thoughts bisected mine. "I feel like Ozymandias, today," he said softly. "Sometimes I wish I would stay away from book-stores. If you are too curious, the forgotten past, all the centuries that man has lived, have a new way of reaching out and grabbing you with their bony fingers, and crying: 'Here I am. Don't forget me.' Men or women long dead who once tried to evoke in words the meaning of life. Thousands of people who lived and died, and with them all their effort and striving and everything they held valuable or dear. Some of these books are like a pitiful call across the centuries. People pleading, 'Listen, listen. I lived once, too. I knew all your problems and tried to solve them! I held in my hands *The Memoirs of the Cardinal de Retz, The Memoirs of Duc de Simon,* plays by playwrights of the seventeenth century, unknown today. *The Yellow Book,* source book of the crime that impelled Browning to write *The Ring and the Book* . . . and as I flipped the pages, read here and there, and regretfully put them down, I felt sad for man who dreams such magnificent dreams, has so many things to tell other men that might give them the answers they so desperately need. There is no time for the past. The men who thought they might bridge the centuries or even the decades will ultimately receive little hearing or even recognition of the few fundamental truths they spent a lifetime learning and attempted to communicate.' "

I kissed Stanley. "Ecclesiastes . . . Vanity . . . vanity . . ."

"No, vanity is too simple," Stanley said. "Chiding men like your father or me for their strong drives doesn't prove anything. Preaching the folly of ambition doesn't answer the question why. It leads only to negativism and hopelessness. Just so long as we are driven to find the answers to what our individual and collective meaning is in the world, then we have a purpose for living. Since it is probably insoluble it is a good quest. From the perspective of man, at least."

I hugged Stanley. "I wish somehow I could relate Daddy's death to my own life . . . to our lives. When I first came to Harrad I had a sense of futility as the minor motif to all my thinking. It came down to this. 'What does anything matter in this world? In life? Why bother to study, for example! What does it matter whether I am Phi Beta Kappa, or just a bored rich girl! Either way I'll die, and that will be that.' And then I found you, and the feeling was no longer autistic, it embraced us. Now I go around praying that somehow a moment like this could be ever frozen for us, not for the world to view like Keats' Greek vase, but just for us . . . both of us, immobile forever, but sentient. You see, my selfishness now includes you. But it is better, somehow, because I know I need you more than I need my own life."

"Your father never even achieved that much," Stanley said, kissing my neck and tracing the contours of my ear with his fingers. "When I think about Sam, I can't feel he was really brave, and yet I know he was braver than I would have been. At least, typically and necessarily for Sam, he was the final 'master of his fate.' "

Lying with Stanley deep inside me, his arms around me, neither of us seeking anything but a joyous loss of personal identity as I had numerous times, I reviewed the last weeks in August and the days in Houston and Newport before Daddy took his own life.

When Harrad closed in June, Stanley and I went to Houston. As he had the summer before, Stanley worked on the top floor of the headquarters in an office next to Daddy's.

"You could start at the bottom and work up," Daddy

told him. "But that doesn't mean a thing today. Horatio Alger heroes would get clobbered in the business world today. Take me, for instance, I don't run an oil business anymore. I play a never-ending chess game that involves national and foreign politics, local wars, labor leaders, foreign affairs, economic cycles, competition and the movement and direction of top executives who have all the fun doing the job that I used to do; the producing of oil and gasoline and selling it. It's a world which operates without love. The grease that keeps the wheels turning is what it will profit you."

While Daddy continued his unremitting campaign to prove that even his own daughter was simply an interesting adjunct to the more vital world of business, I infiltrated the Office of Grove Employee Welfare. This department, a necessary evil that Daddy shrugged off as a damned fool development, cost Grove Oil several hundred thousand dollars annually because people today not only wanted a job and endless fringe benefits, but expected their employer to be a great white father and love them in spite of all their foolish little woes and misfortunes.

Much to Beejee's surprise, Stanley and I slept together in one of the guest rooms, drove Daddy back and forth to work each day, swam in the swimming pool naked, and generally lived as if we were on our own private island. Beejee, dressed, or in a bikini, occasionally watched us from a pool side chair. A drink in her hand, trying not to stare at Stanley's nudity, and quite obviously disapproving of me, she would propose various dinners and social gatherings, or dances with other young people who she was sure would interest us.

"You two will get bored to death with each other," she said one day, unable to control her thoughts any longer. "I'm not your mother, Sheila, but if I were I would never have permitted you to start this sex business so young. Not even married. God! In a couple of years you'll be absolutely fed up, weary to extinction with each other. Waiting to divorce or just die. What have you got to look forward to?"

"What are you looking forward to?" Stanley asked her. "You're only thirty-six."

"More of the same," Beejee said. "And I'm thirty-three. At least all my surprise packages weren't opened at twenty-two."

"Stanley and I have found the secret of everlasting surprise," I said, grinning at her.

"What the hell is it?" Beejee demanded, and looked rather sour when I told her.

"Curiosity, wonder. Maintaining a child's mind in an adult world. Essentially not giving a damn about all the silly little conventional problems of being what people expect you to be, or what you think they expect you to be . . . and being just yourself. Come on, Beejee! Take off your bikini and dive in the pool! Yell at the cook and your maid who are watching us through the venetian blinds. Tell 'em to come on in and swim bare-ass with us."

"You are nuts," Beejee said. "Even your Daddy would grow faint at the idea of two Negroes swimming in his white marble pool."

So the summer was a lovely love summer, and Stanley and I were oblivious to the world. The thought of death was for people who die . . . not us. We were immortal. Then, one afternoon in August, Daddy told Stanley he was going to London. Typically, he left on the afternoon plane without saying goodbye. Beejee was more than a little exasperated. Daddy had promised her that the last week in August, all of us, Beejee, Stanley, Asoka and I would fly up to New England,

pick up the company yacht, Shebee (named after me
and Beejee), which was moored at a marina near
Gloucester, and from there cruise along the coast arriving in Newport for the Cup Races in September.

"This is a marriage?" Beejee asked me angrily. "I'm
simply one of your father's possessions. Occasionally
he remembers that he owns me. Then he smiles fondly
at me. Insists that I tell him that he is really nice. All
the while he is fawning and offering me blandishments,
his mind is a thousand miles away. Just why did he
have to go to London now?"

Stanley didn't know, but Daddy told him he would
join us in Gloucester on Labor Day weekend.

Beejee exploded. "God damn him, anyway! I have
to learn what my husband's plans are through his
flunkeys. No aspersions on you, Stanley. If it hadn't
been you, it would have been Miss Graves, his pursed-
lipped efficient Man Friday."

In retaliation for Daddy's treatment, Beejee immediately set in motion plans for a houseparty. Guests
started arriving on Friday and were still going strong
a week later. When all bedrooms were filled new ar-
rivals from all over Texas slept on the lawn and beside
the pool. No one escaped initiation: being tossed in the
pool, clothes and all. The timid ones were issued dry
cotton dresses from Beejee's enormous wardrobe or
chinos from Sam's. The brave ones simply walked
around naked until their clothes dried out.

The rumor spread that a continuous blast was in
progress at the Grove mansion. Departing friends, unable to face another drink, were replaced by strangers
who didn't even know that Beejee was the mad hostess.
Finally, some days later, Tim Shoaty, our butler, discovered Stanley and I hiding out on the flat L roof
where we were spying on the proceedings like visitors

from space. Tim informed us that thus far two thousand dollars worth of liquor had been consumed, several sofas had been set on fire by female inebriates. The front living room was covered with foam from fire extinguishers that two drunks had aimed at each other in great good humor, one of Daddy's Etruscan vases etched with a man and woman copulating had been used as a football and missed on a forward pass . . . and if Stanley and I were going to continue to camp out on the roof and ignore the whole mess, he was quitting.

Over Beejee's protest (it was her house and if she wanted to reenact the Fall of the Roman Empire, well, it was her own damned business), Stanley and I closed the bar, kicked out twenty or so pie-eyed Romans, telephoned Asoka, who was attending summer school at Harvard, and escorted Beejee (who after three days, suddenly discovered that she had a god-awful hangover and pounding head) to the airport.

The next day, the Saturday before Labor Day, we were all quietly aboard the Shebee. Beejee swore off liquor trying to convince "Snowy" the Captain and any of the crew who would listen, that drinking was absolutely suicidal. She would take the pledge if they would.

Daddy arrived on Labor Day. Within an hour we were underway. He told us he cabled "Snowy" to load up with supplies. We were well enough stocked to stay at sea until the races started at Newport.

"Your father is acting strangely," Stanley told me when we were in our cabin the first night out. "I know Sam pretty well, Sheila. Something has snapped out of place. I wonder if he is having problems with Grove Oil!"

I watched Daddy the next few days. The only change I could notice was that he seemed much too intent on all of us having a good time. He followed Stanley or me or Asoka around the boat telling us he knew we were bored, he knew this hanging around, reading or sunbathing, or just looking at empty ocean could get awfully dull. Did we want to pull into some yacht club? Did we want to anchor and fish? Should we head for Newport right away? He tried to sunbathe with Beejee and drove her crazy, apologizing. "I just felt the need to get away from people," he kept saying. "Not you . . . not my family. Just the mad chase."

He didn't even react when Beejee confessed about the party. When she told him his very special, two thousand dollar Greek vase had bit the dust, he just hugged her, called her "old girl," and told her he didn't blame her a bit. He would have done the same thing if he were a woman and had married Sam Grove.

The morning of the fourth day out, neither Daddy nor Beejee appeared for breakfast. Around noon Beejee came out on deck looking quite radiant. "I don't know whether to cry or shout for joy," she told me. "Your father made love to me most of the night. He was wonderfully gentle and affectionate. Then this morning he slept in my arms like a baby. I don't dare ask him what has happened." Beejee sighed. "In our twelve years of marriage, I've never known Sam could be like that. Pray for me, honey. Pray that it lasts."

Poor Beejee. It didn't last. The next night after dinner, even before the dishes were cleared away, Daddy started drinking heavily. Most of his meal had been liquid and he only dabbled with his steak. When all of us refused further drinks, telling him it was too soon after dinner, Daddy grinned and said hollowly, "It's not too soon for me. It's too late." He slumped on one of the sofas and stared at us. "Sometime tonight I'm going to get drunk enough to walk down to the stern of this ship and consign what remains of Sam Grove to his maker."

"Sam, please. I told you to go easy on the liquor," Beejee said. "Let's play gin rummy and stop talking crazy. I'm really quite fed up with drinking and all the stupidities that people say under the influence of alcohol."

"You are right," Daddy said grimly. He hurled the remains of his drink, glass and all, out the door of the lounge, and over the rail of the boat. "If I'm going to do it, and I must, then I'll do it in full control of my senses."

"What's bothering you, Sam?" Stanley asked. "Has something gone wrong with Grove Oil?"

"Not Grove," Daddy said. He was silent for a long time. "Not Grove. Just Sam Grove. The machinery is giving out. In less than three months Sam Grove will stop running. In four or five at the latest, he will be dead. I have incurable cancer in my stomach, and upper bowel. They opened me up in London to make sure. After taking a long look, they told me a colosotomy and wearing a bag of shit would get me nowhere, that I might as well prepare to meet my maker."

Daddy poured himself another Scotch. "It's true enough," he said quietly. "I'm not the type that would make a joke out of death. I'm going to die. I have had two weeks to think about it, and I'm still not adjusted to it. I suppose we are all going to die, but I've been too busy to think about it before this."

Desperate, we all started talking at once. There must be some hope. When did he first know about it? Why had he been so secretive? The doctors could be mistaken.

Beejee tried to tell him about a distant acquaintance who had had a colosotomy. It was more than ten years ago. He was still living. She sat beside him and held his hand. "Sam, you mustn't give up."

"It's no use, Beejee," he said. "I've explored every avenue of hope for several months now. I'm dying and I must face it. I've made thousands of decisions in my life. The only difference between all of you and me is that I know roughly, give or take a month or two, when I'm going to die. I also know that the final month or two will be a slow, agonizing process with me wanting to die, and the doctors morally obliged to fill me with morphine and keep me breathing. At that point I won't be Sam Grove any longer but a shell with a heart that refuses to let go; beating feebly in a body that is already dead. I've had friends go that way. All that anyone could say was, 'If only God would take him. If only he would die and get it over with.' That's not going to happen to me. I am going to die with dignity. All I am asking you, the only people who really care one way or the other, is not to get maudlin about it. A year from now, the month or so longer that I might have lived isn't going to make a damn bit of difference. Please, Beejee," Daddy patted her hand. "Stop whimpering and listen to me . . . you, too, Sheila."

Stanley had listened to Sam dry-eyed but fascinated. "Sam, why do you want to be so dramatic about it? Why prey on our emotions? Are you looking for pity? If I were deciding to kill myself, I'd just do it. I wouldn't make a production out of it."

I looked at Stanley horrified, believing that he had at last revealed an unsuspected cruelty in his character. "Do you have to be so cold blooded, Stanley?" I half-sobbed, half-screamed. "Daddy isn't going to do anything crazy. Daddy needs love and sympathy. We're not discussing the weather or politics." Stanley told me later that he couldn't shake off the feeling that Daddy's dispassionate appraisal wasn't real. . . . "We all must be dreaming it."

Daddy shrugged. "Please let's look at it calmly. If I killed myself in a conventional way, I could do it à la Hemingway, and blow my brains out. A very virile ending, and rather in character for a man who has lived like I have. But unfortunately it would have a disastrous repercussion on Grove Oil stock. All the stock holders would be looking for financial reasons. After giving it a good deal of thought it seemed to me that scattering my brains around a room and leaving my relatives to pick up the mess is not only pretty dramatic, but downright shocking. I could do it à la Hollywood, a painless exit, caused by an overdose of sleeping pills. But the truth is that I lack the courage for such a slow approach. I might even change my mind at the last minute and start yelling for a stomach pump. Now the way that I have decided has several advantages. First, it gives me the opportunity to discuss it with you as rational human beings. I can give you brief assurances that your financial security will be no problem for any of you. Second, I plan to do it very quickly. I never learned how to swim . . . too busy making money. I have some trousers with lead weights sewn in. . . ."

"Oh, my God, Sam!" Beejee gasped. "This is in-human!"

Sam ignored her. "I'm not looking for an audience. A man dies better alone. I'm just telling you what I must do. The third point that I want to make is I am hoping that none of this discussion is ever reported to the press. When you all dock in Newport tomorrow, Stanley can call the police. Snowy will back him up. The crew will keep their mouths shut." Sam grinned. "Money is useful sometimes. Here's your story. We were out about thirty miles. Sam was in pretty high

spirits . . . pretty well oiled. Gotta keep oil in it somehow." Daddy grinned and patted my shoulder. "Sam
Grove must have fallen overboard. That's all there is
to it. Sam Grove drowned. Cut off before his time. It
will only make enough news to last one edition. There
will be no body to worry about. No mourners. No display of the last remains. No ugly burial. Come on, have
another drink with me. I think it is a damned fine idea.
What's your reaction, Asoka? You've been mighty
silent."

"I'm a Hindu, Sam," she smiled. "Thanks to you I
have learned some of the philosophy behind my religion. I believe there is no death. There is only ceaseless
life that assumes many forms. The form called Sam
Grove will disappear, but the essence of what creates
the form will live forever."

A bitter expression on her face, Beejee scowled at
Asoka. "I'm a simple uneducated person," she said
dully. "I love you, Sam. I don't even know why I love
you. All I know is that I can't sit here and calmly discuss you dead. I want you to stay alive just as long as
it is humanly possible. God, Sam . . . Can't you hope!
There could be a miracle. Maybe you could live a much
longer time than you think."

"I've been all through that," Daddy said adamantly.
"If I hang on too long I'll lose the power of choice. I'll
be kept breathing as long as possible without regard to
whether I am suffering. I'm not going to die that way.
I could be bitter about the fact that I have to die, but
I am not. That's the way the ball bounces for Sam
Grove. I can't really say that another twenty years of
doing what I have been doing is anything special to look
forward to one way or the other. I've done it all. The
rest is repetition. Let's stop talking about it. I want to
talk about all of you."

"Is it so bad to suffer?" Beejee demanded. "Maybe God expects that man should suffer. All your life you've tried to play God, Sam. Why can't you die like a man?" Beejee said the words coldly. To me she seemed as shockingly cruel as Stanley had been.

Daddy simply guffawed. "That's better, Beejee. No damned pussy-footing around. You may be right. The truth is, I am probably a coward. For the first time in my life I'm in a jam and I can't buy my way out of it. I only have one answer. I'm afraid to die like a man. To be blunt, I think dying like a man is just plain horse-shit. I personally don't like the way a large majority of men have to die; blubbering tunes of glory."

The conversation suddenly stopped. Daddy had closed his business deal, and with one flat statement wrapped it up. Beejee was still crying. Although all of us were obviously shaken, no one seemed to have any words left to say.

"All right, Daddy," I said finally. I tried to keep my voice from trembling. "You said you wanted to talk about us. I want to talk about me. Did you ever really give a damn that most of my life I never really had very much love or affection from you or mother. I suppose I really should be the most shocked one here. I do love you. But not as a father. As a man, yes. A person who has obviously been nice to me. Why was it this way? Can you tell me why? If I really knew, maybe I could feel something more than I feel. More than the shock I would feel about anyone's death. Oh, God," I said, unable to stop crying. "Please, Daddy, I don't know what I am saying. Do you know? Do you understand?"

He stared at me a long time, and then he said, "I guess I know what you mean, She. It comes to this. Why in hell can't people give each other the love they need in this world! I don't know what to tell you. I am

what I am. Maybe it would have been different if your
mother could have gone along with me. We met in high
school. Both of us came from poor families. My old
man drove an oil truck. I have two brothers. They've
come a little further up the income scale. One of them
operates a couple of Grove Oil filling stations. The
other is a manager of a chain store. They have never
liked me. I let them sweat out their own living. I'm
leaving them a half million dollars each." Daddy
grinned. "It's no favor. The money will rock the boat
of their nice middle class lives. They'll gorge themselves
with cars and boats and trips around the world, and
eventually drink themselves to death." Daddy paused.
He looked thoughtfully at all of us. I had the feeling he
wasn't even seeing us. "I suppose you think I'm a pretty
cold-blooded bastard. I guess I am. The desire to be
something more than a truck driver helped me discover
the world was for the tough and ruthless. Five years
after I married your mother, I was the sole distributor
for Standard Oil in the state of Connecticut. You were
two years old, She. I had done it. I was a successful
man. Not a millionaire, but rich enough. But somehow
I had lost your mother along the way. I guess we never
really understood each other. She wanted a husband
who was a part of the social life of our town. To me
the clubs, the bridges, the teas, the cocktail parties,
charity balls . . . all the little people trying to prove
their superiority with new fifty-thousand dollar homes,
trips to Europe, the latest cars, were a colossal bore.
I had met some really wealthy men, powerful men. One
of them lived in a twenty-thousand dollar house and
drove a car that was ten years old. He was a millionaire.
Money to him was simply a big power game. He spoke
my language. This was exciting. The getting was a hell
of a lot more interesting than the idle spending. Without

telling your mother (she wouldn't have been interested, anyway), I put most of our money into oil leases. Suddenly, I had made my first million dollars. All I wanted in the whole damned world was someone to tell me how good I was. I wanted your mother to grab me and hug me and say: 'Sam, you're wonderful. I love you.' Of course, I wasn't wonderful. I was a damned surly bastard to live with. I was generally, by most standards, somewhat anti-social. I knew it. But I didn't need daily confirmation of it from your mother." Daddy grinned flittingly. He shrugged. "All I've needed all my life is to have someone love me enough to understand."

"Understand what?" Beejee demanded. "You never gave me the impression you wanted to be understood or be too close to anyone."

"Christ, I could never give a long tearful explanation of my behavior," Daddy said. "All I needed was tacit, sympathetic realization that I was driven, that I couldn't help it . . . that I was my own worst enemy. I was like a hamster in a cage, whirling on the wheel not because he wants to, but because he *has* to. My drives . . . where they came from weren't important . . . maybe if I went to a psychiatrist, he would say that I was sexually frustrated. . . ."

Beejee scowled and shook her head. "Now I've heard everything!"

"I mean it," Daddy said. "I guess it started with your mother, She. In bed we were a couple of people with a job to do. We did it, and that was that. Neither of us could get close to the other. We couldn't break through to the little sacred people that lived inside of us. We simply ignored each other's emotional needs. I don't mean sexual needs. Hell, I don't know what I mean, maybe just the need to say a million words to each other while we both listened and did our best to understand."

"Have you ever managed that with any woman?" Beejee asked.

"Occasionally," Daddy grinned. "Not with you, Beejee. When I was younger sometimes I took the complete plunge. Dropped my defenses. Then I suddenly discovered that no woman I ever met really wanted to know the real Sam Grove. Hell, I don't even know the real Sam Grove anymore. He lived in another time . . . in another world. If I met him today I'd think he was a pretty sad character. It's too late. I've worn the mask so long, there's no face underneath it. I'm sorry, She. There is no answer. Maybe you wouldn't have become a Phi Beta Kappa, if you had the love and affection you missed. Maybe you would only be a richer version of your mother. And the joke is maybe you wouldn't be one whit happier. You could ask me why you were born. I could tell you that a contraceptive failed. Your mother was shocked, but douches and ergot couldn't stop your rush for life. I was glad. I guess eventually so was she. But it didn't give you what you needed . . . love. Who in this world ever really has it, anyway?"

"Everyone has it, Sam," Asoka said. "The trouble is, most of us don't ever learn to give it. We think if we give love and don't get it in return somehow or other our supply dwindles."

Daddy smiled. "That will never change. It's the nature of the beast. For God's sake let's not talk anymore. I just want to sit out on the rear deck and look at the stars."

Beejee grabbed Sam and hugged him. "I love you, Sam. Please . . . Please don't. . . ."

Asoka and I clutched his arms. Neither of us could speak. Daddy looked at us with tears in his eyes. He kissed my forehead and patted Asoka's head. "Look," he muttered. "I talk a hell of a lot braver than I really am. I'm glad I got it off my chest. I might think about it . . . but I really haven't got the nerve. The next few days we'll watch the Cup races. When they're over I'll check into Mass. General Hospital. Maybe they've got some new miracle cure." He hugged Beejee. "Honest, I promise. All I want to do is get some clean salt air in my lungs."

We watched him through the portholes. He waved at us, and then sat down on a canvas deck chair facing the stern.

"God," Beejee sobbed. "What should I do?"

We tried to talk to each other . . . to comfort each other, and at the same time keep a watch on Daddy. Stanley went out on deck and sat down beside him for a while.

"He's all right, I think," Stanley tried to reassure us. "He just wants to be alone."

At midnight he was still there.

Somehow, exhausted, our nerves shattered, we must have stopped watching.

At ten minutes past twelve, Beejee looked out. "Oh, my God. My God! My God!" she screamed. "He's gone!"

When we started searching the boat, Snowy came down from the bridge. "It's no use," he said quietly. "I saw him go overboard."

Stanley held his arms around Beejee and me. "When I went out to talk with him he told me to tell you that he loved you both. No one could stop him, She. He said if you were going to cry . . . to cry for the living."

During the past six weeks the thought keeps recurring to me, how very much alone each person is in the world. Not one of his three wives ever understood

Daddy, and I guess he never was close to any of them. Will Stanley and I do better? I pray that we will. And that's funny. Pray to whom? "You don't have to pray," Stanley told me. "All our lives we will work at one goal . . . *being each other*. What we achieve between us we can multiply. In many areas we've already multiplied it by six. It's more than being your brother's keeper. It's *being* your brother."

When Beth and I first decided we would be married in our senior year at Harrad, we knew a church wedding couldn't possibly be right for us. Whatever beliefs we individually had in God, a Supreme Power, call it what you will; the beliefs didn't function in the framework of any religious theologies. On the other hand, a civil ceremony performed perfunctorily by a city clerk or a justice of the peace seemed inadequate, quick . . . without meaning. Valerie got into our discussions because she and Jack had decided to get married too. The boys just listened, amused by our desire for some kind of ritualistic marriage ceremony.

Beth tried to explain. "It's not really a ritual we want. I think Sheila, Val, and I feel the way we get married should somehow reveal our deep feelings for each other as individuals. Maybe we're just being feminine. Maybe we want something to remember . . . something that will give the commitment we will make to each other real meaning. Something neither the church nor the state can provide. The church rituals are meaningless to us. The state ritual is nothing more than a legal contract."

"Why not write our own marriage ceremony?" Stanley suggested. "If we make it interesting enough, we can invite all the classes at Harrad. Maybe Margaret and Phil will let us use the Little Theatre."

We discussed it with the Tenhausens, who were immediately enthusiastic. They had a friend who was a justice of the peace and could legally marry us. Whatever else we wished to add to the conventional state contract was up to us. With typical enthusiasm InSix ploughed into the problem.

Last night, when it was all over and Stanley and I, Beth and Harry and Val and Jack were married, we agreed that our ceremony was a success. The weeks of discussion needed for planning each step paid off, not only for us, the participants; I think everyone at Harrad found it a memorable experience.

At quarter of eight, the Little Theatre, lighted with electric candles that flickered in all the windows, cast a friendly glow and made soft shadows on the faces of the students. The second movement of Beethoven's Ninth Symphony was playing softly. We had taped the music, amplifying it from four speakers and timing it so that the Chorale Movement wouldn't start until everyone was seated. Jack had made a new translation of Schiller's poem *The Ode to Joy,* so that everyone could follow the Chorale which is sung in German. We had multigraphed this onto the programs. The programs also gave the marriage vows we would take. The timing was perfect. As the chorale *Hymn to Joy* began, growing out of the searching music as it does, a hush fell over the audience. The flickering lights of the candles and the rapture of the music created a feeling of time and people encapsulated, as if momentarily, we were all living in a new dimension and every person in the room was interlinked by a mysterious unity.

As the Chorale Movement concluded, the electric candles were dimmed and the stage was bathed in a blue light that gave the floating quality of swirling mist and fog. Valerie, Beth, and I, in white linen dresses, walked on stage left of center facing Harry, Jack and

Stanley who appeared right of center wearing black trousers and white short-sleeved shirts, open at the neck.

In measured steps, as the quiet opening of Gliere's *Concerto for Voice and Orchestra* filled the theatre, we walked toward each other, and then turned to face the audience. Three separate groups, our fingers interlaced, we listened, facing the guests, while the exquisite voice of a coloratura soprano, wordless, but using her voice as the ultimate orchestral instrument in soaring flights of pure sound led the orchestra and probed love, life, God and beauty. After about fifteen minutes of sheer emotion and feeling, when the final measures of the concerto were reached, the students were watching us in hushed silence. We waited silently for a few seconds, and then we spoke in unison.

"I Stanley, I Sheila, I Harry, I Beth, I Jack, I Valerie, having experienced deep love and warm affection with the person whose hand is laced in mine, having joined our bodies many times in a small attempt to convey to each other our love, having experienced the ineffable wonder of surrender of ourselves into the unity of something beyond our comprehension, having the desire to express this feeling in the culmination of the creative act available to all human beings; our children, who will link us with the future of all men and women and perpetuate us in time, as man knows it; having full confidence that our abiding faith in each other as human beings will last our lifetime; seek permission, petition and enjoin the State of Massachusetts to recognize us and bind us in responsible marriage, asking not that our love for each other be circumscribed for a lifetime of single devotion, but recognizing that as our love and understanding grows it may encompass others without harm or deprivation to the one with whom we are legally joined."

We had learned the words perfectly. Spoken together by the six of us, they carried the simple majesty of a Greek chorus. Then through amplifiers, our unseen Justice of the Peace responded in a warm, friendly feminine voice.

"The State of Massachusetts has through me, Sarah Forstner, investigated the physical health of the petitioners and found it good. In full confidence that each of you will approach your lives together in a continuous proud and happy realization of your love and the love of your children, by the laws vested in me, I pronounce you, Sheila Grove and you, Stanley Kolasukas; you, Beth Hillyer and you, Harry Schacht; you, Valerie Latrobe and you Jack Dawes, man and wife. May you treasure this trust and responsibility and live fully happy lives. And now if the respective males have some tangible symbol of their affection they wish to give their wives they may do so before these friends and witnesses."

The rings the boys placed on our fingers were simple gold bands engraved with our names and the word "Mizpah." We kissed excitedly. And then the six of us, tears running down our cheeks, hugged each other for a moment, and walked slowly down the center aisle. The voice in Gliere's Concerto filled the theatre in one final trill of ecstasy.

"It was lovely," Beth marvelled before we were joined by the entire Harrad student body milling around us and happily congratulating us. "We wrote it ourselves, rehearsed it, and yet when it actually happened for real, I was so trembly and awestricken I thought I would burst into tears."

Val and I were crying happily. "We are married, Sheila," she grinned through her tears. "I can't really believe it. Somehow, we are all married to each other, too."

And we were married. Not just for better or worse, or richer or poorer, or in sickness and health, but somehow with an even deeper commitment that transcended all of these. We had learned to like each other, and discovered that liking was the leaven of love. Poor Daddy, he loved a lot of women, but he didn't like them much.

FROM THE JOURNAL OF STANLEY COLE

January and February, the Fourth Year

Before graduation, all seniors must turn in a joint thesis to complete their work in the seminar on Human Values. Phil Tenhausen assigned the project in September, with the papers due in May. The subject is "How our present Western Society might evolve, could, or should evolve within the next hundred years into a society where each individual could live lives that realized their full potential as human beings."

The Tenhausens have insisted that we try to keep our projections within the realm of possibility, hence capable of evolving out of the framework of the present economic, social, and religious environment of a reasonably democratic country. We are given two assumptions. One, that with all its deficiencies Western democratic society as we now experience it is probably superior to any form of social, economic or political system now, or previously in existence, in the world. The second condition is that the type of "Psychologic individual," who must ultimately dominate our projected society, has been investigated in a preliminary way by Abraham Maslow in his many analyses of the "self-actualized" healthy human being, and described in some detail in Maslow's book *Motivation and Personality*.

So far as I know, none of the seniors' roommates have started their papers, but all of us have spent hours of discussion, kicking around various approaches; arguing and disagreeing on the fundamental principles involved in such a society. When we all started to talk about our Utopias, Phil tried to kill this approach. He pointed out that Maslow had offered the idea of "Eupsychia," a Utopia where all men were psychologically healthy. From what Maslow claimed he knew of healthy people, he felt he could predict the kind of culture that would evolve if a thousand psychologically healthy families migrated to a desert island where they could work out their destinies as they pleased.

Phil feels the desert island approach is unrealistic, and was evolved to its ultimate stupidity by Irving Wallace in his novel *The Three Sirens*. So Phil is challenging us to a far more demanding solution by insisting that we work within the reality of the Harrad experience and extend the insights we have gained to a larger social environment.

Aside from discussion, Sheila and I had found no logical approach to our thesis. Sam's death and our marriage kept the cross-currents of our thinking from coming into focus. A few days before Christmas, Sheila's mother and her husband drove up to Boston to discuss the details of Sam's will. Reluctantly, Sheila met her at the Charter House Motel in Cambridge. From there they were going to the Boston lawyers who had transcripts of the will and full information for the heirs. Sheila knew in advance that her mother was disgruntled and unhappy at her share in Sam's estate. "I suppose she expects that I'll give her more," Sheila told me grimly, then laughed. "What the hell, maybe I will . . .

and then I'll shake hands and say Goodbye Mother for this lifetime. I hope we don't meet the next time around."

I decided that Sam's money was none of my business even though Sheila and I were married. I promised to meet her later in the Harrad gym when she returned. A group of us congregated at the end of the pool and were discussing our thesis in terms of a book called *Images,* by Daniel Boorstein. His analysis of our culture, which depends so much on pseudo-events and pseudo-news, and numerous books in the same vein by Vance Packard and others seemed to show a straight path to an Orwellian future with little hope that reasonable people could halt the roller coaster ride to hell. None of these critics of our society had any real solutions, and were perhaps making their "Reality" even more real by identifying it and then walking away without answers.

Phil and Margaret joined us and our discussion switched to whole-hearted approval of Margaret's well-formed body. Last year she had been pregnant. She and Phil had a daughter aged six and a boy eighteen months. With three children, she still remained as trim as a girl in her twenties. Margaret was trying to convince us it was simply a matter of calories and judicious exercise when Sheila, pattering along the edge of the pool, her breasts bobbling unconcernedly, her face wearing a preoccupied frown, joined us, a little breathless.

"God," she sighed. "It's good to be back after a day among the philistines. I heard what you said, Margaret. It's not only calories. It's middle class stuffiness. Millions of Americans are inflated not only by food but by their own pomposity. My mother used to be a fairly simple woman. She claims she left Daddy because she couldn't stand his drive and aggressiveness. She married

Harold because he was an uncomplicated person whose hobbies of fishing and home carpentry left plenty of time for clubs, television, and Sunday family togetherness.

"Daddy discovered a very nasty way to prove to her that all men are corruptible. Three years ago, Harold was suddenly promoted from the accounting department of Grove Oil to eastern Vice President and Controller. From eight thousand dollars a year, Harold now earns forty thousand dollars a year. His once simple life has become complicated by a big house in Saybrook, a cabin cruiser, two automobiles, and the kids in private schools. Mother and Harold are enamoured with their prestige and new status in the community. They are owned by their possessions. They spend more than they earn to maintain their new image of success. Mother has passed from girdles to corsets. Harold's favorite occupation is hotel size steaks, which he proudly barbecues with the help of a handy man and maid for his summer guests, while everyone present consumes oceans of liquor and tasty hors d'oeuvres. The men discuss business and tell each other dirty jokes while the women courteously rip apart all their friends."

I interrupted her tirade. "Why did your mother come up to Cambridge?"

"That's the second installment of the sad story," Sheila said grimly. "She's quite upset about Daddy's will. She, and Daddy's second wife, whom they are trying to locate (she married an Iranian prince), received two hundred and fifty thousand dollars each. Beejee got all the property and a million dollars. Asoka got two hundred and fifty thousand. I inherited five million dollars. The balance of the estate is largely the stock of the Grove Oil. It went into the Grove Foundation. I have the entire voting control of the Foundation.

Mother is more than exasperated. She feels that I could spare at least a million."

While Sheila had told me the details of Sam's will, the others were surprised and a little shocked by so much money. "Good God," Jack Dawes whistled. "I knew you were rich, but I never thought you were filthy rich. When are you kissing goodbye to Harrad and your proletariat friends?"

"Damn all of you if you feel that way," Sheila flashed. "I'm not interested in money. It can do nasty things to you. Look at my mother. She got a quarter of a million dollars because she slept with Sam Grove a few years and had me. Now she firmly believes that she is entitled to more. And if she had it, what would she use it for? A villa on the Riviera, a house in Palm Beach or Palm Springs, a bigger yacht. A life of sheer waste. As far as I'm concerned, Daddy played her a dirty trick. The two hundred and fifty thousand dollars will give her and Harold sufficient delusions of their own importance to make them completely intolerable."

"What are you going to do with your money?" Beth asked. "Foundations have to disburse all their money. . . . Ye gods!"

"Sheila is going to underwrite experimental movies," Jack said mischievously. "Now we can finish the *Meshugana Ape*."

Sheila giggled. "I think it would be better, Jack, to set you up as a fashion designer. Such originality as Fanny Fashions should be encouraged. Seriously, I'm going to see that a lot of the Foundation money goes to Harrad. From that point on I'm open to suggestions. With the income from my personal estate plus the Foundation money, the lawyers tell me I'll have about four million dollars a year to get rid of. At the moment, several hundred people are eager to help me figure how to spend it," Sheila grinned. "My only friends are right here at Harrad."

Hilariously, we made Sheila stand up while we all kissed our naked Santa Claus. Phil was last in line. He picked Sheila up, whirled her around joyously, and jumped in the pool with her. We all jumped in after them. Sheila came to the surface gasping, her hair plastered over her head. "Oh gosh," she yelled. "I love you all."

It's strange, the way ideas spring into being. I couldn't offer Sheila any really good suggestions on how to disburse the Foundation money, but the thought of it was in the background of my mind. Maybe the way to have a steady source of new ideas is to treat your mind like an insatiable, giant hopper. Keep tossing everything and anything into the pot. If you don't try to start grinding, eventually when you get enough in the mill, the gears will start turning themselves.

For the past few weeks, in a course in Political Science which I have been taking, we have been studying election returns in the various states. While perhaps I should have been aware of it, I was conscious, for the first time, that the total vote for both candidates for governor of certain states was only a few hundred thousand votes, and the winning margin in many cases was exceptionally small. Theoretically, in those less populous states it was easier to run for governor, both financially and in the area of actual political contact, than in states like California or New York. On the other hand, an exceptional governor of even a small state could very readily create national political interest in himself as well as his state.

I was taking a shower with Sheila, soaping her breasts and belly and pussy, and I suppose my mind should have been preoccupied. She was shampooing her hair and enjoying my playing . . . when somehow *The Idea* snapped into place.

"Eureka, I've got it! I've got it!" I yelled and hugged her soapy body against me getting soap in my eyes and mouth as I kissed her excitedly. "I've got a practical proposal for how a unique society could develop within the framework of the United States. Suppose a group like InSix, backed with sufficient money and a complete social program, infiltrated one of the smaller states and gradually developed it as a show-case society for the rest of the country to emulate. That Sheila, my love, is the launching point we can take for our thesis in Human Values."

"Sounds way-out and mad," Sheila said practically as she rubbed me down with a towel. "What state? And how could you change the people within a particular state? After all, for good or bad they're all Americans with much the same perspective, values, and outlook on life. There is no fence around any state."

In no hurry to dress, we lay on my bed and discussed it. "Several states in the Northwest jump into my mind," I told her. "Obviously, the people in these states have some of the pioneering spirit left. Where could we start? Let's visualize a group of six or more men and women with a definite social program designed to help people live to their full potential. Let's assume this Utopian group would take up residence in this State, which they have carefully preselected and studied statistically in every possible way. Our group is thoroughly acquainted with the economics of the state, the racial groups, the political problems, the religious groupings. They would plan the first stage of their program to take a minimum of ten years. The first goal to be accomplished would be a complete rewrite of the state laws. One of the group would have to be a lawyer. Fortunately, most of the laws governing marriage, divorce, censorship, education, wages, and working conditions, all crucial to the new society they have envisioned, are within the province of the state and can be changed, for the most part, without Constitutional conflict. It would even be possible to make changes in the State laws, knowing they conflict with the Constitution, and then wait until these laws have been tested in the Supreme Court. This is where money would come in. Our dedicated group, backed by a foundation with plenty of money available like the Grove Foundation, would carefully plan its long range propaganda and project a complete approach that eventually would give them political control of this State. Once our group is functioning within the State, they would go all out to attract within their orbit all the thinking citizens of the state. Within a few years their plan would be to control the political machinery and elect a sympathetic Governor and legislature."

"My God Stanley," Sheila rolled on top of me, a big grin on her face. "Are you talking about our thesis . . . or are you picturing yourself as Governor of this mythical State?"

"At the moment, I'm writing our thesis," I laughed. "But honestly, I believe it is within the realm of possibility."

Sheila must have helped me because I was suddenly aware that my penis slipped inside her. "I like the idea," she sighed happily. "So now tell me. What laws do we change?"

"Hey, give me time! Twenty minutes ago I was Stanley washing your pussy. You are making it difficult to make the transition to His Excellency Governor Stanley Kolasukas!"

I couldn't let the idea alone. Within the next few weeks I got InSix deeply involved in it. When we approached

Phil, he agreed that if the six of us wanted to attempt it as a joint thesis, we could do so; but he expected at the very least a paper of one hundred and fifty pages with detailed analyses of our plans and proposals. So, with some groans from Harry, Jack, Valerie and Beth, who complained that even in our final year Phil was still a slave driver, InSix entered the discussion phase to see what we could come up with.

Jack decided we couldn't work in a vacuum. We'd have to pick a definite state in the United States that would be our theoretical guinea pig. After a week or two of argument and plenty of statistical research we have chosen the State of X.*

We all agreed that the most important task would be to change the entire system of education within the State. In this way, within twenty years, we would have re-oriented most of the younger generation. Simultaneously we would have to do our best to re-educate the older generation. We knew that on a wide scale this would be impossible, but we felt that if we worked slowly, within a period of two or three years, we could develop a central committee of sufficient educators, politicians, businessmen and religious leaders who agreed in principle with what we wished to accomplish. From this group we would gain political strength, and ultimately be able to sway the average voter. We knew that we could not reveal our entire program even to this strong central committee. Many of the changes in the basic social structure of the State that we would ultimately make would require that a previous change had become firmly entrenched.

* In a recent letter to Phillip Tenhausen, Stanley mentions that InSix still retains great interest in the proposal offered in their thesis. For this reason the identity of the State they chose for their proposal has been concealed.

Our base premise was: if democracy was to really function and survive in a situation of exploding populations, it depended on a citizenry educated in much greater depth than at present. The present pattern of a generalized high school education, with a small portion of students taking college courses and the majority receiving a very thin general education, was developing citizens without historical perspective. Few people had any understanding of meanings and values in the world either historically or personally. We would aim immediately for a State supported educational system which would expose all students in depth to world history, English, languages, social sciences, art, music, etc. Students who showed early promise in the Sciences and mathematics would be allowed to specialize but even these students would be required to have thorough grounding in the humanities. In our State-supported high schools, there would be *no* trade or practical courses. From the first grade, through a potential fifteen grades, all education would be directed to producing the educated, well-rounded man or woman, and developing for each person a complete psychologic understanding of himself, his abilities, and his relationship to society. For the exceptional student, capable of doing the work at a rapid pace, there would be swifter promotions from grade to grade, providing always that the student's emotional adjustments kept pace with his mental growth.

No student would be permitted to complete his education in state-supported trade schools or colleges until he was eighteen. Thus, students capable of moving faster would progress in high schools to a thirteenth, fourteenth or fifteenth grade. Graduation to state-supported colleges and trade schools could occur either from the twelfth grade or the fifteenth grade. The upper third of all the twelfth and fifteenth high school grades would go directly to three year colleges, which would be completely reoriented to the revised high schools, and not waste the freshman year doubling back on education already acquired at the high school level. These three year colleges would continue the education in the humanities, in depth, allowing specialization in the second year only in the area of the sciences and mathematics. All upper-third graduates of these colleges would go on to state-supported graduate work in whatever area the student wished to pursue.

Students who graduated from the high schools below the upper third of the class would go on to state-supported professional and trade schools and there, in two or three years, complete the training they preferred, acquiring the skills necessary to function as an economic unity in the state.

In the early years of grade school, major emphasis would be placed on developing reading ability. All studies in the first nine grades would be oriented around this objective. The student entering the tenth grade would be able to read rapidly and would receive continuing awards and citations to develop pride in this ability.

From the first grade on, all students would take a required course similar to the Harrad College Human Values course. In the early years, the purpose of all teaching in this course would be to counteract the spurious values in our culture and put the individual's life in perspective in relation to values being destroyed by any advertising and any of the arts which overemphasized materialistic goals as the basis of success. All the schools would continuously help the students to evaluate the mass communications of our society such as television, radio, newspapers, magazines. All teachers in the Human Values courses would be equipped to tackle and expose the false values being propagated and aimed at particular age levels. These teachers would not hesitate to expose any element of society, whether it was government, business, religion or literature and the arts, which were inculcating values that denied the ultimate goodness and excellence of man.

Since our Utopian planners invading the State of X would be working with a long term master plan, the broad outline of which could not be revealed at the beginning, the relative speed of initial accomplishment would be slow. After some analysis, we selected the City of Y which is the largest city in the state. Here, our Utopian planners would take up residence. Slowly and methodically, several of the group would be groomed to run for the State legislature and ultimately Governor. Our platform of a state supported educational program (which we believe would have wide appeal) would guarantee any citizen, regardless of race, color, creed or financial ability, a complete education in keeping with his intellectual abilities, and would develop his full potentials as an economic citizen as well as a human being. To further implement the educational program, no citizen of the State, after the fifteen year initial program was under way, would be allowed to enter the employment market until he or she was twenty years of age. In addition, these newly educated citizens would be encouraged to leave the employment market at the age of fifty-five. To develop this aspect of our program we envisioned a State Social Security program supplementing Federal Social Security which would guarantee any individual who had been working for thirty years an income equal to the minimum State hourly wage rate.

Citizens of the State leaving the employment market at the age of fifty-five would be guaranteed an additional state-supported educational program of not less than two years, the purpose of which would be to re-orient them into various programs of continuing study and research, both for their personal growth and possible additional contributions to the state in the form of literature, art, science, etc. All persons retiring from the area of economic employment would automatically be required to pursue further optional programs of study at the expense of the State.

In our various discussions, Jack Dawes took over the economic planning of the State, realizing the necessity of adjusting and fitting this into the entire economic scheme of the United States so that the State of X would be financially able to implement the educational and social security proposals. Jack proposed that, eventually, when our candidates for the legislature were firmly entrenched, a complete program of tax and wage and internal price control within the state could be legislated. The first step would be to raise the minimum wage to $2.50 per hour, and concomitantly adopt State-wide price control, freezing all prices at the level of the previous minimum wage. When the wage rate was raised to $2.50 per hour, the work week would be simultaneously relegislated to a nine hour day, five days a week. The new forty-five hour work week would be without time and one half for overtime. All Saturdays and Sundays throughout the state would be State holidays with the only business permitted to operate being those devoted to leisure pursuits.

A flat ten percent of all income after Federal taxes would be collected by the State in taxes, at the source, to underwrite the educational and social security programs. In Jack's opinion, manufacturing industries would be eager to enter the state because while the minimum wage was high the longer work week would increase productivity. Additionally, the total wages paid an employee would not exceed other states working on a thirty-five hour week with time and a half for the additional ten hours. Jack also proposed a state tax on all corporations which would be reduced dollar for dollar on all money spent by a particular corporation for expansion and development of facilities within the state.

Jack also proposed a New Resident Tax to discourage population shifts to this State by individuals who wished to benefit but had not contributed through work and the State income tax. The New Resident Tax would be computed on the amount of taxes paid by a citizen within the state (in the same income bracket as the new resident), and would be payable from the commencement of the program, but could be prorated for a maximum of five years.

All State finances would be put on a pay-as-you-go basis. Complete income and operating statements of the state, in a detailed breakdown, would be published mandatorily in all newspapers of the state on a quarterly basis. The citizens of the state would, by means of all forms of communication within the state, receive through indoctrination (from non-governmental sources) a constant progress report on the state's affairs and achievements.

We assumed that by the third State election, a period of six years, after the original invasion of our Utopian group, that they would have elected a Governor and a dozen or more state representatives who were in over-all agreement on the portions of the program disclosed by the group thus far. It would now be possible to initiate changes in state laws. Radio and nonnetwork television stations would have been drawn into the orbit. A nonprofit, but commercial radio and television station with a distinct editorial format, subsidized by the Foundation, would have been for several years propagandizing for various reforms in the State laws. Within six to ten years, the time would be appropriate for the first proposals for new laws that would diverge sharply from the past social modes of the State.

As soon as the education program had been revamped by changes in the State laws and was now under a State subsidy with a non-political, non-elective education board (to determine all school and college policies, courses and programs of study thus preventing domination by any future non-sympathetic political group) our Utopian planners would demand laws abolishing all censorship of any kind. We estimated that this could occur within ten years, but our group would keep a close pulse on the changing conditions within the state and initiate the proposal sooner if possible.

The moment laws were passed abolishing censorship of any kind, the schools, radio, television, the newspapers and all avenues of communication would be ready to combat the influx of any hard core pornography either published within the state or coming in from the outside. A broad general policy defining hard core pornography would not attempt to censor it, but would subject it to wide examination and reveal its lack of human values, showing in actual examples as they occurred in print, in the arts, or in stage presentations, how the sadistic, and abnormal elements in hard core pornography denied the real warmth and love that one individual was capable of toward another. Without anxiety or fear, the teachers, editorialists, commentators and religious leaders of the state would show on television, quote in print and read aloud examples of devalued sex portrayals and involve citizens of the state in a deep search of the value and worth of any presentation of the sexual impulses, that denigrated man and woman for each other. The weapons would be laughter, ridicule, and a constant revelation and exposé of the stupidity of rutting sex . . . showing its lack of meaning, beauty, esthetic values or love for the participants. Working with a population conditioned through twelve or fifteen years of the new schooling techniques, (some of us felt that all censorship could be eliminated within six years) our feeling was that hard-core pornography would be laughed out of the State.

With the abolition of censorship, we expect the portrayal of the nude human body would quickly appear in all areas of communications within the State. Graphic depiction, in any form, of heterosexual intercourse would become commonplace. Children would grow up accustomed to the portrayal of the act of sexual intercourse and the birth of children, in all the arts. Judgement of the value of particular portrayals would be on the aesthetic side, and portrayals of the act of intercourse which failed to measure up to the enlarged sense of human values of all citizens of the State would tend to reflect back disparagingly on the person or persons responsible. Our State would "censor" by unanimous disapprobation of its citizens.

As the portrayal of nudity became a commonplace, actual nudity on beaches, in and around the home, would become a matter of personal choice and convenience. When the State finally came around to revising the laws regarding nudity, it would be a matter of the law catching up with the actual moral codes and practices within the State.

Beth pointed out a side effect of the complete elimination of censorship: magazines of the *Cool Boy* ilk would simply languish and die for lack of interest. Once nudity was generally acceptable on the beaches, in public performances, and casually around the home, the voyeur aspects of seeing the naked human being would be supplanted by the wonder, delight and amazement of the male and female body. Magazines and movies whose sole purpose was to cater to a natural desire to see the human body of the opposite sex naked would become superfluous.

We came to the conclusion that a complete elimination of censorship within the State, would have emphatic results. Under the aegis of a Statewide program to explore the lack of human values and meaning of hard core pornography, as well as a considerable portion of sexually titillating material now being sold as literature and drama and promoted without regard to human values, we would finally have the net effect of eliminating most of these neurotic substitution desires for such material.

To further uproot sexual neuroses, and reorient the individual solidly in society and in the world, our Utopian planners would gently start propagandizing for a complete revision of the marriage and divorce laws within the State, with the ultimate purpose of passing completely new laws. This would be a long-term project needing twenty years. After the younger generation had been thoroughly schooled in new concepts of the meaning of love, and with a new understanding of the taproots of jealousy, we would be ready for sweeping changes in the concepts of marriage and the family.

We finally agreed on the following revisions. Premarital living at the State-supported trade and regular colleges, along the Harrad pattern, would be generally available. Marriage would become mandatory on the impregnation of the woman. Marriage prior to the birth of a child would be optional. Divorce would be readily available to childless couples, but probably not much used, since few would get married until they had a mutual desire to have children. Divorce where there were children under twenty would be permitted but would be discouraged and rather difficult to obtain unless *both* parents were willing to sever all ties with their children and permit them to be adopted into happier environments. Divorce in families where all children were over eighteen would be relatively easy to obtain, but we felt that few couples would avail themselves of the opportunity since the new marriage laws of the State would permit group marriages to a maximum of six couples. Group marriages, we felt, would in many cases inject new interests and a revision of values into marriages dulled by familiarity, as well as providing greater meaning and security for the new group families. Four or six couples desiring to marry as a unit would be given rigorous psychological testing to determine their adaptability to this type of marriage. Group marriage could be dissolved in whole or in part by petition to the State providing the remaining couples were willing to assume all responsibility for the children. Obviously, with the new concepts of marriage and the family, adultery would have no meaning. The centerpinning of the family would be children and mutual love and esteem of the partners. Bigamous marriages to a maximum of two men and one woman, or two women and one man, would be permitted if all the participants were in complete accord and desirous of such a marriage. Divorce of any of the parties in a bigamous marriage would forfeit all children, under eighteen, to the State.

Since the attitude of the State would be the preservation of the dignity and excellence of the individual human being and the insistence that all children were raised within some form of happy family environment, the entire philosophy of the State through its educational systems would be to encourage a free sexual environment, with love, in its wider sense, and not romance dominating all sexual matings. The keynote would be interwoven individual responsibility.

The other night we discussed these initial proposals with Margaret and Phil. While Phil accepted most of our premises, he insisted on more detailed documentation on showing how we would, in actual practice, accomplish our various objectives.

"There are a couple of points that I would like to raise, also," Margaret said. "When you are finished, do you still have a democracy or will the natural conflicting 'isms' of democracy defeat your whole program? This leads to the second point. While you have allowed yourself twenty years to accomplish your objectives, your most difficult opponents will be organized religion, and individual religious leaders themselves."

"Of course, we'll have opposition, and plenty of it," I said. "But we would have several advantages. We would be operating with a thoroughly planned program, and would make no attempt to label it or publicize it as a whole. Properly conceived, those who disagree would find themselves boxing with shadows."

"You see, Phil," Beth said, "if the first stages of our State-supported educational program are developed so they have popular appeal, and we believe they can, then subsequent social changes would grow out of this quite logically. Furthermore, we would operate, on the surface, by completely democratic means. But democracy as an instrument of social action never functions without direction. Most citizens of any society are disinterested. The personal processes of existence and making a living in our culture, coupled with inadequate education, produce a mass man who must be directed.

Some group of individuals, or a specific individual, democratically elected, decides what they (or he) believes are the goals and purpose of a particular society at a particular time. Then, whether it be a Napoleon, a Hitler, a Roosevelt, or a Kennedy, the leader uses any means society permits to accomplish his or his group's personal beliefs. While democracy is presumably the will of the majority, in recent years, the majority no longer means a substantial majority. When elections (and subsequent policies and changes in social direction) are determined by as small as a one or two percent majority, the democratic processes simply force an almost equally large minority into submission. I don't believe we would be subverting democratic processes with our planned society. Our Utopian Group would simply be deciding what is best for the State, as politicians have done through the centuries, and then force these decisions into reality through the power of money and repetitive mass communications. We believe that the beneficent results of our planning would entrench the social gains that we would make. Which political party, ultimately had State power, would not matter, since, in any event, we would be careful not to identify our program with a particular political party."

Sheila tackled the problem of opposition from organized religion. "We have studied the State of X's religious groupings very carefully. The total Catholic and Jewish faith is a minority. The large majority of the population is Protestant, and hence may be somewhat more receptive. Keep in mind that we would not be challenging any beliefs in God."

Margaret smiled. "But you would be in conflict with most theologies, particularly in relation to sex and marriage."

"That's true," Sheila said. "But we would not be

offering a *laissez-faire* society. Once the educational aspects of our program are sold (and keep in mind even today we have a climate of much greater sexual freedom which the churches and religious leaders have already had to adjust to) it will be obvious we're offering the basis of social strength and religious strength based on a strong family-centered system. The approach to marriage and divorce that we're proposing could be easily assimilated into church doctrine. Whether our beliefs in man's ability to raise himself higher on the evolutionary ladder are limited to man's faith in his own ability or man's faith in God, the goal amounts to the same thing."

Phil chuckled. "Margaret, we have done it!" he said enthusiastically. "It really doesn't matter whether you kids make your pipe dream a reality. The important thing is that you can think creatively, and not be afraid to posit a different world. The truth is that Harrad has only begun to solve the problem. Man exists in society. If a few men could find the answers to the sexual confusion of modern times, and make people aware that hate and jealousy are not instinctive behavior but learned reactions, then they will have at least created an outpost in the vast jungle of human inter-relationships. You'll have to remember constantly that your group would be fighting an unceasing rear-guard action. Intelligent men and women who have achieved a greater ability to reason are vastly out-numbered by the normal, the average, the great mass of people who will label them with rubrics and castigate them as deviates, and in the long haul they will wonder whether it is worthwhile to be the innovators in society."

"Phil . . . Phil," Beth interrupted him. "We know the words of your song by heart. It sums it up to the fact that mass man, untrained and vastly uneducated, can do little with his hard won liberty except to eventually surrender it. But I'm disappointed in your reaction."

"Why?" Phil asked, puzzled.

"You called our thesis a pipe dream, and inferred that we couldn't make it a reality."

Phil grinned. "Considering the world as a whole, your approach is a little way-out with elements of youthful, wishful thinking."

Jack laughed. "You can say the same thing about Harrad College."

"If we are all nothing but your pipe dream, Phil," Val said, "you better not stop smoking. I couldn't stand the shock."

"You are all safe," Phil said, chuckling. "I promise if I stop pipe dreaming, it won't be until all my actors are one hundred and two years old!"

FROM THE JOURNAL OF HARRY SCHACHT

May, the Fourth Year

Today, Beth and I were cleaning up our rooms chucking out a four-year accumulation of stuff we wouldn't need in Graduate School. I came across my Journal in a bottom drawer. Looking back over the first years and the incredible amount of stuff I wrote, I read parts to Beth and I couldn't help smiling. I haven't written anything in these pages for a year. What happened to all the qualms and fears of Harry the Beast? Would I have ever believed it possible that Beth and I would be married, that she would be calmly walking around the room wearing nothing but my shirt and humming a happy little tune as she surveyed with great pride the new roundness in her belly, or that Stanley and I would watch with joy and laughter as Sheila and Beth, naked, compared their speed of maternal growth? In a few weeks this phase of our life will be over. What can I say that sums it up? In a few words I can only echo Beth: "Oh, Harry . . . I am so happy. I love you. I love everybody!"

It's amazing to me how Beth and I, and InSix as a group, have developed such a fundamental rapport (really, an inadequate word) with each other. Last week is only one example I could multiply a hundred times. So here it is, Phil, nothing important really, just a windup to this Journal of mine in case you want it, as you once said you did.

Sheila insisted on treating InSix to tickets for the Metropolitan Opera on their Boston road showing. "If we are all going to live together in Graduate School," she said, "I want to be sure that you are all willing to try to enjoy something outside your own interests. Jack and Stanley have made us experts on folk music, Beth and Harry play symphonies and concertos incessantly. Valerie has dragged us to jazz festivals. I like opera . . . so you will all have to suffer."

Jack groaned that operas had some good music but damned silly plots. None of us really suffered. The girls were ecstatic over *La Traviata.* Jack, Stanley and I watched Anna Moffo through binoculars as she sang *Manon.* Between the acts of *Manon,* Stanley was admiring the blooming bellies of Sheila and Beth.

"I can't help it," he kidded them. "I have fallen in love with Anna Moffo. That's the way it is in opera. Love happens just like that! Manon meets Des Grieux. Five minutes later she runs off to Paris with him. Actually, you know the minute she meets Des Grieux, she can't wait to wiggle out of her knickers for him."

"Opera is opera," Sheila said. "You don't confuse it with life. Tragic opera gives you an emotional catharsis, maybe even deeper because of the addition of music, than any Shakespearean or Greek tragedy."

Jack disagreed. "Most of the popular operas were written nearly one hundred years ago. In those days adultery, spurned love, rabid jealousy and uncontrolled hate were even more than now the modus operandi of life. Today, we are more sophisticated. We can't believe

Lucia de Lammermoor would marry someone she didn't love. She'd just tell her brother to go to Hell."

But when Joan Sutherland sang the "Mad Scene" from Lucia, all of us stood up. Tears in our eyes, we cheered and clapped.

"See," Sheila said unabashedly drying her eyes. "For a moment you believed! For a moment you felt all the longing and terror of Lucia gone mad for love."

Back in our rooms at Harrad we were still arguing about it. "I wasn't crying for Lucia," I said. "I was emotionally involved with Joan Sutherland's voice as she led the orchestra, reaching feelings beyond the power of any man-made instrument. I listened truly spellbound."

"Which proves a point," Jack said. We had all crowded into Sheila's and Stanley's room and were drinking champagne in glasses we'd expropriated and carried off in bulging pockets from the Music Hall's Champagne Bar. "If the Harrad experience is valid, and ever becomes a large factor in the world, a large portion of what we label our cultural heritage in literature and in the dramatic arts such as Shakespeare, opera, classical literature, as well as ninety-five percent of every drama, and novel written in the past fifty years will have absolutely no meaning."

"It's a good point," I agreed. "Given an entire society educated as we have been, the common fare of the dramatic arts or literature, based as they are on adultery, jealousy, hate, war, murder, sexual sadism, sexual aberrations, petty misunderstanding and the simple inability to communicate . . . such material will only have antiquarian interest. It will seem as dull and boring as the medieval astrological writings."

"My God," Beth said. "I don't know as I would envy

such a world. The long history of man's arts, his quest for beauty and truth in the world, is the only stable thing that we have left. The plot of Lucia, for example, may be silly by today's standards but the idea of love and the heartbreak of Edwardo's *bella inamorata,* in fact all of Donizetti's music represents the tragedy of man caught in his own circumstances, destiny, fate . . . call it what you will. If you wipe out the idea of Laöcoon, man struggling to rise above the evil in himself, you have wiped out the essence of man as he knows and understands himself."

Jack smiled. "After four years at Harrad, do you still believe man is of necessity a dualistic creature doomed by his very nature to always have good and evil in conflict within him?"

"No, I don't," Beth said. "But in our future Utopian world with no conflict, with everyone in full accord finally, with no wars, no murders, no hate, no jealousy, what in heaven's name will be the subject matter of the arts? Not to harp on Lucia . . . but it is a good example; what forces in the world will inspire a Donizetti to create his music, or a Sutherland to sing it? I'm sure that man, no matter how good he may be and how much he is in control of his emotions, needs the purge and sudden realization of his insignificance that a great dramatic tragedy can give him."

"There's a thousand subjects," I said. "Imagine a drama and literature built on the principle of Greek drama. Man not against himself but against the gods. For us in the twentieth century the gods are the unknowns. Man against disease. Man against premature death. Man against mass hatred. Man crying for security, or solitude, or love. Man against war or poverty or misunderstanding. Man against greed or corruption.

Man against his own desire for achievement. Man trapped on this planet and yearning for the stars. Man against his own ignorance. A new kind of Faust. In this kind of drama and literature the individual good man, the protagonist, the hero, would once again assume his heroic stance. His failure against unknowns, and not the failures of his own petty personal misfortunes, would assume all the grandeur of real tragedy."

"I think you may have something," Valerie said. "A modern Donizetti could write a modern Lucia. Lucia could be a southern white girl in love with Eduardo, who could be a Negro. Lucia's brother could be a white supremist. With these elements, you could write a new tragic libretto to Donizetti's music."

"Or a new Donizetti could write new music," Stanley chuckled.

"In the new Harrad world of the next hundred years," Jack grinned, "when all of us are coffee colored, and the Negro-White problem has passed into history, that conflict will be just as antiquated as the present Lucia."

"Isn't that a point?" Stanley asked. "Man should use his arts to express the strivings that have meaning for his time. We need new literature and new arts to point the way. Valerie's idea is contemporary . . . but there will always be Harry's universals."

Beth just walked over and sat in my lap. "What are you writing?" she asked. "May I read it?"

When she finished she kissed me. "Feel my belly. I'm so proud of it! Aren't you?"

I admitted that I was.

And that's Harrad, Phil. Millions of things to wonder about and discuss, and new lives eager, if we will help them, to pick up where we leave off. Right now, Beth is waiting to continue this discussion, in a somewhat lower key, with me inside her, and her new belly pressing against me. I'm afraid our conclusions, if any, may never get written down!

A LETTER FROM BETH SCHACHT

December, after the Fourth Year

Dear Margaret and Phil:

We received your letter asking for news of the first class to graduate from Harrad. As we told you last June, we decided somehow that InSix would hang together. Like other couples that grouped together at Harrad, the six of us seem to have developed a built-in unity that seems to sustain us. As secretary of InSix, I have been elected to bring you up to date.

First and most important, Sheila and I gave birth to baby boys, Arnold and Abraham, respectively . . . born within ten days of each other. Valerie is five months pregnant, but (Jack to the contrary) it seems dubious at the moment whether she will agree to suffer through what happened to Sheila and me at delivery time.

But to go back. When Harry and I were accepted at the University of Pennsylvania Medical School, Sheila decided to do graduate work here in music. After some juggling, Stanley switched from Harvard Law to U. of P. Law. Valerie gave up Western Reserve and is here working in sociology, while Jack is doing graduate work in economics at Wharton.

It sounds simple when I write it but it took a whole

summer of juggling and argument to get us all settled in one spot for another four years. Then it took Sheila, Val and I at least two months of heated disagreement to settle on a house where we could all shack up together. InSix is now the proud owner of an old ten room house in a convenient but run-down section of this City of Brotherly Love. The house cost InSix a down payment of five thousand dollars, and was all hell to work out with the staid Philadelphia bankers who looked down their long noses but finally succumbed to Jack's financial genius. If they knew the whole truth, and not the simple fact that we are poor but deserving students, I fear the sky of Philadelphia would be lighted with the word SIN in red neon; to guide and warn the faltering steps of the good progeny of William Penn and Benjamin Franklin, against a similar immoral course. No, not old Ben! . . . He was a gay dog. I'm sure that if he had thought of it, you and Phil would have been several hundred years too late with Harrad. What a different world it would have been!

I was about to say that Val, who under Harry's tutelage, made an excellent midwife to Sheila and me, is not sure that she wants to be the next "victim."

Safely ensconced in our own beds, Sheila and I had our babies at home. It was no picnic, and it was none of this natural childbirth stuff. It was just plain rugged, but now, as we recall it, neither Sheila nor I can help smiling. We are twentieth century heroines in a world where most births are cut and dried, where mothers labor on a production line, carefully planned for the convenience of doctors who so far as possible keep normal working hours. Our future citizens come into the world in the most modern aseptic conditions. Healthy and antiseptic, I suppose, but definitely lacking something so far as the "poppa" is concerned and maybe even the "mamma." Keep in mind that none of us are advocating a return to primitive child bearing. Sheila and I are still deep admirers of modern hospitals. Only, as Harry pointed out, the modern birth process omits one very vital phase of child bearing . . . the male love, his interest, curiosity and identity with his wife and child at the moment of birth.

Try as he would, Harry could not persuade the doctors, the hospital or the medical school that he and Stanley should have the privilege of witnessing the birth of their children . . . and maybe even hold my and Sheila's respective hands as we labored on our joint productions. It simply would not be possible. No hospital with their crowded labor rooms was set up for such sentimentality. Oooh, did that word make Harry mad. He gave the doctor an extended dissertation on the difference between love and sentimentality.

It didn't take Harry and Stanley long to figure out a simple solution. All Sheila and I had to do was to sweat it out. Inevitably we would give birth. Frankly, about this time Sheila and I were beginning to have doubts. With his usual thoroughness, Harry jumped ahead in his medical studies and stayed up night after night becoming an expert on obstetrics and every facet of childbirth. Then, just to make sure, Harry assured the doctor who was looking after Sheila and me that he would be summoned if the blessed event arrived suddenly and without warning.

When I awoke at four in the morning on October fifteenth, no one had to tell me I was in the first stages of labor. Harry suddenly changed his mind and was going to call the doctor and rush me to the hospital, but I crossed my fingers and told him that I was game if he was. After all, I assured him, I had acquired such a thorough knowledge of what was going on inside me that I really didn't want to be an inert, half-conscious, contracting lump of flesh. My brain wanted to know what was really happening to the rest of me. Little did I know what I was in for.

The first ten hours seemed to last an eternity, but I wasn't lonesome. Since all parents make a fetish of taking pictures of their offspring Jack decided that Harry and I should do it right and start from scratch. Yes . . . you guessed it! Thanks to Jack, the frustrated movie mogul, and over my howling protests and later Sheila's, we have the nicest movies you ever saw of the birth of our babies. I've watched the film of my stardom, my finest performance, over and over again with awe and pride that I, Beth, accomplished this miracle.

I won't bore you with details. We will bring our movies up to Harrad soon and show them to you. You'll see me with the most amazing grimaces, and Val and Sheila flitting over me like mother hens, wiping my face or rubbing my back while Stanley watches in amazement, and Harry with our good doctor friend (he arrived about nine o'clock with plenty of scowls for all concerned). They finally stopped arguing over recumbent me and counselled each other.

Harry insisted that I would have an easy birth. He should try it! About noon they propped me into a semi-sitting position. Since I had been measured and studied thoroughly day by day for the past four months and also given endless advice by Harry, I was contracting and relaxing on schedule with much happy cheering from the sidelines. Finally it was over. If I was the heroine, Jack deserves the cameraman's Oscar. He condensed the long hours into about forty-five minutes of dramatic deep feeling. He captured my tears and pure joy, and Harry's proud grin when he held Abraham up and slapped him on his fanny. He interspersed this with all the faces of our friends, showing unconstrained, amazed, happy wonder. Of course, Jack doesn't need compliments. He now envisions a new age of home movies, with him as the precursor and founder of a new kind of movie studio devoted to the business. Imagine, newly-marrieds would be able not only to show you movies of their honeymoon (omitting of course the hours of implantation) but would then proudly pass onto the next reel and show junior being hatched.

Now, we are back to normal! I missed two and a half weeks of lectures and classes, but, since we are taking identical courses, Harry kept me up to date. Sheila took three weeks off, but her schedules are more flexible than med school. Sheila and I nursed our babies for a few weeks. We even exchanged the little rascals, who didn't seem to care from which teats they got their sustenance. Before Abraham went on a bottle, Harry tried a taste or two, but wouldn't recommend it for a diet. Now that both babies are on bottles and we have developed an easy schedule, most of Sheila's classes are in the afternoon, so she is morning boss. I take over maternal duties about two-thirty on most days. We have about two hours a day when the boys or Val, or a nice motherly neighbor who lives next door, takes the daily watch. Mostly there are no problems since the kids are sleeping.

Do you wonder how our communal life works out in practice? Believe me, it is never dull. First, money. Jack and Valerie, our President and Treasurer, pay the bills. As you know for the past three years we have pooled all our resources into our corporation, InSix. The purpose of InSix is to provide the education and all expenses for the six of us for the next four years. When we started in September, InSix had about twelve thousand dollars from our total summer earnings over the past three years. We also had the income from our record royalties of seventy-six hundred dollars and one thousand I got for posing for the famous Cool Girl picture. After the down payment on our dilapidated mansion, we had about eighteen thousand, so we ought to have enough money to last all of us for at least two years.

We had a stormy family conference here early in October, and the only point of agreement was, that even though Sheila was more than willing and enthusiastic to subsidize all of us, that we would make it on our own. You should have seen us showing the house to Val's, Jack's, Harry's and my father and mother. Such wailing and consternation and fears of perdition for their brood! I can't make up my mind whether Sheila and Stanley were better off; they had no explaining to do. Anyway, Jack made a sporting proposition to the three fathers who were present. If we got into financial difficulty, they would loan InSix a maximum of four thousand dollars each, which Sheila would match with four thousand. So much for finances. We are confident that within four years the world will be blessed with two doctors, one lawyer, and three sundry Ph.D's.

As for day in, day out living, our home is our castle and fortress. Sheila, Val and I do the shopping and plan dinner, the only meal we all manage to eat together. We have one downstairs room strictly for study, with desks, chairs, lamps etc. purchased from various junk shops. Very comfortable. Only one rule in this room, absolutely no conversation. If you don't want to study, but feel unconversational, you can sit and stare and no one would even dare ask what you are thinking. We made one room a music room and here we have a piano (Sheila's donation) and record player. Here we sing, play music, write kooky stuff for records we hope to make and generally horse around. The dining room and living room off it are for eating, discussion and guests. God, do we have guests! Some never want to go home, and on weekends some don't. We find them Sunday morning sleeping on the floor, and the discussions that started Saturday night are still going strong Sunday noon. Naturally, we attract all the screwballs and curiosity seekers from here to New York City. Discussions range from sex to Zen, communism to existentialism. You name it and some one is available for a "pro" and someone for a "con."

Upstairs is the sacrosanct headquarters for InSix. There are five bedrooms but only one damn bathroom. Fortunately this house was built in the days that bathrooms were big. It measures nearly twenty by twenty feet. Since the boys are rather uninhibited about not only their, but our excretory functions, Sheila, Val and I (who are definitely inhibited) made them enclose the toilet with a four wall partition, and that, at least, has a door and lock on it! However, anything can happen . . . and since the partition doesn't reach the ceiling, which is at least twelve feet high, I discovered one night that all the giggling on the outside was caused by reflection of Beth sitting on the pot and being stared at in a mirror Jack had ingeniously propped on an appropriate angle.

Bathing, showering etc. is strictly public. None of us, including the boys, has any trouble getting his or her back scrubbed . . . or any other part of our anatomy, if we show the slightest interest.

Naturally, sex is somewhat uninhibited. Now that Sheila and I are back in circulation, and after Val has her baby, we've decided not to attempt any more progeny until we've finished our education.

A few weeks ago, on a rainy Saturday afternoon, we were all sprawled across Sheila and Stanley's bed, and

Sheila plunged into the discussion of whether we were going to continue monogamous or return to the more or less informal sex life of our Harrad days, and if the latter, how? She suggested that if the mood seized us, we might occasionally want to switch bed mates, but only on the basis of prior non-alcoholic discussion and one hundred percent agreement.

Harry disagreed on the method. "What I can't figure out," he said laughing, "is that if I asked you to sleep with me, Sheila, and if you didn't want to, or Stanley didn't want you to, or if Beth didn't want me to, how in the devil would you solve it? All I'd have done is create tension with the three of you. It's really an impossible thing to discuss."

But we did discuss it . . . for nearly three hours. We concluded how impossible it would be to avoid exchanging partners. We were bound to be attracted physically to each other, living as we did. We were married as a matter of direct responsibility to each other, but marriage didn't preclude the feeling of love, and just plain sexual attraction we had for each other. I suggested it would eliminate tension to sleep with our "proper" mates Saturday through Tuesday, and our "improper" mates Wednesday, Thursday and Friday. Stanley protested that this didn't include Val and Jack, and once Val was "back in the lists as a combatant" it would change the sequence. Harry's argument was more fundamental. As much as he enjoyed sex, he wasn't about to make it a "duty" to make love to three different girls in one week. Not that he wouldn't try occasionally, but if he felt sleepy on a particular night he didn't want to arrive on the sacrificial couch with an engraved guarantee.

We finally solved it by agreeing to exchange our spouses for one week at a time with Valerie and Jack included. This is working beautifully. Sheila, Val and I were discussing it last night. If you dig back into the history of marriage, particularly in Briffault's famous study *The Mothers* you'll find that originally most marriages were group marriages. Isn't it possible within the framework of modern society that some of the beneficial aspects of such marriages might be retained? What have we gained in our little society? Whether I am sleeping with Harry, Jack or Stanley, it is not a lustful experience or orgiastic. It is very definitely not casual. We are deeply good friends, and we do not take each other for granted. Each of us brings something a little different to the other, and it sparks our lives with a real *joie de vivre* and a deep commitment.

Val summed it up. "Every Sunday when my new husband for the week joins me in my room, I feel like a new bride all over again. Sometimes I wake up in the night and for a sleepy moment I may forget whether I am with Stanley, Jack or Harry, and then I feel warm and bubbly. Me . . . Valerie . . . too tall and with big feet and sometimes too bossy . . . three men love me and care for me . . . and I . . . I love us all!"

Really sex with all of us is warm laughter and deep mystery existing almost simultaneously. What will happen when we finish our education? We talk about it once in a while. We know that inevitably economics and the problem of making a living will separate us and we will pursue our monogamous lives and have our children in a more conventional pattern. But we know, too, that we will plan our holidays and vacations together with the sure knowledge that the pressure of society to conform will never break the bond that we have formed, not only because of sex and the desire for variety within our monogamous lives, but even more because all of us will continue to respond to the chal-

lenges of living. And when we meet in the future we
will not be dull suburbanites passing an evening of alcoholic boredom, and repressing our sexual feelings. We
will be alive, vital, inter-acting, intensely curious and
wondering human beings who care deeply for each
other.

A couple of things sum us up pretty well. A week
ago, we all went up to New York to visit with Bad Max
and some of Jack's friends in the Village. Here is a
vignette of those who think they are challenging the
conservatism and conformity of society. First, we
watched a Flashlight Parade and Rally to protest the
harassment of the Arts in New York City. A motley
crowd of students, artists, beardos, and what not, all
wearing black as a token mourning for the Death of
Freedom in the city, were protesting the Licensing of
Movie Films, the Censorship of Books, Seizure of Art
Works as Obscenity, Harassment of Coffee Houses by
the police etc. Later we watched another group spon-
sored by the New York League for Sexual Freedom
who were picketing the Women's House of Detention
carrying placards which read: "Free the Prostitutes."
"If it weren't for Sex you wouldn't be here." "32-69
come and join our Picket Line." "Whoop-de-doo, I
want to screw, how about you?" "Ballin is good for the
Soul" etc. etc. . . .

I'm afraid the six of us felt like visitors from another
planet. What these people thought was rebellious and
provocative seemed to us pitiful and foolish. For if men
and women want to change society, the effective way is
the Harrad way. Not sticking your tongue out, or spending your time wailing at the superficial manifestations
of man's stupidities or making a greater ass of yourself
than those you are protesting against. No, far better to
live your life as a totality . . . slowly and methodically,

with a sure knowledge of what you wish to accomplish. The kind of personal rebellion that will change the world is summed up by John Gardner in his concept of the "self-renewing man." "What is he? Who is he?" Here is how Gardner describes him in the Carnegie Corporation Annual Report:

"The self-renewing man is versatile and adaptive. He is not trapped in techniques, procedures, or routines of the moment. He is not the victim of fixed habits and attitudes. He is not imprisoned by extreme specialization . . . In a rapidly changing world versatility is a priceless asset, and the self renewing man has not lost that vitally important attribute. He may be a specialist but he has also retained the capacity to function as a generalist. The self-renewing man is highly motivated and respects the sources of his own energy and motivation. He knows how important it is to believe in what he is doing. He knows how important it is to pursue the things about which he has a deep conviction. Enthusiasm for the task to be accomplished lifts him out of the ruts of habit and customary procedure. Drive and conviction give him the courage to risk failure. (One of the reasons mature persons stop learning is that they become less and less willing to risk failure.) And not only does he respond to challenge, but he also sees the challenge where others fail to see it . . . For the self renewing man the development of his own potentialities and the process of self discovery never end. It is a sad but unarguable fact that most human beings go through life only partially aware of the full range of their abilities. In our own society we could do much more than we do now to encourage self development. We could, for example, drop the increasingly silly fiction that education is for youngsters and devise many more arrangements for lifelong learning

. . . But the development of one's talent is only part, perhaps the easiest part, of self-development. The maximum 'Know thyself,' so ancient, so deceptively simple, so difficult to follow, has gained in richness of meaning as we learn more about man's nature . . . as Josh Billings said, 'It is not only the most difficult thing to know one's self, but the most inconvenient.' It is a life-long process . . . that brings us to the recognition that the ever renewing society will be a free society. It will understand that the only stability possible today is stability in motion. It will foster a climate in which the seedlings of new ideas can survive and the deadwood of obsolete ideas be hacked out. Above all it will recognize that its capacity for renewal depends on the individuals who make it up. It will foster innovative, versatile, and self-renewing men and women and give them room to breathe."

That's it, Margaret and Phil . . . that's Harrad . . . that's us! We hold the key to the future. The door is unlocked and open. Those who pass through are going into a new era, a new age. Not a Golden Age. My God . . . how dull that would be! No . . . rather an Age of Continuous Wonder . . . an Age of Creative Insecurity.

Love from all of us,
Beth

BIBLIOGRAPHY

During the four year seminar in Human Values, Harrad students cover more than a thousand books in the general area of psychology, history, sociology and sexology as well as selected novels and autobiographies. With the feeling that any college or university could offer a similar course on a one year basis, either at the freshman or sophomore level, here is a listing of a few of the germinal books used at Harrad College. These books are not technical, but they *are* dangerous. Any reader who is exposed to all of them may find his entire sexual as well as religious thinking quite drastically re-motivated.

While at first glance some of these writers and books may seem incompatible, they do have one thing in common; their purpose, whether explicitly stated or not, is to point the way to an exciting new world where men live life to its full potential without shame or neurosis. Thus, as a group, these writers exceed their own limitations and charter a world where man has finally achieved the mission of all religions . . . to give love without asking for it in return. Do not look for Krafft-Ebing, Havelock Ellis, Kinsey or similar encyclopaedists in this listing. Their cataloguing job has been thoroughly done. What the world needs now is men and women to weigh the facts and fictions of the past and *dare* to propose new solutions.

Allport, Gordon, *Becoming,* New Haven 1950, Yale University Press

Bertocci, Peter A., *Religion As Creative Insecurity,* New York 1958, Association Press

Bloch, Iwan, *The Sexual Life of Our Times,* New York, Allied Book Company. n.d.

Boorstin, Daniel, *The Image, A guide to Pseudo Events in America,* New York, 1961, Atheneum

Breedlove, William and Jerrye, *Swap Clubs,* Los Angeles, 1964, Sherbourne Press. Sherbourne is courageously documenting many of the fundamental changes taking place in our sexual mores.

Briffault, Robert, *The Mothers,* The Matriarchal Theory of Social Origins, New York 1963, Grosset and Dunlap

Chesser, Eustace, *Unmarried Love,* New York, 1965, David McKay

Cooke, Charles E. and Ross, Eleanor, *Sex Can Be An Art,* Los Angeles, 1964, Sherbourne Press. One of the new type marriage manuals that contains quite a bit more than "how-to-do-it" sex.

Cuber, John F. and Harroff, Peggy, *The Significant Americans, A Study of Sexual Behaviour among the Affluent,* New York, 1965, Appleton Century

Bassett, Marion, *A New Sex Ethics and Marriage Structure,* New York, 1961, Philosophical Library

Berg, Louis and Street, Robert, *Sex: Method and Manners,* New York, 1953. The McBride Company. A sex manual with a quite different approach.

Ditzion, Sidney, *Marriage, Morals and Sex in America, A History of Ideas,* New York, 1953, Bookman Associates

Ellis, Albert, *Sex Without Guilt,* New York, 1958, Lyle Stuart. Ellis will go down in the history of the sex revolution as the first man to dare to lift the curtain and reveal the smog behind it.

Ellis, Albert and Arbarbanel, Albert, *Encyclopedia of*

Sexual Behaviour, New York, 1961. Hawthorn Books. A two volume work that should be more publicly available.

Ellis, Albert, *The American Sexual Tragedy,* New York 1954, Twayne Publishers

Ford, Clellan S., and Beach, Frank A., *Patterns of Sexual Behaviour,* Harper Brothers, New York 1951

Frankl, Victor E., *Man's Search for Meaning,* New York, 1963, Washington Square Press

Fromm, Erich, *The Art of Loving, An Enquiry into the Nature of Love,* New York, 1956, Harper and Row

Gardner, John, *Self Renewal, and the Innovative Society,* New York, 1963, Harper and Row

Garrison, Omar V., *Tantra, the Yoga of Sex,* New York, 1964, Julian Press. An introduction to a fascinating way to reach Nirvana via the extended act of sexual intercourse.

Goldberg, B. Z., *The Sacred Fire, The Story of Sex in Religion,* New York 1932, Horace Liveright

Guyon, René, *Sexual Freedom,* New York, 1950, Alfred Knopf

Hefner, Hugh, *The Playboy Philosophy.* A continuing study of sex in all its aspects appearing in *Playboy Magazine* in 1964 and 1965. By the time Hefner gets ready to publish it in book form he may have to write an addenda justifying *Playboy.*

Hegler, Inge and Sten, *An ABZ of Love,* New York 1963, Medical Press. The kind of Sex Manual the younger generation should read early in life.

Henriques, Fernando, *Love In Action,* The Sociology of Sex, New York, 1960, E. P. Dutton

Hunt, Morton, *The Natural History of Love,* New York 1959, Alfred Knopf

Key, Ellen, *Love and Marriage,* New York, 1912, G. P. Putnam. This book published more than fifty years

ago by a Swedish writer reveals how Sweden beat the
world to a saner view of love and sex.

Kirkendall, Lester, *Pre-Marital Intercourse and Interpersonal Relationships,* New York, 1961, Julian Press

Knight, Richard, *Sexual Symbolism, A History of Phallic Worship,* New York, 1957, Julian Press

Lamont, Corliss, *The Philosophy of Humanism,* New York, 1949, Philosophical Library

Legman, G., *Love and Death,* New York, 1959. Breaking Point. This is a study of censorship laws that permit sadism and murder, on television and in motion pictures, but forbid the depiction of love. Some publisher should get G. Legman to update it

Lewinsohn, Richard, *A History of Sexual Customs,* New York 1958, Harper Brothers

Lindsey, Judge Ben B., *The Companionate Marriage,* New York, 1927, Garden City. A proposal written many years ago that is well worth reviewing.

Lipton, Lawrence, *The Erotic Revolution, An Affirmative View of The New Morality,* Los Angeles, 1965, Sherbourne Press

Mace, David and Vera, *The Soviet Family,* New York 1963, Doubleday and Company

Malinowski, Bronislaw, *Sexual Life of the Savages,* New York, 1929, Harcourt, Brace & World

Maslow, Abraham H., *Toward a Psychology of Being,* New York, 1962, D. Van Nostrand, Inc. Abe Maslow will someday be widely recognized and perhaps be considered as influential as Freud on future developments in psychology.

Maslow, Abraham H., *Motivation and Personality,* New York, 1954, Harper Brothers

Montagu, Ashley, *The Meaning of Love,* New York, 1953, Julian Press

Mounce, Mervin. While he has not, as yet, been published in book form Mervin Mounce, as President of the American Health Alliance, the Official Nudist Association, has a long editorial record of maintaining a humanistic position toward sex love and, of course, nudism.

Neill, A. S., *Summerhill, A Radical Approach to Child Rearing,* New York, 1960. Hart Publishing Co. A. S. Neill, of course, pointed the way to Harrad College.

Reich, Wilhelm. *The Sexual Revolution,* Maine 1945, Orgone Institute Press.

Reiss, Ira L., *Pre-marital Sexual Standards in America,* Free Press of Glencoe, Illinois, 1960

Robie, W. P., *The Art of Love,* New York 1921, Eugenics Publishing Company. Dr. Robie is one of the great men who wrote on sex and love. The complete edition of this book is far more than a sex manual.

Russell, Bertrand, *Marriage and Morals,* New York, 1929, Horace Liveright. Old Bertrand led the parade when Albert Ellis wasn't even a beam in his father's eye!

Schur, Edwin M., *The Family and the Sexual Revolution, Selected Readings,* Indiana University Press, 1964

Scott, George Ryley, *Phallic Worship, A History of Sex and Sex Rites,* Mental Health Press

Scott, George Ryley, *Curious Customs of Sex and Marriage,* London, 1953, Torchstream Books

Sorokin, Pitirim, *The American Sex Revolution,* Boston, 1956, Porter Sargent, publisher

Taylor, G. Rattray, *Sex in History,* London 1953, Thames and Hudson

Von Urban, Rudolph, *Sex Perfection,* London 1952, Rider and Company

Watts, Alan W., *Nature, Man and Woman,* New York 1958, Pantheon Books. The first part of Watts' book is somewhat difficult for those not versed in Oriental philosophy. The last section should be required reading for anyone contemplating marriage.

Wilson, John, *Logic and Sexual Morality,* Baltimore, 1965 Penguin Books, Inc.

Wallace, Karl Miles. *Love is More than Luck, An Experiment in Scientific Match Making.* New York, 1957. Wilfred Funk Inc. This book precedes the present Operation Match which is burgeoning in the collegiate world and ultimately points toward the development of many colleges patterned on the Harrad College principle.

Young, Wayland, *Eros Denied, Sex in Western Society,* New York, 1964, Grove Press

ABOUT THE AUTHOR

A graduate of Bates College and the Harvard Graduate School of Business Administration, ROBERT H. RIMMER resides in Quincy, Massachusetts and directs a nationwide business from his Boston office. Two earlier novels, *That Girl from Boston* and *The Rebellion of Yale Marratt* investigate controversial social and moral issues. Mr. Rimmer describes himself as a writer who thinks he can move the world, and he is busily trying to find a place to put the fulcrum.